A Jenetta Carver® Adventure

A GALAXY UNKNOWN®

CHANGING
OF THE
GUARD

Book 11

BY

THOMAS DePRIMA

Vinnia Publishing - U.S.A.

AGU:®

Changing of the Guard
A Galaxy Unknown® series – Book 11

ISBN-13 (print): **978-1-61931-033-9**

ISBN-10 (print): **1-61931-033-3**

ISBN-13 (eBook): **978-1-61931-032-2**

ISBN-10 (eBook): **1-61931-032-5**

Cover image from: Shutterstock.com

Photo manipulation by: Thomas DePrima

Appendices containing political and technical data highly pertinent to this series are included at the back of this book.

To contact the author, or see additional information about this and his other novels, visit:

http://www.deprima.com

Acknowledgements

Many thanks to Michael A. Norcutt for his suggestions, proofreading,
and for acting as my military protocol adviser,
and
A special thank you to my copy editor Myra Shelley and her
proofreaders who always do such a tremendous job.

Novels by the author:

A Galaxy Unknown®...

A Galaxy Unknown®
Valor at Vauzlee
The Clones of Mawcett
Trader Vyx
Milor!
Castle Vroman
Against All Odds
Return to Dakistee
Retreat And Adapt
Azula Carver
Changing of the Guard

AGU:® Border Patrol...

Citizen X
Clidepp Requital
Clidepp Deja Vu

AGU:® SC Intelligence...

The Star Brotherhood

Colton James novels...

A World Without Secrets
Vengeance Is Personal

When The Spirit...

When the Spirit Moves You
When the Spirit Calls

Table of Contents

CHAPTER ONE
~ March 11th, 2290 ~

The gallery area of the enormous Admiralty Board Hall on Quesann was filled to capacity. Space Command and Space Marine officers, Galactic Alliance senators, and members of the mass media had arrived early, although that didn't improve their seating options. All seating was by reservation only, and all seats had been spoken for days earlier. The reason for the extraordinary interest in this regularly scheduled A.B. meeting was simply that the first new Supreme Commander in thirty years would be chairing this meeting. The former Admiral of the Fleet, Richard E. Moore, had retired and returned to his home in Region One, so the day's meeting would be chaired by his replacement, Admiral of the Fleet Jenetta A. Carver.

Live imagery from the Admiralty Hall was already being broadcast to the enormous convention center building directly across the park-like quad for those unable to reserve seats. Huge monitors distributed around the main convention arena were projecting the events for those turned away from the Admiralty Hall due to lack of space. The G.A. political campus on the planet Quesann had never seen such activity for any assembly.

The session would also be broadcast live to all Space Command bases, all ships in the First and Second Fleets, all Space Marine bases, and all G.A. offices, although it would literally take days for the S-band transmission to reach the farthest points in Galactic Alliance space. As with Senate meetings, the mass media would televise the session for civilian viewing, although the signals would likewise take many days to reach their audiences.

Senior officers who hadn't requested and received seating assignments for the scheduled session at least three days prior were standing against the wall around the outer perimeter of the gallery seating area. The attendees forced to stand considered themselves fortunate merely to have an opportunity to witness the historic session in person. Once the SRO space had been filled, everyone, regardless of position or rank, was being directed to the convention center. With guest accommodations for special visitors, the center had mainly been constructed to provide a space for special exhibits when planetary representatives other than G.A. Senators came to Quesann for meetings. Although the main exhibit hall could hold several thousand conference-goers, it was not available for commercial use because a special security clearance was required just to set foot on the planet.

The front three rows of the A.B. Hall gallery seating had been reserved for— and were now occupied by— invited newsmen and newswomen representing the largest media organizations in the G.A. Immediately behind them were the G.A. senators who had reserved their seats as soon as their staffs notified them of the scheduled meeting and the requirement to reserve seating. And behind the seated G.A. senators were the Space Command captains and Space Marine generals and colonels who had requested seats before all seating was assigned.

A few minutes before the meeting was scheduled to begin, admirals began entering the hall through the door behind the large horseshoe-shaped table with an opening that faced the gallery seating. All were seated when Jenetta entered the hall with her two Jumakas and approached her chair at the center of the table. The slight delay wasn't to make an *entrance*, but to make sure her uniform looked perfect in every respect, and ensure that every hair on her head was in its proper place. She knew that millions, perhaps billions, of G.A. citizens would be watching her first appearance.

Although attendees had been asked not to make any noise during the session, a member of the press stood up and began to clap. This tribute resulted in a spontaneous reaction in the room as other press members stood and joined in the applause. Within seconds, the rest of the crowd joined in and the building seemed to reverberate with the clapping and then cheering. They all knew that Jenetta had done more to protect the people of the G.A. from outside invaders than any of her predecessors and perhaps more than all of them combined. It was the most rousing response Jenetta had received since giving speeches at both NHSA and SHSA on Earth years earlier.

Jenetta smiled, took her seat at the conference table, and pounded the gavel on the sounding block once to signal that the regularly scheduled session was about to begin.

The attendees stopped clapping and all conversations ended as they took their seats. Jenetta pounded the gavel once again and said, "I call this public session of the Space Command Admiralty Board to order." As the highest ranked active-duty officer in the service, Jenetta's position on the A.B. was mandatory, and her role as chairperson was automatic. Tradition held that each member of the Board had an equal vote in all matters, but technically their votes were nonbinding upon the Admiral of the Fleet. He or she could accept the consensus of the attending admirals— and almost always did— or choose to override their opinions and simply order that a particular action take place as long as it was in accordance with Galactic Alliance law.

"Before I begin the formal proceedings," Jenetta said, "I want to again thank the G.A. senators, their staffs, and all Space Command and Space Marine officers, enlisted personnel, and our civilian staff for the exceedingly warm welcome I received upon my return to Quesann, with a special thank you to the members of the Admiralty Board. While on my extended leave of absence, my thoughts were never very far from the problems and issues facing my military brothers and sisters, as well as those facing the G.A. Senate. In addition to the regular members of the Admiralty Board— Admiral Roger Bradlee, Admiral Shana Ressler, Admiral Arnold Hillaire, Vice-Admiral Brian D. Holt, Vice-Admiral Raymond Burke, Vice-Admiral Raihana Ahmed, Vice-Admiral Lon Woo, Rear Admiral (upper) Loretta Plimley, and Rear-Admiral (upper) Lesbolh Yuthkotl, I want to welcome the visiting admirals who have joined us at the table today— Admiral Evelyn Platt, Commander of the First Fleet, and base commanders Rear Admiral (upper) Jorge Mendez, Rear Admiral (upper) Vincent Sprague, and Rear Admiral (upper) Rebecca Colsey. I also welcome retired Rear Admiral (lower) Stanley Bendzet.

"It's wonderful to be back and I look forward to the years ahead as we work to establish and maintain the rule of law within the greatly expanded boundaries of Galactic Alliance space.

"Before we begin today's agenda, I have a personal announcement for everyone here on Quesann and for the people of the Galactic Alliance, wherever you might be."

Standing up, Jenetta walked around the table and stopped a few meters from the center of the gallery section before she began to speak. While in the A.B. Hall, an admiral's implanted cranial transducer, usually referred to as a CT, sent their spoken words directly to the speakers mounted around the room, so it wasn't necessary that any carry a portable microphone. Cayla and Tayna had immediately assumed their customary places on either side of her once she left her seat.

"A great many people in the G.A. know that two Jumakas from the planet Taurentlus-Thur have been my constant companions for many years. On my left is Tayna, and on my right is Cayla. What most people don't know or even suspect about the Jumaka population is that they are sentient beings."

The hall suddenly became so quiet that you could hear the proverbial pin drop as jaws dropped and attendees seemed to stop breathing momentarily.

"Yes, it's a fact. Jumakas *are* sentient beings. I've known since our first day together that Cayla and Tayna were highly intelligent, but even I didn't fully appreciate their sentiency until the King of the Hudeerac Order gifted me with a male Jumaka. When I saw my two wonderful friends calmly conversing with the male and realized they were communicating information and sharing values just as you and I would, I was greatly surprised, but pleasantly so. So I began looking for a way to communicate with them also, but their speech is so unique that my language translator failed to offer anything intelligible. I contacted a Terran wildlife expert, Mr. M.A. Wilkerson, who had been studying the Jumaka population on Taurentlus-Thur for a number of years, in an effort to learn if he had made any progress with their language. Although considered a foremost expert on Jumakas, he'd actually had little success with direct sightings. The Jumakas were always aware of his presence immediately, regardless of how well he concealed himself. They would then quickly disappear into the dense forest. He had to be satisfied with recorded imagery produced by cleverly concealed miniature cameras.

"A number of annuals ago, Taurentlus-Thur enacted a law that makes removal of Jumakas from the planet a very serious crime, but authorities there allowed Mr. Wilkerson to bring a male to my estate on Obotymot because they knew I had two females. I'm very grateful to the officials on Taurentlus-Thur who permitted the transfer, and I want to again assure them that Nicky— as Dr. Wilkerson named him— is quite healthy and happy at his new home. Once Mr. Wilkerson and Nicky arrived, Wilkerson was able to begin a real study of the Jumakas because Cayla, Tayna, Nicky, and Thor were just as anxious to converse with us. They willingly donated their time and effort to the cause. I can't tell you how excited and overcome with emotion I was when the first crude translation device allowed a basic two-way communication with my wonderful friends.

"Improvements to the translation device have progressed rapidly since the first bulky devices constructed by Mr. Wilkerson, and they are now small enough that my friends can wear one. They appear like the collars placed around the necks of pets on Earth and other planets, but I assure you they are not there to control or dominate my friends. Rather, they free my friends from the inability to communicate with Terrans and other species. I realize that Cayla and Tayna look very much like the jaguars of Earth, but aside from general appearance, they have little in common. Many of you probably know that Cayla and Tayna saved my life when an assassin tried to end it. Terrans who witnessed the event were frightened by the ferocity they saw, but my friends only did what any bodyguard would have done, which was necessary on that occasion. The observers were frightened because the only weapons Cayla and Tayna had available to use for self-protection and to prevent the attacker from injuring me or anyone else that day were those they were born with. They have never attacked any other person in our many years together.

"I will soon be presenting a petition to the G.A. Senate requesting that they declare Jumakas sentient beings, and in doing so, extend to them the rights, privileges, and freedoms held by all sentient beings in G.A. space. All Jumakas presently caged in zoos or forced to perform guard activities must be freed immediately, as would be the case with any other sentient species. And anyone caught imprisoning a Jumaka after an established date must be charged with slavery. People currently using Jumakas for guard duty must establish an employment contract that gives the Jumaka the right to terminate their employment subject to the terms of the contract agreed to by both parties and within the labor laws of the planet that covers work regulations for all sentient life.

"I'm sure the members of the media wish to ask a few questions, so Cayla and Tayna will answer directly. The hall's public-address system has been linked to the frequency of their collar translators for this occasion. The overhead speakers in the hall will carry their responses so everyone may hear. Cayla will go first. Does anyone have a question for her?"

A newsie in the first row of seating raised his hand and stood up. "I'll start," he said.

"Please identify yourself and your employer."

"Jonah Tidestrum, Earth Today News Syndicate."

"Go ahead, Mr. Tidestrum."

"Uh, Cayla— do— you— understand— my— words?" Tidestrum asked in very precise, loud, and condescending speech.

"Of course I understand you, Mr. Tidestrum. But why are you speaking in that very unusual manner?"

Subdued ripples of laughter floated through the gallery area. Even Tidestrum chuckled.

"I'm sorry, Cayla. I wasn't sure how well your translator worked."

"The translator is so *you* can understand *me*, Mr. Tidestrum. I can understand you without it."

"Cayla and Tayna understood what I was saying from the very beginning," Jenetta said. "I've since learned they had picked up Amer by listening to the freighters while being transported. They also have a good understanding of other languages they've heard while in captivity and since they've joined me as my companions."

"Aren't they in captivity now, Admiral?" another newsie asked.

"Your name and employer, please?" Jenetta said.

"Leslie Hearst, Intergalactic Freedom Press."

"No, Ms. Hearst. They are not. Ask them."

"Tayna, are you free?"

"As free as you I imagine, Ms. Hearst. Freedom is a relative term. If you're asking if we stay with Jenetta because we have to, the answer is no. Jenetta offered to take us back to Taurentlus-Thur and endeavor to locate our relatives, but we declined. We were taken from the jungle when we were extremely young, and we don't remember very much about it. We would be strangers there. Jenetta also offered our spouses, Nicky and Thor, the opportunity to return to the planet. They've declined as well. Besides, Jenetta belongs to us."

"I'm sorry. I don't understand. Admiral Carver *belongs* to you?"

"Perhaps I can clarify that," Jenetta said. "It's the way Jumakas think of family unity. I belong to them and they belong to me. Their cubs belong to them, and they belong to their cubs. The cubs also belong to me and my children, and my children and I belong to them. I suppose it's like a mutual adoption process. We're all free from any restrictions on our movements, actions, or choices once we reach the age of consent, subject of course to the laws of the society where we live. That naturally varies with the species. Jumakas mature much sooner but also have a shorter lifespan than Terrans. Do you understand?"

"I think so, although it's a foreign concept that a Terran could belong to a pet."

"Ah, that's where the difficulty in fully understanding the premise lies. Cayla, Tayna, their mates, and their children are *not* pets. That's the whole purpose of this discussion. I want everyone to understand that Jumakas are not pets or domesticated creatures and shouldn't be treated that way. They are entitled to their freedom just as much as you and I are. They don't need us to care for them throughout their lives, as is normally required with pets. Everyone has to stop seeing them as either wild or domesticated animals that don't have a capacity for intelligent reasoning and thought. When someone sees a Pledgian or a Milora, they don't see a wild animal. They see an intelligent individual who simply has a distinctive appearance that is unique from that of Terrans and other species. That's all they should see when they see a Jumaka."

"Excuse me, Admiral," another newsie said. "The voices we're hearing are coming over the speakers in the ceiling. How do we even know that what we're hearing is what the Jumakas are saying? There could be someone responding from a back room."

"A fair question, Mr.—?"

"Petraro Visconta of the Galactic News Service."

"What you've asked is a fair question, Mr. Visconta. Tell me, when you attend a press briefing where the speaker is talking into a microphone on a lectern in a language unknown to you, how do you know you're hearing the right message over the loudspeakers or even through your personal translator?"

"Uh, I guess we— take it on faith."

"But you don't have such faith in me that I'm telling you the truth?"

"Admiral, I didn't mean to imply that *you* would lie to us. Perhaps you're not getting the correct translation as well. You said the translation database was developed by an M.A. Wilkerson."

"I trust that every word I hear from the translator is accurate, although you're correct that Mr. Wilkerson alone developed the vocabulary database used by the new translation collar while in my employ. I trust the translation is accurate because, as Cayla said, they understand Amer and have verified that the Amer they hear played through speakers is exactly the message they were attempting to communicate. The Jumakas all understand how very important this issue is to their species, and they're anxious to cooperate in whatever tests the appropriate government agency devises to assess their intelligence and sentience as long as the tests are non-invasive and are the same tests used to attribute sentiency to other species."

"And Cayla and Tayna have verified the accuracy of every single Amer word Mr. Wilkerson associated with a Jumaka word or phrase?"

"This was not an overnight project. My friends worked with Mr. Wilkerson for many months in developing the translation database. Where Amer words had no equivalent meaning in the Jumaka language, they adopted one. It's entirely possible that a Jumaka on Taurentlus-Thur may not understand what a particular Amer word means, but that's true in any meeting with other species. I have stated that the translation is one-hundred-percent accurate, and I accept that without question or reservation."

As Visconta retook his seat, Jenetta asked, "Are there any other questions?"

"I have another, Admiral," Leslie Hearst said. "How long do you believe it will take for sentience verification?"

"I really don't know, but I *can* say there's no question in my mind of their sentiency, and I intend to keep pressing for that status under G.A. law. I also appeal to planetary governments to individually recognize the rights of Jumakas as sentient beings because new regulations can sometimes move slowly here at the Senate level. As representatives of their worlds, senators must often communicate with their home world politicians and citizens to determine how they should vote on different issues."

"Have the officials of your birth planet, Earth, agreed to this?"

"I haven't been in touch with anyone on Earth, but I can assure you that on my home world of Obotymot and also on Nordakia, Jumaka sentiency is already law. The people on my planet know that Jumakas aren't dangerous unless dramatically provoked, and treat them just as they would any other resident of the planet. No one runs away in fear or cowers when they see a Jumaka walking down a village street. In fact, the children on my planet love to come over and walk alongside the Jumakas and play with the cubs. They know my friends don't pose a threat to anyone. This is the first time I've presented the sentiency request outside of the Nordakian sphere of influence. I wanted to wait until the original translation database was refined to a point where normal conversation was possible. I believe we've reached that point, but Dr. Wilkerson continues to work on improving it and expanding the dictionary."

"How can he do that with Cayla and Tayna here with you?"

"Nicky and Thor are on Obotymot, as are most of their cubs. Dr. Wilkerson recently completed a translation database that converts the Jumaka language into Nordakian, and begun work on a database that will convert Amer into the Jumaka language. When the cubs were born, their parents had to translate Amer for them because they had all they could do to learn their own native language. We knew that Amer would come later."

"How many cubs do you have?"

"Cayla gave birth to four. Their names are Orlando, Cheri, Kera, and Ruby. Their father is Nicky, the Jumaka Dr. Wilkerson brought from Taurentlus-Thur. Tayna gave birth to four as well. They are named Jake, Alex, Autumn, and Chelsea. Their father is Thor, the Jumaka presented to me by the King of the Hudeerac Order."

"Why didn't you bring any of them today?"

"Six of them are back on Obotymot with their fathers, who have responsibility for their education. Ruby and Jake are here, and their mothers will educate them. I didn't bring them today because they're still quite young and can be a little rambunctious at times, like Terran infants that have reached their fifth birthday. During the work day they stay at my residence with my children, Kaycee and Kyle. The cubs have bonded with my children and want to remain with them, just as Cayla and Tayna stay by my side most of the day."

"So your children have their own protectors?"

"It's by choice. All of the cubs wanted to come, but if you could see the way they race around the house and grounds all day, you'd understand why I had to limit it to the two who made the first request."

"So you can't control them?" Visconta asked.

"They're like Terran children— full of energy and always looking for fun and games. When it's necessary to tone down their enthusiasm, their parents speak to them, although sometimes they must be reminded several times, just as Terran children must be reminded sometimes. But when they're around my babies, as they often are, they are as gentle as Terran kittens, although they're quite a bit larger."

"So you're not afraid they'll injure your babies?"

"Of course not. But if anyone else tries to harm my babies, Ruby and Jake will ensure the assailant certainly regrets it, if he or she lives."

"So you do use the Jumakas as protectors."

"Use? No. The Jumakas are our friends— our family— not pets, protectors, or security animals. But— they have a sixth sense for danger, and they will protect us if necessary, as Cayla and Tayna have already done for me and as most family members would do for another member of their family.

"We seem to have reached a plateau in the questioning," Jenetta announced, "so I suppose it's time to adjourn this discussion for today and allow everyone to think about the information that's been provided. Thank you."

As Jenetta turned and walked back to her seat, Cayla and Tayna followed and took their usual places at her side.

Jenetta pounded the gavel once and said, "We'll now continue with regular business, beginning with a reading of the minutes from the last general session."

After the old business had been discussed, new business of a general nature was discussed. With the completion of that, the day's open session was ended.

"I thank everyone for their attendance today and for the welcome I've received," Jenetta said. "The board will now take a brief break before convening in executive session. Thank you."

With that, the admirals rose and filed out through the rear door that led to their office areas. A lunchroom reserved exclusively for the admirals and their aides was the destination of most, while the clerks headed for the A.B. staff dining hall on the opposite side of the kitchen.

As Jenetta sat down at an oval table large enough to accommodate all of the admirals, she looked down at the two Jumakas and asked, "What'll it be, girls? Milk?"

"Yes, please," Tayna said.

"Me too," Cayla said. "And perhaps a few biscuits with peanut butter."

Admiral Plimley, looking on, asked, "Did they answer?"

"Yes. I received the signal via my CT. Both said they would like some milk, and Cayla said to include some biscuits with peanut butter. Girls," Jenetta said, addressing the Jumakas, "Why don't you activate the speakers on your collars so the other admirals can hear you when you speak."

"Okay, Jenetta," Cayla said, the words coming from her collar this time.

"That is just so amazing," Admiral Hillaire said. "I never would have suspected she was speaking a language because the vocal sound she was making seemed, to my ears, to be a low growl. My little terrier makes a great deal of noise, but I know of no translator that could convey what he might be saying, if anything."

"I don't mean to offend you or demean your terrier, Arnold," Jenetta said, "but the intelligence level of Jumakas is far superior to the reputed levels of most Terran canine species. Canines do make wonderful companions because they're loyal, loving, and protective, but I don't believe they can communicate with each other except on very basic levels using vocal loudness and frequency, as well as through body movements and positions. Dolphins, whales, and other marine life do verbally communicate with each other, but even they fall far short of how we define sentient life. The Jumaka body is ideally suited for life in the jungles and forests of Taurentlus-Thur, but the lack of a hand with opposable digits for gripping imposes severe limitations in a world designed to suit hominoids. However, that shouldn't exempt them from being declared sentient."

"I believe you have the support of everyone on the Board," Admiral Platt said. "I witnessed the Jumakas interacting with you, your family, and the staff at your estate on Obotymot. There's no question in my mind that they're highly intelligent and sentient. However, the G.A. Senate will probably require extensive testing by anthropological, ethological, zoological, and biological scientists. Then the cognition scientists will seek to determine their intelligence levels while the behaviorism psychologists will seek to establish their ability to fit in with hominoid society."

"I think hominoid society will have more difficulty fitting in with Jumakas than the other way around."

"They're afraid of us," Tayna said. All eyes at the table immediately looked down to where the two Jumakas were seated next to Jenetta. Only their heads and necks were visible above the edge of the table.

"On Dakistee, they ran when they saw us coming," Cayla said.

"That'll change once they understand you won't hurt them unless you're attacked first," Jenetta said. "Once the G.A. Senate confirms sentience, I believe attitudes will change almost overnight as the press spreads the word throughout G.A. space."

"I hope so," Tayna said. "We only want to live in peace and raise our families."

"We know, Tayna," Admiral Ressler said, "and I have no doubt that Jumakas will be accorded sentience status in G.A. space with all the rights and privileges that entails. But democratic governments work ponderously slow at times so it may take awhile."

"We understand, Admiral Ressler," Cayla said. "Jenetta has explained the process to us. We will be patient because for the first time since hominoids began capturing or killing our people, we can see a day coming when we will be free everywhere in G.A. space."

"Jen, if I might be permitted to change the topic of conversation," Admiral Holt said after a few seconds of silence at the table. "While on leave, you were receiving summarized reports, but now you need to delve into the full text. You have an enormous amount of catching up to do."

"I realize that, Brian. And I've been spending every minute possible reviewing past sessions of the Board, both general and executive, and reading all filed reports."

"Yes, but the reason I bring it up is because of the situation with the Denubbewa."

"They've come back? After that last drubbing we gave them?"

"We don't think they ever left!"

CHAPTER TWO

~ March 11th, 2290 ~

"I haven't come across any reports on that topic in my reading. I thought the Denubbewa were gone after the last encounter that found them building motherships much closer to this base than we ever anticipated."

"Our fleet stung them hard, really hard, on that occasion," Admiral Bradlee said, "but the latest intel is very eye-opening. Most of my people believe the Denubbewa are on the verge of making an all-out push to arrogate much of Region Three. We don't think those walking computers would attempt that unless they believed they had a good chance of accomplishing it."

"Do you suspect they've developed a new defensive strategy against our weapons and tactics?"

"We don't know. But we do know they're very quick studies. And the information we've collected indicates they may have already assembled a vast armada in Region Three. It's even possible they've been reinforced by motherships from their home territory. My best people fear that the new war about to descend on us will make the deadly war with the Uthlaro seem like a practice drill on a target range."

"That's extremely troubling, Roger," Jenetta said. "Why do you suspect they're after Region Three? It's true our presence in that region has been very limited during the past decade given the size of the territory we've been forced to annex and our limited military resources, but what makes your people believe the Denubbewa have established it as an arrogation objective?"

"Reports from freight-haulers have been increasing at an alarming rate."

"Have the Denubbewa been hijacking cargo ships and killing the crews again?"

"No. They've not attacked any shipping lately— as far as we know. My people suspect they're presently avoiding all contact with shipping because of what we managed to do to them here in Region Two in retaliation for their attacks on our military vessels and again after we learned they were hijacking freighters for their ore cargos. But we believe the Denubbewa are out there in considerable numbers— and growing."

"If they fear us and our weapons," Admiral Burke said, "what would persuade them to remain in G.A. space? It seems any sensible enemy would flee once they understood we can destroy them at will, wherever and whenever we encounter them."

"I can only report that the sightings of Denubbewa warships have increased to an enormous and unprecedented level, and it has my best people worried. We've spread the word to every freight hauler in Region Three that we need them to report any and all sightings and estimated courses of Denubbewa ships, and the reports have been flooding in. The locations of the reported sightings are too far apart to represent the same Denubbewa ships, so it appears we're talking about an enormous fleet. Those vicious cyborgs must be up to something big."

"There's only one reason I can imagine for why they haven't turned and run," Jenetta said.

"I'd love to hear your theory," Admiral Plimley said.

"They've logically concluded that our technology in certain scientific fields is far more advanced than their own. They have to know by now that our ship speed is significantly greater, so they would naturally want to add our capability to their own ships. Also, with our double-envelope technology, they're unable to see us coming or going when we attack. For a war-centric civilization apparently intent on conquering the galaxy, if not the universe, that has to be the driving motivation. I wager they want our speed technology so badly they're willing to sacrifice innumerous ships and cyborgs to secure it. Our ability to attack them while never being observed has to be driving them crazy. I know that in their place I would give almost anything to learn how an enemy is able to attack and destroy my vessels without alerting my forces to an imminent attack or even their presence."

"They could have gotten the double-envelope FTL technology when they destroyed the *Yenisei* or the *Salado*," Admiral Hillaire said. "They had plenty of time to study the ships."

"I'm assuming they were unaware of our speed advances back then," Jenetta said. "Believing themselves to be far superior to the biologically developed life they'd encountered in this galaxy, they obviously failed to study the ship's propulsion capability from the perspective that it might be superior to their own."

"It's sort of comforting to know they're not perfect," Admiral Woo said. "But if they're not hijacking cargo freighters, where are they getting the raw materials they need to build new ships and cyborgs?"

"We suspect they're doing what we do and everyone else does," Admiral Bradlee said. "They've probably established mining operations on remote planets, moons, and asteroids to collect their own ore because it's far safer than tangling with us."

"They might even have entered into pacts with our enemies," Jenetta said.

"Which enemies?" Admiral Burke asked.

"Pick one. The Raiders, the Uthlaro, the Tsgardi— no, scratch the Tsgardi. We have them pretty well bottled up in their own solar system, and we've been keeping a close watch on their activities since they breached their containment that one time. But the Gondusans are also a possibility. When they later became a signatory to the THUG pact, we took back the territory we had allowed them to recover with the fall of the Milori government. That certainly didn't endear us to them."

"Why not the Milori?" Admiral Hillaire asked. "We took control of their *entire* empire after they surrendered and then we appended it to G.A. space."

"I don't think they'd participate in this. They have the best of all worlds now. They're legally able to exploit the wealth of all previously unclaimed resources in G.A. space without fear of reprisal. I honestly believe most Milori are tired of war and only want peace. But it could be someone we haven't fought yet, such as one of the numerous crime syndicates in Region Three. Perhaps all of them. They may have merged into another Raider-like force while I was on leave. I'm sure you remember that the Raider organization was created when all of the small and independent crime groups in Region One and the surrounding territories were united into one criminal force."

"Yes. We certainly don't need another Raider-like organization," Admiral Burke said.

"I'm surprised the Raiders have allowed the small crime organizations in Region Three to flourish," Admiral Woo said.

"That might be owed to the former Uthlaro military dominance in Region Three," Admiral Plimley said. "They probably kept the Raiders in check."

"But that military policing is gone now," Admiral Yuthkotl said.

"Yes," Jenetta said. "And it's no doubt left a tremendous power void that will naturally be filled in some manner. If Space Command can't successfully pick up the reins, some other organization will. The situation is one that, in physics, we refer to as 'horror vacui.' A more common articulation is 'nature abhors a vacuum.'"

"Yes," Admiral Plimley said. "A truism originally postulated by Aristotle, I believe."

"So are we looking for Denubbewa fleets or crime lords?" Admiral Burke asked.

"The Denubbewa— always," Jenetta said. "But let's not ignore the criminal element. We must try to keep the criminal groups from uniting— if they haven't already. And once we get the Denubbewa situation cleared, we can start putting pressure on the crime groups to pare down their illegal activities."

"I wonder if the Raiders will try— or are trying already— to bring the independents into their organization," Admiral Plimley said.

"I have a couple of top SCI teams and a number of independent agents now operating undercover in Region Three,"

Admiral Bradlee said. "It takes time for them to work their way into positions of trust, but they'll get there. And when they do they'll begin providing the invaluable intel we require to make decisions on how to proceed."

"While we're trying to gather intel about the independents, perhaps we should take a closer look at the Raiders," Admiral Bradlee said.

"Yes," Jenetta said. As the mess waiters approached the table with food and beverages, Jenetta smiled and said, "I make a motion that we suspend further work discussion until we convene in executive session following our break."

"I second the motion," Admiral Woo said. Punctuating his statement with a smile, he added, "I missed breakfast."

"Any objections?" Jenetta said. When no one objected, she smiled and said, "I guess the motion carries."

◆

Once the admirals, their aides, and the clerks had taken their seats in the Hall, Jenetta called the executive session to order.

"Before we resume the conversation we began in the dining room, I want to share a few thoughts. As you can certainly appreciate, there were a few months during my pregnancy where my mobility was considerably— restricted. As a result, I spent a lot of time lazing about and mulling over the problems I faced on Obotymot, as well as the problems being faced here in Regions Two and Three. I developed one idea in particular I wanted to present for consideration if I decided to return to Space Command.

"I'm sure you're all familiar with the details of the numerous covert missions conducted in Clidepp space by Lieutenant Sydnee Marcola and her crew. As you know, during her first mission she and her crew experienced a series of calamitous issues stemming from a design flaw with the temporal envelope chamber. The novel approach her people took in their effort to repair damage to the CPS-14 temporal generator resulted in the significant performance enhancement we now enjoy. That modification, and a few other necessary improvements, resulted in the small tug being re-designated as a

CPS-15. Additionally, all other new vessels include that enhancement, and all existing vessels are being retrofitted.

"I doubt anyone would argue that the Scout-Destroyer was a wonderful addition to the fleet. The smaller crew requirement gives us the ability to cover substantially more territory in less time than we could with full-sized warships. The development of the CPS-15 added another step forward in downsizing the crew size of ships with considerable warship capabilities. We were able to replace one Scout-Destroyer in every pair of SDs tasked to seek out and destroy Denubbewa motherships. Since a Scout-Destroyer has a crew complement of one hundred eighty-five and a CPS-15, when fully staffed, has a crew of just twenty-five, every attack pair requires one-hundred sixty fewer crewmembers than two Scout-Destroyers require. The savings in personnel allows us to have far better coverage as we search space for Denubbewa vessels and motherships. At this time, I'd like to propose that we again alter our attack-pair configuration to consist of just two CPS-16s. The bombs currently being ejected from an SD can just as easily be dropped from special habitat containers attached to the keel of a CPS-16, so each new attack pair will result in another savings of one hundred sixty fewer crewmembers. What does everyone think?"

The room was silent for a few seconds as the other admirals thought about the suggestion. The silence was broken when Admiral Burke said, "The idea has merit. As we well know, our biggest problem out here has been insufficient staffing and equipment levels. We simply don't have enough officers, enlisted, and ships to cover the vast areas of space in the G.A. given the expanded borders, even with the new speed enhancement."

"You said CPS-16, Jen," Admiral Plimley said. "The highest designation right now is CPS-15. Are you also proposing a ship upgrade or redesign?"

"Yes. The reports I've read about the missions into Clidepp space indicate that the quarters aboard a CPS-15 are far too small for extended voyages. The captain's combined office and sleeping quarters are smaller than the quarters assigned to an ensign aboard a destroyer."

"That's because the CPS-14 was originally intended for minor tasks of very short duration and distance."

"Exactly. But now we're talking about permanent shipboard assignments and long-duration missions. Aside from the captain, no crewmember aboard a CPS-15 has private quarters. Officers and enlisted all sleep in a single cabin area. They can only have complete privacy when they lower the special panel on their bunks. I'm proposing that the ship be elongated sufficiently to provide private quarters for the officers and petty officers, and two-person cabins if the new configuration includes enlisted below the rank of petty officer. An expanded mess area must also be provided. The captain should continue to have an office near the bridge— one that allows him or her to have private meetings with up to six other individuals— and a separate sleeping quarters area at least consistent with the space allocated to lieutenants aboard a destroyer."

"I thought the redesigned habitat containers had addressed most of those problems," Admiral Woo said.

"They've made things more bearable, but they were still only intended to alleviate issues on voyages of fairly short duration with the crew returning to a destroyer when the mission was complete. I'm suggesting permanent shipboard postings aboard CPS-16s, as have become routine with Scout Destroyers, and that all crew quarters and the crew mess hall be part of the ship rather than a level in a habitat container. The smaller ships, the CPS-14s and CPS-15s, will continue to be used for voyages and tasks of relatively short duration. Also, all ships must be able to transport up to thirty-two containers at any time, without modifications."

"Thirty-two?" Admiral Bradley echoed. "I thought the CPS-14 and 15 models were only designed to accommodate eight at a time. Why do we need a fourfold increase?"

"The CPS-14 was actually designed to accommodate twenty-four at the very beginning," Admiral Plimley said, "because one of the original intended roles of the CPS-14 was to deliver food and supplies to remote locations when a Quartermaster vessel wasn't readily available. However, the original build specification called for just one computer interface unit to be installed prior to delivery. That allows the monitoring of only eight containers. There were two additional but vacant console areas where additional computer interface units could be added, and the system could be upgraded and tested by any decent engineer to add a new interface unit within a week's time if additional interface units were needed. The computer interface units are actually included in the spare parts inventory at the time the builder turns the ship over to Space Command. During early production of the CPS-14, an additional interface unit was added, allowing an additional eight habitat containers on those ships."

"Why do the ships need so many interface units?" Admiral Hillaire asked.

"The container system itself is very similar to that of freighters in that you can keep adding just as many containers as you wish," Admiral Plimley said. "A freighter's only restriction is the ten-kilometer length limit imposed by the G.A. for travel safety. But a freighter's container-monitoring system is very unsophisticated. It's only needed to monitor temperature and pressure in the containers so the bridge will be alerted if someone opens a top hatch on the container or the container's basic environment is affected, either internally as by fire or from external damage to the container. The control system in CPS ships is a thousand times more complex because the habitat containers become an integral component of the ship once attached. Some containers are used for housing so the engineers must have a system that constantly monitors and controls the complex environmental systems on each deck of every container. Other containers house the ship's defensive and offensive weapons systems and are tied directly to the tactical station on the bridge. Still others are used to control and support flight operations, food storage and preparation, etc., etc."

"I see," Admiral Bradley said. "That all makes perfect sense."

"I have a question, Jen," Admiral Ahmed said. "If we make the modifications you're suggesting, will the new CPS fit inside the bay on a destroyer?"

"Good question, Raihana," Jenetta said. "At this time, I'm assuming the answer would be no. I've envisioned the final ship to appear as if someone cut a CPS-15 in half and stuck a large new section in the middle that would better accommodate the crew on their missions. The beam and diameter of the ship would remain the same, but the length would be greatly enhanced. Doing it this way would result in the least redesign work. The bridge and engineering sections of the CPS-15 are fine. We can use the bow and stern sections from the existing design. We just have to design a new three-deck mid-section. As I envision it, the new space on the top deck would contain all of the officer's quarters. One deck down, the new space would be used for the enlisted quarters and the new mess hall. The third deck would add a number of lockers for storage or other purposes. To accommodate the new design in a destroyer, the temporary airlock inside our newer destroyers would have to be greatly extended, assuming the basic diameter of the new CPS remains consistent. But the CPS-16 is not intended as a mere adjunct to the larger warships. The CPS-15s and Scout-Destroyers can continue to fill that role. The CPS-16 will be used for paired patrol duties until the Denubbewa are eradicated from G.A. space and then possibly as independent patrol ships in the future, which can also aid in search and rescue operations."

"Then you're suggesting we stop building large warships such as battleships?" Admiral Plimley asked.

"Not at all. We've already reduced the construction schedule of battleships and cruisers substantially over past decades. I believe the current production level is adequate. There's still a need for such vessels, albeit in a reduced role from what was once envisioned, and we'll need replacement ships as the current ships reach the end of their maximum useful life. Right now we need quantity over size. If Roger and his people are correct in their assessment of the situation, we must get as many ships as we can build and staff out there searching for and destroying Denubbewa vessels. Not just motherships, but Denubbewa warships as well."

Jen took a deep breath and asked, "Roger, how many reports of Denubbewa motherships have been included in those sightings you mentioned?"

"None."

"None? No motherships? Not a single one?"

"From the descriptions, we believe all sightings have been standard Denubbewa warship configurations."

"That doesn't make sense. With so many sightings, *someone* must have sighted a mothership."

"There's no way a Denubbewa mothership can possibly be confused with a warship. It would be like comparing a minnow to a whale on Earth. The display in a DeTect system would light up like an evening sporting event in a stadium. So I have to assume the reports are accurate. We distributed descriptions and images of the two different configurations to all freight companies and independents. Every report states the sighted vessel was a warship."

"Then I have to wonder where their motherships are," Jenetta said.

"Perhaps the motherships are in incredibly distant and remote locations," Admiral Hillaire said, "and the warships have been ordered not to make contact unless absolutely necessary to avoid being followed to the motherships."

"Perhaps," Jenetta said, nodding her head in thoughtful agreement.

"Maybe the Denubbewa have changed tactics since learning that we can destroy their motherships so easily," Admiral Yuthkotl said. "Perhaps they've weaned themselves off motherships and now operate as totally independent vessels."

"Possible, but unlikely," Jenetta said. "The motherships have to be their resupply and maintenance centers. Without them, they'd be forced to establish bases on planets. But given their seemingly mobile nature, it's hard to imagine them establishing fixed bases."

"The need to hide their presence from us may be outweighing their need for complete mobility," Admiral Bradley said.

There was silence around the table for a couple of minutes as everyone thought about the problem.

Jenetta broke the silence with, "I've just had a thought. What if the Denubbewa have taken a page from the Raider handbook? What if they've built bases inside asteroids?"

"Yes," Admiral Bradley said, nodding. "That's possible. Or what if they've simply begun disguising their bases as asteroids by collecting smaller asteroids and attaching them to their hulls so they appear as large chondrite asteroids?"

"Also a possibility," Jenetta agreed. "When the Raiders began hollowing out asteroids for use as hidden bases in space, we made a great effort to locate bases we knew existed. We had little luck finding them, but we were able to commandeer the two we did locate and adapt them for use as Space Command bases."

"We can't possibly search all of Region Three looking for hidden bases inside asteroids," Admiral Plimley said. "When they see we're searching in the vicinity, they'll simply close the entrance and go silent until we're gone. We don't have the resources or the time to minutely examine every asteroid looking for signs it might contain a hidden base."

"That won't be necessary," Jenetta said. "We've become far better equipped to search for disguised asteroid bases than we ever were before."

"I don't understand," Admiral Burke said. "How are we better equipped now than we were a decade or two ago? We still have to evaluate the composition of the asteroid and determine if it could house a base, then locate the entrance opening. And there are hundreds of thousands of enormous asteroids in G.A. space."

"Forget the old search-and-identify tactics," Jenetta said. "All we need do is have ships capable of double-envelope travel fly through every asteroid as they do with motherships. Instead of dropping bombs, we take a few images. In a fraction of a second we'll know if an asteroid is hollow and there's a hidden base inside or if the asteroid is really a disguised Denubbewa mothership."

"Brilliant!" Admiral Hillaire said. "Absolutely brilliant. Why haven't we thought of that before?"

"I suppose it's as the old Latin proverb says, 'Mater artium necessitas'," Jenetta said. "In Amer that sort of equates to the popular saying, 'Necessity is the mother of invention.' When we were searching for the Raider bases, we didn't have double-envelope capability. Once we developed the capability, we were focused on finding and stopping the Denubbewa and only used the new capability for planting bombs in the motherships. But now we can also use it to identify disguised Denubbewa bases, if that's what they're doing. And we can do it at Marc-One speeds."

CHAPTER THREE

~ March 11th, 2290 ~

Jenetta climbed into the rear area of the oh-gee limousine waiting on the roof of the Admiralty Building and plopped wearily into a plush chair. She was followed immediately by Cayla and Tayna, each of whom selected a seat according to their personal preference from among the variety of chairs and small couches in the large sitting area. The limo provided the ultimate in comfort for the weary. Since oh-gee vehicles didn't have to compete with other ground vehicles on narrow highway lanes, the limos used by G.A. officials on Quesann more closely resembled small floating cabins than the automotive limos used in previous centuries on earth.

Protocol dictated that security vehicles accompany any vehicle in which the Admiral of the Fleet was a passenger wherever he or she traveled on the planet, despite the fact that the assigned Dakinium-sheathed limo was very nearly impregnable. So Jenetta's ride home more closely resembled a parade than a simple commute.

Jenetta's first day at the Admiralty Hall had been long and exhausting, and she looked forward to getting home and possibly relaxing a little. Unfortunately, she had hours of reading ahead of her, or at least hours of listening as the small viewpad she carried read aloud to her.

The home assigned to Jenetta on Quesann was the one she'd occupied as Military Governor of Regions Two and Three. The enormous mansion, built to appear exactly like her family home on Obotymot— although it had one less floor— had been vacant since she left for extended leave. Admiral of the Fleet Moore had considered it too ostentatious for him because his family was still in Region One. He had chosen a more modest six-bedroom home on Admiral's Row for his quarters while on Quesann.

When moving to her family home and then returning to Quesann, it seemed like she'd never really left home at all. Admiral Holt, who had taken command of the Second Fleet while she was on extended leave, had remained at the beautiful home on Admiral's Row built for him when he'd first arrived on the planet to become Jenetta's second in command. There had been little occasion for Admiral Holt to entertain visiting dignitaries since the G.A. Senate had naturally taken full responsibility for the governance of Regions Two and Three when Jenetta left on extended leave. The task had been theirs all along, but their remoteness while on Earth meant that Jenetta was best suited to handle that role from inside Region Two. Her promotion to Admiral of the Fleet meant that her full attention would now be required for that military role.

Day-to-day governorship of Regions Two and Three was now in the hands of civilian administrators who had arrived with the G.A. Senate. Since all civilian employees were required to live in homes built on the government housing campus rather than on the military reservation, Jenetta's home on Quesann had remained vacant during her absence.

As the limousine lifted off with its escort and trailing security vehicles, Jenetta whimsically wished she could drive herself. She knew she'd never have an opportunity to pilot a ship again, at least not while she remained in the position of Admiral of the Fleet. Some people appreciated being chauffeured everywhere, but she longed for the days when she could occasionally jump into her private fighter on Quesann and zip through winding canyons on land or wave-hop across the oceans at maximum atmospheric speed. Her position allowed her to simply order that she be given control of the vehicle, but it wouldn't be seemly and would probably wound the egos of the people chosen to chauffer her.

When the small convoy of vehicles approached the location of her home, no building was visible at that location. It appeared merely to be a small park with lovely gardens. When someone in the lead vehicle gave the proper identification, the protective bubble dissolved and the house and real grounds became visible. The security vehicles then broke off and returned to other duties as Jenetta's limo landed on the pad near the front entrance of the house. The protective bubble immediately reappeared to hide the house from the eyes of anyone outside the perimeter of the grounds.

The bubble wasn't merely a disguise. It was also a force field that would cause any vehicle or object attempting to penetrate the grounds to lose all power and crash as it tried to cross the perimeter or to explode before it could penetrate the barrier if it was a weapon. Oh-gee vehicles that strayed from the designated driving paths had to fly high enough to avoid the invisible protective domes covering homes on the military base and the government housing areas. And anyone flying high enough to avoid the domes would immediately find themselves being chased by security vehicles or aircraft.

As the limo set down on the pad outside the house, a security officer hurried from the house to lend any assistance required. Normally, security personnel remained hidden from family view, but there were times when they emerged to offer help with carrying luggage or whatever bundles the residents carried.

Upon entering the house, Jenetta headed first to the nursery on the third floor. She found Ruby and Jake playing on the carpeted floor with Kaycee and Kyle. The children, now six months of age, were naturally as helpless as any Terran child at that age. The young Jumakas, having just celebrated their first birthday, had almost reached their full adult size, but they were as gentle with the children as they had been when they were still kittens. And they loved playing with the twins. Kyle was presently atop Jake, who was lying on his back so Jake couldn't move, but Ruby ran over to greet Jenetta, Cayla, and Tanya. Celona, the Nordakian maid who had come with them to help with the children, stood as Jenetta entered the room.

"Celona, I've told you that you don't have to jump up when I enter the room."

"My parents taught me I must always show the proper respect, Your Grace, no matter how close we become. I'd feel very uncomfortable not standing."

"I understand," Jen said with a sad look. Turning towards the young Jumaka, Jenetta smiled and said, "Hi, Ruby. Are you and Kaycee having fun?"

"Hello, Jenetta," the young Jumaka said, the words issuing from her collar translator. "Yes. I love playing with Kaycee, but I wish she could talk with me."

"I know, dear. It may be another year before she can have conversations with you, but it will come. Just be patient."

"I will. Momma has explained it to me. You know, I can't imagine how you all got along before you made our collars. I'd go crazy if I couldn't talk with Terrans."

"It would have been wonderful if I could have spoken with Tayna and Cayla from the start of our time together, but we managed to communicate and show our love for each other in other ways."

"Jenetta told the people at the meeting today that she wants us to be treated as equals with Terrans and all other in-telligent races in the G.A.," Cayla said.

"Aren't we already treated as equals?" Kaycee asked.

"In this house and on Obotymot, always. But outside the grounds here, you might find people who will react to you as if they'd just encountered a deadly beast. You've been fortu-nate not to have been exposed to the treatment we knew at your age, and Jenetta says it will continue to get better for Jumakas now."

"It won't happen overnight," Jenetta said. "It may take a little time, but it *will* slowly get better until all Jumakas are accepted as sentient beings with all the rights and privileges Terrans enjoy." Walking to where Kaycee was sitting, she picked up her daughter, checked her diaper, then hugged her gently. She then smiled widely as she held the child at face level just slightly away from her body. "How's my beautiful little girl today? Are you having fun playing with Ruby?"

Kaycee stared back at Jenetta and smiled, obviously not understanding a word but fully understanding the expression of love, caring, and gentleness directed towards her from her mother.

Jenetta then moved over to where Kyle was lying atop Jake. "And how are you today, Jake?" she asked.

"Hi, Jenetta," the young male Jumaka said, looking up from the floor. "I'm fine. Welcome home."

"Thank you. How are you and Kyle getting along today?"

"Good. He's getting strong. When he pulls on my belly fur now, I can really feel it."

"Just be patient with him. He doesn't understand yet that it hurts a little."

"Oh, it doesn't hurt. At least not yet. Perhaps in another year it will."

Jenetta smiled. "Hopefully by then we'll be able to make him understand that he shouldn't pull it at all."

"I don't mind."

"Good."

Just then the door opened and Jenetta's mother entered the room.

"Ah, you're home at last, dear. We've been holding dinner. Come on, everyone. Dinner is ready."

Celona picked up Kyle, checked his diaper, and began walking with the other adults towards the door while Ruby and Jake raced out of the room at breakneck speed. They needed to stretch their legs after hours of lounging in the nursery while they played with and watched over Kaycee and Kyle.

Jenetta had accepted the promotion of Admiral of the Fleet solely because of the children. She could perform her duties with the military and still be home most evenings to be with her kids, just like other working moms with more normal jobs. During the day, her mother, her maid Celona who had requested she be allowed to accompany them, and the two young Jumakas would watch over and protect her progeny. If that wasn't enough, there was always a squadron of Marines on duty in and around the house to protect the occupants of the home and the staff.

◆

"When were you going to tell us, dear?" Annette Carver said as they began to enjoy their meal.

"Tell you what, Momma?" Jenetta replied.

"About Jimmy's promotion to Captain, that his new command was a brand-new destroyer, and about the ship being assigned to the Second Fleet at Quesann."

"You already knew. I heard from Jimmy today and he said he was sending the news to everyone in the family."

"Why didn't you tell us his promotion was pending?"

"I didn't know. I was pretty involved with managing the immigrant situation at home and dealing with a mission for King Tpalsh, so I fell behind on reading the Admiralty Board minutes. I'm still trying to catch up."

"What was it you did for the king, dear? You never told us."

"My mission was to give the President of Dakistee a formula developed on Nordakia that would cure the planetary sterility problem plaguing the Dakistians, while at the same time cementing a new bond of friendship between Dakistee and Nordakia."

"And did you complete the missions?"

"I believe so. Only time will tell if it lasts. The President of Dakistee maintains a lot of personal hostility towards the people of Nordakia, even though the ones who wronged her people died twenty centuries ago. I'm afraid I might have angered her myself because I had to resort to a sort of blackmail to accomplish my mission. But it was the only way to help her people and ours."

"Blackmail?"

"Sort of. I told her we had the cure for her planet's problem but that she would have to mend fences with Nordakia if she wanted to receive it. I told her she must first appear before planet-wide media and declare her friendship with the Nordakian people and announce that they were forever welcome on Dakistee. Only then would the ambassador from Nordakia turn over the cure."

"And she agreed to that?"

"Yes, she agreed. Reluctantly. And she made a face like I had forced her to drink a gallon of lemon concentrate at one sitting."

"Do you think she'll stand by her word?"

CHANGING OF THE GUARD

"She's a politician. Who can know what politicians will do or how long they'll stand by their solemn promises? Most will turn on a dime when it's in their personal interests to ignore everything they've promised. But at least she declared in front of the national media that Nordakia has provided the cure to the sterility problem and that it didn't cost them a single G.A. credit. The people will remember, even if the politicians conveniently forget."

"Wonderful. I'm sure that when she thinks it over, she'll be glad you forced her to do the right thing. By the way, when can we expect Jimmy to arrive here at Quesann?"

"If everything is found to be satisfactory when he completes the initial space trials with the new ship, he'll be directed to proceed to Quesann. The voyage to Region Two will provide them with a good shakedown cruise where the crew will have an opportunity to get comfortable with other crewmembers while not having a bunch of shipyard inspectors constantly looking over their shoulders and watching their every movement during duty hours. Jimmy should arrive here in less than six months if everything goes well."

"That would be wonderful. It's been such a long time since he's been able to come home for a visit."

◆ ◆ ◆

Aliana Shanara grimaced and kicked off her heels as she entered her apartment after a hard day at the office. As she walked over to her favorite chair in the living room and plopped into its soft comfort, she ordered a tumbler of scotch on the rocks from her automated butler.

Aliana wanted to return to her Mikel Arneu appearance, or even a male with another identity, but she remained stuck in the body of a woman because the Upper Council refused to allow her to change back into a male. Their latest comment was that she was so much more pleasant as a woman. Besides that, the full transformation back to a male could sideline her for as much as a year. Since Aliana had first been appointed to head the Lower Council, she had been known throughout the organization as a cast-iron bitch who never gave an inch or smiled even once during the workday. It was rumored she derived pleasure from sneering and cursing out her subordinates. One thing that could not be argued was that the company had become significantly more profitable since she'd been appointed to the position. The Upper Council certainly didn't want that to change. Aliana knew that if she simply let the profits slide in a disguised effort to be replaced, the Upper Council would most likely dispose of her rather than fire her. So she was stuck as she was unless the Upper Council suddenly had a change of heart. And since Aliana knew that the Upper Council members had no hearts, she would only be able to get away if the entire Upper Council ceased to exist. That thought was never very far from her mind, but she knew the entire Upper Council would have to die at the same time, and a means of accomplishing that had so far eluded Aliana.

While she waited for her scotch, she turned on the evening news. It was a good thing she hadn't yet received the tumbler of scotch when the top story of the day was reported or it would have been decorating the whole-wall media screen after the tumbler smashed against it. The story announced that Admiral Jenetta Carver had been promoted to the rank of Admiral of the Fleet and had just conducted her first Admiralty Board meeting. Shanara scowled because she knew Carver was almost definitely beyond her reach now— at least for a number of years. The Admiral of the Fleet was always surrounded by a plethora of security people whenever he or she was out in public, an occasion that was in itself very rare. But neither Aliana nor Jenetta would die a natural death for thousands of years, so Aliana would just bide her time until another opportunity presented itself.

The news station was actually reporting events that had occurred days earlier because the Admiralty Board was now ensconced on the new base at Quesann. When the Board had been on Earth, the news reached the planet Centrasia, where the Raider headquarters was located, in just one day. Naturally, the Raider Corporation never used their real identity on legal documents. On Centrasia they were known as Weltez Commercial Industries, or WCI. It was the perfect cover for the criminal organization. On Centrasia, the government never looked closely at conglomerates that paid their taxes promptly while also paying healthy bribes to the government people tasked with regulating corporate entities.

Aliana scowled at the success Carver had enjoyed since their first encounter. Every time she had attempted to commit Carver and her sisters to a life of slavery in a Raider pleasure resort, have them killed outright, or even kill them personally, she had failed.

Aliana's attention was brought sharply back to the media report when Jenetta walked to face the newsies in the visitor gallery. Two large animals that appeared to be Terran Jaguars with black fur, accompanied her. Jenetta then presented an appeal to the public that her pets be declared sentient. Aliana started to laugh, believing it was some kind of prank, but she returned to seriousness as the cats began speaking to the newsies. Her disbelief that the two Jaguars were actually producing the speech she heard slowly turned to belief as the interview process continued.

Aliana had first learned of the two animals owned by Carver when an assassin hired by the Raiders had tried to terminate Jenetta's life on the base she had 'liberated' from the Raider organization. At the time, she had attributed their action simply to pets protecting their owner. But this made far more sense. If the cats Jenetta referred to as Jumakas were sentient and actually understood Amer, they would be invaluable as bodyguards. She could use a couple of bodyguards who would protect her with their lives and couldn't be bribed to look the other way, disappear at a critical moment, or commit the act themselves. Carver had indicated during the appeal for a sentiency proclamation that her two females had just given birth to a total of eight cubs. That indicated there might be many other Jumakas outside Taurentlus-Thur. And if there were, cubs must be available. Aliana was now determined to get a mated pair before they were declared sentient. Her final thought before downing the scotch in one gulp was to wonder how long it would take a pair of Jumakas to rip out the throats of every Upper Council member as they gathered for a session.

◆　◆　◆

The Space Command shipyards had terminated production of CPS-14s when the upgraded model became the primary vessel in the class. The CPS-15s were similar enough that ninety-two percent of the completed hull sections and components constructed for the 14s could be used for the more powerful ship without any modification. While CPS-15s would continue to be built, their production schedules were suspended as work crews immediately began constructing CPS-16s. Once again, the new design was similar enough to the previous ship in the class that most of the completed CPS-15 hull sections and components could be used for the extended CPS-16 without modification. In computer model simulations, the redesigned ship worked to perfection. Since the bow and stern sections of the two ship designs were identical, as were the sub-light engines, the first CPS-16s could be ready to begin space trials in less than three months. Production of the CPS-15s would recommence in a limited fashion when the priority order for ninety-eight CPS-16s was filled to satisfaction.

At the same time that work on the CPS-16s began at the Lorense-Three shipyard, work on the new habitat containers that would house and deploy the bombs began at the Mars shipyard. The bombs dropped by the Scout-Destroyers had been so successful that the design would not change, but the quantities produced would increase tremendously for at least a year. Since their missions were expected to last a considerable time, the CPS-16s would bring most of their ordnance with them. That was why all CPS-16s had to be able to handle up to thirty-two habitat containers.

Planners envisioned that the commanding officer of a Scout-Destroyer, likely a Space Command officer with the rank of commander, would coordinate the search activities of a squadron of twenty-four CPS-16s operating in pairs as they sought to root out and destroy Denubbewa motherships and warships. Jenetta had had no moral issues with the search and destroy missions against the cyborgs ever since the Denubbewa had, without provocation, destroyed the *Yenisei* and *Salado*, killing most crewmembers outright and mutilating the bodies of survivors in some sort of medical experiment. It was therefore a proven fact that the Denubbewa would maim and kill Space Command and Space Marine personnel at any opportunity. The invaders should have vacated G.A. space long ago. Their destruction now would be owed to their own failure to accept that they were violating a claimed and occupied area of space where they were not welcome and where the occupants were fully capable of defending their space.

The newly recognized threat posed by a deadly enemy gave shipbuilding efforts the highest priority. Work schedules on new battleships and even destroyers where the hull had been laid would be delayed until the CPS-16 design was in full production. The CPS-16 docks would receive whatever they needed as soon as it was available. The shipbuilding crews, unaware of the reason for the revised scheduling and urgency, joked that Carver, with so many firsts in so many areas, probably wanted to set a new record for the most ships ever produced by Space Command during her first year as Admiral of the Fleet. But they all knew, to a person, that Admiral Carver didn't pursue such foolish recognitions and responded to the work demands as if war was about to break out any day. Most had been working at the yards when war did break out with the Milori and then the THUG pact, so they knew that such heightened shipbuilding activity only preceded a situation where the safety and security of the G.A. was at stake.

CHAPTER FOUR

~ May 23rd, 2290 ~

"Excellent," Jenetta said several times to the shipyard manager, Commander Tildroy, as she toured the first CPS-16 completed at the Lorense-Three yard. "The crew will have decent quarters for long-term voyages. Let's look at the two special habitat containers."

Ten minutes later, the viewing party of four admirals, the senior yard officer, and four senior members of the commander's staff entered the first special container. As always, Cayla and Tayna were at Jenetta's sides.

Special containers had previously been constructed for housing Marines, defensive and offensive weapons for the ship, and aircraft, but this one was a special container for the crew. Manufactured at the enormous underground facilities on Mars, the first group of thirty units had just arrived a few days earlier.

The top level was devoted to an oval running track. No longer would CPS crews on long voyages have to run back and forth in a corridor for exercise. The oval track would be a welcome addition. Going down, the next two levels each housed two courts that could be used for squash or handball. The next level contained a swimming pool suitable for swimming laps and a spa that accommodated up to six individuals. The lowest level in the container was devoted to enormous tanks that could suck the pools dry in minutes and store the water if battle action was expected. The CPS-14 had been designed so that side-mounted external tanks could be added in place of two shuttles in case the mission called for the ability to submerge the ship for concealment. With the new container attached, the ship would always have negative buoyancy when landing in water. In the event of an emergency, the water in the storage tanks could be pumped out of the habitat container in minutes to restore buoyancy.

"Better water and sport amenities than you see on some cruise ships," Admiral Woo joked.

"Our people may have to spend many months or even years in space on long, boring missions," Admiral Plimley said. "They deserve a few recreational diversions."

"I agree," Woo said. "I was just making a witticism."

"Our people in these small ships should enjoy some of the same exercise apparatus our people posted to destroyers and larger ships enjoy," Jenetta said. "A long voyage with nothing to do can seem like an eternity."

"The crews assigned to these ships are going to have it better than our people in Scout-Destroyers," Admiral Ressler said. "As far as I know, no Scout Destroyer has a pool or hot tub."

"That's true," Admiral Plimley said. "Once they learn the CPS-16s have one, they'll all want one. But the SDs would need a major redesign to include a pool."

"Can't we simply add a docking collar beneath the SDs to accommodate one of these containers?" Admiral Woo asked.

"Perhaps not simply, but it's definitely possible," Admiral Plimley said. "The problem is that the docking collar and container would prevent the ship from performing as a bomber. I'll have to look into it to see if there's some way to accommodate a recreational container."

"At least all of the full-sized warships already have running tracks, handball courts, and pools," Admiral Ressler said, "so we won't have to break the budget converting them."

"The new destroyers already have docking apparatus for a habitat container, so we'd only have to give them a container like this one if they needed it," Admiral Woo said.

"Let's take a look at the container that lets this ship earn its pleasurable new accoutrements," Jenetta said.

Over the next half-hour, Commander Tildroy gave a detailed explanation of how the new container functioned, from automatic ordnance reloading from a destroyer's weapon stores when the CPS-16 was docked with a destroyer to targeting and deployment of the bombs.

When the tour was over, Jenetta and the other admirals thanked Commander Tildroy and his staff and transferred to

Jenetta's CPS-15 barge for the trip back to Quesann. The Admiralty Board dining room staff had arranged for a lunch to be served aboard the barge on the return trip.

"The new ship is impressive," Admiral Woo said as they took their seats at the table. "That was a good idea, Jen. The crews will be much better rested on long voyages. And well-rested crews are better prepared to handle whatever comes at them. I especially liked the lifts in the new habitat containers. Our people will no longer have to climb ladders while a CPS-16 is on the ground or use weightlessness when the ships are in space. Normally it's fine, I suppose, but when you have to move something, it can be extremely difficult not to have the use of your hands to hold whatever you're moving."

"We've designed the lift tubes to be an integral part of the container, not the ship," Admiral Plimley, the director of Weapons R&D and SC Shipyard Management, said, "so they are immediately available for use in every model since the CPS-14. Of course, a lot of existing containers will have to be retrofit. But we gain more room because we can remove the stairways used in some containers. In the event of a system malfunction, the elevator shaft becomes a gravity-free tube in space. On the ground, there're ladder rungs built into a re-cessed area on the side of the tube."

"Loretta," Jenetta said to Admiral Plimley, "how soon will we have a squadron of CPS-16s available to deploy?"

"If the space trials go smoothly, the first squadron can de-ploy in as little as 60 days. That's assuming we reduce the normal space trial period from ninety days to thirty."

"A CPS-16 certainly doesn't have the complexity of a de-stroyer," Admiral Woo said, "and most of the ship has been proven for some time. A good crew should be able to put their 16 through its paces in thirty days."

"That's a reasonable assumption," Admiral Ressler said. "We'd better get busy assembling crews. What about the SDs necessary to command the squadrons?"

"The Second Fleet took delivery of four new SDs two months ago," Jenetta said. "I asked Brian at that time to re-serve them for this project. So all we need are the crews. They're going to need some practice time so the paired CPS-

16s can release their bombs at exactly the right nanosecond. The computer systems will have all the proper software installed. We'll just need to make sure the control systems aboard the ships are properly synced before squadrons deploy on their missions."

"Where should they begin?" Admiral Woo asked.

"Region Three, naturally," Jenetta said. "That's where all the sighting reports are coming from."

"But where in Region Three?" Admiral Ressler asked. "Region Three is three times the size of Region One."

"We'll have to see where the greatest concentrations of sightings have occurred and begin at that approximate location."

"And our ships should destroy all Denubbewa they encounter?" Admiral Woo asked.

"The general orders should be to simply follow any Denubbewa warships the CPS-16s encounter."

"You're hoping they'll lead us to their motherships, Jen?" Admiral Plimley asked.

"Yes. Since we've had no sightings of Denubbewa motherships, their warships will have to show us where they're hiding."

"And if they don't?" Admiral Woo asked.

"If there's no contact between Denubbewa warships and motherships, I suppose we'll have to assume that there are no motherships associated with the warships we're following."

"And how long will we continue to follow them?"

"Unless the warships lead us to a mothership or attack someone in G.A. Space, we'll simply follow them until new orders are issued. At that time, we unload on them until there's nothing left but small chunks of cyborg servo mechanisms and spaceship."

◆　◆　◆

The morning's Admiralty Board meeting had ended and Jenetta was in her office working at her desk when her viewpad chimed once, very softly. Tapping a touch point on the face of the device, she learned that a vidMail from her sister Christa had been added to the incoming queue. She needed a break so she activated the full wall monitor that faced her desk, then selected the vidMail from among all the others that had arrived that day.

As the image of Christa took shape on the wall, Jenetta leaned back in her chair and smiled. The image was a recording so Christa couldn't see the smile, and it simply indicated that she was happy to hear from her sister.

"Hi, sis," the larger-than-life image appeared to say. "I've been so busy that I haven't vidMailed you in over two weeks. I guess it's been the same with you. I hope you, Kaycee, Kyle, Momma, Cayla, Tayna, Ruby, Jake, Celona, and everyone else are fine. Whew! That list seems to get longer every time I say it. Perhaps in the future I'll just refer to them as 'the gang.' I'm doing fine, but I've been busy wrapping things up here. Sometimes it's hard to believe I've been here five years, but other days it seems like I've been here forever. The scuttlebutt is that something big is brewing because the shipyards are busy 24/7 making warships—warships on the small side perhaps, but still as deadly as they come. I want in, and I'm hoping you can help me get to wherever it is we're preparing to go and whatever we need to do. The rumor system is good, but nobody yet has a clue exactly why the shipyards and munitions plants are working around the clock.

"So how about it, sis? Can you use another experienced officer in this upcoming fight? I know you said you'd find me a second seat on a battleship, but I suspect the smaller ships are again going to see most of the action, as was the case when the THUG pact made a move on Region Two. So, do you need an experienced commander for a Scout-Destroyer mission? I hope so because I'd hate to be sitting at my desk on Dakistee while our comrades are fighting to protect the G.A. from whatever threat now faces us.

"I'm going to send Momma a vidMail after I finish this one, but I won't be mentioning anything about the new danger facing the G.A. Let me know as soon as you can.

"Love ya.

"Christa Marie Carver, S.C. Commander, North Pendleton Marine Base, Dakistee. End of message."

Jenetta took a deep breath and then released it. Christa had been on assignment to Dakistee for more than five years, although she hadn't technically been in a posted position there for that amount of time. She had been sent there to investigate a new underground facility discovered by archeologists and was supposed to return to her real posting when she completed the mission. The brief mission turned into a five-year tour because she was the best qualified to help the Dakistians after directly being involved in awakening them. And she was too valuable an asset to be left sitting at a desk on Dakistee while Space Command was gearing up for possible action.

Jenetta reached out and touched a contact spot on her viewpad that would send a message to her aide, then said aloud, "See if you can reach Admiral Holt."

A voice said, "Right away, Admiral."

Several minutes later Jenetta heard, "Admiral Holt is on your com channel."

"Thank you," Jenetta said before touching a different spot on the viewpad. The full wall monitor lit up again, this time with a live image of Admiral Holt. A camera would also be projecting a live image of Jenetta, unless she chose to block it. She didn't. A tiny blinking green light on the edge of the wall monitor indicated that the communication was being encrypted in both directions. The highly secure encryption scheme on the base changed daily, and it was virtually impossible for anyone to listen in or even record the transmission for later disassembly and transcription.

"Good afternoon, Brian. I hope I'm not pulling you away from something important."

"Hi, Jen. No, I'm just working in my office. And apparently you are as well."

"The paperwork never ends. Brian, the reason I'm calling is because I have a superior officer who's wrapping up a duty tour and is in need of a good assignment. I'm not trying to influence your decision regarding the assignment of officers for the four new Scout-Destroyers, but I wanted to offer you the services of this officer if you're interested. Have you completed your appointments for the new ships you received?"

"I've decided on two officers and have eight more under consideration. Two of the remaining eight officers lead the pack by a decent measure. None have received reassignment orders yet. Who did you have in mind? Christa?"

Jenetta smiled and said, "You're always one step ahead of me."

"We both know that isn't accurate, but sometimes I can almost keep up. As a matter of fact, I was going to call you to see if she might be available soon."

"If you want her for one of the SDs, she's yours."

"I want her."

"Okay, I'll start the process to free her from Dakistee and bring her here."

"Wonderful. We're going to need the brightest and best for this upcoming engagement. The Denubbewa aren't a JV team. That makes three top officers. I only need to decide on one more."

"Who are the other two?"

"Commander Burl Kalborne and Commander Walter Fareman."

"I'm familiar with their records, although I've never met either of them. They appear to be good officers."

"As soon as I decide on a fourth, I'll be submitting the list to the A.B. for approval."

"If the fourth is as good as the first three, there won't be a problem with the approval."

"You don't happen to have another sister who might be interested in the seat, do you?"

Jenetta laughed. "Eliza is very happy aboard the *Ares*. But if she learns that the warships are not going to be a part of this operation, she might start angling for a change. I'm not going to offer it to her though. Larry would be angry with me if I took away his second in command."

"Jen, Larry wouldn't be angry with you if you took away his entire bridge crew. He'd only get angry if he was beached. And even then he'd never be angry with *you*. He holds you in the same high regard I do. We're all friends and always will be."

"If you really want me to recommend someone, I will."

"I'm listening."

"My former aide, Commander Lori Ashraf, might be interested. She's second seat on the destroyer *Stuttgart*."

"I remember her. How're her command skills?"

"Top shelf. She was my second when I commanded the SD *Colorado* against the THUGs, so she's had quite a bit of command and battle experience."

"If you recommend her, I want her. Do you want to contact her?"

"It would be more appropriate if the initial contact came from you. But you can mention that I recommended her."

"Okay. I'll send a vidMail today, enquiring about her interest. The *Stuttgart* is on patrol about a week away. If she's interested, I'll order the ship to return or find someone else to bring her here. What about Christa?"

"I'll make arrangements to get her here as soon as possible, but since she's on Dakistee, three weeks is the absolute best time, even at Marc-One. And that's only if an upgraded DS ship is headed this way from somewhere in the vicinity. If I have to send my barge, it'll be six weeks."

"Each squadron will deploy just as soon as the unit is complete, Jen, but as I understand it, all ninety-six of the CPS-16s needed for the four squadrons won't have wrapped up their space trials for at least six months. Some of them haven't even had their major hull sections assembled yet. We have enough time to get all personnel prepared and in place."

"It's not necessary to have the entire task force assembled before we begin operations. Once you have the first squadron complete and ready, you can deploy them to their assigned territory."

"The other school of thought is that once we find and destroy the first Denubbewa mothership, the others may pull back and make themselves even more difficult to locate."

"Yes, that's a consideration. Another perspective is that if the motherships are on the move to avoid us, they'll be easier to spot. Well, the decision is yours as commander of the Second Fleet, Brian. You know I trust your judgment implicitly."

"As I do yours. We'll see how things progress at the shipyard and with the space trials and possibly revisit the deployment strategy as the first squadron nears its readiness point."

"Okay, Brian, we'll wait and see how things progress. Have a great day."

"You also, Jen. Holt out."

"Carver out."

Jenetta leaned back in her chair and thought about the conversation— specifically about Commander Ashraf. They hadn't seen one another since Jen had left for her extended leave, although they'd communicated with vidMails as much as once a month. Jen had known that Ashraf was second seat aboard the *Stuttgart* and wondered if she'd give up such a position to accept command of a much smaller ship. If she did as good a job in an SD as she'd done previously as second-in-command, it might even enhance her chances of promotion to captain of a full-sized warship. Jen shrugged and decided not to get involved with the decision. It was entirely up to Lori.

◆　◆　◆

"You may go right in, Admiral Hillaire," Jen's aide said. "You're expected."

Hillaire nodded and approached the office door. As he stepped into the area where the door sensor could identify his CT, the doors slid open.

"Come in, Arnold, and have a seat. We're all ready to begin."

All of the other members of the Admiralty Board were already seated in the large office. Admiral Hillaire was the last to arrive.

As Hillaire got comfortable in the lounge chair he'd selected, Jen said, "I want to thank you all for coming to this unofficial meeting of the Board today. I've been told this is highly unusual because we have no aides and nothing said here will be recorded, but as many of you know, I've always preferred to keep certain plans secret. The possibility that our enemies might learn of our plans before we have a chance to implement them has always worried me."

"We can talk openly in executive session," Admiral Ahmed said, "without fear of having our discussion recorded."

"Yes, Raihana, but our aides and clerks would still know what we discussed."

"But they all have a Most Secret security clearance," Admiral Yuthkotl said.

"Yes, Lesbolh, but they still might talk among themselves and someone without a Most Secret clearance might catch part of the conversation."

"So what's so hush-hush, Jen?" Admiral Bradlee asked. "Are you planning a coup of the G.A. Senate?" The smile that accompanied his question showed that he was kidding.

"No today, Roger. But what I wanted to discuss might seem that way to some."

"I was just kidding, Jen," Admiral Bradlee said.

"I know, Roger, but I'm not."

"Don't keep us in the dark, Jen," Admiral Woo said. "Tell us what this is about."

"Okay, Lon, here it is. When we discussed the actions of the new CPS-16 deployment, there was something else I wanted to discuss, but I hesitated to mention it even in executive session. I wouldn't even mention it in the lunch room where none of the clerks would be because the mess attendants could possibly hear. So here it is. I want every ship in Space Command that has double-envelope capability to fly though every asteroid in G.A. space."

"Looking for Denubbewa?" Admiral Plimley asked.

"Yes, Loretta. And also for Raider bases or the bases of any other group, organization, or military that is seeking to hide themselves from us. Naturally, they won't enter Dixon or Stewart, but every other asteroid should be searched."

"That's an enormous task," Admiral Hillaire said. "It was overwhelming when we were just talking about doing it in Region Three."

"Yes, I know, but I believe it will be worth it. Every ship with double-envelope capability flies though every asteroid at top speed and takes images of the interior. If the asteroid has been hollowed out, even partially, we'll know, and the occupants will never suspect we visited them. We can create a database of hits and put it aside until we wrap up the Denubbewa threat. Then, when our current plate is clean, we go after the Raiders or anyone else who may be hiding their presence and illicit activity in G.A. space."

"So far I haven't heard anything that even remotely sounds like something we're not currently empowered to do," Admiral Bradlee said, "or something of which the G.A. Senate might disapprove."

"Okay, here's part two of my wish list. We use the information we've gathered to begin putting an end to slavery in Region Three. We've been so busy defending G.A. space from incursions by enemy nations that we haven't addressed that very important issue, but it's one that must be resolved. We can't continue to denounce slavery in the Clidepp Empire while we're ignoring slavery here."

"We're not ignoring slavery here, Jen," Admiral Bradlee said. "Unlike the Clidepp government, which openly embraces slavery of Terrans and even profits from it, the G.A. Charter denounces slavery in every form for every sentient species and makes it illegal in G.A. space. We just haven't had the resources to stop it. My people have been working to identify where all of the so-called pleasure resorts are located in preparation for the day when we have the resources to begin eradicating slavery in Region Three. But identification is one thing, and stopping it is quite a different matter. The space station locations will be difficult, but not impossible, to commandeer. However, where slavery is perpetrated on a planetary scale, stopping it is another issue entirely. The Galactic Alliance Senate has never established a ground force because the charter forbids intervention in planetary matters. Our Space Marine forces are only charged with maintaining shipboard security or for performing limited Special Ops missions on planets."

"Roger makes a good point, Jen," Admiral Woo said. "You've ably demonstrated with the Tsgardi, the Milori, and the Uthlaro that Space Command is quite able to conquer an enemy by destroying their space fleets and even laying waste to their planets from outside their sensible atmosphere. What we seem to be talking about now is taking over an entire planetary government *without* causing considerable infrastructure destruction and inhabitant death. But we've never had the ability to invade a planet and take over a government without first destroying the infrastructure."

"Exactly," Jenetta said. "That's where I was headed. It's time we create a large Marine ground force specifically trained to handle significant hostile situations on planet surfaces."

"That's going to be a really hard sell in the G.A. Senate," Admiral Burke said. "I'm sure some of the Senators will immediately assume the worst. It's always seemed to me that one of their greatest fears is that Space Command would one day grow too powerful for them to control."

"I agree that there will be a great gnashing of teeth," Jenetta said, "even though we've never done anything to support a fear we might attempt to wrest power from the Senate. We're a military organization that operates under civilian authority, and we've always been careful not to violate the power and authority they've vested in Space Command and the Space Marines.

"If we're forced to deploy ground forces," Jenetta continued, "I'm not sure we could avoid inflicting a considerable amount of death and destruction. We've all studied the tactics used on Earth and other worlds during periods of war. Destruction of the enemy's infrastructure has always been the main battle strategy when conquering a government that still refuses to capitulate as a more powerful force moves in. When I said ground forces, I was thinking more of police actions, but it might not be possible to take command of a planet without resorting to considerable violence and force as the planetary protection forces are subjugated. If our goal is to liberate a significant part of a population that's being held in slavery, a surreptitious effort to create a fifth column on the planet—assuming one doesn't already exist—might be the best place to begin. Then, in time, we can begin a ground assault with the support we've been able to establish on the planet.

"I realize the enormity of the task ahead of us. Even discounting the ongoing threat from the Denubbewa, we've only got a tenuous handle on protecting our territory and bringing the rule of law and order to Regions Two and Three. We still have a major uphill battle ahead of us. All we want is peace, freedom, and security, but there seems to be a never-ending effort by others who are greedy for power and wealth to deny us that. We must have a way to enforce the rule of G.A. law on those planets that refuse to adhere to the few restrictions we demand, such as no slavery, no G.A. credits forgery, and no narcotic distribution outside a planet's atmosphere. In the past, we've had planets request that we step in to help them deal with serious criminal elements or civilian uprisings, but the G.A. Senate has always refused because it violates our Charter. It's time to amend the Charter— slightly."

"I believe you have the full support of the Board, Jen," Admiral Platt said, "but as Raymond speculated, it might be a hard sell in the G.A. Senate. A very hard sell."

"I'll have to tread carefully lest I create the wrong impression regarding our need for a ground force. If anyone has a better idea before I begin working on my proposal to the Senate Council, I'm listening."

CHAPTER FIVE

~ June 28th, 2290 ~

"Commander Carver has arrived, Admiral," Jenetta heard on her viewpad.

"Send her in," Jenetta said as she stood to come out from behind her desk.

The pocket doors to the outer office slid open a few seconds later. Christa entered and came to attention a meter from the desk. "Commander Christa Carver reporting to the admiral as ordered," she said.

As the doors silently closed and no one in the outer office could see, both women giggled and rushed to embrace.

"Welcome to Quesann, sis," Jenetta said as they hugged.

"Thanks, sis. You have no idea how happy I am to be here."

"Are things that bad on Dakistee?" Jenetta said with concern.

"Deadly," Christa said with a fierce expression, then added, "Deadly dull, that is. All I've done for the past few months is approve requisitions or deny them. I hate clerical work."

"How's Madu?"

"She's healthy. But I haven't seen her very much other than on the vid."

"Is she still upset with me?"

"I doubt she'll ever get over the fact that you forced her to make nice with the Nordakians. She never speaks ill of them in public anymore, but I'm sure the hatred is still there. She just doesn't want to appear to be a hypocrite after the way she acted in front of the cameras in order to get the formula."

Jenetta shook her head. "They gave her a formula that ends sterility on their planet, one that saves their entire race at no expense, and she still hates them."

"Yeah. I don't think she'll ever truly welcome their presence. The rest of the population doesn't seem to feel that way though. Everywhere you look you see happy women with big bellies, and it's not just because they're getting fat from eating too much. Well, I suppose they *are* eating a lot more."

"Because they're eating for two or more now?"

"Yeah. I expect the Dakistee population to increase by about fifty percent within the next year. It's practically a law that all women must become pregnant as soon as possible to rebuild the planetary population. Some women haven't yet managed to become pregnant, but some are carrying twins or triplets. It appears that the predicted demise of the Dakistians was greatly exaggerated."

"That's wonderful," Jenetta said with a smile.

"Yeah," Christa said with a hint of melancholy in her voice.

"Are you having regrets about not yet finding a mate for yourself after seeing so many women, including your sister, happy to be pregnant?"

"Are you telling me you're pregnant again?"

"No. I haven't even seen Hugh since he came to the Obotymot Mansion, although we do vidMail each other at least twice a week."

"Oh. Uh, no to your question. Well, maybe a little. But Eliza and I decided to wait and see how your pregnancy turned out. We were very concerned that the Raider DNA modifications might affect our offspring. And then there's the not-so-minor issue that it would pretty much mean an end to our time in space, as it's done for you."

"I don't regret it for a second, although I thought I would once. Kaycee and Kyle are about as healthy, happy, and beautiful as two babies could be. Wait until you see how big they're getting."

"I have. Momma's been including pictures every time she vidMails the family. She seems as delighted with her grand-children as any grandparent could possibly be."

"I know how happy she is. But she never told me she was sending pictures with *every* vidMail. Now that you're here, you can see them in person."

"I've watched them as they've grown because every time Momma records a vidMail, she's holding one of the children. And either Jake or Ruby are always in the picture as well."

"The cubs rarely stray very far from the kiddies during the day, and they sleep in the nursery at night. I think the only time during the day they don't have the kids in visual range is when I arrive home at night. As soon as I enter the nursery, they dash out and complete some laps around the house and gardens to get some exercise because they've been sitting or lying around all day watching over the babies. Sometimes I think they're even more devoted to Kaycee and Kyle than Cayla and Tayna have been to me."

"I wish I had been able to bond with one of the cubs while I was on Obotymot."

"It wouldn't have mattered. They had to remain with their fathers while they were educated. But the next time you see them, they can leave if you establish a mutual bond with one of them."

"There are six still unpaired— so far— and six of us Carvers when we count the boys. Do we all get one?"

"You don't *get* one. The pairing must be mutually decid-ed. I've told Ruby and Jake that Kaycee and Kyle must accept them of their own volition when they reach an age where they're old enough to decide."

"Come on. There's no way Kaycee and Kyle are going to refuse a lifelong bonding with Ruby and Jake after they've grown up together. And by the way, where are Cayla and Tayna?"

"Being tested— again."

"Again?"

"Again."

"Why aren't you with them?"

"The testers refuse to let me look on. I think they suspect my presence might affect the results. But Cayla and Tayna always tell me everything that occurred during the tests. I want to make sure the testers aren't going too far."

"Just how long have the tests been going on?"

"Off and on— almost since I petitioned the G.A. Senate to declare Jumakas sentient beings. I understand though. The decision will affect the entire population of Jumakas, not just Cayla and Tayna. So the testers want to be thorough and don't want to risk any possible chance that the results could be influenced by my presence."

"How's it going so far?"

"They refuse to release any of their findings until the information is presented to the full Senate for a vote on the petition."

"No other alien species has ever been subjected to this kind of lengthy testing for sentience. Even the Pledgian population was simply accepted as sentient from the beginning, and they've never produced any great thinkers. They haven't even sent an elected representative to the Senate, although they're entitled to a seat. I'm quite sure they'd never get off their home world if they didn't hitch a ride with visiting freight-haulers."

"I believe the Jumakas weren't immediately accepted as sentient because they've never had an ordered society. That's probably because they've been hunted for centuries on Taurentlus-Thur for use as guard animals and such, so they've had to avoid the Thurians. Since there was no way to communicate with them, even the indigenous people of the planet never suspected just how intelligent the Jumakas were until this century. And they certainly never believed them to be sentient."

"If— I mean when— they're declared sentient, it might start a review of other species that appear marginally sentient. For example, there are those horse-like creatures on Noe d'al.

They, too, can't converse with Terrans or anyone else— yet, but they seem amazingly intelligent. Perhaps they'll find someone to petition on their behalf."

"Perhaps. Maybe that's why the testers are being so careful with the Jumakas. They want to make sure their findings are ironclad. Hey, have you spoken with Admiral Holt today?"

"No, he's not available today, but I have an appointment for tomorrow morning. I've already accepted the position of SD captain, pending approval by the A.B."

"There's no problem there. I've discussed it with the other board members. However, the A.B. can't vote on it and make it official until Admiral Holt makes the recommendation official. Don't worry about it. It's just a formality."

"I'm not worried. I'm just anxious to get settled in the new ship and get to know her. Or is it him?"

"The rule of thumb was always to use the male pronoun for warships, destroyers and above, and the female pronoun for everything else. Only destroyers required an officer with the official rank of captain to be named as captain of the ship. When Scout-Destroyers became independent search-and-destroy vessels during the THUG war, the lines became sort of blurry. I guess we can refer to any ship that carries offensive weapons as a him."

"So the CPS-14s and up should also be referred to as him since they can carry offensive weapons."

"I guess. Now, until everything is formalized, you'll stay at my residence."

"Thanks. I've already had my things sent over. I'll get out of your way now and go visit with Momma and the gang. See you at dinner."

"Okay, sis."

◆ ◆ ◆

"It's so nice to have all three of my daughters here at once," Annette Carver said as they sat down to dinner.

The *Ares* had just arrived back in port and Eliza had talked the ship's third watch officer into switching duty shifts with her. Since they were in port, all watch duty was usually boring. Eliza had to be back at the *Ares* before midnight for third watch, but she could enjoy a leisurely visit at Jenetta's home before then.

"It's too bad none of the boys could be here," Annette said.

"Jimmy will be in Region Two in a few more months, Momma," Jenetta said. "And we might even see Richie this year. Quesann is now the hub for the G.A. and we have a lot of cleaning up to do."

"Do you think your father will ever be sent out here, dear?"

"There's not much chance of that until he moves up to captain a new battleship, Momma. But large warship construction has slowed in favor of the new smaller ships."

"I've heard the shipyards are working 24/7, turning out new CPS-15s, Jen," Eliza said. "What's up?"

"The CPS-16. It's an extended version of the 15. Unlike the 15, which was designed for temporary assignments and relatively short voyages, the 16 will be a regular posting. Crewmembers will not have any other posts to return to after a mission is over, so they'll remain with the ship until they head out again."

"That I hadn't heard."

"And I know you won't pass it on until it's formally announced in a few months."

"You say an *extended* version of the 15," Christa said. "How extended?"

"It allows every one of the officers to have private quarters as large as the quarters a lieutenant would have on a battleship. Petty Officers will also have private quarters, although a bit smaller than that of the officers. Lower rank enlisted will be doubled up in PO-sized quarters. But even the enlisted who're doubled up will have significantly more space than anyone currently has in a 14 or 15."

"Sounds great," Eliza said. "But it would probably still seem cramped to anyone used to a battleship."

"I suppose, but the new oval running track, squash/handball courts, swimming pool, and hot tub will make up for it a little."

"You're kidding— right?" Eliza queried.

"Not at all," Jenetta said.

"Wait just a minute," Christa said, raising her voice slightly. "Are you telling us that the new CPS-16 ships are all going to have a running track, squash/handball courts, a swimming pool, *and* a hot tub? Just how much are you lengthening the ships?"

"The improved recreational capacities should ease the boredom on extended voyages and permanent postings," Jenetta said.

"But there's no swimming pool, squash/handball courts or hot tub aboard my new SD command."

"Have you changed your mind about accepting the command? It's not too late, you know."

"Okay, what gives?" Eliza said. "I recognize that tone in your voice. You're putting us on, aren't you?"

"Not at all. I'm being perfectly serious."

"Then you're not telling the whole story," Eliza said. "What did you leave out?"

Jenetta couldn't hold the ultra serious expression any longer. As her face broke into a huge grin, she said, "Everything I told you is true, but..."

"But? But what?" Christa asked.

"The yard engineers have modified the SD plans to include a docking collar for the keel of all new Scout-Destroyers."

"So we can dock with one of the CPS-16s and use their facilities?"

"No, so you can have your own facilities. The running track, squash/handball courts, swimming pool, and hot tub are part of a special habitat container that can attach to any ship with the right docking capability. All new destroyers already have that capability so they can transport multiple habitat containers without stowing them inside the ship. Now, all new SDs will have the docking capability as well. And we'll be retrofitting all older SDs so they can enjoy the same recreational features as the new ships."

"So both my ship and each CPS-16 in my squadron will have them before we depart on our first mission?"

"Yes."

"Great. I can hardly wait to go."

"Well, at least finish your dinner before you rush off to jump into a hot tub," Annette said with a grin.

"Yes, Momma," Christa said, returning the grin.

At that moment, Kyle, who was being fed by Celona, burped up some food and all attention became focused on the babies.

"I hope you'll both be able to come to Kyle and Kaycee's first birthday party on August 9th," Jenetta said to her sisters.

"That's up to you, Admiral," Eliza said with a grin. "Will we still be in port?"

"Christa should be here unless she has problems with her shakedown cruise. I'm not sure about the *Ares* at this time."

"Then let's just say we'll definitely be here unless our Space Command duty takes us away," Christa said.

◆　◆　◆

When Christa arrived in the outer office of Admiral Holt the next morning, his aide told her to go right in. Christa paused for just a second as she approached the doors to his inner office and straightened her uniform before stepping into the area where the sensor would acknowledge her presence and open the doors.

"Come in, Christa," she heard Admiral Holt's booming voice say as the twin entrance doors temporarily slid into their storage pockets. Christa walked directly to Admiral Holt's desk and then braced to attention.

"Commander Christa Carver reporting to the Admiral," she said, looking straight ahead.

"At ease, Christa," Holt said. "Have a seat."

Christa sat in one of the oh-gee armchairs facing Admiral Holt's desk but remained rigid.

"We've known each other long enough that you can relax a bit more than that in my presence."

Christa smiled and relaxed her posture as she said, "Yes, sir. It's wonderful to see you again."

"And you. I'll bet you're glad to be out from behind that dirt-side desk."

"Yes, sir, I certainly am. I'm really looking forward to being back in space again."

"I can imagine how you feel." Smiling wistfully, Holt added, "If only I was young enough to captain a ship once again..." His face relaxed into seriousness as he dismissed the thought. "Well, if wishes were G.A. credits, we'd all be wealthy beyond belief. What has Jenetta told you about your mission?"

"Just that the number of sightings of Denubbewa warships in Region Three has been increasing at an alarming rate and our job is to track them down and destroy them."

"That's all?"

"That's all she told me. She said you'd brief me completely at the appropriate time. Is there more?"

"Yes, quite a bit. It's accurate that we want you to take your squadron of CPS-16s and hunt for Denubbewa. But we don't want you to destroy them immediately. We want you to tail them and see if they lead you to any motherships. After destroying the mothership, you can destroy the warships. The reason for not destroying the warships immediately is because there has only been one reported sighting of a Denubbewa mothership in Region Three during the past eighteen months, and there has to be more than one out there."

"Just a single mothership sighting with all these warship sightings? That's a bit unusual, given what we know of them and how they operate."

"That's why we need to follow them and see if they lead us to where the motherships are hiding. The A.B. believes they may be using a tactic utilized by the Raiders— hiding in hollowed-out asteroids. Or they might possibly just have assembled a number of small asteroids and attached them to the mothership's exterior to mask its presence."

"That's an interesting theory."

"So we can't destroy the Denubbewa warships at first sight, as much as we'd like to. When you spot a warship, assign one of the vessels in your squadron to tail them discreetly while the rest of your ships search for others. And there's another task you're to perform. We want you to fly through all asteroids in your search area and take images of the interiors to see if they're hollow to any degree. This last task is Top Secret. We don't want anyone to learn what we're doing. All information gathered as a result of the fly-throughs is to be stored in your SD computer system under tight security until you're ordered to submit it to SCI in a Priority-One communication."

"Are we looking for something other than Denubbewa motherships?"

"We're looking for anyone who has created a place of concealment. It doesn't matter if it's the Denubbewa, Raiders, Uthlaro rebels, or simply smugglers. While we have star charts of Region Three that show all of the planets large enough to support life, we need more information. We want to chart every planet, asteroid, space station, and derelict ship that could be used by criminals, slave traders, or smugglers."

"That's quite a task."

"Yes, but double-envelope capability and the new Marc-One speed makes it practical to commence such an operation."

"So we're not just hunting Denubbewa. We're hunting criminals and making new star charts."

"All these tasks are crucial if we're to maintain law and order in Region Three and destroy enemies of the G.A., such as the Denubbewa."

"Anything else, sir?"

"I think the tasks I've enumerated should keep you busy for a while," Holt said with a grin.

"I suppose how long we're busy depends on the size of the territory we're assigned to cover."

"It's sizeable. You'll get the actual location specifics with your orders after the A.B. officially approves the officers I'm naming for command."

"Do you know when that will be, sir? I'm anxious to get the crew shakedown cruise out of the way."

"All four of the new SDs have completed an initial space trial with skeleton crews experienced in SD operations, as well as with shipyard inspectors, so you'll really only be evaluating the crew performance of the people assigned to the new ship. Most are experienced hands. The only question about the vessel is its performance with the new docking collar and special habitat container. As you know, the SDs were re-designated by Jenetta to drop bombs after the Denubbewa showed up, but attaching a container to the keel makes that function extremely dangerous and almost impractical. However, each SD will carry a full load of WOLaR bombs, and in the event it must serve as a bomber, the habitat container can be released and then recovered later after the enemy is destroyed."

"How long does it take to eject the container and prepare for a bombing run?"

"I'm told the ship can make the initial transition in less than two minutes, but it can take as long as thirty minutes to recover the container and link up afterward."

"That's not a problem if the Denubbewa, or any other enemy, have been destroyed."

"The first SD to receive the new docking collar— your ship— still needs to have the release and recovery tested by SC personnel in open space. That's one of your tasks during the shakedown cruise. Your engineering staff will use a couple of small robotic tugs to recover the container after it's detached from the SD and you perform a simulated bomb run."

"Yes, sir."

"Are you staying with Jenetta or in the BOQ?"

"Jenetta wanted me to stay at her house until I ship out."

"Good. You'll probably hear of the appointment approvals from her first, but your new orders will be sent to you about the same time. I guess that's about all for today, Christa."

Standing up, Christa said, "Thank you for your confidence in me, Admiral."

"As soon as I heard you were available, I wanted you to be part of this. You've done spectacularly in every position you've held, and I know you'll perform with that same degree of intelligence and fortitude in this new role. Dismissed."

Christa braced to attention briefly, then turned on her left heel and left the office. Admiral Holt smiled as the door closed, then returned to the report he'd been preparing when Christa arrived.

CHAPTER SIX

~ June 29th, 2290 ~

One of the innumerous tiny ships normally used to ferry workers, inspectors, security personnel, and crewmembers around the shipyard in orbit around Lorense-Three floated gently towards an enclosed dock at the end of two long rows of tethered spaceships. Everywhere one looked there was activity, and the sight wasn't lost on the six Terrans crowded around the viewing bubble at the bow of the shuttle.

"The rumors are true," Vyx said. "They *are* working like there's no tomorrow."

"But they only do that when there may not be a tomorrow," Byers said. "Where's the *Scorpion*, Vyx? I don't see it anywhere."

"The yard manager told me it's inside that enclosed dock directly ahead."

"Why?" Nelligen asked. "I thought the work was done."

"Probably because it might attract too much unwanted attention if it was out in the open. It's not a Space Command ship or military vessel. It was originally made in an Uthlaran shipyard, so it really shouldn't be here in the retrofit shipyard."

"It's a shipyard, isn't it?" Brenda asked. "And the ship belongs to the SCI. Why wouldn't it be here?"

"Because this is a Space Command shipyard for the construction and refitting of Space Command vessels, not for retrofitting undercover vessels. We don't want people questioning our presence in a Space Command shipyard unless they have adequate security clearance. Many vendors supply materials and parts to Space Command, and that stuff is delivered by ordinary freighters. They might mention what they saw to the wrong person."

"It sure took them long enough to make some simple modifications," Kathryn said.

"Simple?" Vyx said. "What makes you think they were simple?"

"You said they were going to increase our speed. Aren't they just adding something to the engine?"

"First, as you can see, they're extremely busy here," Vyx replied. "I'm grateful they were able to do the work at all. Second, much of the increased speed will be owed to the work performed on the hull. We've seen just how vulnerable we are in Region Three, so they've sheathed the whole ship in Dakinium. We need both extra speed to keep one step ahead of the criminals in Region Three and better hull protection. Okay, we're here, so let me concentrate on aligning this ship's airlock with one on the dock."

"Aren't we going to need EVA suits?" Byers asked.

"No. The spacedock is fully pressurized. It makes it a lot easier to do the work if you don't have to wear a bulky spacesuit during an entire shift. But be careful because I've also been told there's no gravity where the ship is being retrofit. That has to make the heavy lifting work required for building new ships and retrofitting older spaceships a snap, but we'll have to take care not to float off the deck. They didn't give me any magnetic boots. I assume there are lots of handrails inside."

Vyx deftly maneuvered the small shuttle alongside the dock, then used short bursts with the thrusters to align the ship with the airlock. When he believed it was perfectly aligned, he touched a contact point on the console. The ship confirmed the positioning and extended a robotic arm to attach to the spacedock and pull the small ship tightly against the floating building. Once the ship was abutted against the dock, an airlock seal inflated to make the small tunnel airtight. When the computer confirmed the seal, Vyx opened the hatch and the six passengers transferred to the dock.

As they entered the building, they found themselves on an enclosed observation track that extended three-quarters of the way around the area that housed ships being built or modified. The observation track had gravity decking set to Earth Normal so they were able to walk without a problem. Large observation windows into the work area allowed them to see the *Scorpion.*

"It looks exactly the same as when we left it three months ago," Byers said. "I thought you said they were supposed to sheath the outside in Dakinium."

"According to the yard manager, they have," Vyx said.

"They couldn't have. Wouldn't it be black now? That's not Dakinium. It's still the same tritanium outer skin. How long is it going to take to have the hull covered?"

"I've been assured that it's Dakinium. The scientists at Space Command have learned how to colorize the Dakinium to any color they want now. I told them I wanted them to match the old hull exactly so that no one would know it was Dakinium. You'll see the difference the first time I open her up. We should be able to reach Marc-One now."

"Marc-One?" Ursula said. "What's that?"

"It's still Top Secret, so don't repeat this. It's the fastest speed anyone can currently travel. It was named after the captain of the ship that discovered how to modify our existing technology to significantly increase the speed. It's roughly Light-14,686."

"Holy krapolie," Byers said. "Fourteen thousand, six hundred eight-six *times the speed of light?* That's, uh, about thirty times our old speed. We're going to get wherever we're going before we even leave the place we were."

"*Now* you guys all know why I was pushing extra hard to get the new skin for the ship. It's the special sheathing that makes the speed possible. But that's *also* Top Secret so don't tell *anyone.* I sold SCI on the idea that Region Three is so huge that if we don't get the new skin, we'll never get anything done out there."

"And we still get the Dakinium advantage of being almost indestructible?" Byers asked. "I mean with the color not being black."

"According to Admiral Bradlee— yes."

"Great," Nelligen said. "Now we can either outrun everybody or just let them pound us until they run out of ammo."

"It's even better than that," Vyx said. "The new skin allows us to go *out of phase* with normal space. If anybody fires a missile at us when we're out of phase, the missile will go right through us."

"What?" Byers said. "Right through us? Out of phase? That's crazy."

"I didn't dream it up. I'm only telling you what I was told."

"Is this another one of Carver's inventions?" Byers asked.

"Admiral Carver?"

"Yeah."

"Well, as I understand it, she pioneered it. By accident."

"Accident?" Nelligen said. "How do you develop something like this by accident?"

"Many of Earth's greatest advancements have been the result of accidents down through the centuries. Fortunately, the people credited with discovering them were smart enough to realize what they had, or what had happened and what it took to duplicate it. Until Carver discovered the speed advantage and then the out-of-phase advantage, everyone thought Dakinium was only useful to make a hull impregnable to most attacks. Of course, that's pretty damn important when someone is shooting at you, but the other Carver discovery is just as important. If she hadn't stumbled on the speed advantage, we might still be limited to Light-480. I suppose someone else would have eventually had the accident and discovered it, but who knows if they would have realized what had happened and how to do it again."

"Right time, right place, and the smarts to recognize the discovery," Nelligen said. "Makes all the difference."

"Now hold on a minute, Vyx." Byers said. "Look at that hull plate just ahead of the forward hatch opening. It's a different color. That's the plate we had to replace after that cargo container shifted during loading and damaged the previous plate. They haven't sheathed the hull with tritanium-colored Dakinium, and there's the proof."

"We'll, it certainly looks like the plate we used to fix the ship. I suppose the color difference *could* be owed to the way the lights in there are illuminating the hull. But there's only one way to tell for sure."

Vyx turned and walked to a door that opened into the area where the *Scorpion* floated.

"Vyx," Brenda said loudly, "What are you doing?"

"I'm going to take a look."

"You don't have an EVA suit on, you reckless fool."

"Don't need one, my love. According to the gauges here, the air pressure is equal on both sides of this wall."

"But you don't have a tether."

"It a sealed chamber. I can't get lost in space."

Vyx depressed a button on a panel next to the door and they could hear locks releasing. In no more than seconds, the massively thick door opened about an inch and stopped. Vyx grabbed hold and pulled it open enough to squeeze through. Then, while Brenda held her breath, he kicked off from the wall area on the other side of the observation door and sailed slowly across the roughly fifteen-meter distance to the *Scorpion*.

There were no handholds on the ship in that area, so even though Vyx was able to easily check his forward progress when he reached the ship, he had no way to stop and move to where he wanted to go. He managed to grab a small cover over an exhaust vent and come to a complete stop. Then it was a matter of moving slightly downward to where the discolored plate was located without pushing off a little too hard. He did it near perfectly and managed to get a good look at the hull plate. But he continued to slide slowly down the hull until the hull curved under and he was no longer in contact with the ship. For several minutes he made exaggerated movements like he was trying to swim, but it got him nowhere. Although the area was pressurized, it was gravity-free and there was nothing to push off from.

Byers and Nelligen were in hysterics, but Brenda was beside herself and about to go look for help when a worker with a propulsion pack came along and towed Vyx to the door he'd entered. Once he was safely back on the observation deck in the observation tunnel, the worker grinned and returned to his assigned area.

"Well, that was definitely a different experience," Vyx said, as he pushed the door closed and locked it.

"Are you nuts?" Brenda said after he'd closed the door. "You could've been stuck out there."

"With the yard fully staffed and workers everywhere? Not a chance. And it wasn't like I didn't have all the air I needed to breathe. All I really needed was a means of propulsion. It was actually a lot of fun. But back to business. It looks like Al is right. It's not the lights. That panel is definitely a different color. Let's find the work supervisor."

It took fifteen minutes to track down the supervisor, and then they had to wait thirty more until he completed a conference with some of his foremen.

"Well, Trader," the work supervisor said, "I hear you went for a swim and one of our guys had to rescue you. That's why we lock the doors."

"I knew I was in no real danger. The pressure gauge showed the work area was pressurized."

"Unless we needed to open the outer doors."

"Can you do that while the observation tunnel door is wide open?"

"Uh, no. You're right. The safety interlocks would have prevented it. But you could have been stuck out there for a while."

"It was fun being in zero gravity and not wearing an EVA suit. I knew that if I couldn't get back and no one showed up to help me, one of my associates would have gone for help."

"What was so important you had to get out to your ship?"

"We have a question about the hull. It was supposed to be sheathed with Dakinium."

"It has been sheathed with Dakinium— every square nanometer. You're protected from everything except those damn acid warheads the Denubbewa use on their missiles. Our people still haven't found a realistic solution to those. Of course, if you're out of phase, even those don't present a danger."

"I went out to look at the hull because one of my associates noticed a hull plate that hadn't been swapped out. It's one we had to replace after a freight container accident."

"You're referring to the plate on the starboard side just ahead of the front freight hatch?"

"That's the one."

"That's a Dakinium plate. We made that one special so it appeared exactly like the one it replaced. Admiral Holt insisted that nobody be able to tell the difference between the *before* ship and the *after* ship. And they won't, unless you decide to jump to Marc-One while someone's chasing you. And I guess our work was successful if even *you* couldn't tell the difference."

"I apologize. I'm amazed and extremely grateful that you went to such lengths."

"Just part of the service. You people risk your lives to protect our asses and we want you to be safe and able to keep on doing whatever it is you do."

"I always thought it was impossible to alter the color of Dakinium."

"It was— until the scientists found a way to so it. We irradiate it very carefully and we can make any identification pattern now or make the Dakinium any color, including hot pink."

"I can't imagine anyone in Space Command wanting hot pink. I think the bronze color of tritanium is perfect. You say you irradiate it? Uh, is it safe afterwards?"

"Perfectly. Dakinium absorbs all energy that strikes it, so it absorbs the radiation. And it never reflects energy back. If the Dakinium has an abundance of energy, it safely disperses it, but we've learned how to collect and store it now, so we're actually charging storage cells when the ship's being bombarded by cosmic radiation in flight or solar radiation when a ship is parked anywhere near a star. We no longer have to use antimatter to generate electrical power for shipboard use."

"I see. So there's no possible chance of radiation burns if we touch the hull while we're on the surface of a planet?"

"Not from the Dakinium. But bring plenty of DNA lotion in case you're skin is exposed to a star's radiation."

"Wonderful. So if we're all set, we'll get out of your hair."

"Just about. Why don't you board your ship and I'll have some of my people come over and explain the modifications we made to the bridge and engineering areas."

"Great. Thanks."

"Just part of the service, Trader."

◆

"Everyone comfortable with the changes?" Vyx asked after the shipyard people had all vacated the *Scorpion*. Everyone seated at the kitchen table indicated that they were satisfied either by mumbling something unintelligible or nodding, so Vyx said, "Great. Then let's have dinner. The best time to leave the barn is in about four hours. At that time, there shouldn't be any freighters in or near the shipyard to see us leave. What's for dinner, Al?"

"Wernallo cutlets, smashed bonque, gomort spears, sacolio buns and butter, and numeshi pie for desert. Plus coffee and ale, of course."

"A meal fit for king," Brenda said. "It's so wonderful to have a man around who can cook. You're a real treasure, Al."

"I'm happy to cook as long as you ladies do the dishes afterward."

"I can push the button on the dishwasher as well anyone aboard this ship," Katherine joked. "But I can't seem to master the coffeemaker."

"As long as you ladies can handle laser pistols and rifles like pros, we'll overlook all minor imperfections," Nelligen quipped.

"Stop joking and bring the food," Vyx said. "There's a man starving over here."

◆ ◆

For the first ten light-years after leaving the shipyard, Vyx held the *Scorpion* to single-envelope travel, although he pushed the ship to the maximum speed of Light-480. He wanted to make sure the ship still *felt* the same at the former maximum speed. When he was confident that all was well, he dispersed the single envelope and built a double envelope. As he engaged the drive, the stars became like streaks of color on the front viewscreen. Vyx smiled. *It almost makes you feel like a god*, he thought.

◆ ◆ ◆

"I've located a Jumaka for you, Miss Shanara," Aliana heard in her right ear when she activated her com connection. "The price is quite reasonable compared to what they were going for before Carver started this sentience nonsense. I convinced the owner that if he delays he'll soon have to free the beast and lose his investment, so he wants to move fast before the market bottoms out completely."

"I want to see it."

"It's part of his private zoo. I'm sure we can arrange a viewing."

"Do it and let me know where and when."

"I'll get back to you as soon as I can arrange it."

◆

Less than an hour later the exotic pets dealer called again.

"You can see the animal tonight any time after eight, if you wish."

"I wish."

"Okay, I'll give you the address where we can meet and then head over to look at the animal."

Aliana wrote the address and time down, then terminated the connection.

◆

At half past eight, Aliana and her bodyguards entered the home of the Jumaka owner. He then led them through the enormous house, passing through a number of rooms with large cages containing exotic animals, to the room where the Jumaka was kept. As soon as Aliana and her small entourage entered the room, the Jumaka began snarling. Aliana told the others to stay back, then turned to approach the Jumaka.

"Don't put your hands anywhere near the cage," the owner called out, "or you might lose them."

"I'll be careful," Aliana said as she walked to within four feet of the cage. Turning to look back at the others, she said, "Would everyone leave me alone? I'll be very careful."

The owner and dealer didn't want to leave the room, but Aliana's bodyguards made a few motions with their hands and convinced the two men they should honor her request.

Once she was alone with the animal, Aliana said in a very soft voice, "I'm certain you're a lot smarter than you let on. And I'm pretty sure you can understand every word I'm saying, even if you can't respond in Amer. I'm in a position to take you home with me, and you'll never be kept in cage again. You'll have the complete run of my apartment and enjoy far more freedom than you've known in a long time, if ever. Does that interest you? If it does, stop snarling and sit down."

The Jumaka stopped snarling and stared at Aliana but didn't sit down.

"You're not sitting. Does that mean you're not interested in coming with me, becoming my companion, and being free?"

The Jumaka abruptly sat down.

"Good choice. I'm sure you and I are going to be great friends. Someone has invented a device that allows species other than Jumakas to understand what you're saying when you speak. To us it just sounds like growling, but we know now that your species is intelligent and has remarkable language skills. I might be able to get you one of those collars so we can converse, and you can also converse with everyone you meet. Would that be something you'd like? Nod your head if you would."

The Jumaka stared at her for a few moments, then nodded its head up and down.

"I thought that might appeal to you. I know someone at the company that manufactures the device. I'll start working on getting you one right away. It's a collar, but it's not like a pet collar. It's just a band that holds a tiny microphone against your throat and converts everything you say into Amer. Would you be willing to wear such a collar?"

The Jumaka nodded again and Aliana smiled.

"Yes, I think you and I are going to be friends— close friends— and companions."

CHAPTER SEVEN

~ July 9th, 2290 ~

"There's a Commander Ashraf to see you, Admiral," Jenetta heard as she touched her viewpad in response to the chime sound that indicated her aide was attempting to contact her.

"Send her in."

Lori Ashraf entered the large office and walked to the desk where she braced to attention and said, "Commander Lori Ashraf to see the admiral on a personal matter."

Jenetta smiled and stood, then walked around the desk to where Ashraf was standing. "At ease, Commander. It's wonderful to see you again. It's been such a long time since we worked together."

As Ashraf opened her mouth to speak, Jenetta reached out and pulled her towards her as she took the final step closer to embrace her old friend. Ashraf just smiled and responded to the embrace in kind.

"I've missed working with you, Lori."

"And I've missed working with you, Admiral. I look back on those years as the happiest I've spent in Space Command. Not that I'm unhappy now, but those were special years as you worked to bring law and order to G.A. space."

"As *we* worked to bring law and order to G.A. space."

"I've wanted to thank you for recommending me for command of a squadron of CPS-16s."

"Admiral Holt asked me whom I would appoint and I immediately thought of you."

"I appreciate the recommendation. I've been working closely with your sister Christa, developing the protocol we'll employ once we've deployed. It's a monumental task."

"Yes, it is. And the most important one we've ever faced. I now believe the Denubbewa don't simply want to take over the galaxy, they want to kill all sentient life in it and populate it with cyborgs like themselves. I'm confident that was the reason for the amputated Terran limbs we discovered when we sifted through the wreckage of the Denubbewa warship that attacked the GSC Scout-Destroyer *Salado*. I believe they were studying our physiology so they could transplant our brains into cyborg bodies after wiping the Terran memories and implanting Denubbewa memories."

"That's a gruesome thought."

"It's the only one that makes sense. Among the wreckage, we found deceased cyborgs that had brains from a dozen different species, all of whom are unknown to us. The biological brain is the only non-artificial component we've found in the cyborgs."

"And you believe they've decided that Terran brains are their next target of acquisition?"

"Among the sentient species in G.A. space, there are only a dozen or so with brains as evolved as those of Terrans."

"Does that include Jumakas?"

Jenetta smiled before saying, "It may. The scientists testing them have yet to release their findings. I'm anxious to hear their evaluation regarding the Jumaka's ability to reason, how well they retain new information, and their capacity to live free among other sentient species. As far as I'm concerned, it was only the Jumaka vocal incompatibilities that prevented them from being accepted as a sentient species eons ago."

"I watched your A.B. debut speech with great interest. Like you, I knew your Jumakas were highly intelligent, but I never suspected they were sentient. They just seemed like well-trained pets that could provide security when necessary."

"I received a message from the Planetary Council on Taurentlus-Thur recently. They informed me that a law has been proposed that the Council declare Jumakas to be the second sentient species native to their planet. The proposal will have to be discussed at length before a final vote because there are innumerous derivative issues, such as native land property rights and such, but they've passed an interim measure that calls for anyone convicted of hunting Jumakas to be tried for either murder or attempted murder."

"Wow. It sounds like they've already made up their minds and just have to determine how Jumakas can fit into Thurian society."

"It does sound positive. At the very least, Jumakas will finally be safe in the jungles from big game hunters and slavers."

"How did Cayla and Tayna take the news?"

"They're very excited about this next step forward and the possibilities for additional advances."

"Do you think they'll want to return home once the planet is safe for them?"

"I— don't think so. I believe they consider Obotymot their home now. It's where they first mated and where their cubs were born. They're part of my family, and I'm part of theirs. I certainly hope they don't choose to live on Taurentlus-Thur, but if that's what they decide, I won't stand in their way— and I'll arrange for their transportation to the planet."

"The others too? I'm talking about the males and the cubs."

"Yes— for the males. Obotymot is the only planetary home the cubs have ever known, but yes for them as well. Although we should probably start referring to them as children or offspring. They've grown so big so fast, they've almost reached their full adult size."

"Is there any chance I could get one?"

"There's always a chance, but I won't distribute them like puppies. They have to make their own decision to bond with someone or not. And I'd guess my sisters and brothers have the inside track with this litter since they're members of the expanded Carver family that includes the Jumakas. Plus there's the fact that the offspring have already met several of my siblings and begun to establish bonds with them."

"I see. I thought that might be the case. Well, perhaps a future litter."

"Perhaps."

"I remember you telling me what a comfort Cayla and Tayna were for you when you rose to a command position. I guess I hoped I might enjoy the company of a good friend like them now that I'll be in the top job aboard my ship."

"It's often said that it's lonely at the top. I can verify that. But don't rush into anything. Whether you bond with a Jumaka or a less intelligent friend, make sure the relationship is solid and that you enjoy spending time together. I would probably avoid a relationship with a fish or amphibian. A companion you can hug and cuddle would be best."

"Well, I guess getting a goldfish like the one I had when I was a little girl is out."

"If it gave you pleasure, don't rule it out."

"It was exciting at first, but the thrill wore off after a few weeks. As you said, we couldn't cuddle. And we certainly never shared quality time together."

Jenetta grinned and then said, "I'll keep it in mind that you'd like to bond with a Jumaka, and if any opportunities open, I'll try to arrange an introductory meeting."

"Thank you, Admiral."

"Christa has dinner at my home several times a week. Why don't you join her when you can?"

"Thank you, Admiral. I will."

"It's been wonderful having you visit me here. I look forward to getting together with you under less formal conditions."

Commander Ashraf smiled and said, "I guess that's my cue to take my leave."

"Too obvious? I didn't gesture towards the door."

"I was your aide for a long time, Admiral. I guess I'm still attuned to the intimations."

"I would love to sit and talk for the next hour, Lori, but I'm working on a very important briefing for the G.A. Council and I have to get it done today because they need time to review and discuss it among themselves. If the Council approves, it will be presented at the next full Senate meeting for discussion and a vote."

"I understand, Admiral. I'll get out of your way. I look forward to joining you for dinner at your home when both our schedules permit it. Good-bye for now."

"It *has* been wonderful talking with you and I look forward to our next meeting as well."

Commander Ashraf braced to attention, smiled, and left the office.

Jenetta's smile lasted only as long as it took to get back to her briefing notes, and she let out a sigh as she read over what she'd written. "Is this any way for an intelligent military officer to make a living?"

◆　◆　◆

"I understand Lori Ashraf dropped in to see you at your office," Christa said during dinner a day later. "She said you couldn't spare very much time for her then because you were working on something very important for the Senate. She said you invited her to come here for dinner with me when our schedules permit."

"That's true. I could only spare her a few minutes."

"That was the first time you've met face-to-face in a couple of years, wasn't it?"

"Yes, in a few days it will be two years since I left Quesann to take my extended leave. That was the last time we'd talked in person."

"She's told me she was devastated when you informed her you were retiring. She said she was so delighted when you decided on a leave of absence instead."

"I know. I'd gotten that same reaction from most people, including Eliza. But by the time I talked to Eliza, I had already submitted the leave-of-absence paperwork instead of a resignation."

"So if you didn't have time to talk after not seeing her for two years, you must have been working on something super important. Is it anything you can talk about?"

Jenetta finished chewing the bite of chicken in her mouth and swallowed before replying. "As Admiral of the Fleet, everything I work on is super important. And no, I can't talk about anything I work on unless I initiate the conversation. Sorry, that's just the way it is."

"When will you be able to tell me? My squadron will be deploying within ten days."

"After you've reached your search area and before you actually begin the search, you'll receive new instructions. Those instructions will give you a clue."

"A clue? A clue to what?"

"A clue to what's going down. Your intelligence will allow you to put together a scenario that's probably pretty close to the truth. But don't discuss it with anybody because we don't want others to put it all together just yet."

"Put *what* all together?"

"You'll see. That's all I can tell you at this time. And don't repeat a word of what I've said tonight."

"But you haven't said anything."

"When you think about this conversation later, you'll have enough that it will all come together when you get your final instructions for your search mission."

◆ ◆ ◆

"Atten-shun," someone called out as Christa and three of her senior officers from her Scout-Destroyer command entered the massive meeting room. Actually, it was more like a college lecture hall where each row of attendee chairs facing the speaker was slightly higher than the last. The room was capable of seating over a hundred, but there were only forty-eight in the audience area when the SD officers entered.

"As you were," Christa said loudly and the attendees retook their seats. When the hall was again quiet, she said, "I know all of you are anxious to know the particulars of our deployment. Today you'll learn our mission objectives." Christa paused for effect for a couple of seconds. It seemed as though everyone in the hall was holding their breath. "We're going on a Denubbewa hunt. SCI believes the Denubbewa have aspirations towards a complete takeover of Region Three. We're going to stop them. We're not in this alone. You forty-eight represent the two most senior officers aboard each of the first CPS-16s to deploy, but there will be three more equally-sized squadrons out there with us in the next few months, each searching their assigned area and taking this fight to the enemy. For weeks, you've all been training in bombing operations. Each of your crews has reached a proficiency level that qualifies your ship to come with my Scout-Destroyer and blast those metal-headed monsters out of existence.

"Our twenty-four CPS-16s pack more power than a battle-ship when you consider the area we can simultaneously cover and the specialized function we perform as bombers. Just because the Denubbewa are manufactured on an assembly line rather than born to a biological mother doesn't mean we can underestimate them. They attacked and viciously destroyed both the SC Scout-Destroyer *Yenisei* and the SC Scout-Destroyer *Salado*, either killing all hands on board in the action or taking them back to their own ships and dissecting them in medical experiments. But that was before we knew what we were up against or even that they sought to destroy all biological life forms in the universe and were therefore our enemies. They had the element of surprise, but we now have more advanced weapons, far greater speed, and an intimate knowledge of the enemy. We haven't lost a ship since the *Salado*, and I don't intend to lose any ship from this bombing squadron or learn that any CPS-16 on this mission has fallen to the enemy. The one fact you must never forget, not even for an instant, is that while in double-envelope mode the enemy cannot harm us. They can fire ten thousand of those nuclear weapons with acid-filled warheads and never hit us because the missiles will simply pass right through us. But let's not get too overconfident. The enemy is known for their ability to adapt quickly. So we want to remain as invisible as possible to their sensors and cameras. We intend to always know where they're hiding but never allow them to know where *we* are or when we'll come for them. I don't know if cyborgs fear death, or even if they're concerned for their personal safety, but if they do or are, I want them quaking in their iron skins when they even think we're about to strike.

"You've all received instructions for proceeding to an assembly area roughly one light-year away. You're to have your ship and the full complement of crewmembers assigned to your vessel there no later than 0600 two days from today. We'll jump off at 0800 and proceed at Marc-One to the coordinates in the orders you'll receive no later than 0700 two days from now. You are not to relay anything you've heard here today to any crewmembers until after we're underway in two days. And once we deploy, we're going dark. Tell your

crews to send messages home to friends and relatives informing them that they will not be hearing from you until our extended mission is complete. Personal messages may be
queued but are NOT to be sent until you've been informed the
mission is over. Any questions?"

When no one spoke or raised their hands, Christa said,
"Then you're dismissed."

As Christa turned to leave the lecture hall, the attendees
jumped to their feet. When the doors closed behind Christa
and her three senior officers, the CPS-16 officers began discussing the upcoming deployment among themselves.

◆ ◆ ◆

Christa entered the bridge from her briefing room on the
Scout-Destroyer *Koshi* GSC-SDH101 and glanced around,
noting that all personnel were at their duty stations. The
bridge was almost identical to previous Scout-Destroyers, except in one very obvious respect. Where on all older SDs
there was only a single console for communication, the SDH
model had two stations. The extra station was to help with
coordinating a full squadron of CPS-16s while the original
station concentrated on maintaining all normal communications and monitoring.

"Navigation, is the course laid in for the deployment assembly location?"

"Aye, Captain."

"Tac, is the DeTect system clear?"

"The board is green for that course, Captain."

"Helm, is the double envelope built?"

"Aye, Captain. We're good to go on your command."

Christa sat down in the command chair and relaxed before
saying, "Helm, take us there at Marc-One."

"Aye, Captain. ETA is thirty-five minutes, forty-nine seconds. Engaging."

As the helmsman touched a contact point on his console,
the Scout-Destroyer *Koshi* disappeared in the blink of an eye.

◆ ◆ ◆

"Our main objective is to locate any and all Denubbewa
ships here in Region Three," Christa said to the officers

aboard the twenty-four CPS-16s assembled at the area where they would begin their search. They'd been traveling for over a month to reach this location, and a video conference was now being held in the privacy of the captain's office aboard each ship. Only the captain and first officer aboard the CPS-16s were permitted to attend the high-security, live presentation. Aboard the Scout-Destroyer *Koshi*, Christa had been joined by her first and second officers before the conference began. "Denubbewa warship sightings have been increasing significantly for some time and we've been sent here to find out what they're up to. We have the honor of being the first squadron of four dedicated to this task. Each of you captains will shortly receive orders specifically prepared for your ships. Since our squadron consists of twenty-four CPS-16s and one Scout-Destroyer, we'll advance through our assigned territory in a five-by-five formation with the *Koshi* in the center. All ships will broadcast an Alpha-Six rotating-frequency ship-protection code so we can maintain the proper distance from the other ships in the squadron. As you know, our De-Tect range is limited to four billion kilometers, so we'll proceed on a common course with all ships spaced five-point-five billion kilometers from the ship on their larboard and/or starboard, and on their sail and keel. This will provide a swath twenty-seven point five billion kilometers high and wide with sufficient overlap to ensure we miss nothing. In the event a ship must stop to investigate something, all ships will come to a halt until the issue is resolved. At all times you will maintain your double envelope unless I personally give permission to cancel it. That will both protect us from attack and also help to further conceal our presence. Our Dakinium sheathing protects us from everyone's sensors, and the double envelope makes us literally invisible even with a sun behind us since we'll be out of phase.

"Upon opening my own sealed orders this morning, I learned we have been given a second objective. This other objective is Top Secret and should not be made known to crewmembers without a need to know. That will probably limit the knowledge to the bridge crew. As we search for Denubbewa at Marc-One, we'll also search for hiding places.

Even though there have been almost constant reports of Denubbewa warship sightings, there have been no reported sightings of Denubbewa motherships. This is more than a little unusual. SCI suspects the motherships may be hiding inside hollowed-out asteroids— a trick learned from the Raiders— or that they may have enclosed themselves in a tight asteroid field. They might have even attached asteroids to their hulls to further conceal themselves. When we encounter any asteroid or asteroid cluster large enough to offer concealment, the squadron will stop to investigate. The ship whose course takes it closest to the object will then fly through the object, taking as many images of the interior as possible.

"Should there be any indication that the asteroid is being used as a place of concealment, we first have to decide who is using it. If it's the Denubbewa, we'll back away and watch for a while. If it's Raiders, smugglers, or someone else, we store the information in the computer and proceed with our search.

"Any questions?"

"How long will we watch the Denubbewa ships we locate before destroying them, Captain?"

"I've been given special orders from Admiral Holt that dictates when and if that will happen."

"Yes, ma'am. Did you say *if*?"

"I did say *if*. And no one, I repeat, no one will begin an attack on any Denubbewa ship or base until I first order it. I want to destroy those metal-heads just as much as everyone else. But unless your life and the lives of your crew are in imminent danger, you will not commence such an attack without my authorization. And as long as your ship is inside a double envelope, your life can't be in imminent danger. Am I clear?"

"Yes, ma'am. Clear as crystal."

"Good. Any other questions?"

After a brief silence, Christa said, "Okay, no questions. Pass the course information on to your navigator when you receive it, which should be in a few minutes. Advise your Tac, Helm, and Com of the formation particulars. When your bridge crew is ready, take your position relative to the *Koshi* and prepare for the search effort, then notify us that you're in position and ready to begin the search. I'll send the order to proceed when all ships are in position and ready to commence the operation. That's all."

Forty-six minutes later all ships were in position, had their double envelope built, and were ready to begin the search. Christa sat back in the command chair on the bridge and gave the order to advance. The com chief responsible for all formation communications passed on the order and the entire squadron disappeared as if by magic as the helmsmen engaged Marc-One speed.

◆ ◆ ◆

A week later, Christa prepared her second report to Admiral Holt from her office. The first had merely informed him that the squadron was commencing the search.

"Message to Vice-Admiral Brian D. Holt, Commander of the Second Fleet, Quesann Headquarters, from Commander Christa Carver aboard the GSC *Koshi.*

"Good day, Admiral. We've completed the first week of searching for Denubbewa and I have to report we've seen no trace of them. To date we've investigated twenty-three asteroids, but none were hollow. We located four derelict ships, all of which had been destroyed by unknown attackers, but all attacks had to have occurred decades ago. Scavengers had picked the ships so clean we had trouble finding identifying information. Corpses aboard the ships were all Uthlaran. We've logged dozens of freighter sightings, but we didn't stop them since they weren't Denubbewa ships. We continue our mission to locate the Denubbewa.

"Christa Marie Carver, Commander, Captain of the GSC *Koshi.* End of message."

Christa leaned back in her chair after forwarding the message to the bridge com chief with instructions for immediate transmission. The *Koshi* squadron was operating in an area where the reports about Denubbewa activity had been the highest. Christa had expected to see at least one Denubbewa warship by now. Were the sighting reports false? Had the Denubbewa left the area? Or had they learned a Space Command attack force was headed this way and gone into hiding? And if they were in hiding, *where* were they hiding?

CHAPTER EIGHT

~ December 3rd, 2290 ~

After months of searching, the *Koshi* squadron had still not sighted a single Denubbewa warship or mothership. They had located a hollowed-out asteroid that was serving as a base for someone, possibly Raiders, but hadn't alerted the occupants to their presence. Christa simply sent the information and images taken by the CPS-16 that had passed through the asteroid to Fleet Command as was specified in her latest orders.

The squadron had now examined several hundred asteroids, located and investigated thirty-two derelict ships, and spotted hundreds of freighters in transit.

The squadron was presently stopped while one of the CPS-16s investigated derelict ship thirty-three.

"Captain, this is XO Mollago," Christa heard in her CT. "We just received a strange message from the *Karl Linne*. The captain reports that there appears to be something blocking out the light from several distant stars, but their sensors say there's nothing there. They want to know if they should investigate, wait until the *Boll Weevil* completes its investigation of the derelict ship and then investigate, or simply ignore the anomaly completely."

"We do not ignore *any* anomalies. Has the *Boll Weevil* confirmed the derelict is permanently out of action?"

"Yes, ma'am. They're just trying to download any intact computer files so we can identify the ship and the attackers if possible."

"Very well. Tell the *Karl Linne* to move in close enough to identify the anomaly, using extreme caution. They have permission to drop their double envelope only if necessary and I want a report as soon as they learn anything."

"Aye, Captain. Mollago out."

"Carver out."

Very few things could blot out the light from distant stars and yet not provide sensor readings. A gaseous cloud of space dust could account for the missing light, as long as the light from distant stars was weak enough and the cloud dense enough, but there should have been some sensor readings.

◆

Some forty minutes later, XO Mollago called Christa again.

"The *Karl Linne* reports that the anomaly appears to be a ship of some sort, Captain. They circled it twice at close range."

"A ship? A ship that's invisible to sensors?"

"Aye, Captain."

"Get us there, XO."

"Permission to drop the envelope so we can use sub-light engines and thrusters?"

"Granted. Tell the *Karl Linne* to maintain a discreet distance. Has the *Boll Weevil* completed its work?"

"Almost, Captain."

"Tell the investigative team to drop whatever they're doing and get back aboard their ship. I want the *Boll Weevil* to have their double envelope built within fifteen minutes."

"Aye, Captain. Mollago out."

"Carver out."

Christa jumped up from her desk chair and rushed out to the bridge. Mollago started to rise from the command chair as she emerged from her office, but she waved him down and began to pace the deck as the *Koshi* moved towards the strange anomaly.

It only took five minutes to position the *Koshi* roughly one hundred kilometers from the object. At one time all ships had standing orders never to approach a potentially hostile ship closer than twenty-five thousand kilometers to reduce the risk of damage from laser weapons. But that was before the fleet had Dakinium sheathing and double envelope capability. Christa didn't like to drop the envelope, but it was necessary for improved maneuverability. As the *Karl Linne* had reported, the dark object blocking out the light of distant stars did appear to be a ship.

"It's a ship alright," Christa said as she studied the silhouette of the object on the large monitor at the bow of the Scout-Destroyer.

"But what kind, Captain?" Mollago asked. "And whose ship?"

"It's very difficult to see the outline clearly from this distance, especially without a sun nearby. Com, check with the *Boll Weevil* to see if they have their double envelope built yet."

"They report it will be complete in twenty seconds, Captain."

"Good. Let's wait those twenty seconds."

"The *Boll Weevil* reports that their double envelope is built, Captain," the com chief said some fifteen seconds later.

"Tac, any movement of the dark ship?" Christa asked.

"None, Captain."

"Helm, take us closer."

"Aye, Captain," the helmsman said. "Uh, how close, Captain?"

"About a kilometer— close enough to clearly identify that object. But at the first sign of any movement or activity from that ship, get us far away and erect our double envelope."

"Aye, Captain."

"We want to be on the opposite side from the *Karl Linne*. Com, tell the *Karl Linne* to put on every exterior light they have. Tac, light us up also so the *Karl Linne* sees a good silhouette."

As the tac officer acknowledged the order, exterior lights on the *Karl Linne* suddenly illuminated.

"It's a Denubbewa ship," Christa said at the same instant as her XO. "The design is unmistakable."

"It's enormous, Captain."

"From what I can make out, it appears to be one of their largest warships."

"But what's it doing just sitting there?" her XO said aloud.

"Tac, any sensor readings from that ship now?"

"Negative, Captain. It's as if there's nothing out there. All I'm getting is a small reading from the *Karl Linne's* exterior lights where the covers have been retracted."

"Just like us," Mollago said, "when other ships try to scan us and the Dakinium absorbs all electronic signals."

"Exactly," Christa said.

"But how can that be?"

"There's only one answer to that question. The Denubbewa have Dakinium— or something damn close. XO, I have some messages to send before we do anything further. But tell the captain of the *Karl Linne* to get two investigative teams ready to board that ship, and have our Marines prepare for a little trip."

"Aye, Captain."

◆

Once back in her office, Christa sat down at her desk and began composing the most distressing communication she had ever sent.

"Priority-One Message to Vice-Admiral Brian D. Holt, Commander of the Second Fleet, Quesann Headquarters, from Commander Christa Carver aboard the GSC *Koshi*.

"Admiral, I have very serious news. We've just found a ship that so far appears to be a derelict. I wanted to send this message before we do anything else, so we haven't yet had time to investigate further. Admiral— the ship doesn't show up on our sensors. It appears to be sheathed in Dakinium, and— Sir, it's not one of ours. The only reason we discovered it is because it happened to be near a derelict that *did* appear on our sensors. While we were waiting for the *Boll Weevil* to complete their inspection of the derelict we'd stopped to identify, someone aboard the *Karl Linne* noticed that the light from some distant stars appeared to be blocked out. I thought at first that it might simply be a gaseous cloud of space dust, yet sensors indicated there was nothing out there.

"I ordered the *Karl Linne* to investigate the anomaly. As they moved closer to this *hole* in space, more light from distant stars was blocked. The captain of the *Karl Linne* then ordered his helmsman to circle the *darkness*. In so doing, they determined without question that an invisible object was somehow responsible for the blocked starlight.

"I immediately ordered the *Boll Weevil* staff to end their onboard investigation of the first derelict and get back aboard their own ship so they could erect their double envelope. Once that was done, I had the *Koshi* move to the immediate vicinity of the anomaly. When we were on what we believed was the opposite side of the anomaly, I had the *Karl Linne* turn on their exterior lights. From the silhouette we could observe, the anomaly is definitely a ship— and it has a decidedly Denubbewa appearance. I believe it's one of the Denubbewa's largest warships.

"When I've completed this message and sent it, I'm going to notify the commanding officers of the other two Scout-Destroyer squadrons about our find. It now seems logical to assume the reason we've had such poor luck locating even a single Denubbewa ship is because we can no longer locate them with our sensors, as would be the case if they were sheathed in Dakinium or some similar energy-absorbing material. That's all I have to report for now, Admiral. I'll send an update as soon as we know more.

"Christa Marie Carver, Commander, Captain of the GSC *Koshi*. Message complete."

The *Koshi* was currently operating some two thousand light-years from Quesann, which meant that travel time at Marc-One was about forty-eight days and communication time was about twenty-five days each way.

◆

"Com, get me the captain of the *Karl Linne*," Christa said as she returned to the bridge. "Put him on the front monitor."

"Aye, Captain."

A few seconds later, the large monitor at the front of the bridge changed to show an image of the *Karl Linne* captain, Lt. Kurt Aston, sitting in his bridge command chair. He was in turn receiving an image of the *Koshi* bridge.

"Captain," Christa said, "I've just sent messages to Fleet Command and the commanding officers of the other two Scout-Destroyers operating in Region Three, informing them of your find. Now that they know what's happening out here, it's time to investigate that new derelict and learn everything we can. I want you to send your two investigative teams over to that anomaly with orders not to enter until ordered to do so. I have my two platoons of Marines suiting up. One of our shuttles will bring one platoon to the ship in question where they'll enter the ship first. After they secure a position inside the ship, or if they meet any resistance, the other platoon will join them. Once we've eliminated any armed resistance, your people can move in and learn everything they can about this ship. I'll notify you when that will be possible."

"Aye, Captain. My people will be ready. I'll move the *Karl Linne* in a little closer and send them over in maintenance sleds."

"Very good, Captain. Stand by until we hear from the Marines."

◆

The bridge monitor of the *Koshi* became a patchwork of images from the Marine's helmet-cams as they deployed from the shuttle and made their way over to the strange ship. They managed to open an airlock large enough to allow two Marines in EVA suits to enter with each cycle. The first ones in then secured the area around the airlock as more and more of their Marine brothers and sisters entered the ship until the entire platoon was inside.

Ever since the first Space Command vessel, the Scout-Destroyer *Colorado,* had been sheathed with Dakinium, there had been difficulties with personal communications between ships. The problem was with the Dakinium and the immediate absorption of all signals coming into contact with its hull. Bridge communication signals were sent and received via a special antenna on the outside surface of the hull. It was large enough to handle any incoming and outgoing communications without interfering with the establishment of the ship's envelope. But no signals other than those sent and received through the ship's bridge communications system could be sent or received from inside the ship. Signals from CTs implanted in officers were always routed through the ship's communication system, so a CT could be used to communicate with officers on other ships or enlisted personnel with special RF equipment, using an RF scrambled signal. RF frequencies were employed because they were so slow that were anyone to intercept them, the senders would be long gone before anyone could follow the signal back to the source location. However, since the Denubbewa ship wasn't equipped to handle Space Command communications, another method had to be used. When the Marines first reached the ship, they mounted a tiny antenna on the surface of the ship using a vacuum seal to make it stay where placed. Like the antenna on the Space Command vessels, it wasn't large enough to invalidate the ship's sensor invisibility. A millimeter-thick line was then run through the airlock to the interior of the ship. It was so thin that it didn't interfere with the door's seals, which were still able to effect one-hundred-percent airtight efficiency. Once inside, the wire to the antenna was attached to a portable communications transceiver that allowed full communications between the Space Command vessels and the ship being boarded, regardless of how it was sheathed. The helmet-cams of the first Marines to enter the Denubbewa ships went black until the transceiver was set up inside the ship.

"There's power in here and it's pressurized," Lt. Toleder reported as they began to investigate the interior. "The gravity plating is working, but there doesn't seem to be any oxygen."

To his platoon, he said, "Do metal-heads breathe? Anybody know?"

When no one replied, Toleder said, "Guess nobody knows."

The EVA suits were too bulky to wear inside the ship so the Marines had stripped them off and dropped the suits by the airlock before proceeding to clear the way. The personal armor worn by all of the Marines provided a rebreather unit, but it had a limited-duration cycle when the exertion of the wearer taxed the unit. After a time, the air could start to become stale so the Marine platoon carried a few small oxygen-supply bottles. When their suits told them to replenish with fresh oxygen, they could refill their limited personal supply in seconds.

The bridge crew of the *Koshi* and every ship in the squadron watched as the Marines walked around inside the ship, expecting to be jumped at any minute, but they met no resistance.

"Captain, there doesn't seem to be anyone aboard," Toleder said after about ten minutes of wandering the corridors. "I guess it might be safe to send in your investigators."

"Very well, Lieutenant, we're sending them in. Each team should be assigned two of your Marines for protection. Keep a sharp eye out. It doesn't make sense that anyone would simply abandon a nearly invisible ship that hasn't been damaged. It could be a trap of some sort." Christa turned to the com chief and nodded.

As the com chief sent the message to the *Karl Linne*, informing the captain that he should send in the four-person investigation teams, Christa said to Mollago, "What do you think?"

"I agree with you. It doesn't make sense that a crew would abandon a ship that hasn't been damaged. There must be a problem we haven't encountered yet."

As the investigators from the *Karl Linne* began to enter the ship, the images being broadcast from their helmets were added to the patchwork on the bow monitor. They didn't have personal armor so they would have to wear the very bulky EVA suits the whole time. They'd brought along their own portable oxygen tanks so they could stay aboard the alien ship for an extended period if necessary. Their EVA suits also contained a rebreather unit and small oxygen supply for replenishment of stale air overtaxed by exertion.

"Tac," Christa said, "remove a few of the helmet cam images where we have two or more individuals sending the same basic view."

"Aye, Captain."

Although not every image would appear on the monitor, every image was being recorded and could be played later if a question arose about something that happened. Removing redundant images increased the size of the displayed images.

With Marines providing security, the investigators began to move out. One team went in search of the bridge, while the other team went to look for engineering. The Marines who weren't providing security for the investigative teams were involved with a thorough check of the entire ship, opening every compartment carefully in case Denubbewa were waiting to pounce.

More than an hour had passed before the first sounds of alarm were heard.

"Captain," Lt. Toleder said excitedly, "we've found Denubbewa."

"Alive?"

"Uh, I don't know, ma'am. How do you tell? They all appear dead until they move, right?"

"Are they moving at all?"

"Uh, no, Captain. But the one I'm looking at has a tiny illuminated red dot on its forehead, just above the bridge of its nose."

"I'm not seeing any image from your helmet-cam. Stand by. Tac?"

"Sorry, Captain, I guess his cam was one that got turned off to make room for others. Here we go."

Toleder's helmet-cam image replaced one from an investigator on the bridge. The Marine officer was in a large room with dozens of Denubbewa lying on tables. None were moving.

"I see what you mean, Lieutenant. They all appear to be dead, but I have to wonder what that light is. Do any of the others have it?"

Walking around the room, Toleder said, "Yes, ma'am. They all appear to have that red light, and it's on."

"And where do those wires go?"

The wires Christa was referring to rose from a hole in the top of each table near one edge and were plugged into the torso of the Denubbewa on that table.

"There's a sort of metal box mounted on a shelf beneath each of the tables. They might be charging units."

"Don't disconnect any of them. You might wake them up."

"This is strange, ma'am. You'd think that if they are alive but unconscious while being charged, someone would have been watching over them to wake them up in case something happened. A guard, sort of."

"Yes, Lieutenant. I agree. Don't interrupt anything. I'm going to send a couple of engineers to your location to take a look." Turning to the com chief she said, "Have the captain of the *Karl Linne* send two engineers to where Lt. Toleder and these men are located."

The com chief relayed the message and Christa turned back to watch the front monitor.

It took almost ten minutes before the engineers were escorted into the room where several dozen Denubbewa lay perfectly motionless on the tables. The two squads of Marines had never relaxed their attention for a second and had spent the time moving around, searching for any sign of weapons. They'd found none, but if any of the Denubbewa had awakened and reacted violently to their ship being invaded by Terrans, it would draw more fire than it could possibly imagine.

After a brief look, the senior engineer said, "I concur. It looks like they're being charged."

"Can the table be moved without waking them?" Christa asked.

"Uh, it appears it can, Captain. The table is on wheels like a medical gurney. I just have to release the locking mechanism."

"Then release it so we can move this one out of the room. Let's get him, or her, or it away from the others before we try to wake him."

"Him or her?" the junior engineer echoed. "Do the Denubbewa have sexes, Lieutenant?"

"How the hell would I know?" Lt. Toleder said. "Just unlock the wheels."

Slowly and carefully, the two engineers and two Marines rolled the table out of the room, followed by Lt. Toleder.

"What now, Commander?" Toleder asked Christa.

"Let's see if we can get it aboard the *Karl Linne* without waking it."

"Can they survive space without an EVA suit?"

"One way to find out, I guess. We have plenty more if we lose one or two," Christa said.

"Oo-rah," the lieutenant said.

When Toleder, the two Marine enlisted, and the two engineers from the *Karl Linne* arrived at the airlock, they realized they were going to have to disconnect the Denubbewa's wires to get him outside the ship because the table wouldn't fit through the airlock door.

"I've got an idea," the senior engineer said. "I saw some shipping containers that reminded me of coffins. Let me get one of those and we can transfer this guy to that before he's fully awake. We'll be able to get the container into the airlock."

"You're assuming he won't wake up fully alert?" Lieutenant Toleder said as sort of a question.

"Uh, yeah, I guess I am."

"Well, I don't have a better idea, so let's try it. If he gets too violent during the transfer, we'll just put him down for good."

"It'll probably take me about ten minutes to get back here with the shipping container. This EVA suit wasn't designed for this sort of activity. I'll need some help."

"I'll go, sir," one of the Marines offered.

"Good. We should still be here when you get back, Corporal. We're not going anywhere— unless our sleeping friends wake up."

"Uh, yeah, sir."

The engineer and the Marine corporal returned about twelve minutes later with a shipping container that was about two and a half meters long. They set it down on the deck and opened it.

"I'll be damned," Toleder said, as he peered down at the open container.

The interior of the container was lined with some sort of packing material like solidified foam and was cut out in the shape of a Denubbewa cyborg.

"Do they ship these things in these containers?" the corporal asked the engineer.

"How would I know? I just saw them when we were looking for the engineering areas."

"How many more of these cases did you see?" Toleder asked.

"There're hundreds down there."

"Are they all empty?"

"I didn't investigate."

"We need to know before we leave this ship." Activating the Com 3 channel in his helmet, Toleder said, "Staff Sergeant Kroger, send a squad of your people to the airlock. We have to investigate a cargo area."

"Yes, sir, Lieutenant," Toleder heard back. "They'll be there in a few minutes."

When the Marines showed up at the airlock, Toleder sent them to the cargo area with the corporal and the senior SC engineer. Toleder, the junior SC engineer, and the other two Marines then waited at the airlock for the squad leader to report in.

It was another fifteen minutes before the sergeant with the squad reported to Toleder.

"Sir, we're in the cargo hold and we've examined the shipping containers. Only a few dozen appear to be empty. The rest appear to each contain one of those sleeping cyborgs."

"Do any of them have a red light on their forehead that's lit up?"

After a short pause, Toleder heard, "The senior SC engineer says no. The light is not lit on the Denubbewa in any of the cases we opened."

"Okay, Sergeant. Post two of your people outside that cargo area to keep an eye on things in case those cyborgs suddenly come alive. Then come back to the airlock."

"Yes, sir."

When the squad showed up at the airlock, Toleder explained that they were going to disconnect the Denubbewa from the wires that seemed to be charging the cyborg and then place it in the packing container.

"As soon as it's disconnected, we lift it up and put it in the open container. Use appropriate force if the metal-head resists us, but try not to kill it— yet. The commander wants it intact for study. Okay, let's do it. I don't know how much these things weigh, but they can't be too heavy from the way they seem to be constructed. Okay, let's do it."

As the engineer unplugged the wires, the Denubbewa's eyes suddenly lit up. It had no eyelids and was incapable of facial expression, but it looked evil. One of the Marines raised his laser rifle in an automatic reflex.

"Hold your fire, Marine," Toleder said. "It hasn't made any threatening moves yet. Okay, Marines, lift that thing up and lay it gently in the packing case. If we don't damage it, it might not react to our handling."

"It's heavier than it looks, sir," one of the PFCs said. "I'd guess it's about two hundred fifty pounds."

"Just take your time. It hasn't reacted in opposition yet."

As the Denubbewa was placed into the container, its eyes stopped glowing and the red light above the bridge of its nose winked out.

"It looks like it's going to sleep," the sergeant said.

"It might be conditioned to react to the shipping container that way," the SC engineer said.

"Let's close the cover and the latches before we get too lax," Toleder said.

Once the container was latched, the Marines at the airlock, except Toleder, suited up in EVA suits and began the process of transporting the Denubbewa to the *Karl Linne*. The airlock was large enough to hold the shipping container when it was upright, so they had the container outside the Denubbewa ship and in one of the maintenance sleds within several more minutes. The table, once the legs were collapsed, could also fit upright through the airlock. So that and what appeared to be a charging unit were sent over as well. The SC engineers remained behind in the Denubbewa warship.

"Okay," Toleder said to the Marines outside the ship, "transport it to the *Karl Linne*. You Marines will remain with the container at all times. Never leave it until you receive a different order from either myself or the watch officer aboard the *Koshi*. You will sleep with it in shifts and eat next to it until relieved. Understand?"

"Oo-rah," the Marines said as the maintenance cart began to move slowly towards the *Karl Linne*.

"Captain," Toleder said as he and the engineers began walking back towards the area where they'd found the Denubbewa, "are you still observing?"

"I'm here, Lieutenant. Good work."

"What are your orders, ma'am?"

"Leave a few of your people in the area where the Denubbewa are on the tables in case they awaken and continue searching the ship. And I'd also like to get an exact count of the number of Denubbewa still in those shipping containers and learn if there are any more such containers anywhere in the ship. Keep an eye out for any Denubbewa activity. As you said earlier, there should have been at least one on guard duty. I'm sending over the other platoon to assist in the search of the entire ship."

CHAPTER NINE
~ December 3rd, 2290 ~

While waiting for further word from the Marines and engineers aboard the Denubbewa ship, Christa went to her office and sent an updated report to Admiral Holt and the two other CPS-16 squadrons in Region Three that were hunting for Denubbewa. Given the great distances, the first Priority-One transmission to Admiral Holt hadn't even really begun the long journey to Quesann, and it would be several days before the other squadron commanders received the reports sent to them, but Christa wanted to document everything that was happening in case it all just suddenly went south and there was no one left to tell the tale.

The bridge crew continued to watch the front monitor as the Marines went about their assigned tasks. No one could dispute their thoroughness. After they completed the count of Denubbewa in the storage hold and restacked the containers, they began moving through every part of the ship that was accessible. Happily, they encountered no other Denubbewa either awake, sleeping on tables, or even entombed in shipping containers.

◆

It took almost eighteen hours to search the enormous ship with just the two platoons of Marines, but when they were done, the bridge crew aboard the *Koshi* could confirm that they had been as thorough as if searching for a lost cache of diamonds that included a significant finder's fee for the team that located it.

Christa immediately sent another round of messages that included the precise count of Denubbewa found aboard the ship.

Then it was time to confront the Denubbewa they'd removed from the ship. The shipping container, table, and charging unit had been transported via shuttle to the *Koshi* and placed in a hold especially prepared for the confrontation. Engineers aboard the *Koshi* had fashioned steel chains to be used when the Denubbewa was unpacked.

Christa would watch on a monitor as the Denubbewa was uncrated and lifted onto the table. She wanted to be in the hold, but as the commanding officer, she had to remind herself that she had a duty to remain as safe as possible so that order and the chain of command was maintained during this potentially dangerous period.

The container was placed near the table and opened, but the Denubbewa didn't stir until several Marines started to lift it out. At that point, its eyes glowed and the red light on its forehead lit up, but nothing else changed.

As the Denubbewa was laid on the table, engineers fitted the prepared chains to various parts of its body. The shape and flexibility of the Denubbewa's wrists and ankles meant they couldn't be used to secure the cyborg, so the engineers routed the chains through openings in the protective plate covering the cyborg's torso. During the process, the cyborg moved its eyes to follow the actions of the engineers, but it never resisted or otherwise even moved.

When the engineers were finished, no one doubted that the Denubbewa could not get up off the table unless it was first unchained. Christa then came to the hold and moved over to the table. A squad of Marines was standing by, just in case.

"Do you understand my words?" Christa asked.

The cyborg just stared back at her as if it didn't have the slightest clue what she was saying.

Looking at the engineering officer who had supervised securing the cyborg, Christa said, "It appears it doesn't understand me. That's to be expected. I want you to mount a monitor above it and begin running some basic Amer language instructional vids. Perhaps it can learn enough Amer that we'll be able to communicate with it on a basic level."

"Aye, Captain. We'll have it set up within the hour."

"Carry on, Lieutenant," she said to the Marine officer responsible for security.

After transmitting an update on the situation with the Denubbewa, Christa sat down to think. There were Marines posted in the holds aboard the Denubbewa ship, and every bridge in the squadron was monitoring the helmet-cam transmissions so they'd know immediately if a situation developed. The *Koshi* and the CPS-16s couldn't simply leave the area with the Denubbewa still alive, and she didn't want to destroy them and the ship because they represented an incredible intelligence resource. She was in a quandary, but she knew there was one thing she should do immediately.

"Lieutenant Kurt Aston," Christa said after touching her Space Command ring.

"Aston here, Captain," she heard the captain of the *Karl Linne* say.

"Captain, I want a piece of the material from that Denubbewa ship's hull. But I don't want the missing piece to interfere with the ship's invisibility or mobility. If other Denubbewa are hunting for it, I don't want them able to locate it. We know it's not emitting any homing beacons, and we're prepared to stop it should one start up. I want us to remain invisible for as long as we're here."

"That's a tall order, Commander, but I'll get my engineers working on it. I can't promise they'll be able to remove a piece though. If it really is Dakinium, we'll never get a piece off the hull with cutting-torches or anything else we have on board."

"There is one way."

"Seriously?"

"Seriously. But it's dangerous."

"What isn't?"

"While the Marines were searching the ship for Denubbewa holdouts, I was watching the helmet-cam images. At one point, they searched an armory, and I thought I saw some of those small missiles the Denubbewa use, like the ones used against the *Yenisei* and the *Salado*. If they are the same, those missiles have a warhead topped by a highly corrosive acid that can melt through Dakinium. That's how they managed to kill the crews of our two destroyers."

"Yes, I read the report on the tactics employed by the Denubbewa and also the confidential report about those missiles."

"Then you probably know that Space Command personnel were able to recover one of the unexploded missiles that missed its target and went ballistic in space. And— that they were able to disassemble it."

"Yes, I recall hearing that."

"The information for how to disassemble the missile is in the Space Command Tactical Weapons Database. Your engineers should be able to accomplish that as well. But they'll have to be extremely careful because that acid eats through practically everything except glass. And it's not safe to disassemble one of those missiles inside one of our ships, so it should be done in a shuttle, far enough away from the ship so the nuclear explosion does no other damage should they be the slightest bit careless."

"Are you ordering me to have my people disassemble a nuclear device so we can retrieve the acid?"

"No. That would have to be a voluntary action."

"I'll discuss it with my people. As I said, I'm not even sure we can remove a piece of the hull without destroying the ship's ability to remain invisible to all sensors. We'd have to determine that first before asking for volunteers to disassemble a nuclear device."

"I know. And I'm sure your people will do their very best. Carver out."

"Aston out."

◆

It was close to seven hours later when Lt. Aston contacted Christa.

"Captain, my engineers have completed their examination of the hull. They tell me there's a flat piece of metal that doesn't appear to have any function other than covering a vent. It absorbs all electromagnetic particles that contact it. They believe the acid could be used to cut off the plate, and we could replace it with a spare Dakinium vent cover we have aboard the *Koshi*. The exposed area would be minimal to begin with, and our vent cover would ensure the cloaking nature of the ship remains intact. Would a piece of the metal only twelve centimeters by about eighteen centimeters be sufficient for your needs?"

"Yes, I believe the scientists back at Quesann will be able to analyze the composition of the metal from a sample that size."

"That's too bad."

"Why?"

"I was sort of hoping you would say no. Now I have to search for a couple of volunteers to disassemble a nuke."

"Such tasks are always difficult, but it's why they pay us the big credits."

Aston chuckled and said, "If money was such an important consideration, we wouldn't be able to find enough people to fully man even one battleship."

"I know, but that line is always good for a laugh. If you can't find anyone to volunteer for the task, I'm sure I can find someone aboard one of the other ships."

"I'll get back to you as soon as I've had chance to talk with my crew."

"Okay. And thanks. Carver out."

"Aston out."

◆

"I've found two volunteers for the missile disassembly. Actually, almost everyone aboard the ship wanted to volunteer, so I had to require that one is a pilot and the other an engineer. If neither was a pilot, I'd have to send a third person out."

"Very good, Lieutenant. Have them both review the disassembly instructions and confirm they fully understand the process before they're allowed to leave. I'll contact the Marines aboard the Denubbewa ship and have them deliver a missile to the *Karl Linne*. Then your people can begin whenever they're ready. The most important task is naturally the safe disassembly of the missile, but of secondary importance is the safe handling of the acid. That stuff will eat through almost anything, so if they spill any, it will eat completely through the shuttle deck and won't stop until there's nothing left to eat or the acid is neutralized. The atmosphere inside the ship will be long gone by then."

"We understand, Captain. The two individuals are presently reviewing the disassembly instructions with our entire team of engineers. They'll be ready when they leave here."

"Very good. Carry on, Lieutenant. Carver out."

"Aston out."

Christa leaned back in her office chair. In battle, she didn't hesitate to place people in dangerous situations that might result in their deaths. It was a necessary part of the job. But when there wasn't someone shooting at her and her people, asking for volunteers to risk their lives was, for her, the most difficult chore in the universe. She did it without hesitation, but it always ate away at her.

◆　◆　◆

"Okay," Ensign Barbara Culchech said as she cut the engines on the shuttle, "we're far enough away that we won't harm anyone else if we go boom."

"Go boom?" Lieutenant Harris Lockwood said with a wry expression.

"It's an advanced technical term. It refers to an explosive force of significant intensity in a closed environment."

"I see. Say, are you sure you graduated from the Academy? I mean you didn't just stow away on a freighter one day and happen to find yourself on Quesann?"

"Shhh! Don't say that too loud. Someone might start an investigation."

"You're something else, Barbie."

"But *what* else you don't know, Harry."

"No, but I'm hoping to find out one day."

"Well, let's get started on this task. Tonight's pizza night and I want to get back before it's all gone."

"The number one rule when dealing with a nuclear weapon is never hurry."

"Yeah, yeah, yeah. Now hurry up!"

Harris laughed and climbed out of the right cockpit seat, then moved to the rear compartment as Culchech activated the cameras in the rear compartment. The other ships would get the images, but voice communication wasn't enabled so as to avoid possible distractions. As Harris opened the case containing the missile, he paused and took a deep breath.

"It doesn't look very deadly, does it?" Culchech said. "I mean, it's so small."

"Just one of these could kill everyone aboard the *Karl Linne* if it went boom while inside the ship. And it will definitely kill both of us, so let's get serious."

Lockwood lifted the missile out of the storage case and placed it in a makeshift rack constructed by the *Karl Linne* engineering department.

"Okay. I'm all business. What's first?"

"First, we remove the warhead. Once we separate that from the nuclear second stage, the greatest danger is past. We just have to hope this missile isn't different than the one our people in Region Two were able to disassemble."

"Okay, let's do it. What do I do?"

"You reviewed the disassembly videos, right?"

"Of course. I was standing right next to you the second time. Lieutenant Aston insisted those instructions be burned into our memories."

"Right. So you will hold the second-stage part of the missile steady while I attempt to remove the warhead."

"Right."

"So kneel on the deck and grab hold of the second stage now that I've placed the missile in the special rack. And hang on like your life depends on it— because it does."

Culchech knelt and placed both hands on the body of the missile to keep it from moving on the rack as Lockwood knelt by the head.

"Ready?" Lockwood asked as he held a ceramic probe near the warhead.

"Of course. Get on with it. I'm starting to sweat a little."

"That's good. It tells me you're taking this seriously."

Lockwood held the tip of the ceramic probe near a small hole in the warhead where it met the nuclear stage of the missile. Taking a deep breath, he inserted the probe slowly until he met resistance. He placed his left hand beneath the warhead to hold it in place and steadily applied pressure on the probe. When he heard an almost inaudible click, he felt the full weight of the warhead in his left hand. Slowly he pulled the warhead away from the nuclear stage. As it came completely free, he lowered it into a small packing case with interior padding designed to secure it from moving about. He slowly closed the case and snapped the latches. Then he released the breath he'd been holding and took another deep breath.

"You can let go now," Lockwood said.

Culchech relaxed and sat back on her heels, then released the breath she'd been holding and took another full breath and released it. "Okay, what's next? That's all they showed in the video."

"That's it."

"That's it? We're done?"

"We're done here. The most dangerous part of this operation is over. I just have to put the missile back in its storage box and we can head back to our ship."

"There's no more danger?"

"This was just the first step but by far the most dangerous. There's still a level of danger as this effort progresses, but the number of personnel in danger of imminent death has been reduced to a handful. The next step is to remove the acid in the warhead so we can use it to cut off a small piece of that Denubbewa ship's hull for analysis. If the proper procedures are followed and there're no slipups or accidents, everyone will be fine."

"It's almost anticlimactic."

"I guess it's like that sometimes. You prepare for the worst while hoping for the best."

"Okay. Then let's wrap it up and head for home."

"Yeah, I'm kind of looking forward to pizza myself now."

"I hope we get there before all the pepperoni's gone."

"Maybe they'll hold one just for us. We're heroes."

"I think that works for most things but never on pizza night."

◆　◆　◆

As the shuttle piloted by Culchech docked with the *Karl Linne*, a shuttle from the *Koshi* was docking on the opposite side of the CPS-16. The hatchways to both small vessels opened into the *Karl Linne* at the same time. An engineer from the *Koshi* hurried in and carefully took the case containing the acid from Lockwood, who was emerging from the shuttle with Culchech.

"I've got it," the lieutenant from the *Koshi* said. "Thanks." He then turned and reentered the *Koshi* shuttle. A Marine waiting at the hatchway then closed the *Karl Linne* hatch. Within a minute, the shuttle's hatch was closed and sealed. The diminutive ship then returned to the *Koshi*.

"I guess our part is done," Lockwood said.

"Yeah. Hey, let's go grab some pizza."

"Okay, but first we have to put the rest of the missile into the armory locker so no one gets curious."

"Who would want to tinker with a nuclear weapon?"

"You just never know. And if we go boom, we don't get any pizza."

◆　◆　◆

The acid was delivered to the engineering section on the *Koshi* for the next step. Christa believed the much larger engineering staff aboard the Scout-Destroyer was better equipped to handle the dangerous fluid than the CPS-16 engineering section. That point probably wouldn't be disputed by Lockwood or anyone else.

◆

"Captain," Lt. Mollago said from the command chair on the *Koshi* bridge, "the acid has arrived and been delivered to engineering."

"Very good, XO. Keep me apprised."

"Yes, ma'am. I've just been told that the Denubbewa prisoner is getting agitated."

"Agitated?"

"He keeps mumbling something."

"He's talking?"

"Not Amer. It's just gibberish."

"I'll go take a look."

"Aye, Captain. Mollago out."

"Carver out."

◆

As Christa entered the hold where the Denubbewa was chained to the table, she saw three engineers standing around the table, looking down at the cyborg.

"I understand the prisoner is getting agitated," she said to one who turned and approached her.

"He began to utter nonsense when the first vid teaching basic Amer ended, Captain."

"What kind of nonsense?"

"He's saying something like ma, ma."

"Ma?"

"That's what it sounds like."

Christa walked past the engineer and approached the table. The Denubbewa looked up at her and said, "Ma, ma."

"He seems to think you're his mother, Captain," one of the engineers said with a grin.

"And this started when the vid ended?"

"Yes, ma'am."

"Could he be trying to say *more*?"

"Uh— I suppose that's possible," the senior person said.

"Let's put on the next vid in the series and see what he does."

As the second vid started playing on the monitor, the Denubbewa stopped talking and calmed down.

"It seems that's all he wanted," Christa said.

"Do you think he understands it, Captain?"

"I don't know, but it can't hurt. We have no other way of communicating with him. Just make sure he doesn't get access to any technical data."

"Yes, ma'am."

◆　◆　◆

"The acid warhead doesn't contain any explosive capability," Lt. Burton, the chief engineer aboard the *Koshi* said to Christa during a status meeting in her office. "We've succeeded in moving some of the Denubbewa acid to a separate glass container that can be used in a weightless environment so we can attempt to remove that small piece of the Denubbewa ship for analysis."

"Very good. Coordinate with the engineers aboard the *Karl Linne*. They've identified a place where a piece can be removed and still allow the ship to maintain its sensor invisibility. They deserve to be involved."

"Aye, Captain. I'll contact them."

"After the acid eats through the Dakinium, does it become inert or remain dangerous?"

"According to the engineers who examined the *Salado* and *Yenisei*, the acid became inert. But we don't know if that's a property of the acid or because of the nuclear explosion that occurred immediately after the acid ate through the hull. The Space Command database paper that presented the findings of the scientists who analyzed the orb of acid retrieved from the undetonated weapon recovered in space never expounded on that aspect of the weapon."

"That's too bad. I'm sure it was merely an oversight."

"Of course."

"When do you expect to attempt the hull material recovery?"

"Tomorrow, if the *Karl Linne* engineers are agreeable. We'll use a very small sample of the acid and see how long it remains active. If a single drop shears off the entire piece and is still active, we'll know we've got a problem. We've rigged up a special glass container to hold the piece we cut off so it presents no danger to our ship once we've detached it from the Denubbewa ship."

"And if the acid remains active after the single drop cuts the piece off?"

"We have a second glass container for that contingency. We'll use a piece of cloth to capture the drop and immediately put the cloth into the glass container. Hopefully, that will prevent any other damage."

"How long will it take to analyze the material and determine if it's Dakinium or some other material with similar properties? We need to know if it has any weaknesses."

"We can only perform a very preliminary analysis— not the kind of in-depth analysis you want, or really need. We can confirm the general properties of near indestructibility, absorption of all energy so that no sensor data is ever reflected, and that it *appears* to have the other basic properties that we expect of Dakinium. As you know, it took years for the Space

Command scientists to duplicate the material sample your sister discovered on Dakistee, and even then, they couldn't match it exactly. They continue to experiment— their goal being to offer the virtual indestructibility inherent in the original plus the properties they've managed to add, such as the latest feature of producing Dakinium in any color of the rainbow with all tints and shades. A full analysis can only be performed at Quesann, which now houses the laboratories that were formerly located on Earth."

"Get me whatever you can. I need more information to make my decision regarding the ship we've found."

"You'll know almost as soon as I do, Captain."

"Thank you, Lieutenant. Dismissed."

◆ ◆

Several hours later, Christa was still in her office and still staring up at the overhead as she examined her position and weighed all her options— repeatedly. Her squadron couldn't remain at this location forever, but they also couldn't leave an intact Denubbewa ship here. If they were forced to leave, she would have to destroy the ship and that represented the loss of a potentially invaluable intelligence resource. Space Command had never been able to capture an intact Denubbewa vessel before and certainly not one with live cyborg prisoners. She believed she couldn't simply destroy it unless it was ordered by the Second Fleet Commander at Quesann. Of course, there was always the danger that the entire crew of the ship would simultaneously awaken and pull weapons from— somewhere. In that case, she'd have no choice. And the only way to destroy the ship was to have one of the CP-16's drop an bomb inside. Since the hull appeared to be Dakinium, it would probably remain intact while the insides were reduced to scrap.

Christa was brought up out of her deliberative state by a call on her CT.

"Captain, this Lt. Burton. The prisoner is demanding to speak with you."

"The cyborg is demanding something?" she queried after touching the face of her Space Command ring. "In Amer?"

"Yes, ma'am."

"Is he speaking in gibberish like before?"

"No, ma'am. This time he's talking whole sentences."

"I'll be right down."

◆

As Christa walked into the hold where the prisoner was being held, she noticed that the Marine guards had their weapons at the ready.

"Has the prisoner tried to escape his bonds?" Christa asked Lt. Burton.

"No, ma'am. He's just been very— insistent— that he be allowed to see you immediately."

Turning towards the Marine sergeant she said, "Lower your weapon unless the prisoner actually presents a threat."

"Yes, ma'am," the sergeant said.

The two other guards lowered their weapons without being directly ordered to do so.

Christa walked closer to the table and looked down at the cyborg. "Have you been asking to see me? I'm the Captain of this ship."

"Captain," the cyborg responded in almost perfect Amer but with a slightly raspy voice, "you must release me and allow us continue our journey unimpeded."

"And why must I do that?"

"Because we are not Denubbewa, and the safety of the G.A. depends on you releasing us."

CHAPTER TEN
~ December 4ᵗʰ, 2290 ~

"*Not* Denubbewa? You certainly look like a Denubbewa."

"The Denubbewa conquered my planet and enslaved our entire race a millennium ago. Then they began to slowly take my people away. We never knew where they were being taken until *we* were taken. Once they had us aboard one of their ships, they extracted our brains from our bodies and put them into these mechanical bodies. Then they cleared our minds of all memories and implanted Denubbewa memories so we would become part of their collective. Fortunately, the Denubbewa didn't know how our minds worked. We have the ability to retreat into an unconscious state where their memory erasure procedure couldn't reach us. But we did absorb the new Denubbewa memories, and that enabled us to fool the collective. Once we had been accepted as faithful Denubbewa slaves, the Denubbewa stopped watching us so closely and we could allow our previous memories to flood back into our consciousness. We have the memories of two lives, but we know which is real and which is fake.

"We've waited and planned for many annuals, and we finally had an opportunity to take over a Denubbewa ship and escape the collective. We made it to where you found us, but we had been awake for weeks and our minds desperately needed rest, even though the Denubbewa bodies could continue on without rest.

"That's why you must release us. We are not your enemies. We are only attempting to escape the Denubbewa and find a planet where we can again establish our own civilization, just as you would do in our place."

"You want to establish a new civilization in this sector of space?"

"No, no, no. It must be as far from this place as possible. The Denubbewa intend to colonize this part of space for many thousands of light-years in every direction. And when they control that, they will move on and conquer another enormous sector of space. And then another until they eventually control the entire galaxy. Their goal is to one day control the entire universe."

"That's a pretty ambitious plan."

"It won't happen tomorrow. They know that. But they are infinitely patient and know it will happen one day. We need to find a place where we can rebuild our society and prepare for the day when we must again confront the Denubbewa. The first time we met, we welcomed them as travelers with whom we could trade. Before we knew what was happening, they had become our masters."

"Your Amer is very good. I didn't think you could speak it at all."

"Your instructional vids allowed me to correlate my own language with yours. The Denubbewa don't normally use verbal speech as you do and as we once did. I'm finding that the more I use the voice box built into this body, the more comfortable I am with it. Cyborg communication with other cyborgs is limited to electronic signals."

"If Denubbewa only use electronic communications, why do they install voice boxes in the body?"

"Because almost all cyborg bodies are constructed from a single design, and some cyborgs need to communicate with species being assimilated until the individual has had their brain extracted and inserted into a cyborg body."

"I see. We employ personal electronic communications as well, but we prefer verbal speech whenever possible."

"I know. I've been receiving your electronic communications ever since I awoke. But I didn't understand the language so I simply stored all communications until you gave me a reference for the many words I was hearing. Now that I understand the meaning of the words, I've been reviewing all the communications I've stored."

"You're able to intercept our electronic communications?"

"Yes. And it's a relief to be away from the Denubbewa. We were constantly besieged with communication messages there. You never have a moment, a single moment, where you can enjoy some peace and quiet. Since only your officers here seem to use electronic communications, there are long periods where I hear nothing."

"How many of the Denubbewa cyborg bodies we found in your ship are occupied by your people?"

"All of the cyborg bodies on the tables and most of the bodies in the shipping containers. Those in the shipping containers are on minimal life support. They can remain that way indefinitely if we recharge them once every annual."

"Is that the meaning of the red light on your forehead? If it's lit, you're conscious?"

"No, when lit it means I'm not on reduced life support. I can be either awake or asleep."

"And the others? You said most are your people."

"There are a few Denubbewa puppets there. We kept them only for spare parts until we can produce biological bodies for our brains."

"You'd return to biological bodies after being in mechanical bodies?"

"Biological bodies can repair themselves if an injury isn't too serious, or they can usually be repaired by doctors if the injury is serious. These mechanical bodies are easy to repair, but they have no sense of touch or feel, at least not the way biological bodies do. We hate these bodies and want to be Elobians again."

"That was the name of your race? Elobian?"

"Yes. We were a civilization of peaceful citizens long before we even dreamed of space travel. We know now how foolish we were to be so trusting of the Denubbewa when they arrived. We assumed that because they were so advanced, they must be benign. We accredited our own values to the Denubbewa, and we learned the hard way that intelligence and beneficence do not go hand in hand."

"The two are not mutually inclusive but neither are they mutually exclusive. Every civilization must be based on its own merits without preconceptions based on the merits or misconducts of other civilizations."

"True."

"What is your name? How should I refer to you?"

"The Denubbewa named me R398QBE4391AX843L. My name before the Denubbewa enslaved me was Sywasock Devollneost."

"Then I shall call you Sywasock. I'm Captain Carver."

"I am pleased to make your acquaintance, Captain Carver."

"And I yours. Do you need anything, such as food, water, lubricant?"

"I would like to be unchained."

"I'm afraid I can't do that— yet. Trust is not given, it's earned."

"I understand. My appearance is that of a Denubbewa and your history with the Denubbewa is like that of my own race."

"Exactly. You've made a good start here today towards establishing trust, but we have a ways to go."

"Then could I have one of the guards plug me into the power supply each night? Once fully recharged, we can unplug ourselves, but we cannot plug ourselves in."

"I'll take care of it. You said before that the safety of the G.A. depends on us releasing you. What did you mean by that?"

"I apologize, Captain. I was just trying to get you to listen to me. I got a little carried away."

Christa just nodded and said, "Goodnight, Sywasock."

"Goodnight, Captain Carver."

Christa's first stop after leaving the cyborg was the bridge. She walked directly to the com console.

"Chief, I want all CT transmissions blocked immediately until further notice."

"Yes, ma'am. I'll shut down the system. Uh, is there something I should be aware of?"

"Our guest under guard just told me that he hears and automatically records all electronic messages transmitted within the ship. Until we know we can trust him, there are to be no CT transmissions."

"Yes, ma'am. What about communications between ships?"

"We have no choice, but we have to be careful with what we say for the present."

"Yes, ma'am."

Christa left the bridge and walked through the corridors to think. She was glad she was aboard a Scout-Destroyer and not a CPS-16 or she would have quickly run out of corridor and wound up retracing her steps.

She suddenly realized what she had to do and stopped the first person she passed. He happened to be a cook's assistant.

"Find the XO and tell him to come to my office— immediately. Then find Lt. Burton and give him the same message."

"I can use a com to have them paged, Captain. Will that do?"

"No. I want you to tell them in person."

"Aye, Captain."

Christa returned to her office to wait for her officers and think about her discussion with the cyborg.

Lt. Mollago arrived first. His sweats were soaked with perspiration.

"I'm sorry, Captain, but I was told you wanted to see me immediately."

"Come in, XO. I also sent for Lt. Burton. We'll wait for him before I start. Need a towel?"

"Uh, if you have one handy, ma'am. I was in such a hurry to report that I forgot to grab one."

Christa opened a drawer of her desk and produced a clean towel. Mollago hadn't even finished wiping his head before Lt. Burton showed up. He was wearing a robe.

"Sorry, Captain. I was in the hot tub. The messenger reported that you said immediately."

"Yes, have a seat. We have a serious problem. I spoke to the cyborg prisoner a short time ago. He's learned to speak our language. But what's even more remarkable is what he told me."

Christa then related everything the cyborg had told her about being able to intercept all electronic messages.

"Do you believe him, Captain?" Mollago asked when she was finished.

"We can't afford *not* to believe him. I've had the CT system shut down until we can secure it."

"Secure it, Captain?"

"I'm hoping Lt. Burton can arrange that. There must be some place on this ship where we can place the cyborg where he can't intercept communications messages—say next to a power supply junction room or something. There must be someplace where an officer can't make or receive CT communications."

"The ship designers have gone to a great deal of trouble to prevent that from happening. But I might be able to rig some kind of a low voltage power barrier around a storage locker that will prevent signals from penetrating into the locker."

"Good. Do it. As quickly as possible. The entire routine of the ship is going to be turned upside down if we can't use our CTs."

"Captain," Mollago said, "do you think he's been communicating with the other cyborgs on the Denubbewa ship?"

"No, I considered that but then dismissed it. Our hull is sheathed in Dakinium, so no radio signal can get through. Also, the Denubbewa ship is sheathed in something like Dakinium that absorbs all electrical and electronic signals. And I seriously doubt he'd be able to send and receive signals using our temporary transceiver setup."

"So we only have one possible breach of security so far?"

"I believe so. Lt. Burton?"

"I agree, Captain. The cyborg may have been able to receive transmissions within the ship but not send or receive messages with anyone or anything outside the ship."

"Good. Why don't you get going on that project? XO, I want to talk to you about a different matter."

After Burton was gone, Christa said, "I'm going to relate everything the cyborg said to me, and my impressions. I recorded it, but I want you to know now in case something was to happen to me. But you're not to repeat it to anyone *unless* something happens to me."

"Of course, Captain."

◆

"That's quite a story," Mollago said when Christa had finished.

"Yes."

"Do you believe him?"

"I'd like to. And he was pretty convincing, but I just don't know. He went from not knowing a word of Amer when he came aboard to speaking like a professional on a lecture circuit in just two days. So, did he learn everything from the vid instruction courses with the combined information from all of the messages he intercepted, or has he been stringing us along? And he originally said that the safety of the G.A. depended on my releasing him and the others. But when I questioned him about that, he said he was just trying to get my attention. There's more there than he's admitting."

Mollago just shook his head slowly to show he had nothing to offer on the topic.

"And it adds another dimension to where we go from here. If we'd had to leave the area without being able to take the Denubbewa ship, I would have ordered it destroyed, along with all of the Denubbewa aboard it. But now, knowing that most of the Denubbewa might actually be captured aliens who are aware of their previous lives and only want to be free makes such a decision much harder."

"I'm glad I don't have to make that decision."

"Your time will come. You're an excellent second officer and will move into the top spot one day."

"Thank you, Captain."

"Of course, it may not happen if you keep coming to your captain's office dripping sweat all over her carpet." She punctuated the humorous remark with a smile.

Mollago smiled and said, "Sorry, Captain. And next time I'll bring my own towel."

◆ ◆ ◆

"Captain," the Com chief said, "a Priority-One message for you has just come in."

"Send it to my queue, Chief."

"Yes, ma'am."

Commander Lori Ashraf was working in her office aboard the Scout-Destroyer *Seeker*. She leaned in so the computer could perform the retinal scan before she was allowed access to the message. When the computer was satisfied, the message began to play. She was surprised when she saw that it was from the *Koshi*.

"Hello, Lori," the image of Christa Carver said. "I have some distressing news. I've already forwarded this information to Admiral Holt, and I'll be sending it to Commander Fareman as well.

"In a nutshell, we've found what appears to be a derelict Denubbewa warship. More importantly, it appears to be sheathed with Dakinium. If that's accurate, it might explain why we haven't spotted a single Denubbewa ship before now. And we only discovered this one because we stopped to investigate a derelict freighter that *did* appear on our sensors. While my people were investigating the freighter, someone noticed that the light from a group of distant stars wasn't visible.

"That's all for now. I'll message you again when we know more. We're going to attempt to board the Denubbewa ship. I'm appending our coordinates so you'll know where we are if we fail to report in again.

"Wish us luck.

"Christa Marie Carver, Commander, Captain of the GSC *Koshi*. End of message."

Commander Ashraf immediately notified the watch commander to have the entire squadron proceed to the new coordinates she was sending to the navigation station.

◆　◆　◆

"Working with the engineers from the *Karl Linne*," Lt. Burton said to Christa and Lt. Mollago during a meeting in Christa's office, "we were successful in removing a piece of sheathing material that covered a vent on that Denubbewa ship."

"Excellent," Christa said. "And the acid issue?"

"A single drop of the acid went inactive after several seconds on the Dakinium. It only scored a deep slice about a centimeter in length. We had to use quite a bit to cut the sample off."

"That's good news. Have you begun the analysis of the material?"

"We began that work this morning."

"Is the Denubbewa ship still invisible to all sensors?"

"Yes, ma'am. Captain, this ship gives us an incredible opportunity to learn about the Denubbewa. Have you decided when we can begin examining their systems?"

"We cannot begin examining their systems until we first ascertain that nothing our people do can result in any sort of an automated signal being sent to the Denubbewa fleet— at least not until we're ready for a signal to be sent to them."

"I don't understand," Burton said. "Why would we want to have an automated signal sent to them?"

"Why does a hunter bait a trap?"

"Oh."

"Exactly."

"But we can never be sure that we won't accidently cause an emergency signal to be sent to the Denubbewa when we begin examining electronic systems. If that happened, they'd know their secret was out."

"There is one way."

"Not examine the systems?" Mollago said.

"Okay," Christa said with a smile, "there are two ways."

"Then what's the other, Captain?" Burton asked.

"As I've mentioned before in our meetings, I've been sending a stream of updates regarding our find to Admiral Holt and the other two squadron commanders searching for Denubbewa to keep them fully apprised of developments. In one of my first updates to Admiral Holt, I suggested that he send one of the newer ship transports the Second Fleet now has operating in Regions Two and Three. That would enable us to send the Denubbewa ship back to Quesann for study. Unfortunately, the distance to Quesann means that they haven't yet received even the first message I sent.

"Yes," Lt. Burton said. "If a DS Ship Transport were to arrive, we could put the Denubbewa ship inside and be confident that no emergency beacon or automated message could ever reach the Denubbewa because the transport ship's Dakinium outer hull would prevent it."

"Until we have some safeguard such as that in place, or we actually want to summon the Denubbewa fleet, we can't start messing around with alien technology that we don't yet understand."

"Of course, Captain. And that's fine. I don't really expect that ship to be going anywhere. I'm just kind of anxious to play with the new toy."

"While we wait, what's the situation with our prisoners?"

"We continue to rotate the guards every watch," Mollago said. "There's been no activity among the Denubbewa on the tables, and there's nothing going on where the inactive Denubbewa are in shipping containers."

"Very good. Well, there's just one more thing to discuss before we adjourn. Lt. Burton, have we made any progress with the attempt to block all communications within that storage area we want to use as a holding cell?"

"We're still working on it. The power envelope we've created around the storage locker so far is blocking all communications in *most* of the interior. We continue to work to achieve one hundred percent in the entire room. Perhaps it will be ready by tomorrow."

"I hope so. It's darn inconvenient not having the CT system working."

"I know, Captain. And I agree. I keep finding myself trying to use mine throughout the day until I remember it's been deactivated."

"Okay. If that's all, we're done. Carry on."

◆ ◆ ◆

By the next afternoon, work on the temporary holding cell was finished. Lt. Burton guaranteed that no electronic signal could possibly be received or sent from inside the storage locker. The prisoner was moved immediately. Following completion of the move, Christa ordered the com chief to restore the CT system. Every officer aboard ship was delighted to once again have their CT fully operational. It was commonly said that a person never appreciated something they used frequently until they were suddenly without it.

◆ ◆ ◆

Several days later, the *Seeker* and twenty-four CPS-16s arrived in the sector. They had used the coordinates sent by Christa, but in the vastness of space, with everything constantly spinning and shifting, coordinates were not as accurate as they would have been on a fixed plane. And with the *Koshi* and all of the CPS-16s being sheathed with Dakinium, the small task force was not visible on sensors. The *Seeker* was able to locate the *Koshi* by first locating the derelict ship the *Koshi* squadron had stopped to investigate. The *Koshi* squadron ships had all turned on their exterior lights at minimum intensity once each hour so the other ships could verify everyone's position, and the same policy was employed when shuttles needed to navigate among the twenty-five unseen vessels. When a message arrived from the *Seeker* in which Captain Ashraf announced that her squadron was nearby, Christa ordered all ships to illuminate their exterior lights at half brightness until the arriving ships could establish their exact positions. Communications among the ships, naturally encrypted, was accomplished via narrow band laser signals rather than open S-band in order to assist their concealment.

◆ ◆

"Commander Ashraf's shuttle has arrived at the shuttle bay, Captain," Christa heard through her CT.

"Thank you. I'll go down to greet her personally."

Ten minutes later the shuttle had entered the bay and settled onto the deck while the outer hatch sealed and the temporary airlock was pressurized. When the airlock's transparent walls rose up out of the way, the shuttle moved to the only available parking location in the small bay and settled to the deck. Christa entered the bay as the shuttle's ramp was extending to the deck and watched as the passenger hatch was opened.

"Lori, it's wonderful to see you again, especially under such difficult circumstances," Christa said with a smile when Commander Ashraf emerged from the shuttle and walked down to the deck.

"And you, Christa. Are the circumstances difficult here? I got the impression you had everything under control."

"Let's go to my office and I'll fill you in."

CHAPTER ELEVEN
~ December 13th, 2290 ~

"Congratulations," Ashraf said as soon as the doors to Christa's office closed and before they had even taken their seats.

"For?" Christa said as she sat down.

"For securing an undamaged Denubbewa ship and dozens of Denubbewa prisoners. SCI must be beside themselves with joy and anticipation."

"I doubt they even know yet. We're a very long way from Quesann."

"Even if they don't know now, they'll know soon enough. And when they do, they'll be toasting your name."

"I'm glad you've come, Lori. We may have to defend that ship and the prisoners with everything we've got."

"Have you confirmed that the hull of the Denubbewa ship is sheathed in Dakinium?"

"Not completely. We've determined through analysis that the material shares many of the same properties as Dakinium. But the final verdict will rest with the Space Command scientists who've been studying it for years."

"It's black, it's virtually indestructible except for that acid the Denubbewa have, and it absorbs all energy beams and electronic signals?"

"Yes."

"Sounds like Dakinium to me. I guess the real question is: Where did they get the formula so they could manufacture it?"

"I'm hoping they acquired a piece of Dakinium when they destroyed either the *Salado* or the *Yenisei* and reverse engineered it."

"Why hoping? Because the alternative means someone sold us out?"

"Exactly. And it wouldn't be just Space Command or even Terrans being sold out. The one cyborg that is talking to us says the Denubbewa aren't here to conquer and control G.A. space. He says they're here to conquer and destroy all sentient life so they can replace it with their own cyborgs. He claims the cyborgs are just mindless slaves to the real Denubbewa."

"Are the real Denubbewa cyborgs, or do they have a biological body?"

"During one of our conversations he said he doesn't know. He claims never to have met one. Apparently the cyborgs work in designated clusters, and each cluster receives their directions from a single supervising cyborg who gets his marching orders from a higher supervisor, and so on."

"Sounds like a standard military hierarchy."

"Yes, except only one cyborg in each cluster ever gets to communicate with a higher up, and he only sees one level up. We, on the other hand, always know who's in the chain of command above and below us."

"So you're just going to sit here and wait to see what happens?"

"What else can we do? I can't destroy that Denubbewa ship with all the cyborgs inside and simply continue on with our mission. The intelligence loss, were I to do that, would be immeasurable. Besides, the mission is a bust if we can no longer detect Denubbewa ships with our sensors."

"I was thinking we should take the ship back to Quesann in order to save time, or at least as far as we can get it before we meet a Transport."

"I requested a Transport be sent, but that message hasn't even reached Quesann yet. And we don't know their systems well enough to pilot it. We might accidentally engage some sort of a self-destruct mechanism or send out a signal that attracts every Denubbewa in Region Three directly to us, and we wouldn't even know they're coming."

"True, but we don't have to fly it. We have forty-eight tugs available. That *was* the designed purpose of CPS-14s after all before they became a reconfigurable ship that could be customized for any mission. The CPS-16s have been modified quite a bit, but they can still be used for that purpose."

Christa grinned. "That's true. I've been so focused on the other issues that I never even thought of that."

"You're a Carver, not a god, although some folks think of you three ladies that way. I managed to *almost* keep up with the admiral while I was her aide, and I was ahead of her only a very few times during our many years together. And when I was actually ahead, it was only because the issue was extremely complex and I considered an option she missed because she was focused on issues I didn't even know about yet. Are there any issues here that I'm not aware of?"

"Uh, maybe one."

"I bet it's a big one."

"Uh, yeah."

"Can you talk about it?"

"Yes, but you can't repeat it."

"Your sister always trusted me to hold confidences sacred."

"I know. Okay, hang onto your seat."

Christa then related everything she had heard about the Elobian race in multiple conversations with the cyborg down in the special holding cell.

When she was done, Commander Ashraf said, "Wow!"

"Yeah."

"Who else knows about this?"

"My XO knows everything I've told you. And the guards have overhead parts of it, but I've sworn them to silence under threat of court-martial for anyone who speaks of it."

"Not Admiral Holt?"

"I've told him a little, but only the highlights. I didn't want to put too much in a communication— even a Priority-One communication."

"I don't blame you. This is Corplastizine on steroids."

"I like your suggestion about using the CPS-16s as tugs. Let's do it."

"Okay. As soon as we're done with our conversation, I'll inform my senior engineering officer and he can work with your senior person to figure out what we'll need to do it. Have your people produced images of the ship that we can use to determine attachment points?"

"No. I hadn't considered towing it to Quesann as an option. Until we learned of the sheathing, I had intended to destroy the ship because we're so far from Quesann that bringing a Denubbewa ship to the base seemed like a waste of time. Although we've never captured an intact Denubbewa ship, SCI has had enough pieces of destroyed ships that I believed there were no surprises in this one."

"Then we should have them begin work on that right away so our engineers can develop the plan for towing it."

"I hope they'll be able get it working with a double envelope," Christa said. "Do you have any idea how long it would take us to get back to Quesann at Light-480?"

"I suppose it would take about— eighty-four years. Half a lifetime. I'd say— that would definitely make it worth waiting for a Ship Transporter."

Christa started laughing, and that started Lori laughing.

◆ ◆ ◆

The best engineers among the fifty ships present devoted themselves to preparing the Denubbewa ship for being towed in a double envelope. At first, they attacked the problem as if they might have to actually tow the Denubbewa ship with multiple tugs and account for control and inertia, but then they decided to forget all that and simply concentrate on building an envelope large enough to encompass one CPS-16 and the Denubbewa ship. The envelope generator of the CPS-16s had been designed to handle massive loads, but nothing so large as a Denubbewa warship that dwarfed Space Command's largest battleships. Working around the clock, the engineers came up with a plan to dramatically increase the power output from a CPS-16 envelope generator. They hoped their modifications wouldn't burn out the generator, or even worse, short out the electrical system in the entire ship.

Rather than ropes or cables, each CPS-16 carried a dozen sections of two-inch-thick rods, each rod being just over three meters long and made of Dakinium. Once fastened together, two rods, each 18 meters in length, would extend from the CPS-16 to the Denubbewa ship. The rods were probably strong enough to tow a planet, but strength wasn't the primary requirement. Once the rods were connected to both ships, the

CPS-16 would activate its envelope generator and the two ships should then be able to move as one. Should any gap suddenly open in the connection, the envelope would dissipate and the Denubbewa ship would suddenly be at a dead stop in space while the towing ship continued on until it learned it had lost its load. The honor of towing the Denubbewa ship to Quesann was given to the *Karl Linne* because it was the bridge officers from that ship who had noticed the light from distant stars being blocked out by an anomaly, which led to discovering the black ship in the blackness of space.

Once everything was ready, it made no sense to hang around where they'd been for the past twenty-four days so the convoy of fifty-one ships prepared to head for Quesann.

◆ ◆ ◆

"Admiral, Admiral Holt is calling," Jenetta heard from the viewpad sitting on her desk. She tapped a couple of contact points and the large monitor facing her desk illuminated with the image of Brian Holt.

"Good morning, Brian."

"It isn't, Jen. It may never be again."

"Are you alright?"

"I'm a little sick. I just received a message from Christa."

"Christa? Is she alright? I haven't heard from her in weeks."

"She appears to be healthy, but the message she sent came Priority One."

"What's wrong?" Jenetta asked, concern now showing on her face.

"Christa's squadron has found a Denubbewa warship. It appears to be a derelict— so far. She wanted to inform me immediately so the Marines hadn't yet entered the ship to investigate when the message was sent. She says she'll continue to send updates anytime she learns anything new. Jen, Christa says she believes the ship is sheathed in Dakinium."

"Oh, no! Please tell me today is April 1st and this is a joke."

"Sorry. No joke. That's why I'm not alright. It looks like we've just lost our major edge in the fight with the Denubbewa."

"If it's sheathed in Dakinium, how did Christa even find it?"

"It was a fluke. As per their orders, they had stopped to investigate a derelict freighter that appeared on their sensors and someone on the bridge of a CPS-16 noticed that a strange anomaly was blocking the light from a group of stars. Christa investigated and they discovered the Denubbewa warship. I'm awaiting any updates with new information, but I wanted to give you what I had."

"How far away are they, Bry?"

"Communication-wise— about twenty-five days."

"Twenty-five days," Jenetta said with a sigh. "A lot can have happened in twenty-five days."

"Yes."

"I'll need to call an emergency executive session of the A.B. We have to discuss this new development. But I should wait until we have a little more information. If the Denubbewa are able to manufacture Dakinium, the whole tide of war could shift against us."

"Christa says she believes the Dakinium has to be responsible for her inability to locate any Denubbewa ships other than the derelict they found. And neither of the other two squadrons has seen a single Denubbewa ship since they've been in Region Three."

"I'm going to send a notification to the A.B. members that an emergency meeting will be called as soon as we have more information from the *Koshi* squadron. That way they won't make any plans that prevent them from attending for the next couple of days. Let me know as soon as you hear *anything*, Brian."

"You know I will, Jen. Holt out."

"Carver out."

It had been an interesting week so far. The twins were cutting their first teeth and Jen was running into resistance with the G.A. Council because they couldn't see the need for creating and training a ground force of Marines. And now this.

Jenetta leaned back in her chair and seemed to be studying the ceiling of her office as she devoted her mind to the problem of the Denubbewa having Dakinium.

◆ ◆

"I just received another message from Christa," Brian Holt's image said from the large monitor in Jenetta's office a short time later. "The Denubbewa ship appears to be intact, and the Marines met no resistance when they entered the ship and began their search. They've found Denubbewa cyborgs in two locations. In one, the Denubbewa are lying on tables and appear to be asleep or something. In the other, a storage hold, the Denubbewa are stockpiled in shipping containers. That group appears to be totally inactive. The ship itself appears to be in excellent condition."

"Then why was it just sitting there? And why wasn't there anyone on guard duty, charged with the task of awakening the sleepers if anyone boarded?"

"I suppose we could assume the Denubbewa believed no one would ever locate them. But I hate making assumptions like that. We'll just have to wait for more information from Christa. She's promised to send an update whenever she learns anything worth reporting."

"Damn, I wish they weren't so far away," Jenetta said.

"I wish the speed of our space communications had kept pace with the speed of our space travel. The S-Band communications haven't improved in half a century while travel has gone from Light-75 to Light-14,685.7 with double-envelope capability."

"We definitely need some improvement in communications, but we have other, more serious problems right now. I'm calling for an emergency executive meeting in my office for nine a.m. tomorrow."

"I'll be there."

"Uh, Brian. Why don't we send a Ship Transporter to pick up the Denubbewa warship and bring it back to Quesann for study?"

"It's already on its way. I did that as soon as I got the latest message. The SC Transport Ship *Edison* is in Region Three, just over the border. It was sent to pick up the *Heisenberg*, a science vessel that's unable to sustain an envelope. The *Heisenberg* is fine in all other respects, so I sent orders to the *Edison* to unload the *Heisenberg* and go meet the *Koshi*. I then issued orders for the *Sebastian* to go retrieve the *Heisenberg*. This shifting of assignments will shave six days off the time it takes to pick up the ship Christa discovered."

"Thanks, Brian."

◆ ◆

"Good morning and thank you for coming in," Jenetta said once all A.B. members were in her office. No clerks or aides had been invited to this closed-door meeting. Other than the admirals, only Cayla and Tayna were in the office. They were quietly occupying their usual places against the wall where they could see and hear everything going on. "I realize it's Saturday, but we're faced with a critical situation. I won't mince words. The Denubbewa appear to have acquired Dakinium. Even worse, they appear to have possibly sheathed all their ships with it. That makes it impossible for us to track them down and destroy them with the CPS-16 squadrons as planned because they no longer show up on our sensors."

"The Denubbewa have Dakinium?" Admiral Bradlee, the Director of SCI, said. "This is the first I've heard of it."

"We just learned yesterday, Roger. My sister Christa, aboard the SD *Koshi*, reported that information to Brian after her squadron discovered a derelict Denubbewa warship sheathed in Dakinium."

"Then how did they spot it?"

"Christa reported that they stopped to investigate a true derelict," Holt said, "and someone spotted an anomaly that was blocking out the light from distant stars. They investigated and discovered the Denubbewa ship."

"Abandoned?" Admiral Woo asked.

"No, there were Denubbewa on board, but they were all either asleep or deactivated."

"This is *wonderful*," Admiral Bradlee said excitedly. "We've never had a chance to examine a Denubbewa warship or interrogate Denubbewa cyborgs."

"Yes," Jenetta said, "I suppose there's always a silver lining if you look for it. Right now I'm more concerned with the

Denubbewa having Dakinium. That's been our edge in this fight with the cyborgs. We've now lost that."

"This has to be a mistake," Admiral Plimley said. "The Denubbewa can't possibly have sheathed all of their ships in this short a time."

"I admit it's speculation, but it's based on direct observation," Jenetta said. "We've had three CPS-16 squadrons, a total of seventy-five ships, searching Region Three for Denubbewa ships after months of steadily increasing reports of sightings from freight-haulers. There hasn't been a single report of a sighting for months now. Yes, we're making an assumption about the rest of their fleet, but it's based on solid premise. The question is: If the Denubbewa fleet *isn't* sheathed with Dakinium, then why haven't we been able to locate any of their ships?"

"So what are you proposing, Jen?" Admiral Hillaire asked.

"I'm proposing nothing at this point. I'm groping for ideas on how we can destroy the Denubbewa if our premise is accurate."

"How about your idea that the Denubbewa might be hiding in hollowed-out asteroids?" Admiral Burke asked.

"To date, we've discovered just one hollowed-out asteroid. The ships discovered there are a mix of Terran and Uthlaran manufacture, so it's not a Denubbewa base, although it might be a Raider base."

"So what do we do?" Admiral Plimley asked.

"At this point, it appears we can do nothing except wait and plan possible scenarios. The Denubbewa ship we've captured may give us significant information, or…"

"Or what, Jen," Admiral Bradlee asked when she didn't continue right away.

"Roger, finding a derelict Denubbewa ship in perfect condition is too good to be true. It might very well be a trap. It might be a Trojan Horse of sorts…"

"And Denubbewa soldiers will suddenly materialize from thin air after the ship has been thoroughly searched?" Admiral Plimley said, interrupting.

"There's no rule that states Dakinium can only be used to sheath a hull. It can also be used internally to create places of concealment that our sensors won't penetrate. And since Dakinium absorbs all electronic signals, you'd never receive a warning that an area contained soldiers just waiting to be released. What if the ship has a double hull of Dakinium and the area between the two hulls is filled with Denubbewa warriors just waiting to open a secret door and pour out? But my real thought was— instead of filling it with soldiers, they may just want us to put our best and brightest aboard to learn its secrets. And that's when they detonate it."

"Would they sacrifice their own people like that?" Admiral Ahmed asked.

"They're machines. Do you think a machine cares about a few dozen other machines?"

"I'm not buying it," Admiral Plimley said. "The Denubbewa aren't that devious, Jen. Their actions have always been very direct— overwhelming forces and all-out blitzes. Look at the way they've fired on our ships in the past. They literally launch hundreds of those small missiles when all they need are a few hits in the right places."

"That's only because those missiles are notoriously inaccurate," Jenetta said. "They have no sophisticated guidance systems, so the Denubbewa must fire hundreds in the hope that a few will hit a vulnerable location. I can't help but wonder how many of their own ships have been destroyed when they've run into missiles that have exhausted their fuel and gone ballistic. A Denubbewa battle zone is almost like a minefield afterwards." Jenetta took a deep breath and released it. "Look, we need a lot more information before we can create a plan to combat this new problem. I merely wanted you all to be aware of the situation facing us so you can begin to formulate ideas. And once we have the information we need, we'll be prepared to respond. Thank you for coming in today."

◆

Admiral Holt remained behind after all of the other admirals had left to resume their planned Saturday activities.

Jenetta sighed and said, "Are we the only ones who appreciate the seriousness of this situation, Bry?"

Holt chuckled before answering. "You can't really blame them, Jen. They've got the best mind in the military working on the problem. They know you'll find a solution and send the Denubbewa scurrying back into hiding after their numbers are diminished considerably by a plan born in brilliance."

"But where is that plan coming from? I'm tapped out at the moment."

"But that never lasts for long."

"Not you too?"

Holt chuckled again. "You've always come through for us. I guess we've come to rely on that. While you were on leave, we sometimes felt a little lost and it almost seemed like things would never be the same. And it was while you were on leave that the Denubbewa must have put this re-sheathing operation into place."

"If you're trying to make me feel guilty for taking some time off, it won't work. I haven't regretted taking a leave of absence and I don't believe I ever will. I have a husband I adore and two beautiful children whom I love with all my heart."

"I'm certainly not trying to make you feel guilty. Taking that leave of absence was the best thing you could have done. Since returning you've been a lot like the old Jenetta. I didn't say anything before because you didn't need any encouragement to take that break, but you had really started to look a bit frazzled around the edges before you left. And now we're seeing the Jenetta we know— one rested and ready to take on whatever comes our way. I'm sorry if we appear to rely on you a bit too much, but I'm not sorry you're back. We need you, Jen. And I know that with you and Christa working on this problem, we'll come through in spite of the Denubbewa having Dakinium. And— we knew that eventually someone was going to get Dakinium. Hell, the Dakistians have it. We got it from *them*.

"I'm glad they didn't sell out to the Raiders. And I admit to worrying about how the Dakistians will use their Dakinium and whatever other incredible inventions they have that we don't even know about yet. Their ancestors were brilliant. I mean, look at the technology we know about. There's the Dakinium, of course, but there's also that incredible cloning process. And we certainly can't underestimate the genius behind those incredible stasis beds that allowed the Dakistians to survive, unchanged, for *nineteen* centuries. Can you imagine where the Dakistians would be now if their society hadn't been almost wiped out by the priesthood who feared them?"

"Did you ever suspect that maybe the actions the priesthood took to eradicate the population of Dakistee had some merit? Perhaps there were other projects, ones we don't know about yet, that drove the priesthood to that insane action. Perhaps they believed it was the only way to stop it."

"Yes, I've wondered about that. The people who left the planet— the only home they'd ever known— to seek a better life elsewhere even before space travel had been perfected to a point where the travelers would be safe from radiation and mutations must have truly feared for the future of their descendents if they remained on Dakistee. A mass exodus like the one they planned has usually only been considered if the planet was about to be destroyed by a collision with a giant asteroid or by internal planetary forces that would make living on the surface unbearable or even impossible. If there was something other than religious fanaticism responsible for the priesthood killing off most of the planet's population, I pray that it never resurfaces."

"Amen to that."

CHAPTER TWELVE

~ January 3rd, 2291 ~

"Good Morning, Jen," the image of Admiral Brian Holt said from the large wall monitor facing Admiral Jenetta Carver's office desk. "I just wanted to inform you that I've received a message from Commander Ashraf. She states that she's been in communication with Christa and is proceeding immediately to the *Koshi's* reported location to assist in any way she can. Based on the distances involved and the communication lag, I'm sure they've already joined forces. That will double the size of Christa's fleet in the event this is all some Denubbewa Machiavellian plot."

"I wouldn't elevate it to the level of plotting Machiavelli described in his book *The Prince*, but I'm sure they're capable of devious behavior, despite being machines. Their military advances have been orchestrated by biological brains in a metal body."

"Yes, I'm sure they're capable of exercising a degree of military subterfuge. Without it, they would have been unable to conquer as much territory as they allegedly dominate, let alone maintaining control over it."

"Yes, but brute force and a total disregard for personal safety can take you a long way."

"True." After a brief pause, Holt said, "I've been doing a lot of thinking regarding that matter we discussed last month."

"Which one?"

"Improving the speed of our space communications."

"Have you come up with a suggestion for improving the transmission speed?"

"Not exactly. My thoughts were an offshoot of our discussion about the Dakistians."

"I doubt they'd know of any way to improve the speed," Jenetta said. "They weren't exactly space experienced when they entered stasis twenty centuries ago."

"I understand, but that's not what I was getting at. I was alluding to their innovation abilities and the incredible things they've developed."

"And you think they might come up with something we've overlooked for decades?"

"Something like that, yes."

"I'm always willing to investigate new avenues, but I doubt Madu would even return my vidMail. She was really upset when I pressed her to publicly thank the Nordakians for curing her people's plague."

"Perhaps someone else could approach her. I realize she might hold some resentment towards you personally, but they sort of owe us. By that I mean the G.A. We rescued them from their long slumber and then supported them with food, clothes, shelter, and medical supplies until they got on their feet."

"Perhaps I could ask Evelyn to broach the topic with Madu."

"Admiral Platt would be a good choice."

"Okay, I'll send her a message and explain what we're looking for."

"Wonderful. I guess that's all I've got for today."

"Okay, Brian. Have a pleasant and productive day."

"You as well, Jen. Holt out."

"Carver out."

Jen took in a deep breath and released it. She didn't really think a society that'd had such little experience with space travel would be able to come up with a method for communications speed faster than the current S-band. It simply wasn't needed for planetary communications. However, she would give it a try rather than dismissing it out of hand. But while she was thinking about the Dakistians, her thoughts turned again to the possibility of them having other inventions the G.A. knew nothing about. It was true that their scientists couldn't find a cure for the sterility that plagued their planet so many eons ago. Or perhaps that had been a falsehood.

Were the scientists in league with the people who left the planet? Had they stayed behind purposely to stall and keep the Dakistians from curing the disease?

Jenetta shook her head slightly to clear the thought. She didn't want to always be suspicious of everyone's motives and actions, but sometimes she just couldn't help herself. A small, inner voice always seemed to demand she suspect everyone of being guilty until proven innocent. She tried to tell herself that it was because she was the final judge in so many matters these days and she needed to understand motives and predict misdirections. She smiled to herself as she thought that if she wasn't careful she'd have a heart attack and never see the five thousand years Arneu said she'd live.

◆　◆　◆

"Good Morning, Sywasock," Christa said as she entered the storage locker being used as a holding cell for the Denubbewa prisoner.

"Is it morning for you, Commander? According to my internal chronometer it's quite late in the Denubbewa daily cycle. You haven't visited me since I was moved to this new— room."

Taking a tiny recorder from her pocket, she activated it and then said, "I've been very busy so I've been unable to come before now."

"Have you? I've had nothing to do. I'm beginning to feel very useless. If not for the monitor and the instructional vids, I think I would have gone crazy by now. For so many annuals I have wished for just a little peace and quiet. And now that I have it, I long to again hear the voices in my head. Any voices."

"You can hear our electronic communications, can't you?"

"That stopped soon after our last conversation. I thought you might have stopped it when you learned I could hear them."

"We're still using our electronic communications. That's very strange. Do you suppose it has something to do with being isolated from the other cyborgs?"

"I don't know. It's never happened before."

"Could it be related to bodily requirements? When our species doesn't get the right nourishment, parts of our body begin to shut down. If the shortage persists long enough, we can die. Is there anything you need?"

"Nothing, as long as I'm plugged in each night if I haven't been prepared for long-term storage."

"Your brain is biological. It must require sustenance of some sort."

"I suppose it gets all it needs while we're being recharged. I never thought about it before, but this mechanical body must produce whatever my brain requires from the power unit."

"That's interesting. How long do the cyborg bodies last?"

"As long as replacement parts are available, they seem to go on indefinitely."

"But your biological brain must die at some point."

"I've never observed any cyborg dying, other than during conflict."

"That's interesting. You know, I'd love to hear about your home planet."

"Would you? Then I shall tell you. It's been a very long time since I've talked about it, but I dream about it occasionally."

"You dream?"

"Of course. Don't you?"

"Yes. But I thought you might have lost that ability when they took your brain from your biological body."

"I retained all of my thoughts and memories, even when the Denubbewa were trying to erase them. I believe I've mentioned that all Elobians are taught how to enter a deep state of conscious withdrawal when they're very young. I guess it's what you call being in a trance. We become detached from everything around us and view everything as if it's happening to someone else. It enabled us to protect our memories from being overwritten."

"I see. You were going to tell me about your world before I interrupted."

"Yes. Let's see. Where should I start?"

"Describe it to me."

"I shall describe it as it was before the Denubbewa arrived. It's no longer beautiful, and I don't like thinking about it that way."

"You told me that the Denubbewa invaded your world a millennium ago. Were you born before they destroyed the beauty of your world?"

"Yes, I was."

"How long does your species live?"

"In our corporeal form, my people lived about two hundred of your annuals."

"So your personal longevity is owed to the cyborg body?"

"Yes. As I've said, I've never known a cyborg to die of natural causes."

"And you would give up an incredibly long life to return to a biological body?"

"I would give up an eternity in this form to live just one more annual as I was before the Denubbewa did this to me."

"I see. So tell me how your world appeared before the Denubbewa arrived."

Over the next two hours, Sywasock described his home planet in great detail. He talked about the house where he was raised, his parents, his siblings, and his other relatives. He also talked about family vacations to distant places. His love for his home world was evident from the wonderful images he painted verbally. Christa could envision the mountains, seas, fauna, and flora.

"Your planet sounds marvelous, Sywasock," Christa said when he'd finished. "I wish I could visit it."

"It's gone, Captain. My homeland lives on only in my mind and the minds of my countrymen. The planet is still there, but no one who knew it previously would ever recognize it. When I was transported up to a Denubbewa warship, I could see that my world had been reduced to enormous piles of dirt and rubble as the planet was pillaged for its natural resources. Neither I nor anyone else could do anything to stop it."

"I feel very sad for you."

"Thank you, Captain."

"You must really hate the Denubbewa."

"Yes and no."

"No?"

"Most of the Denubbewa are mindless automatons doing whatever they were ordered to do without ever knowing why they're doing it or even what they're doing in some cases while performing programmed tasks. It's difficult to hate other beings who are being controlled like that."

"Yes. I see. Um, exactly how did *you* avoid doing the evil deeds you were ordered to do?"

"I didn't. Not completely. I did my share of despicable things when to refuse meant death. And as much as I didn't want to live, neither did I want to die. That probably sounds unreasonable."

"No, I think I understand."

"All I have lived for is to escape from the Denubbewa with as many of my former countrymen as I could find and reestablish our species."

"And how exactly do you intend to do that?"

"Every Elobian with whom I could make contact is on the ship you discovered. We were trying to make it as far from here as possible. We know *we'll* probably never see a new homeland, but we believed we could reestablish our species in a biological form that could procreate and send them on their way to a distant galaxy."

"And how do you intend to become biologically corporeal again so you can procreate?"

"A number of the Elobians with me were once brilliant doctors, scientists, and engineers. I'm hoping that with a few cells removed from the brain of each Elobian, we can incubate new countrymen. We'll then teach them everything we know and everything we've learned while we've been prisoners of the Denubbewa."

"You believe you can create a new Elobian from a few cells?"

"We do. A body like ours is simply a collection of chemicals in the right proportions. With the medical equipment on the Denubbewa ship, we believe we can clone our race with enough diversity to avoid the problems of inbreeding."

"Were you involved in any of the Denubbewa warfare?"

"Yes."

"You must have some horrible memories."

"We do. We hope never to see the like of it again."

"And you know how to use the medical equipment aboard the Denubbewa ship?"

"I know how to repair it. Others know how to operate it."

"Did you complete your education before the Denubbewa arrived on your planet?"

"Yes, I did."

"And you had begun your career?"

"Yes."

"What was your occupation?"

"I taught advanced eugenics at an institute of higher education."

"I suspected you were highly intelligent. What was your role as a Denubbewa slave?"

"At first I was simply a repair drone working in the engineering section. Eventually, they came to believe I was trustworthy and, in time, I was advanced to senior repair technician and given all responsibility for the repair of drones that had been injured or that were malfunctioning. That's how I was able to make contact with so many Elobians. They were sent to me because they appeared to be malfunctioning, but the other repair technicians were unable to find any problem. I worked with them and taught them how to fool their supervisors. Over time, I established a kind of— resistance movement."

"You already knew Amer before we brought you onboard, didn't you?"

"Uh— what makes you ask that?"

"You picked it up much too quickly and accurately for someone who had never heard it before."

"I thought I had you fooled."

"I'm not a drone supervisor. We're a bit harder to fool."

"While I served as a senior repair technician over many annuals, I gained the trust of the supervising drone in engineering. When the Denubbewa first entered G.A. space, the ships began intercepting messages from transmissions between freight-haulers. I was given the messages and ordered to translate them. I had access to all materials related to the Amer and Uthlaran languages, so I've been studying your language diligently since then. I applied myself because I believed it might come in handy one day if my people ever got a chance to break away from the Denubbewa while we were still in G.A. space. So what now? Do you kill me for not being truthful?"

"No. You'll only be harmed if you try to escape or if you harm someone aboard my ship. If your story's true, you're very valuable. And if it's true, we'll help you realize your dream of a new planet for your people and even help you create new biological bodies from Elobian brain cells. We might even be able to go one step further."

"Further?"

"I can't promise this, but what if, in exchange for *full* cooperation, we were able to put your brain into an Elobian body created from your own DNA?"

"That's not possible."

"No?"

"No."

"What if I was to tell you that I was not born but created by a machine to be a duplicate of my sister. It's not a secret. Everyone aboard this ship and in our part of the galaxy knows it."

"You're a clone?"

"Yes."

"Grown from an egg produced from DNA? That wouldn't allow me to occupy the new body."

"Mere clones are produced as newborns, with no memories of the host. I was reproduced exactly as you see me now, with all the education and memories my sister had when she was copied."

"And that same technology can be used to put me into a manufactured biological body just like the one I had before the Denubbewa did this to me and my fellow Elobians?"

"As I said, I cannot promise anything. I'm a senior military officer, not a xenobiologist. I was cloned from a healthy, intact original. You would have to be— assembled— from two separate biological components—your brain and a manufactured body. And once your new body was functioning proper-ly, and you'd agreed that you were whole again, your present brain would be terminated. You see, we have very strict rules about cloning, so there can't be more than one of you, or any-one else."

"But there's more than one of you. The original was not—terminated."

"That's true. Seventy-nine duplicates were made before the process was halted. As a result of our creation, a new law was passed. It's now illegal to create duplicates, and even cloning is forbidden on many planets. But the seventy-nine who had already been made were allowed to live, as were the originals. I have a bit of pull with the senior military people who can make construction of a biological body happen, if it's possible with your species, but only one of you can live. And we can't reproduce an entire population of Elobians for you, as much as I wish we could. But to earn the new body, you would have to give up everything you know about the Denubbewa. And I do mean everything. Full cooperation and disclosure. Nothing held back. No falsehoods or half-truths."

"You have it, Captain. Everything I know is yours."

"How did the ship you were in get to the location where we discovered it?"

"We flew it there. By the time we reached that point, the pilot hadn't had a recharge in days. We thought that since we couldn't be picked up on sensors, we were safe from discov-ery. We were wrong, obviously. Anyway, the pilot shut eve-rything down and we prepared for a recharge. When I was unplugged and saw your soldiers standing over us, I expected to be destroyed on the spot, then and there. But instead of de-stroying me, they brought me to this ship. I began to believe that I might not be killed outright and that I might be able to make a deal for my freedom and that of my countrymen. So I began to play along."

"You remember everything the Denubbewa taught you?"

"I do. We all do."

"Is there a self-destruct mechanism aboard your ship?"

"Every ship has a self-destruct mechanism."

"And your pilot knows how to disable it completely?"

"I suppose so. I've never asked him."

"I'll be blunt. You understand that we want all the secrets of the Denubbewa ship and everything else you know about the Denubbewa. That information will be worth the effort of trying to create a new body for you with your memories intact. At the very least, we can produce newborn clones of your species from you and each of your countrymen. Additionally, if you cooperate fully, I promise we'll find you a suitable unoccupied planet where you can build a new home that's protected by the G.A. Space Command or give you a ship you can use for your intergalactic journey."

"And you have the authority to make such a deal?"

"No, but my sister does."

"The biological sister from whom you were cloned."

"Yes."

"Well, that makes sense. If you're going to clone someone, you certainly don't start at the bottom of the gene pool."

"Is that a yes?"

"Yes."

"Okay. Once we get back to our base at Quesann, the experts will be in to question you. If you hold anything back or get cagey with details, all promises I've made will be null and void."

"Quesann? In Region Two?"

"Yes."

"It will take many, many annuals to get there, Captain."

"We're taking a shortcut through a wormhole."

"The Denubbewa have determined that wormholes are a myth. There's no such thing."

"That just goes to show that the Denubbewa don't know everything. We're actually going to surf several wormholes and glide into Quesann in thirty-one of our days."

"What about my ship and countrymen?"

"They're coming also. We're dragging what *used* to be your ship to Quesann. The ship has been confiscated as an enemy weapon of war and is now the property of Space Command."

"How am I going to get to another galaxy if I don't have a ship?"

"You'll be given a ship to complete your journey after our people are satisfied with your truthfulness and your information. But it won't be a Denubbewa warship. Perhaps it will be a small, single-hull freighter filled with whatever food and water you need for the journey. If you wish to go beyond our borders, we'll take you through our extensive labyrinth of wormholes to any place along the edge of our space that doesn't border the territory of another nation and leave you. We'll also give stasis beds to you and each of your biological countrymen that will suspend you just as you are while you cross the vast expanse of space between galaxies."

"You will just let us go free?"

"We are not conquerors. We are a free nation. Our military is only charged with protecting our people and preserving the peace. Where we have absorbed the territory of other nations, it was only done after they first attacked us and made it clear they would never stop attacking us unless we absorbed their territory and policed it as we did our own. We currently have common borders with six other nations and we will never attempt to conquer any of them unless they first attack us. All we want is to live in peace, but races like the Denubbewa envy what we have and want it for themselves. We will defend our territory to the last breath of the last military person, and if necessary, to the last breath of every civilian.

"We've met the Denubbewa in battle a number of times. When the initial contact was made, we weren't expecting an attack. The Denubbewa ship attacked and destroyed our ship before our people understood that the Denubbewa have declared war on all other species in the galaxy. The same was true with our second contact. The Denubbewa ship was able to destroy our ship because we still didn't know we were at war and didn't take the proper safeguards. When two of our ships failed to report, we began to search for them. That's when we learned there was an invasion taking place. Since then, we haven't lost any more military vessels, and at every encounter the Denubbewa ship, or ships, were completely destroyed. When we're finished, there won't be a single Denubbewa ship left in G.A. space."

"The Denubbewa have learned how powerful you are and are using your own technology against you now. They have some, but they want it all because you're so powerful. No one has ever been able to seriously challenge them. You're more powerful, by a factor of ten, than any other force they've faced. They believe that once they conquer you, no one can ever stand in their way again. They will never quit trying to destroy you."

"Wonderful."

"You want them to keep attacking you?"

"We welcome it. It saves us from having to track them down. When a ship or fleet comes at us, we destroy that ship or fleet and then lie in wait for the next attack group. The Denubbewa may have learned some of our secrets, but we have many more—many that no one outside our senior military circles even suspect."

"Such as?"

"I can't tell you. I really shouldn't even have mentioned our extensive network of wormholes. But a lot of non-military people already suspect they exist because they aren't able to understand how we can travel from one end of our vast territory to the other in just a couple of months."

"But I thought travel through theoretical wormholes was supposed to be near instantaneous."

"It is. But the entrances and exits are not always near one another. So we first jump into a wormhole and pop out the other side. Then we may have to travel for days or even weeks to get to the next wormhole entry point."

"But surely your civilians would know about them also."

"No, they don't. You see, you need to emit a special subspace beam to open a natural wormhole. We learned about it quite accidently while testing our ordnance teleportation device."

"The Denubbewa know about that one. They know it's the only way you could have destroyed so many motherships and warships when you'd never had a ship within billions of kilometers of those destroyed ships."

"Yes, military secrets can only remain secret for so long. Once you start using your new equipment, the other side starts to develop a profile of the weapon. Then it's only a matter of time before they know enough to start developing their own. We know we can't keep the wormholes and the ordnance teleportation device secret forever, which is why the greatest minds in the G.A. continue to develop new weapons and search for other natural phenomena we can exploit."

"I'm very impressed, Captain. And hopeful that you can actually destroy the Denubbewa."

"I have to go now, Sywasock. I have a great deal to do, and I've been down here too long. We'll be coming up on a wormhole transition sector soon and I have to be on the bridge to help coordinate the jump. You're sure there's nothing you need?"

"I'd like to have a tour of your ship."

"I'm sorry. That's not possible."

"I understand, Captain."

"I'll come down again when I can."

CHAPTER THIRTEEN

~ January 3rd, 2291 ~

"You were down there a long time, Captain," Mollago said as they sat in Christa's office.

"I was trying to draw him out and determine how truthful and cooperative he's being."

"And is he being truthful and cooperative?"

"It's difficult to tell. The information he's providing might be true, but it might not. Since he's a cyborg, there're no physical telltale signs of lying. But just in case he *is* lying, I've spun a few lies of my own."

"Such as?"

"I told him we use wormholes to travel throughout G.A. space and that's how we can cross great distances so quickly."

"And he believed that foolishness?"

"I don't really know, but a lot of people do still strongly believe that wormholes exist naturally and that wormholes can even be established artificially, although no one has yet proven they could open one that would allow solid matter to pass through." Christa chuckled as she remembered something. "When I was very young, a teacher stood in front of the class and held up an apple. She then took a pen and pushed it through the middle of the apple. She said that she was showing the theory behind wormholes, because by going directly from point A to point B, we saved a great deal of time. I held up my hand and she called on me. When I stood up, I said that geometry shows us the shortest distance between two points is a straight line, but did she think the universe was shaped like an apple. She hesitated for a second before saying that it might be. So then I asked her, if when we look through a telescope at a far distant star, are we seeing something that's actually underneath us? And if it isn't, I asked, how can we reach something faster by going into some hole than we could by going in a straight line? She hesitated and then said that the theory was known as an Einstein-Rosen bridge, but it hadn't been proven yet and that it would be up to my generation to prove it or disprove it. So I asked her how we could prove something didn't exist if it really didn't exist. She thought for another moment and then told me to sit down. I'm sure that whenever I raised my hand after that, she had to take a deep breath before she called on me."

Mollago chuckled. "Is that a true story, Captain?"

"Yes, with one caveat. It was my sister Jenetta who actually attended school when she was young. I have all her memories of the event and actually feel like I was there, but I hadn't been cloned yet. It's a strange feeling to know I was there and yet know I wasn't there."

"I tend to forget you're a clone."

"So do I, most of the time. I'm a real person after all, not a robot or cyborg or anything. And Jenetta's memories fill my head so I feel like I had a childhood and grew up like any normal person."

"What else did you tell the prisoner today?"

"I told him we had discovered wormhole entrances while we were testing our ordnance teleportation device a few annuals ago."

Mollago chuckled before saying, "Ordnance teleportation? He didn't buy *that* one, did he?"

"He said the Denubbewa already suspected we had something like that because it was the only way we could have blown up their ships when we didn't have any vessels within billions of kilometers of the target."

"Okay, I can see how they might be susceptible to believing that because of the lack of visual evidence. But wormholes?"

"Don't laugh. A great many folks still believe that old theory. Einstein's Theory of General Relativity does sort of allow the possibility, which is in contradiction to his Theory of Special Relativity and his belief that nothing could travel faster than the speed of light. Laboratory experiments by research scientists have *seemed* to transport magnetic signals through an artificially created wormhole. I remember reading how excited the scientific community was when the Chinese government on Earth reported that they had successfully transported a single photon from Earth to a satellite in space. People allegedly began predicting that we'd soon be able to send people into space, or to a moon or other planets without a spaceship. But in almost three centuries since that Chinese claim, no one has yet been able to transport a solid mass and have it arrive intact. And after hundreds of years of looking, scientists are still searching for the first provable evidence of a natural wormhole."

"So the burning question remains: Is the alien claiming to be an Elobian really going to cooperate with us and tell us everything he knows?"

"Only time will tell. I really just want to get him, the other cyborgs, and that ship to Quesann so I can turn the problem over to SCI."

◆ ◆ ◆

"Good morning, Lori," Christa said when the ship-to-ship laser communication connection was established.

"Good morning, Christa. How's everything going?"

"Fine. How about with you?"

"Everything's normal. What's new?"

"I just received a message from the SC Transport Ship *Edison*. They've been dispatched by Admiral Holt to take our prize back to Quesann."

"Really! Where are they?"

"I estimate from their reported coordinates that we'll meet up in about four days. I sent them coordinates for where they can take the Denubbewa ship off our hands."

"Okay. Then what do we do?"

"The *Edison's* commanding officer didn't have any new orders for us, so I guess we tag along and go back to Quesann until some new strategy is developed for finding Denubbewa ships sheathed in Dakinium."

"There does seem little sense in remaining out here."

"No sense at all. We can't rely on finding Denubbewa ships by watching for distant stars that suddenly go dark momentarily."

"Yeah. How are you doing with your prisoner?"

"He's told me a lot. I don't know how much is true, but it's an interesting story."

"I'll wait until we can sit down at dinner and you can tell me the whole story."

"It'll take a month of meals. Jenetta wanted you to come to dinner at her home before we left, but I guess you were too busy with the new command. Maybe we can get together there the day we get back. Then I won't have to repeat the story after I tell her."

"You'll probably have to tell your story a dozen times over, so one less time is good."

"Yeah."

"Okay, Christa, have a better one. Ashraf out."

"You also. Carver out."

◆ ◆ ◆

There was nothing to do but wait when the two squadrons arrived at the rendezvous point before the *Edison*.

A few hours later they received a narrow-band encrypted message from the *Edison* requesting that they turn on their running lights for several seconds so the transport could get a fix on their location. Once they had a fix, the *Edison* contacted them by laser signal as the ship headed in their direction.

"Good morning, Christa," Commander Garth Ginsburg, Captain of the *Edison*, said when his ship arrived near the large cluster of small ships. "I understand you have a vessel you want us to haul to Lorense-Three."

"Hello, Garth. Might I ask what your orders are?"

"Just to eject the ship we were transporting and rendezvous with you immediately, if not sooner, to take a disabled vessel on board and then return to Lorense-Three with the vessel. I was told you'd supply any information I required. How large is the vessel we're here to pick up?"

"The vessel is a Denubbewa warship. It's quite large, but you should be able to squeeze it in if you don't have any other vessels in your hold."

"Denubbewa? Is it in pieces?"

"Negative. The vessel is disabled but undamaged."

"Where is it? We don't see any Denubbewa ships on our sensors."

"It's here, but it's sheathed with Dakinium."

"Sheathed with Dakinium? I don't understand."

"This is three levels above Top Secret, but there's no way it could be concealed from you. The Denubbewa apparently have Dakinium— at least enough to sheath one warship. We must get this ship back to Lorense-Three immediately so the scientists there can begin performing tests on the hull."

"I see. But we still can't see the ship."

"Open your hull and we'll push it in."

"Uh, what kind of ship are you in, Christa? I thought the *Koshi* was a Scout-Destroyer, but the number of lights we see suggest that you might be in a Denubbewa mothership."

"I'm in a Scout-Destroyer. The lights you see are from two SDs and forty-eight CPS-16s. All are sheathed with Dakinium."

"Fifty vessels? No wonder you give the appearance of a mothership. And please don't try to push the Denubbewa warship into our hull. We have our own people suiting up and they'll be out there in a few minutes with donkey tractors. Moving even a small ship into our hull is a practiced skill, and bringing a monster of a ship in is limited to senior chiefs. All of our people must finish a hundred hours in simulators and pass a grueling five-hour weightless test before we let them anywhere near a real ship. My chiefs all have several hundred hours of experience. So you folks can just sit back, relax, and watch the show."

Christa laughed and said, "Okay, Garth, it's your baby, and believe me when I say you're welcome to it."

"Thanks, Christa. Uh, where is it, by the way?"

"I'll have the CPS-16 that dragged it this far position itself on the opposite side from you and light it up so it's outlined." Christa turned towards the com chief and nodded. The chief petty officer immediately relayed the message.

About fifteen minutes later, Ginsburg said, "Okay, Christa, thanks. We see it and our people are headed that way on the tractors. That's a really big boy. It's going to be a tight squeeze."

"Yeah, I'm just as glad we didn't have to push it into your ship. I don't think I have enough credits in my account to pay the repair bill if we miscalculated."

"Well, you're still young. You'd have had a lot of years ahead of you to pay it off."

"How long before we're ready to head for Lorense-Three?"

"Oh, probably about three hours."

"After you have the ship secured in your hull, I'll send over all my Marines."

"Marines? What for?"

"To guard the Denubbewa prisoners inside the ship."

"Denubbewa prisoners? You're holding prisoners in there? How many?"

"No more than a few hundred."

"Hundreds? Are you serious? I don't have sufficient staff to guard hundreds of cyborg prisoners. We'll have to space them."

"Most of them are deactivated— sort of. And the rest seem to be sleeping. Some of my Marines are already guarding the Denubbewa aboard the ship, but I want to send the rest of the platoons over so they'll be there to relieve the ones on duty. You only have to feed my Marines. They'll perform the guard duty."

"Does Quesann know you're bringing Denubbewa prisoners there?"

"Do they know? I'm operating on their orders. I bet SCI can't wait to start their interrogations. If it eases your mind at all, I gave my people instructions to immediately destroy any Denubbewa that attempts to break free of confinement."

"That helps a little— if the Denubbewa can be stopped."

"My Marines searched the two holds when the Denubbewa were first located. There were no weapons there, other than the ones in the hands of my Marines."

"I don't think I'm going to sleep soundly until we get to Lorense-Three and unload our cargo."

As the *Edison* crew opened the bow of the ship, the brightly illuminated interior appeared like an enormous flashlight in space that had just been turned on. It was an interesting sight as the practiced donkey tractor operators guided the Denubbewa warship into the hull and secured it. The show ended when the *Edison* resealed the hull in preparation for its return to Quesann.

◆ ◆ ◆

"I've just received orders *not* to approach the shipyard until I receive further orders," Commander Ginsburg said to Christa and Commander Ashraf in a secure, three-way conference call. "I'm to stop at least a thousand kilometers out."

"Do those orders extend to us as well?" Christa asked.

"Neither you nor your squadrons commands were mentioned."

"I assume they're trying to sneak you in," Ashraf said, "so no one will know you're transporting a Denubbewa ship."

"That would be my guess," Ginsburg said. "Third watch is always the slowest time of day there, even though the shipbuilding continues around the clock. Most of the clerical staff only works one watch, and even the freight-haulers bringing in materials and support products are usually nowhere to be seen between midnight GST time and six a.m. That's probably when they'll have me enter the shipyard."

"It might be more than that," Christa said. "They may want to check the Denubbewa ship for explosives before you enter the yard."

"If the Denubbewa were to denote a WOLaR while inside the *Edison,* we could be burned to cinders, but the blast should be largely contained by our Dakinium-sheathed hull," Ginsburg said.

"Yes, but what if the detonation occurred after you moved the Denubbewa ship out of the *Edison*?"

"Well, I suppose it would depend on how well they constructed their Dakinium shell. If the plates aren't secured together as they are on our ships, the blast could possibly cause a chain reaction which might destroy the entire yard."

"Christa might be right about the reason for your orders," Ashraf said. "It makes a lot of sense when you realize that the successful execution of such a Denubbewa plot would set our ship production back at least a year."

"I guess we'll just have to wait and see what HQ has in mind," Christa said. "I've still got Marines on your vessel so I'll hang around to collect them after security from the yard shows up."

"I'm happy to say you were absolutely right," Ginsburg said. "The cyborgs under guard never gave us the slightest problem. I had my Marine security force on standby alert for the entire trip, but they were never needed at all."

"They'll be SCI's problem within a few hours," Ashraf said.

"Hopefully," Ginsburg said. "What now for your squadrons? Going out hunting again?"

"I'm sure the situation will be reevaluated before we deploy again," Christa said. "The latest news I've received states there have been no reported sightings of Denubbewa ships since before we began our mission."

◆　◆　◆

"We've just completed our final wormhole transit," Christa said to Sywasock as the door to the holding cell closed behind her and the guards were unable to hear anything she said. "We're only a dozen light-years from Quesann."

"Then you really were serious when you told me about using wormholes?"

"Of course. We couldn't travel from one end of our territory to the other in mere months if it wasn't for wormholes."

"With the knowledge and technology you have available to you, one might ask why you haven't conquered the entire galaxy?"

"I've told you. We're not conquerors. We only want to live in peace and raise our families. Most of the advancements we've made were accomplished in the name of science to make our lives better, not to dominate others."

"The Denubbewa are just the opposite. They work to make advances in order to conquer. They have no wish to make the lives of the conquered better."

"Tell me, Sywasock, if you can: why do the Denubbewa want to conquer the galaxy and then the universe? What pleasure does it give?"

"Pleasure? It gives no pleasure."

"Then why do it?"

"Why? I suppose it's because— they can."

"That's it? Because they can? But the Denubbewa aren't robots. They have biological brains."

"Whether mechanical or biological, a brain is a brain. When the brain has been stripped of all previous knowledge— or never had any to begin with— and is filled with programming intended only to advance the goals of the senior Denubbewa leadership rather than the individual, one loses the ability to reason and simply becomes an automaton. Surely your society has experienced something like that, albeit on a smaller scale. On my home world, we had what you call politicians. They were very adept at convincing the simpleminded and uneducated people to ignore their own wants and desires and instead devote themselves to what they deceptively called 'working for the greater good.' Of course the 'greater good' to those politicians was anything that enriched the politicians themselves or gave them more power. More power allowed them to control the lives of many more people and thus enrich themselves beyond all dreams of avarice. Our politicians would first enter office as average citizens and be paid a modest, but sufficient salary for their efforts to represent the people. But by the time their political career was over, they had mysteriously amassed vast wealth.

"I've mentioned that during my time as a cyborg, I've heard things that have led me to believe the original Denubbewa were not cyborgs. They were, and possibly still are, completely biological. If that's true, that might be the justification for what the Denubbewa do. All wealth is perhaps being passed back to the original home world. On my world, we also had people we called puppet-masters. They weren't politicians, but they pulled the strings of the politicians and amassed ever greater wealth with each generation, and all without exposing themselves openly. But everyone knew they were there and who they were. I suppose the people who control the most senior cyborgs are like that."

"Yes, the situation is similar on my birth planet. But every so often the people have risen up and violently overthrown the political aristocracy at the top, along with their puppet-masters. And even the puppets at the bottom— usually the uneducated and the students— have finally realized how foolish they've been and how they've been duped. Perhaps that will eventually happen to the Denubbewa."

"I don't think so, Captain. The cyborgs have lost the ability to think for themselves. They simply march in lockstep and do whatever their masters order them to do. They know that if they don't follow orders they might be disassembled."

"Or have their brains destroyed."

"Their brains have already been destroyed. That's why they're incapable of independent thought and march in lockstep."

"I understand."

"What will happen to me now?"

"I imagine our SCI people will come to take custody of you and bring you to their headquarters for questioning. If you convince them that you only want to be free of the Denubbewa and are completely honest and open with all your responses, you'll eventually be released. When that happens, I'll work to help you and your countrymen become biologics again. Then you'll be freed, given a ship for your intergalactic trip, and escorted to the border to ensure nothing happens to you while you're in G.A. space."

"I've been thinking, Captain— I've had nothing else to do. You once said you'd find us a suitable planet here in G.A. space. Is that offer still open?"

"Yes, it is, if that's what you want."

"I'm leaning in that direction. I've begun to think that your G.A. might actually have the ability to stop the advance of the Denubbewa. And there's no guarantee that if we go to another galaxy we won't encounter a race even worse than the Denubbewa. But I'll need to discuss it with my countrymen before I commit us. Would it be possible to see and talk with them?"

"Of course. You'll have an opportunity to see and converse with your countrymen before you have to make a final decision."

"I mean now, so they have time to think about it."

"Right now they're still on the Denubbewa ship while you're on my ship. So I'm afraid there's no way you can communicate with them. Be patient. You'll all be back together again."

"Can't we communicate by radio?"

"The hull material of the Denubbewa ship blocks transmission signals. I'm afraid you'll have to wait."

"Captain, I've been very patient until now. What are you hiding? Have you destroyed my countrymen?"

"No, of course not. I'm just not going to halt this ship in space to make special arrangements for a radio communication."

"I insist."

"And I refuse." Christa took a deep breath and then released it. "I guess our discussion is over for today."

She then turned and walked towards the door.

"Wait, Captain. I'm sorry. I was wrong to accuse you of harming my countrymen."

"I understand," Christa said as she opened the door and pulled it closed behind her.

CHAPTER FOURTEEN

~ February 5th, 2291 ~

"Go right in," Admiral Holt's aide said. "He's expecting both of you."

Commander Christa Carver and Commander Lori Ashraf entered the small corridor leading to the entrance doors of Admiral Holt's inner office and stopped. Before continuing further they took a moment to straighten their uniforms and make sure everything was impeccable. Satisfied, they continued on, the double doors sliding silently open as the duo stepped into the area where they would be recognized by the sensor.

Both women entered the office at once and proceeded to the Admiral's desk, stopping two meters away and bracing to attention. Since Christa had received her promotion earlier than Lori, she was senior. She said, "Commander Christa Carver and Commander Lori Ashraf, reporting to the admiral as ordered."

Holt, standing behind his desk, smiled and said, "At ease, ladies. Welcome back. Christa, congratulations on securing an intact Denubbewa warship for us to study. The scientists, engineers, and SCI are beside themselves. The yard manager was fighting to keep them all at bay while he was still trying to shoehorn that ship into an enclosed dock."

"Thank you, sir," Christa said.

"I have one question though. Why didn't you space those damn cyborgs? They're all brain-dead and never yield any useful information."

"This batch is different, sir. I chose one of them to examine and he turned out to be talkative to the point of distraction. I let him talk."

"A talkative Denubbewa? That's different."

"He claims to have been from a race called Elobians until his brain was harvested from his original body and installed in a cyborg body."

"Did you hear that, Jen?"

"Yes, Brian. I did."

Christa and Lori immediately turned in the direction of the voice. Admiral of the Fleet Jenetta Carver was seated in Holt's informal area, a large alcove containing several over-stuffed chairs and a sofa.

"Why don't we all find seats in the alcove and you two can tell Jenetta and me all about your adventure?"

As they sat down, Commander Ashraf said, "I'm afraid I won't be able to tell you very much. I arrived a week after I learned Christa had found the warship."

"Christa, why don't you tell us your story?" Admiral Holt said.

"I prepared a complete written report, Admiral."

"I read reports all day. I occasionally like to hear firsthand accounts because I can ask questions afterwards."

"Yes, sir."

About an hour later, Christa wrapped up her report with, "That's about it, sir."

"Do you believe this Denubbewa?"

"Uh, I'd like to. I have to admit he isn't what I was expecting. But at the same time— well— I don't really trust him. I'm sure part of that is based on his appearance. I just don't know, sir. That's why I purposely misled him and lied about the wormholes and the ordnance teleportation. If he *is* lying and he manages to get a message back to his base, I want them to be running in circles looking for— or trying to create— wormhole entrances while another group works on teleportation methods."

Admiral Holt laughed and said, "That would be something. I'd almost be willing to set him free to see that happen. But we have a major problem. Our scientists have confirmed what your engineers speculated. The hull material of that Denubbewa ship is Dakinium."

"I expected that determination. It makes their ships invisible to all of our sensors. I wonder…"

"Wonder what?" Holt said when Christa failed to complete her sentence after ten seconds had passed.

"Oh— sorry, sir. I was just wondering if the Denubbewa have found a way to detect the presence of other ships sheathed in Dakinium. In all of the reports I've read regarding their normal operations, they travel in large groups. They must have some way of recognizing the presence of other ships in close proximity so they don't constantly crash into one another."

"Perhaps they use a system like the one developed by Space Command to protect our ships from friendly fire," Jenetta said. "But since the signal is on the standard RF band and can only travel at the speed of light, by the time it's detected by someone else, the transmission source is long gone. We must accept that we've lost the edge we had over the Denubbewa."

"So what do we do now, Admiral Carver?" Commander Ashraf asked.

"Obviously we have to develop a new strategy. Perhaps a direction will emerge from the Denubbewa interviews being conducted by SCI or the detailed examination of the ship being conducted by our scientists and engineers. It's really too early to speculate. Thank you for your work, Commanders. You're excused."

As the two officers stood up to leave, Christa asked, "Dinner tonight?"

"Of course. You're welcome also, Lori, if you're free."

"Thank you, Admiral. I'd love to come."

"Wonderful. I'll see you both tonight."

After the two women left, Admiral Holt said, "Executive session in twenty minutes."

"Right, we'd better get going."

◆ ◆

"That's the situation," Jenetta said as she wrapped up the oral report. The A.B. was meeting in private executive session in her large office.

"So it's as bad as you indicated at the last executive session," Admiral Hillaire said.

"Yes. The Denubbewa have Dakinium and they're sheathing all of their ships with it. We will no longer be able to detect them with our sensors, even when we're parked right next to them, unless they turn on their running lights or exterior lights, or open an airlock or something. Essentially, from a strategic point of view, we're worse off than we were three decades ago. At least back then we could see the enemy coming."

"Weren't our scientists working on something that allowed us to detect Dakinium-sheathed ships?" Admiral Burke asked.

"We've been working on that since we first began covering our ships with Dakinium and we learned our sensors can't detect our own ships, not even when we're in close proximity," Admiral Plimley said. "So far, we've been unsuccessful. That's why the standard practice is to retract the covers over our running lights whenever we're close to another GSC ship or any ship we want to see us. Even if the bulbs aren't lit, the sensor signal bounces back from the lamp surface rather than being absorbed when it encounters Dakinium."

"And nothing has worked?"

"Nothing. The Dakinium absorbs any photons that come into contact with it. It's really an incredible material. Its best feature can also be our biggest problem."

"There must be *something* we've overlooked," Admiral Woo said. "There's always *something*."

"Well…" Admiral Plimley started to say and then stopped.

"Well what, Loretta?" Jenetta said.

"Well, there was something we pursued for a while. In theory it sounded great, but we couldn't make any progress with it."

"What was it?" Jenetta asked.

"It involved neutrinos."

"Neutrinos?" Admiral Ressler echoed. "It's been a lot of years since I was at the academy. Refresh my memory."

"Neutrinos are fermions that interact only via the weak subatomic force and gravity."

Admiral Ressler chuckled and said, "You've lost me already."

"It's pretty complex. Basically, we were interested in using neutrinos because they're electrically neutral."

"Ah, I begin to see," Admiral Ressler said. "Since they're electrically neutral, the Dakinium wouldn't absorb them."

"Correct. But even so, if you were to aim a neutrino beam at something, the neutrinos won't bounce back. They simply pass through whatever they come into contact with. So our approach was to see if we could measure the neutrinos that have passed through a Dakinium-sheathed ship."

"Now you've lost me again."

"Okay, think of it this way. You have a large net suspended a meter above the floor. The openings in the net are six centimeters. Onto that net you drop a bushel of ping-pong balls and a bushel of softballs. Do you see?"

"Uh, not yet."

"Okay, if you evaluate what's on the floor after you pour everything into the net, you see what?"

"A lot of ping-pong balls."

"Exactly. How many softballs do you see on the floor?"

"None."

"Exactly."

"I'm still not clear on what that means."

"Okay, if you would normally see a mix of ping-ping balls and softballs on the floor without the net, but you see only ping-pong balls, you know that a net was used to block the softballs. So knowing that a Dakinium-sheathed ship blocks everything except neutrinos and all you were sensing in a certain direction were neutrinos, what would you assume?"

"That a Dakinium-sheathed ship was present in that direction?"

"Exactly."

"Excellent," Admiral Hillaire said, "That's perfect, Loretta."

"You would think so, which is why we pursued it for a while. Basically, we're not looking for something to be bounced back at us but for something that's missing altogether from the picture of the surrounding space, such as when a Dakinium-sheathed ship blocks the light photons from distant stars. However, we found that we were severely limited with the distance the detection was accurate."

"What was the distance?"

"Only about ten kilometers."

"Ten kilometers is great," Admiral Ressler said. "I expected you to say something like ten meters."

"Ten kilometers may seem like a lot in this room, but in space it's nothing."

"It wouldn't be useful for locating Denubbewa ships at great distances," Jenetta said, "but it would be perfect in situations where fleet ships are operating in close proximity to other ships in stealth situations. It would mean we could stop giving away our positions to everyone by uncovering running lights. Only fleet ships would be able see other fleet ships."

"Yes, in *that* situation it would be effective. But everyone must understand the limitations and not depend on it to reveal the presence of ships beyond the ten-kilometer range."

"You're quite sure it wouldn't be possible to increase the sensitivity distance?" Admiral Burke asked.

"At the time we were working it, we had exhausted every avenue we could think of. But science is always making new breakthroughs, which is why we periodically revisit ideas we had dropped because all avenues were believed to have been expended during the previous research effort."

"How soon can we begin installing this new device in our ships?" Admiral Holt asked.

"Oh, about six months, I would say."

"Okay. All in favor?" Jenetta said.

Everyone agreed by raising their hands.

"Let's try to make it sooner if possible. And perhaps we can reopen that line of research to see if there have been any new breakthroughs that might help us increase the useful range."

◆　◆　◆

"Were there any suggestions put forth at the A.B. meeting today for how we should proceed?" Christa asked Jenetta after they had sat down to eat dinner.

"That's not proper conversation at the dinner table," Jenetta replied. She was holding Kyle and feeding him while

Celona fed Kaycee. The Jumakas were eating nearby, and a server was entering and leaving the room as needs arose at the table.

"You're right. Sorry."

"How did your first ship command go, Lori?" Jenetta asked.

"Wonderful. I have a great crew and everything went smoothly. We encountered no problems on this cruise so I don't know for sure how everyone will react under pressure, but I think they'll do great."

"I'm sure they will," Jenetta said.

Following dinner, as they all sat in the family living room, Christa said, "Tayna, Cayla, how are you doing with the sentience testing?"

"We think they might be done with the testing," Cayla replied.

"At least we hope they're done," Tayna said. "It seems like it's taking forever."

"We think they just can't believe their own eyes," Cayla said, "because our outward appearance too closely resembles that of animals with limited intelligence on their home worlds. If we walked upright on our rear legs, we probably would have been declared sentient months ago."

"That's very possible," Lori said. "But you think the testing is over?"

"They haven't scheduled any more tests in two months," Tayna said. "We believe they're locked in debate over presenting their conclusions to the G.A. Senate for a resolution vote."

"But they can't possibly declare you to be non-sentient," Christa said.

"Why not?" Tayna asked.

"Because it's so obvious that you're sentient. Several worlds have already declared you to be sentient, including the planet where Jumakas originated."

"Only three planets out of the dozens represented in the Senate," Jenetta said.

"Has any planet officially declared that Jumakas are *not* sentient?" Lori asked.

"None," Cayla said, "as far as we know."

"So the score is three and oh," Christa said. "That's a pretty good indication how the vote will go when they actually get around to voting."

"As I've stated in the past," Jenetta said, "governments move ponderously slow at times. It doesn't mean they disagree with the proposal I put forth; it's simply the way political business is conducted in a free and open society. Lori and Christa, join me in my study."

◆ ◆

Christa, the last to enter the study, closed the door and then selected one of the overstuffed chairs for the conference. Once all three women were settled, Jenetta said, "You'll both be receiving orders from Admiral Holt in the morning to return to your search areas and resume your task. Commander Fareman has continued searching his assigned area and Commander Kalborne will soon leave to begin his efforts with the fourth squadron in their assigned territory."

"We're going to continue looking for Denubbewa, even knowing we can't sense their presence?" Commander Ashraf asked.

"Yes, Lori, because we don't know for certain that *all* Denubbewa ships have been sheathed in Dakinium. For all we know, the actual number of ships already clad may be small. So you're going hunting again. There's also the secondary objective of locating bases inside asteroids, and third, indentifying derelict ships and documenting their locations. And if you do happen across a Denubbewa ship that isn't Dakinium-sheathed, don't destroy it. At least not right away. Try to follow it. It might lead you to a mothership."

"What will happen to the Elobian prisoners?" Christa asked.

"First, we have to establish that they're sincere in their desire to separate from the Denubbewa cyborg population and that they're being completely honest and open with us. Once we establish their mindset, we'll make decisions regarding their futures and not before. However, if we believe their stories, we'll do everything we can to help them. We have your reports and a copy of every recording you made when you spoke with the cyborg you took aboard your ship. SCI has been studying them and piecing together a history of the race. Once that's complete, they'll interview all of the others separately and try to corroborate the story and the desires of the others to be free from the Denubbewa. All of the cyborgs have been placed into special Dakinium-sheathed holding areas where they're unable to communicate electronically with the others or pick up information from our communications. So they won't be comparing notes or learning new information regarding our military strength and operations."

"What about the cyborgs in the packing cases?" Christa asked.

"Once we've completed our work with the ones that were on tables, we'll start opening the cases and waking them so we can corroborate their stories as well. Don't worry, we'll treat them properly as long as they don't resist and we know they're not a threat."

"And if they turn out to be a threat?"

"Then we'll deactivate them— permanently— and give the pieces to our scientists to study. What we'll learn from that ship and the cyborgs might be invaluable in fighting them. I have no remorse regarding their permanent deactivation. Although they may now simply be mindless automatons, we must always remember they're deadly tools being used by their Denubbewa masters. The Denubbewa have made it abundantly clear through their actions that they intend to murder all sentient species in the galaxy and replace them with drones. We're fighting for our lives and the lives of loved ones. I'm glad we've had an opportunity to study these cyborgs and their ship, but do not hesitate to destroy any cyborgs you encounter in the future because you think they might simply be victims that can be saved. If you hesitate, you and your crew may be killed before you get a second chance."

"I never bonded with any of the cyborgs," Lori said, "so my commitment to exterminating them has never wavered."

"I didn't bond, either," Christa said, "and I actually lied on a consistent basis to the one who referred to himself as an

Elobian in order to misinform him should he be lying to me. I won't hesitate to destroy any Denubbewa we find, sis."

"Good, because we're a very long way from the end of this war. We know the Denubbewa are already here in great numbers and we have to assume more are on the way. From what the cyborg told you, Christa, we're the first race able to repel their attacks. I'm sure their government back home, wherever that is, knows by now that they're going to have to throw everything they've got at us if they hope to beat us. And we know they're not going to win while any of us still live."

CHAPTER FIFTEEN

~ March 11th, 2291 ~

It was a warm day with just a slight breeze as Jenetta stepped off the shuttle ramp. Large puffy white clouds filled most of the sky overhead and sea birds circled the area, screaming their displeasure at having been disturbed by the approach and landing of the small ship. General Winslow Scott saluted sharply and held it until the salute was returned by Jenetta.

"Admiral Carver," he said as he extended his hand, "welcome to Harrat Island Marine base."

"Thank you, General," Jenetta said, then smiled and shook the proffered hand before adding, "It's a pleasure to visit you here again."

"It's been a long time between visits, Admiral."

"Yes, I've had a lot of catching up to do since returning from my leave of absence. But I'm on top of things again and I wanted to discuss a few confidential matters with you. Since I hadn't been here in such a long time, I decided to come to you."

"You're always welcome, Admiral."

With a smile, she said, "I promise I'm not bringing bad news."

General Scott smiled and said, "That's a relief. Is this a private meeting, Admiral?"

"It is."

"Very well." Gesturing towards his oh-gee limo, he said, "After you."

As Jenetta approached the vehicle, the driver held the door open for her. The General whispered something to his aide, who had started to follow automatically, and the aide turned and walked to another vehicle.

As the caravan of vehicles headed for the Headquarters building, Jenetta said, "Whatever happened to the FA-SF4 fighter I requisitioned for my private use?"

"As I understand it, after you left Quesann the fighter was assigned to Admiral Holt. But he apparently doesn't share your enjoyment of wave-top-clipping and tree-pruning, so it was eventually assigned to an air wing."

"I always enjoyed my little excursions through the canyons and wave-tops."

"Say the word and I'll arrange to have another ship assigned to you."

"Thank you. I'd love to hop into a fighter and enjoy the thrill of flying at maximum speed a meter above the planet's surface again, but now I have to travel with a full security detail wherever I go."

"Yes, we have security in the first two vehicles and last two vehicles in this little parade."

"The security is one of the reasons I avoided putting on the big hat for so long."

"Jen, we're all glad you're back. I mean that sincerely."

"Thank you, Winslow. I am happy to be back. I missed the job and the people. And we have a lot of challenges ahead. I'll explain once we're in a secure environment."

"Is this about the Marine ground force initiative?"

Before responding, Jenetta looked to see if the glass partition between the front and rear compartments was completely closed. When she saw that the indicators attested to the seal, she said, "Where did you hear about that?"

"Are you kidding? It's all anyone's talking about."

"I made a request to the Senate Council for the creation of a ground force a few months ago. It was supposed to remain Top Secret."

"Top Secret? In that political circus? There's no such thing. The secretaries were probably calling their contacts in the media even before you finished your presentation. And the Senators were probably talking about it afterward in the dining room while being attended by civilian waiters and busboys who may not even have a basic security clearance, much less a Top Secret clearance."

"I report to the Senate Council, and we must have their approval in order to establish this new operational force. There's no way around it. And the full Senate must pass the measure for it to become law, not to mention their necessary approval of the required funding. I naturally would have preferred the Council decide whether or not to recommend it to the full Senate before the media, lobbyists, big corporations, and general public begin expressing their opinions, but in the end we need the support of everyone— or at least a majority of the taxpayers."

"From what I'm hearing, there's little support for the creation of a ground force. The senators say that our function is to patrol and secure space outside planets, not interfere in their domestic situations."

"We've had a Marine base located on Dakistee for some time. Whether the Senate wants to acknowledge it or not, they were charged with far more than protecting space around the planet. Our Marines not only patrolled the skies but also protected the planet's population on the ground when the meager security forces of the archeological organizations were unable to cope— which was frequent. And when the Dakistee people were discovered and awakened, our Marines continued to protect the planet from both outside invasion and internal strife. I know the Senate will probably require us to remove all military forces from planets other than Quesann eventually, but at the present time we have extensive ground forces on both Earth and Dakistee."

"While the Senate may not be willing to create a permanent ground force at this time, we can create the nucleus of one right here on Quesann without additional funding. We can initiate training with a small group who will eventually become the instructors in an expanded force when the Senate finally acknowledges its need and permits us to establish the proper framework. Just say the word and I'll begin the operation."

"It's true that our current mandate would legitimately allow us to do as you suggest, but I don't want to commence any activity that might be perceived by the Senate as an end-run around them. Let's allow them to deliberate and argue on the merits and dangers of the initiative for a while. Perhaps they'll see the value of having a trained ground force and realize we're not looking to violate the G.A. charter restrictions that prevent us from interfering or involving ourselves in the operation of planetary governments that aren't violating the written statutes of G.A. law."

"Okay, Jen, you're the boss. I hope the Senate sees it your way because I agree there will be times when we'll need a ground force if we're ever to completely enforce G.A. law in all of our regions. Uh, was this why you came to visit?"

"No. In fact, I hadn't even intended to broach the subject. I have far more important and more secret issues to discuss with you. But let's wait until we can relax with a cup of coffee to begin that discussion. How're your wife, the kids, and the grandchildren?"

◆ ◆ ◆

"This is absolutely amazing. It's hard to believe they got this thing to work," Lt. Daminchic said.

"*Does* it work?" his coworker, Lt.(jg) Stiddant, said. "That's the question."

"It must."

"Why? Simply because it's mounted in this instrument panel?"

"That's usually a pretty good indication that it passed all lab tests."

"Perhaps it was just another test to see if it would work in actual use."

"Maybe, but imagine what it means if it does work," Daminchic said.

The two men were lying on their backs on the deck while they worked to disconnect and remove the device. Only the lower parts of their legs that extended out from under the huge console would be visible to anyone who entered the bridge.

"I can see both good and bad aspects."

"Yes, I can also. But let's concentrate on the good."

"Anyone ever tell you that you're a hopeless optimist?"

"Yeah, my ex-wife," Daminchic said. "Right up until the divorce. I kept telling her we could work out our problems. She kept telling me I *was* the problem."

"You were the problem?"

"She said I was never there for her. I told her I was a Space Command officer and had to go where they sent me and stay there for as long as they said. She knew I was a Space Command officer when we married and she said she understood. But then she started telling me to resign and get a job working for an engineering company on Earth where I could use the skills I'd learned while in Space Command and receive the pay I deserved. I suspect that was her plan all along. Women always seem to think they can change men after marriage and mold us to *their* concept of what they feel we should be or who they want us to be."

"And now?"

"I'm still in Space Command. I'm still going where they send me. I wouldn't trade my life for anything, and my wife is finally off my back. I can tell you this— it's a lot more peace-ful now when I'm on leave."

"What happened to the ex?"

"She's married again. She's now trying to remold number six."

"Six? Which number were you?" Stiddant asked.

"I was the first. We were married right after I graduated from the Academy. Here, hold this wire while I disconnect this other one. Don't let it touch anything that would ground the device out. Anyway, it was when I got my first posting aboard a ship that the problems started. She accused me of abandoning her because I loved Space Command and my work more than I loved her. Eventually she was right because she nagged me endlessly to resign my commission. I didn't contest the divorce."

"You know, this is going to take forever if we have to take this ship apart piece by piece."

"It's the only way to dismantle it without destroying any-thing. And it's not like we're working alone. There are eight-een other ORDER teams doing the same things we are— ob-serve, remove, disassemble, evaluate, and report. We can't afford to rush through the process with technology we don't already know better than we know the back of our hands."

"Like I said, it will take forever."

"But think of the rewards. We'll know the Denubbewa as well as they understand themselves. Maybe better."

"Yeah, we'll be all primed for them when they harvest our brains and insert them into cyborg bodies."

"Never gonna happen," Daminchic said. "I'll put a laser pistol to my head first and make my brain unusable. Besides, with Admiral Carver running the show, the Denubbewa threat is almost as good as over. She's going to kick their tin back-sides back to wherever they came from."

"Oh, no."

"What's the matter?" Daminchic said, afraid something had gone wrong with the removal effort. But he didn't see any problem. Stiddant was holding the piece well away from the instrument panel so it couldn't have grounded out.

"I was just thinking. Carver always absorbs the territory of every enemy she defeats. We could wind up owning the whole galaxy. I'll never get to go home on leave if I have to travel halfway across the galaxy."

Daminchic chuckled. "Don't worry. I think Carver has enough on her plate. She'll just boot the Denubbewa out of our regions and warn them never to come back, as she did with the Milori the first time."

"Yes, but look what happened with the Milori. They came after us again as soon as they'd rebuilt their fleet."

"Well, then maybe you *will* have to travel halfway across the galaxy to visit Earth," Daminchic said with another chuckle. "Okay, it's disconnected. Lower it carefully and stow it in the transport case, then assign the next sequential number and log it on the recorder."

◆　◆　◆

"As most of you already know by now," Admiral Plimley said to the senior officers and civilians assembled in the conference room aboard the headquarters space station orbiting Lorense-Three, "we're looking at the Neutrino Measurement Sensor once again. This is a rush job. We need to be able to install something within six weeks, even if there are no improvements on the previous design. Yes, we know the maximum usable detection range was only ten kilometers when we shelved that project, and even that might be an exaggeration except under optimal conditions. This has our highest priority so we'll take suggestions from anyone at any level. Submit any ideas you might have for improvement to Dr. Ellibock. Any questions?"

"Admiral," a senior scientist named Reed Lanquist said, "has something happened that we're unaware of?"

"I imagine there are always things happening that you're unaware of, Doctor."

A chuckle arose from the assembled group.

"I mean something that threatens Space Command, such as an imminent attack?"

"There have been some new developments, which I'm not at liberty to discuss at this time."

"Are we in danger?"

"This shipyard and the smaller one at Mars are the best protected places in G.A. space. The First Fleet protects Mars and Earth, and the Second Fleet protects us and Quesann. Before any enemy could reach us, our forces would be there to cut that enemy off at the knees. And in the event there was a real emergency detected, you would all have time to get to the planet below and into the underground bunkers deep below the planet's surface. The Neutrino Measurement Sensor is required to give some protection to our brave fighting men and women who will always be on the line between the enemy and ourselves."

"Admiral," another scientist said, "will the project leaders be willing to consider alternatives that were dismissed out of hand in the past?"

"We will consider anything and everything that could possibly give us greater range, provided the technology is advanced enough to incorporate within six weeks. We don't have time for ideas that depend on the perfection of some new material or procedure that's not yet in production. We only have six weeks. But we will entertain any new ideas for future versions if the science is sufficiently advanced for a basic evaluation."

"What happens in six weeks?" Lanquist asked.

"The fourth squadron of CPS-16s deploy to begin their search for enemy ships. We want them to have the device for field testing."

"But it's not effective beyond ten kilometers," Lanquist said. "It can't possibly help them locate enemy ships. Their standard sensor arrays are infinitely more practical and effective."

"Yes, we know Dr. Lanquist. But a new system is being tested for search-and-destroy missions for enemies such as the Denubbewa. As you probably know, each squadron of ships consists of one Scout-Destroyer and twenty-four CPS-16s. When the twenty-five ships congregate for meetings and other reasons, they have to be careful not to make contact with one another. Even though the hulls are sheathed with Dakinium, there are other considerations, such as damage to the sensors or shuttles attached to the exterior of each CPS-16. Currently, helmsmen correct for drift between the *nearly* motionless ships by positioning their ship using the running lights on other ships as their reference points. But that can alert a potential enemy of the group's presence by visual means and negates the secretive presence aspect of the Dakinium. We want our ships to be totally dark while they're lying in wait for an enemy to appear, visually invisible and undetectable to all normal sensors. We're hoping the Neutrino Measurement Sensor can solve that problem by allowing the helmsman to adjust for drift using information provided by the Neutrino Measurement Sensor equipment. The distance between ships is rarely more than one kilometer. However, if we can increase the ten-kilometer effective distance of the device, it will be much more useful when the ships are initially gathering. We recently had a ship rendezvous that required the CPS-16s to go to full illumination with their running lights so the approaching ship could identify their location from thirty-seven kilometers away. Okay, Doctor?"

"Uh, yes, Admiral. I see the reason for the request now. My people, at least those still working for *me*, will give their full attention to this project over the next few weeks."

Admiral Plimley breathed a silent sigh. She hated to lie to these people because they were some of the most trusted scientists, with the highest security clearances, working for the military, but Admiral Carver wanted to maintain full secrecy about the Denubbewa sheathing their ships with Dakinium for as long as possible. She hadn't even informed the G.A. Senate Council yet because she couldn't prevent whatever information she shared with them from being leaked to the media before she'd even left the building. The scientists and military personnel had agreed before learning the particulars of the new research they would be conducting that they wouldn't be free to leave the research location or communicate with anybody outside the research location until the work was complete. Those working inside the Denubbewa ship had actually been sequestered aboard the ship.

◆ ◆ ◆

"We've evaluated all of the recordings provided by Commander Carver," the SCI Captain reported in the executive meeting of the Admiralty Board. "It's our consensus that the cyborg is telling the truth *most* of the time, most especially when he talks about a time on his home planet before the Denubbewa arrived."

"You say most of the time, Captain," Admiral Hillarie said. "When is he not telling the truth?"

"We can't say with any surety. The almost imperceptible flutter in the vocal response could be suggestive of strong anger or could suggest he's lying. We've run the recordings through the computer repeatedly and the computer always says there's a seventy-eight percent chance he's telling the truth and twenty-two percent chance he's being less than honest whenever he talks about his work for the Denubbewa."

"And you interpret that to mean...?" Admiral Woo said.

"Well, he might have been involved in work he doesn't want us to know about, such as the extraction of brains for insertion into cyborg bodies, or perhaps he was charged with developing new weapons or defensive products, such as the Dakinium to clad their ships. The latter would have made it especially easy for him to steal a DS ship. He could have timed it so that as soon as the work was done, he collected his countrymen and absconded with the ship. It would have been much more difficult once the ship was fully manned and returned to active service. That would also support his claim that only a few of the cyborgs in the storage location were not his countrymen. They might have been security people or other drones whose minds had been so thoroughly wiped that they had no desire, or will, to escape."

"So there's no way to ascertain that he's either lying or telling the truth about his work?" Admiral Burke, the head of SCI, asked.

"No, sir, Admiral. Not from the tapes. Our next step is to begin interviewing the cyborgs we have in holding. And then we'll awaken the ones in the shipping containers and interview them. We don't know how they'll react to learning they're in our custody, so we'll be well armed when we activate them. If any resist, we'll do whatever we have to do to protect ourselves."

"That goes without saying."

"Yes, sir. I'm just saying that if we start shooting, it will only be because we believe it's necessary."

"Yes, don't risk your lives. There are lots of cyborgs. If a few are destroyed in the process, no one will mourn the loss."

"Yes, sir."

"Captain," Admiral Burke said, "do you have a list of prepared questions, or are you going to wing it?"

"We have a long list of prepared questions so we can compare answers afterward. But we may also ask questions that arise from the responses of the cyborgs. By the time we're done, we hope to have a complete picture of exactly what went down."

"If all their testimonies match up?"

"No, if all their testimonies are identical, we'll know they're lying because they rehearsed their answers."

"But they're robots. Shouldn't the stories be identical?"

"If they were robots, perhaps. But they're cyborgs. They have biological brains in those tin-can bodies. And biological brains usually record different impressions of the same events."

CHAPTER SIXTEEN
~ May 6th, 2291 ~

Knowing that the Denubbewa had Dakinium-sheathed ships kept the bridge crew of every ship in the three squadrons staring at the stars, expecting to see the lights from distant stars wink out occasionally as a Denubbewa ship passed between them and their ship. But everything appeared normal as they traversed new areas of their assigned territory day after day.

Christa was working in her office when she received a message from the Com Chief.

"Captain, you just received an encrypted message. It's from the *Ottawa*."

"That's Commander Kalborne's ship. Send it to my queue."

"You have it, Captain."

Christa leaned back in her oh-gee chair to listen to the message.

"Commander. We've arrived at our designated patrol area and begun searching. I'm sending notification messages to Commander Ashraf and Commander Fareman as well. Happy hunting. Burl Kalborne, Commander, Captain of the *Ottawa*. End of message."

"Short and sweet," Christa muttered before returning to the log entry she had just started.

◆ ◆ ◆

Six days later, The *Koshi* received another message from the *Ottawa*. Christa was on the bridge but she went to her office to listen to the message.

"Commander, we've picked up a Denubbewa warship with our sensors. It's under power and traveling at Light-480. We've been following it for a short time now, as per orders, and we've intercepted a message that we believe was sent by the Denubbewa. It's encrypted and we can't translate it, but we have a fix on the direction of the transmission. My orders state you're the senior officer among the four squadrons and have been officially designated as the mission coordinator, so I'm reporting the matter to you and requesting instructions. Do we continue to follow the Denubbewa ship or break off and try to determine if the message came from a mothership? Awaiting your orders. Burl Kalborne, Commander, Captain of the *Ottawa*. End of message."

"Message to Commander Burl Kalborne of the GSC *Ottawa* in Region Three, from Commander Christa Carver aboard the GSC *Koshi*.

"Do not break off contact with the Denubbewa ship. You're the first among us to locate a Denubbewa ship under power. We can't afford to lose it. Send a pair of your CPS-16s to see if the new information yields any results. Keep me apprised of any developments.

"Good work.

"Christa Marie Carver, Commander, Captain of the GSC *Koshi*. End of message."

After telling the com chief to send the message, Christa sat back in her chair to think. A Denubbewa ship without Dakinium sheathing was a surprise after all the months spent searching for the Denubbewa without success, finally leading to the now erroneous conclusion that all of the Denubbewa ships were as invisible to normal sensors as were the Space Command ships. She wondered how many more might not be sheathed.

◆　◆　◆

The days passed slowly because the crew of the *Koshi* never spotted another ship of any sort. They were far from the most traveled trade routes, but this was where many of the sighting reports had come from a year earlier.

◆　◆　◆

Nine days after receiving the message from the *Ottawa*, another arrived. The single word 'JACKPOT' preceded a set of coordinates.

Christa immediately sent a set of rendezvous coordinates to Ashraf, Kalborne, and Fareman. The RP she established was about a million kilometers from the coordinates Kalborne had sent, and she estimated it would take about eight days for all four squadrons to rendezvous.

◆　◆　◆

The *Ottawa* squadron and the *Khatanga* squadron were at the RP when the *Koshi* squadron arrived. The *Seeker* squadron was expected in a few hours. After ordering four CPS-16s to picket duty, Christa invited Fareman and Kalborne to join her aboard the *Koshi*.

"Welcome aboard, gentlemen," Christa said as the two commanding officers stepped off the shuttle she had sent to pick them up.

"Thank you, Commander," Commander Kalborne said.

Fareman repeated the salutation.

"Your message was most welcome, Burl. My crew is excited that we're finally going to see some action."

"Christa, you're not going to believe what we've found. My people say they couldn't believe their eyes. It's a smorgasbord of Denubbewa ships. The reason we couldn't locate any is because they've all been here getting new outer skins of Dakinium applied. That must be why there were so many reported sightings. The Denubbewa leadership must have ordered all ships in the region to rendezvous here for the modifications. Some have been completed, many are partially completed, and on some the work hasn't begun yet and are simply sitting there waiting for their turn. My CPS-16 captains took a number of images when they first arrived at the location and then made several more passes because the assembled fleet is so enormous."

"Were your ships spotted?"

"Negative. They flew through at Marc-One, just as if they were planting bombs."

"Did you bring the copies of the images?"

"I sure did. And I can't wait to show them to you and Walt."

"Wait until Lori gets here so she can share in the excitement. She shouldn't be too much longer. Let's go to my office and have some coffee while we wait."

"We should be toasting with champagne."

"Uh, let's wait until the fighting is over and we know the final score."

◆ ◆ ◆

Commander Ashraf arrived about three hours later aboard a shuttle from her ship. The *Koshi's* first officer escorted her to the Captain's office and the officers spent a few minutes renewing old acquaintances before getting down to business. Christa invited her XO to remain.

Kalborne set his viewpad so the images would be displayed on the large monitor facing Christa's desk. As the first images appeared, everyone's jaw dropped while Kalborne chuckled. There weren't dozens of ships in the images, and there weren't hundreds of ships. There were thousands of ships in the images.

"I don't see any motherships," Christa said. "How can there be this many warships and no motherships?"

"They're there," Kalborne said. "They're simply covered with Dakinium so the normal sensors don't show them and the imaging equipment doesn't pick them up. Give me just a second here."

Half a minute later, after he had entered some data, Kalborne tapped a key on the viewpad and an off-color image showed a dozen motherships as a CPS-16 performed a flyby.

"Good Lord," Fareman said. "Look at all of those motherships. They could almost form their own solar system. But how can we see them now if they're sheathed in Dakinium?"

"A new gizmo developed by Admiral Plimley's people. They call it a Neutrino Measurement Sensor. I understand they nearly busted a gut getting it ready before we deployed. In the end, we actually had to delay our deployment by three weeks so they could install the new sensors in all our ships. The modifications are all internal and we brought enough for all our ships. But— it will probably take a few weeks for the engineers to install and test them. The question is: Do we wait until the new sensors are installed or start bombing the hell out of the Denubbewa tomorrow?"

"We wait," Christa said, "and prepare ourselves properly." We all need to be able to see the ships that have already been sheathed, both motherships and warships, but the motherships must be our first attack priority. Each one of them is equal in importance to a hundred warships because they're the glue that holds the Denubbewa fleet together. We must make sure that none of those motherships ever leaves this location. Even limping away is unacceptable. They must be destroyed."

"Okay. Should we remain here or move a bit further away to complete the installation work?"

"Since we really should have the new device working in every ship before we attack and it's going to take several weeks to accomplish the installation, let's move to a different location. I'd say a light-year should be adequate to keep any stray Denubbewa patrols from spotting us."

◆ ◆ ◆

"This conversion is taking much too long," Christa said to her XO during their morning briefing.

"I guess it takes as long as it takes, Captain. The engineers are doing the best they can. I've visited several of our ships where the captains expressed a similar sentiment. Commander Kalborne did say the installation delayed their deployment by several weeks. And that was with shipyard engineers who perform these repetitive activities every day. The experience of our engineers is a lot more general because they're responsible for everything in the ship, and they're sort of feeling their way along with this new equipment."

"By the time they complete this conversion they'll be professionals at this task. And I really don't think a few extra weeks will make any difference. Based on the number of ships we saw waiting to be sheathed by the Denubbewa, they're going to be at it for a couple of years."

"I know. I'm just afraid that every completed ship will be sent out on assignment. We could soon have hundreds of ships out there that no one except us can sense. And the instructions that came with the sensors say they're only effective up to ten kilometers."

"That's not a whole lot of range. I wonder what we'll see beyond the ten kilometers."

"Probably either static or nothing. Admiral Plimley's people aren't prone to exaggeration. If they say it's good *up* to ten kilometers, I wouldn't expect any useful information beyond the specified limit."

◆　◆　◆

"We're ready at last," Christa announced to the small fleet of CPS-16s via a teleconference using encrypted RF transmission to control the distribution of the message. "I'm sure no one expected it would take seven weeks to install the new sensors, but we'll all be able to see the Denubbewa ships now, especially the ones that have already been sheathed in Dakinium. Remember that the sensors are not effective beyond ten kilometers, so at the speeds we'll be traveling during the bombing runs, you won't see the target until the last second. Fortunately, those motherships are so enormous that they're hard to miss. We must take out the motherships first. Once they're destroyed, we'll concentrate on the warships that have already been sheathed. With our double envelopes in place, we don't have to worry about our ships hitting any of the enemy ships or each other. So just concentrate on sending those mothers to the scrap pile.

"Since we've been away from the battle site for so long and the ships there may have shifted positions, one of my CPS-16s will make a surveillance run before we all go in. It will enable us to plan our attack runs on the targets before we actually get there. All ships will be able to view the images produced by the scout before they start their run.

"We'll do this in four attack groups. Since we owe the find to the *Ottawa* squadron, they will have the honor of the first kills. After they complete their pass, the *Khatanga* squadron will make their run. Then the *Seeker* squadron, and lastly my *Koshi* squadron. Once my squadron is clear of the battle site, the *Ottawa* will commence its second run, and so on until either every Denubbewa ship is destroyed or we're out of bombs. Remember, the Dakinium-clad ships are the highest priority, with the motherships being the targets we most want to destroy.

"We'll now move to the assembly area we occupied when we first arrived in the neighborhood seven weeks ago and the scout will perform the flyby to verify the motherships haven't altered their position.

"Good luck and good shooting.

"Carver out."

The one hundred ships headed for the assembly area with the *Ottawa* squadron in the lead. The new Neutrino Measurement Systems worked great. Every ship was able to see every other ship that was within the ten-kilometer range so there would be little danger of collisions when they arrived at their destination if they dropped their envelopes. Upon arrival, Christa issued the order for the selected ship, the *Karl Linne,* to fly through the battle site with its cameras running. As it completed its run and prepared to return, the first images were arriving at the assembly area.

"Where are the targets?" Christa muttered. There wasn't a single Denubbewa ship visible in any of the images.

"*Karl Linne,* this is the *Koshi*. You must be at the wrong location. There are no ships in the images."

"Our sensors say this is the right location, Commander. We don't see a single ship anywhere."

"That can't be. There were thousands of enemy ships at the battle site. Check your navigation again."

"My navigator has checked it and rechecked it. This is the site. And our eyes tell us there are no ships here."

"Good grief," Christa mumbled to herself. "I've just lost the largest enemy fleet in history."

◆

After each of the other squadrons had sent a ship to the battle site to confirm the location information, the navigators got busy and used the stars to compute their position, just in case the installation of the new sensor equipment was disrupting the other equipment. The visual verification results from four navigators confirmed that the equipment was reporting the position correctly.

"What now, Captain?" XO Mollago asked.

"Now we separate into squadrons and each search a quadrant emanating out from this location. They can't have gotten too far. The non-DS-sheathed vessels are limited to Light-480."

"But non-DS-sheathed vessels will probably move inside the DS sheathed motherships, which can travel at speeds up to Marc-One."

"But the motherships can only attain Light-9790 if they haven't yet learned about Marc-One and learned how to manipulate the power fluctuation."

"Shouldn't we assume they have and start our search at the maximum range?"

"You're just full of encouragement today," Christa said with a wry smile.

"I'm sorry, Captain. I'm trying to be realistic."

"I know. I'm trying to be optimistic, but I'm fighting an uphill battle. You're right, we should assume the worst. I keep berating myself for taking the time to install those new sensors."

"You can't hit what you can't see."

"Perhaps I should have allowed the *Ottawa* squadron to take out the motherships when we first got here."

"But then the other ships would have scattered and we would have lost the opportunity to destroy the better part of that enormous fleet."

"Yes, but as it is we've lost the chance to destroy *any* part of that enormous fleet."

"It's too big to hide. We'll find them again."

"I hope so. If the warships all enter the motherships to travel to a new location, we won't be able to pick up the warships that haven't been sheathed yet. And we can only sense the Dakinium-sheathed ships if they're within ten kilometers. In space, ten kilometers is like a grain of sand drifting in an ocean of black water."

◆ ◆ ◆

After several weeks of searching, not a single Denubbewa vessel had been spotted. Christa was about as depressed as she could ever remember being. She blamed herself for losing the Denubbewa fleet. She called the squadron commanders together for a meeting aboard the *Koshi*.

"It seems pointless to keep searching here," Christa said. "The Denubbewa fleet escaped us this time. They could be hiding out there eleven kilometers away from the course we're following and we'd never spot them. So I've decided we'll resume searching the areas assigned to each of us by Second Fleet HQ. Perhaps one of us will get a lead like the *Ottawa* did if we're not all clustered in one small part of Region Three."

"I wish I'd never mentioned the new sensors," Commander Kalborne said. "Then we might have attacked them when we first located them."

"You were doing what your training taught you to do and what Second Fleet HQ wanted you to, just as I was doing what I believed Second Fleet would have wanted me to do when I ordered the delay to install those sensors. It's just fate, I guess. But I can't help feeling I'm missing something. It doesn't make sense that the Denubbewa fleet would just pack up and go before completing the Dakinium sheathing operation. And we know they hadn't yet fully sheathed very many of those warships when we arrived. They must have somehow learned we were here and vacated that site within twenty-four hours."

"Perhaps they have some way of detecting us when we pass by them or pass through them while we're in a double envelope," Commander Ashraf said.

"Perhaps," Christa said. "If they can, we've just lost another major advantage we had over them until now."

"I just had a wild thought," Commander Fareman said. "You told us of the debriefing you conducted with the Denubbewa you brought aboard the *Koshi*. You said the Denubbewa could overhear all communications aboard a ship?"

"That's what the cyborg said."

"Well, how about if he was able to plant a small transceiver somewhere aboard the *Koshi*?"

"He never left the table he was placed on when first brought aboard. He didn't have the run of the ship."

"But he could have dropped something tiny somewhere."

"The Dakinium is supposed to block all signals from passing through the hull."

"Our people just figured out how to make the undetectable detectable. Perhaps they figured out how to make the un-transmittable transmittable."

"Or how about this," Fareman said. "The whole 'seeking freedom' story was a lie. You did find the Denubbewa ship right next to a derelict you would certainly have stopped to investigate. What if there was another Denubbewa, an individual, outside the ship, wearing Dakinium armor or a Dakinium EVA suit. Do cyborgs need to breathe air? Anyway, he would not have shown up on your sensors so he could have planted some kind of bug on your hull and the hull of the *Seeker* when it arrived. Then, when we arrived at the battle site a couple of months ago, they immediately knew we were in the vicinity there so they packed up and hit the spaceways."

"If I wasn't paranoid before, I'm certainly getting there now," Christa said with a grin.

"A Space Command officer I admire very much," Commander Ashraf said, "once told me that the line between paranoia and security-consciousness can be extremely blurry and often invisible."

"Yes, I've heard Jenetta say that. The difference seems to be that the paranoid merely anguishes over things they feel they can't control while the security-aware individual takes action to protect themselves and others."

"So what will it be, Commander?" Kalborne asked. "Anguish or action?"

"Action— always. First we'll scour the interior of this ship for any transmitters the Denubbewa may have planted or dropped. Second, and concurrently, we'll have the exterior of the ship scoured for locator beacons and then scour the *Seeker* and all forty-eight CPS-16s as well. It's going to be a lot of work, but we must determine if we've been bugged or tagged. The Denubbewa had to know we'd arrived near the battle site, and we need to learn just how they discovered our presence before we had a chance to strike."

"I'll get my CPS engineers suited up and externally checking their ships for locator beacons while my Marines and engineers search the *Seeker*," Commander Ashraf said.

"My engineers and Marines can help," Kalborne said.

"My engineers and Marines can assist the *Koshi* personnel," Fareman said. "With everyone working, we'll resolve this issue tout de suite."

◆ ◆ ◆

"I have good news and bad news," XO Mollago said when he entered Christa's office.

She put the viewpad down on the desk and looked up at him. "Give me the good news. I could use some."

"We've ascertained that there's no Denubbewa transmitter anywhere inside this ship."

"Great."

"Plus, there are no locator beacons on any of the CPS-16s or the *Seeker*."

"You've covered everything except the *Koshi*. Is that the bad news you saved for last?"

"Yes, Captain. We found a cyborg on the hull."

"A cyborg? On the hull?"

"Yes, it had fastened itself to a Dakinium latch-pin our engineers use when doing maintenance. And it was enclosed in a Dakinium EVA suit so it could travel with us wherever we went. We think it's been there since we first discovered the Dakinium-sheathed Denubbewa ship."

"Attached to the ship for all these past months? And no one noticed it when we arrived at Lorense-Three and then in the fleet parking around Quesann?"

"It was hidden pretty well, and it was all black on a black hull. So it's understandable that it would have evaded detection."

"Is it still alive?"

"It was when we located it. But it didn't want to be brought inside so it accidently got shot a dozen times in the faceplate during the struggle. The faceplate was the only place it wasn't covered by Dakinium."

"Accidently?"

"I'm assured by the Marines involved that it certainly appeared that way, Captain. The only thing I don't understand is how it recharged. It would have been on the hull for months while we were traveling."

"Sywasock said cyborgs can shut down and not require any power for up to a year. So this cyborg might have done that while we were traveling or when there was no activity. So our hull is now totally free of locator beacons?"

"Uh, yes."

"Why the uh?"

"There's more bad news."

"Lay it on me."

"The Denubbewa had another small device in addition to what we believe is the locator beacon."

"And have we determined what it is?"

"Lt. Burton has begun working on it. He believes it's a mass storage recording device. It was plugged into the cyborg's chest. Burton believes the cyborg was able to store everything he picked up with the telecommunication capabilities built into his body."

"He made recordings?"

"Yes, Captain."

"If there was no transmitter inside the hull, then he couldn't have been receiving anything from someone inside the ship."

"Well, yes and no. When your cyborg was transferred in a yard shuttle, there was no Dakinium shielding him after he left the ship until he was put into a holding cell."

"And you think he might have recorded everything I discussed with him in his internal electronics and then transmitted it to the cyborg hidden on the hull during processing."

"It's possible."

"Yes, it's very possible. It's also possible that the cyborg on the ship was able to record tens of thousands of Space Command conversations, messages, and reports while he was on the hull and the ship was at Lorense-Three and then again when we were with the fleet around Quesann. A lot of it would have been encrypted, but it's amazing what you can learn from ordinary conversations. Tell Lt. Burton to be very careful with that device. If it does contain telecommunications data, we must know what was on it. The Denubbewa cyborg could have transmitted all that data as soon as we got close to the Denubbewa fleet here."

"Yes, Captain."

"Good job, XO. Give my compliments to everyone who participated in this effort."

"Yes, Captain."

CHAPTER SEVENTEEN
~ July 8th, 2291 ~

"Good Morning, Admiral Carver," the G.A. Senate President said cordially as Jenetta was welcomed into the enormous room. She was then escorted to a seat facing the center of the raised dais where the fifteen-member Senate Council sat while conducting business. Cayla and Tayna were, as always, by Jenetta's side.

"Good Morning, President Fluessa," she replied as she sat down. The two Jumakas took their places on the floor on either side of her legs.

"I asked you to attend this closed session of the Council to discuss your request that we approve sentiency for the Jumaka race on Taurentlus-Thur."

"Yes, sir."

"I'm afraid that while much of the Council favors bestowing sentiency status, there is opposition, so we will not be forwarding the resolution to the full Senate."

"May I be permitted to know who opposes it?"

"We are not allowed to disclose how Senate Council members vote on Council business. When a matter goes to the full Senate, the votes are a matter of public record."

"But if the Council doesn't forward a resolution to the full Senate for a vote, there's no voting record for the citizens of the G.A. to learn how senators have voted behind closed doors."

"That's the way it's been since the Senate was established."

"Actually, the Council votes were public information until the Council elected to alter the procedures and keep its voting history a secret from the G.A. public."

There was a silence in the room that lasted a full minute as the Council members looked at one another and then at Jenetta.

"Regardless," the Senate President said, "matters under discussion and the voting history of Council members are not open to scrutiny by the public."

"I understand, Mr. President. And I don't actually need to hear who opposes sentiency for Jumakas. I believe I already know."

"You do?"

"Yes. It's fairly obvious who stands to gain if sentiency is refused. And by that I mean personal gain, not political gain."

Speaking sternly, the Council president said, "I would caution you not to reveal confidential information you learned while attending a Council meeting."

"Mr. President, I haven't learned anything while attending this Council meeting so I can hardly be accused of revealing something I learned here."

"On the contrary, you've— uh— you've learned that the sentiency request will not be forwarded to the full Senate for a vote."

"That's hardly confidential information, Mr. President. The people of the Galactic Alliance are waiting anxiously to see what you've learned in your sentiency investigation. When you fail to send the measure to the Senate for a full vote, everyone in the G.A. will know you've intentionally suppressed the vote. *They* already know Jumakas are sentient. They have the proof of their own eyes and ears. Some planets have already declared Jumakas to be sentient, and more will do so. Those planets are going to demand to see the test data that refutes that declaration. When you fail to make it public because it proves Jumaka sentiency, they'll know you're hiding something for political reasons or personal gain."

"I remind you that as Admiral of the Fleet, you serve at *our* pleasure."

"I serve the people of the G.A. not because I have to, but because I choose to. I serve as Admiral of the Fleet because the G.A. Senate promoted me into this position, and I will step down immediately should the *full* G.A. Senate vote to request or demand my resignation. At that point, I will very happily return to my estate on Obotymot and to my duties there as an Azula and as a Lady of the Royal House of Nordakia. As to the matter of sentiency for the Jumakas, seven G.A. member planets, including their home planet of Taurentlus-Thur, have already enacted legislation that recognizes Jumakas as sentient beings on their planets. Their rights are forever guaranteed there and they are legally protected while on the planet. To keep a Jumaka imprisoned on any of those seven planets is considered an act of slavery. Anyone who keeps a Jumaka imprisoned anywhere else in G.A. space will be arrested as a slaver should they ever set foot on any of those planets. I believe that in time, Jumakas will be recognized as sentient beings everywhere in the G.A., despite the efforts of one G.A. Senate Councilman to block such passage for personal gain."

"Perhaps I should also remind you, Admiral, that you have requested that we, the G.A. Senate Council, approve a Marine ground force and then forward such recommendation to the full Senate for a vote. Irritating a senator who will vote that initiative up or down will not improve your chances."

"I expect the senators to vote the way their consciences dictate, but I would be remiss if I didn't mention that the MGF is not for me personally, but for the citizens of the G.A. I get nothing from it except a heavier workload. I will say, however, that if the Senate ever wants to see the rule of law and order established in Region Three, it must approve the measure. If it doesn't, then anarchy, slavery, counterfeiting, and illegal drug production and dissemination will continue to flourish there. It's your choice, Senators. If you want me to clean up the region, I need the tools and manpower to do that. If I don't get it, you'll have to explain the continued lawlessness to your constituents.

"There's a matter I hadn't intended to bring up today, Mr. President, but as long as I'm here, I guess I will. The Denubbewa are back— in force."

"The Denubbewa?" the Senate President said. "I thought they were all but eradicated."

"No, not eradicated. Space Command gave them a good thrashing, but they keep coming back. A force of some twelve motherships and an estimated four thousand warships were recently spotted in a remote area of Region Three. SCI believes they're making preparations to take control of Region Three away from the G.A."

"This information seems quite convenient, coming as it does following your request for a major appropriation increase."

Opening a folder she'd brought with her, Jenetta handed several photos to the escort who was standing by her side. The escort then took the photos to the Senate president. "These were taken when one of our CPS-16s overflew a Denubbewa fleet a few months ago."

As the photos passed among the senators, jaws dropped. After they'd all had an opportunity to view them, the Senate president said, "How can they possibly have assembled four thousand warships here without anyone seeing them arrive?"

"Space command has been receiving sighting reports of Denubbewa ships for some time. I only learned about it when I returned from my leave of absence. We dispatched four squadrons of CPS-16s to see if they could locate them, and they did."

"Did they engage them?"

"The two CPS-16s that located them couldn't possibly destroy thousands of Denubbewa warships by themselves, Senator. So they pulled back and reported the find. My last message from that sector is that our people are waiting for our forces to arrive so they can attack this one small group of Denubbewa ships."

"One small group? You define four thousand ships to be a small group?"

"Yes, Mr. President. From everything we've been able to learn about the Denubbewa, this is a small group. We assume they're evaluating our defenses. When they attack, they'll reportedly come in numbers that will stagger the imagination. And if those reports are accurate, we don't have one tenth the number of ships and people we will need to patrol G.A. space properly and defeat the Denubbewa when we encounter them."

"Is this an additional request for an increased budget?"

"You have the evidence of what we face in your hands. We do the best we can with what we've got. But if you want us to finally gain control of Region Three, end the lawlessness there, and eradicate the Denubbewa threat, we'll need you to approve the requested MGF appropriation in addition to substantially increasing our annual appropriation for ships and personnel. Senators, the G.A. is roughly six times larger than it was when it only consisted of Region One, yet the Space Command budget is just two-point-one-seven times larger than it was back then when our biggest problem was the Raider organization. And speaking of the Raider organization, we know they control a significant amount of the slavery, drug, and counterfeiting operations in Region Three. If left unchecked, it could spread to Region Two and destabilize the law enforcement efforts we've managed to put in place there only with the help of the Milori."

"Are you suggesting that you'd welcome the Milori Home Guard to join Space Command?"

"The Milori make excellent law enforcement personnel. Their Home Guard has been extremely effective at controlling crime in the sectors where we've permitted them to operate. It would help if we could train them to perform as Space Command personnel and have them adopt our method of doing things."

"I can't believe I'm hearing this," one of the senators said. "Next you'll be telling us we have to give them seats in the Senate."

"They *should* have seats in the Senate. They've shown themselves to be loyal to the G.A., and they are a member planet."

"They've applied, but we haven't formally recognized them as yet," another of the senators said.

"It's overdue. They should be recognized for the progress they've made in restructuring their society away from war and violence and at complying with G.A. law. They deserve a seat at the table."

"At this table?" one of the senators said, gesturing towards the bench that ran the length of the dais.

"I was talking figuratively and referring to the Senate body as a whole."

"The Milori question will be dealt with at the proper time," the Senate President said, "as will the issue of increasing your appropriation and establishing a Marine ground force. Tell us what you intend to do about the Denubbewa."

"We'll do as we've always done. We'll hunt them down and destroy them at every opportunity. They know they'll be treated as invaders every time we encounter them in G.A. space. They've had ample opportunity to leave, yet they keep coming, and in greater numbers every year. We must eradicate them, and we will work tirelessly in that regard. I don't wish to become a cyborg any more than you do, and we know that's what they intend for us should they ever get control."

"What is it you need most?"

"First, many more ships and the personnel to man them. It takes time to build ships and recruit and train new personnel, so the longer we delay, the more dangerous the situation becomes. Second, we need more scientists to help us produce the next generation of weapons. I'm not necessarily talking about arms research. Rather, we need better detection equipment that will help us locate enemies in the vastness of space. Once we find them, we can destroy them. It's locating and identifying the invaders that gives us the greatest problem. If we knew where the Denubbewa were in Region Three, we could send everything we have at them and destroy them. But until we have a better means of locating them, we'll just continue patrolling the Region and hope we run across them."

"What kind of equipment would you like to see in operation?"

"We currently have small satellites we can place into orbit around a planet to watch for problems and automatically report. Those satellites can hold a particular position in orbit or move around— with severe limits on their movement. I'd like to see something like our Distant Detect Grid. Like the satellites I mentioned, the new system should have the ability to travel great distances without intervention and report anything it sees other than natural phenomena. It should have *just* enough intelligence to search out ship movement and report their location. I certainly don't want anything like a cyborg out there, and nothing that's armed. We'd have to craft strict guidelines to prevent that. On an intelligence level, it should be like the small robots that clean our floors and bathrooms. They have one task and can never exceed it because of the strict regulations regarding the development of artificial intelligence units."

"And what would be required for that? How large would the appropriation need to be?"

"I haven't prepared any financial information that I can share at this time. Before a budget can be developed, we would have to establish all the requirements of the device and the design particulars. You asked me what I'd like to see and this has been something I've had in mind, although I haven't acted on it. I've been more involved in the MGF initiative. Before we learned that the Denubbewa were back in force with intentions of taking over the G.A., I'd believed that to be the most important budgetary consideration."

"I see," the Senate President said. "I would like to see and hear more about this automated sentry idea. Please work up some numbers. Do you have any other suggestions for finding and destroying the Denubbewa?"

"No, not at this time. All I can say is that this is the greatest threat the G.A. has ever faced. We must be prepared and equipped to fight them and destroy them whenever and wherever we find them."

◆

After leaving the Council chamber, Cayla said, "Jenetta, does this mean the declaration of sentiency will never happen?"

"Oh no, dear. This is just part of the political game. I told you it would take time and we had to be patient. Seven governments have now declared Jumakas to be sentient. That's a *significant* beginning, and that number will grow as your species travels freely on those planets and the citizens see that your species is as intelligent and peaceful as we've said. Don't get discouraged. Something worth having is worth working for and waiting for. We're already seeing excellent results, and I still have some more cards to play."

◆ ◆ ◆

Jenetta was working in her office when the vidMail from Christa arrived.

"Hi, sis. I've got important news to convey. While we were busy installing the new Neutrino Measurement Sensors in our ships, the Denubbewa fleet disappeared. After we failed to find them again, we started to seriously reflect on what prompted them to leave so soon after we arrived. We decided there just might be a communications transmitter dropped or planted by Sywasock that could somehow send a signal through our hull. Or perhaps someone from his ship might have planted a locator beacon somewhere on one of our hulls. We conducted the most thorough search you can imagine of the interior of the *Koshi* and the exterior of all ships. The interior of the *Koshi* was clean, as were the exteriors of all other vessels. But a cyborg was found clinging to the hull of the *Koshi*. We believe it had been there since we first found the Denubbewa ship. It had anchored itself on the sail area of the ship, behind a raised cover where it was almost impossible to spot. The cyborg's covering and the anchoring material were all made of Dakinium, so it blended in with the black hull and could also travel in our envelope. Here's the really upsetting part. The cyborg on the exterior had what my senior engineer has ascertained is a mass storage device for data. So the cyborg might have been recording every electronic transmission made in the area while we were at Lorense-Three and then also when we went to Quesann. We also believe it might contain all of the collected communications data from Sywasock. When he was taken off the *Koshi*, his communications were no longer blocked by the Dakinium hull. We have the device, so we'll be able to determine what was collected, but I believe the data may have been transmitted to the Denubbewa fleet when we first arrived in their vicinity.

"I'm now concerned that Sywasock was involved in the plot to collect data and I suggest you no longer trust him. The Denubbewa ship had to be a plant because it was conveniently close to where we would stop to investigate the derelict ship. The hull-hugger had the perfect opportunity to affix himself to the *Koshi* because we were occupied with Sywasock and the other Denubbewa. I'm very glad I chose not to share any accurate military data with that tin-head. Were I there at Quesann right now, I would walk into the holding area with a laser pistol and end his undercover activity permanently.

"Anyway, I wanted to pass this information on to you as soon as possible. I'm appending a file containing all the encrypted data we were able to extract from the collection device. Perhaps SCI can evaluate the potential damage. And perhaps there might be something of use to us in there, such as a secret communication between Sywasock and the hull-hugger.

"We haven't been able to again locate the Denubbewa fleet, so we're returning to our assigned territories. Perhaps we'll catch sight of another Denubbewa ship on its way to join their fleet."

"Christa Marie Carver, Commander, Captain of the GSC *Koshi* in Region Three. End of message."

Jenetta stared at the video screen long after the image of Christa faded to black and the Space Command logo appeared and filled the screen. Her mind was racing with thoughts of the potential subterfuge perpetrated by Sywasock. She scowled when she thought of the comments by others that the Denubbewa were not devious. If they hadn't been in the past, they were making up for lost time now.

Jenetta appended the data file sent by Christa to a message she then sent to Admiral Bradlee at SCI as a Priority One. In the message, she related the pertinent facts reported by Christa and asked Admiral Bradlee to investigate and try to determine if any lasting damage might have been caused by the Denubbewa having access to the information in the file.

◆ ◆ ◆

"She's damned impertinent," Senator Fluessa, President of the G.A. Senate, said as he and six other Council members sat eating dinner.

"She was disappointed that we won't approve sentiency for the Jumakas," R.J. Witherea, the senator from Eprikal, said. "I fully support that issue. Jumakas are obviously sentient."

"That's not *my* fault. It's that idiot Sloasku. He won't support my reelection as President of the Council if I allow that resolution to go to the Senate floor."

"Why does he even care?"

"He owns a company that raises Jumakas and provides them to security companies. I've heard he owns thousands, leased to companies all over the planet Kethewit. He'd be bankrupted overnight if he had to free them all."

"He has other companies."

"Nothing as profitable as the security company. The people who lease the animals have to feed them, shelter them, and provide full health care. So he just sits back and collects his monthly payments. It's been illegal to remove a Jumaka from Taurentlus-Thur for a couple of decades, so he has no competition. He began by exporting them when it was legal, then turned to smuggling them off the planet when it was made illegal, until the government really cracked down. That's when he began breeding them. I've heard the females usually have litters of three to seven and can have three litters a year."

"Carver mentioned in her first A.B. meeting that she has a dozen now."

"Yeah, I heard that. But the government officials on Taurentlus-Thur don't object to her having a dozen Jumakas because hers are free to leave at any time."

"So *she* says."

"Yes, but the two that are always by her side say so also."

"But what if word leaked out that she was holding the others hostage on her estate in order to keep these two in line?" one of the other senators asked.

"I thought of that, but it wouldn't work. She's had far too many visitors to her estate on Obotymot and they've all seen that the others aren't caged or being held against their will. I don't know why she's so upset. Obotymot, Nordakia, and Earth have all declared the animals sentient. And now several more have declared them sentient. She's getting what she wants. Eventually, as she said, the entire nation will one day acknowledge their sentiency."

"Everywhere except on Kethewit."

"Yes, except on Kethewit. But Sloasku can't blame me. So Carver has no call to be impertinent and disrespect my person and my office. I've half a mind to send a resolution to the floor calling for her removal as Admiral of the Fleet."

"I've never known you to be suicidal before. The entire G.A. loves her. If she wanted your job, she'd have it in the next election. Before you try removing her, pack up your office because once you start down that road, there won't be a place in the G.A. where you can hide."

"I know, dammit. You don't have to remind me."

CHAPTER EIGHTEEN

~ July 12th, 2291 ~

"Admiral Plimley is here, Admiral," Jenetta heard her aide say. "Are you available?"

Jenetta reached towards the coffee table and lightly tapped a contact point on her view pad before responding with, "Of course. Send her in."

"Good morning, Loretta," Jenetta said from her informal seating area as Admiral Plimley entered her inner office. "Make yourself a coffee and join me."

Admiral Plimley walked to the beverage maker and prepared an espresso, then walked to where Jenetta was sitting and selected a chair on the opposite side of the coffee table.

"Business or pleasure?" Jenetta asked.

"Pleasurable business."

"Oh, good. I haven't had much of that lately."

"The Council decision still got you down?"

"I'm afraid so. But Cayla and Tayna are bearing up, aren't you girls?"

"We see progress," Tayna said.

"Yes," Cayla said, "It's slow but there is definite progress. You warned us it would take time, so we're confident it will happen."

"That's a very enlightened attitude, ladies," Admiral Plimley said. "And you're correct. It will happen."

"So, what pleasurable business is on your mind, Loretta?"

"Jen, I'm so happy to tell you what I just learned, and I couldn't wait until lunchtime. I'm beside myself with joy. This is just so fantastic."

"Then stop gushing and tell me so I can join you in celebrating."

"Okay, here it is. The Denubbewa don't have Dakinium."

"What? Are you sure? It sure seemed like Dakinium. If not, then what is it?"

"Well, it's Dakinium, but it's not."

"Now you've totally lost me."

"Let me explain it like this. When you brought us that door from Dakistee, we couldn't cut it or melt it or anything. We couldn't even scratch it. We knew that we had something incredible, but we couldn't duplicate it. We knew it was a complex compound, not an element, and yet we had no idea where to begin to create the compound. So our people spent months working on it without success. We knew we had one of the greatest finds ever, but it was no use to us if we couldn't reproduce it."

"I remember the stories."

"Then you'll remember that when we finally made some headway and produced a compound *like* Dakinium, we still knew it wasn't as strong as the material used for the door."

"Yes, I remember."

"But it was the best we could do at the time and we decided to sheath a small ship for testing."

"Yes, the *Colorado*. It was the first."

"And you were the one assigned to test it by Larry Gavin."

"Yes. I was his XO at the time."

"And when you proceeded with the final test, that of checking its performance speed under maximum power, you made history by being the first to create a double envelope."

"Wait a minute. Are you telling me what I think you're telling me?"

"Perhaps."

"The compound the Denubbewa are making is not the same compound we use for *our* sheathing?"

"You've nailed it. We believe they must have gotten a piece of Dakinium from— somewhere— and reverse engineered it, just as we did. But they must be perfectionists because their compound is identical to the original Dakinium you brought from Dakistee."

"Do you think they could have purchased it or the formula for making it from someone on Dakistee?"

"I don't know, but where else would they have gotten the original material or formula? I do know that the ship you brought here is not capable of generating a double envelope, and I assume no other Denubbewa ship has that capability."

"But how can that be? Christa brought it halfway back to Quesann in a double envelope. For the second half of the trip, the ship was inside the *Edison*, but for the first half, it was in open space."

"That's why we didn't even check the compound for its similarity to ours— at first. After all, it had traveled in open space in a double envelope. But once we learned their Dakinium is identical to the original, my people began trying to understand how it was possible, and we managed to recreate the situation. If the ship *initiating* the double envelope is sheathed in *our* Dakinium and our ship builds the proper resonance, the other Dakinium somehow temporarily borrows the resonance established by the ship generating the double envelope. Perhaps the ability is related to the way Dakinium absorbs energy and spreads it throughout the compound."

"So the second ship *allowed* itself to be enclosed in the double envelope? That doesn't sound logical. I thought the entire hull had to create the proper resonance."

"What can I say? We're still learning new things every day. You told us about the hitchhiker on the *Koshi*. That's another example of the phenomena. If the Dakinium worn by the hull-hugger invalidated the envelope, they would have discovered it before they ever started back."

"Okay. So assuming that everything you've said is accurate and the Denubbewa Dakinium is not the same as ours, they can't establish a double envelope on their own and are definitely limited to Light-480? Or at least whatever the top speed of their ship is in a single envelope."

"Exactly."

"But their Dakinium is stronger than ours?"

"Yes. But what would you rather have? Light-14,685.7 with an almost indestructible hull and the ability to phase shift so nothing can affect your ship, or Light-480 with an almost indestructible hull that is a wee bit more resistant to attack?"

"Easy decision."

"That's why our people stopped trying to duplicate the original Dakinium compound. We decided that double enve- lope travel was much more desirable. And our hulls are al- most as indestructible as theirs. The degree of difference is not significant."

"How many people know about this, Loretta?"

"About twenty, I would say. And I've already sworn them to silence under threat of cutting their tongues out."

Jenetta chuckled. "You didn't really say that, did you?"

"I wanted them to know how serious I was, but I'm sure they didn't believe I'd ever actually do it."

"Good. Let's limit this information to the people who al- ready know for the time being. There's no need to advertise it. And if nobody else knows, the Denubbewa can't get it out of them during interrogation. We don't want the Denubbewa go- ing back to the drawing board— or in this case, the lab— to try to duplicate our accident."

"I agree we should keep it to ourselves. But that's going to be difficult. The senior officers of the ships will have to know so they're aware they can catch any Denubbewa ship that tries to escape during a battle."

"Yes, you're right. The captain and XO of every ship will have to know, as will the bridge crew. And that means every single bridge crew, including the CPS ships. This is going to be the most widely known Top Secret in the history of Space Command. But— perhaps we can tell them without telling them."

"I'm afraid I didn't follow that statement, Jen."

Jenetta chuckled. "Sorry, I didn't express that properly be- cause I was still thinking about it as I spoke. What I mean is this: We tell the bridge crews that while we have Marc-One, the Denubbewa do not. We explain that *we* didn't even know about double envelope travel capability until we accidently tried to apply more power than the engines were designed to handle, so the discovery was an accident."

"I'm with you so far. I think most people already know that story."

"Yes. So our position is that while the Denubbewa have Dakinium sheathing, they apparently haven't learned about double-envelope capability, and we must keep it Top Secret so the metal-heads don't begin a campaign to learn how we accomplish it. We tell our people they should exploit the speed advantage we have in battle but must *never* discuss it or pass it on to anyone not authorized to know, which includes almost everybody who's not part of a bridge crew."

"You want us to lie to our bridge crews?"

"It's not really harmful if they believe the enemy has the ability but doesn't know they have it and are therefore not us-ing it."

"So we're lying to the bridge crews?"

"Well— yes."

"I love it. We let them think the enemy can employ it should they learn about it, so they must not learn about it from us. That will be even better than simply telling them not to speak about it because they might be even more reluctant to speak about it than they would be otherwise. And if the enemy learned about it from one of our people captured in battle, they'd bust their tin backsides trying to make it work while never understanding why they couldn't do it. Uh, who will tell our crews?"

"I guess that's my job. They have to know about the Denubbewa having Dakinium sheathing anyway. I'll send out a Priority-One message to all ship captains with orders to share the information with just the bridge crews, stressing that no one else aboard should learn. When they go Denubbewa hunting, they'll expect the enemy to only have a top speed of Light-480. That might be the reason our four squadrons didn't find the Denubbewa when they searched for them. They were probably expecting them to be much farther away than they actually were. I'm going to tell them to return for another search but to look much closer to the original location since the Denubbewa can't travel nearly as fast as our ships. Thank you, Loretta. You've brightened my day. Any other good news?"

"No, not yet. We're still investigating technology we found aboard the Denubbewa ships. There are a few things that have our people completely baffled and a few things they think they understand but haven't been able to make work yet. We'll continue to press on, Jen."

"Thanks, Loretta."

◆　◆　◆

When Christa was notified that a Priority-One message had just arrived from Fleet HQ, she dropped her dinner fork and hurried to her office.

Ten minutes later she leaned back in her chair and smiled. Space Command had an edge again, and it was a significant edge. She immediately activated her CT by touching her ring and contacted her XO, asking him to come to her office.

Mollago had the helmsman take the bridge and the navigator move to the helm so he could go into the Captain's office.

"Problem, Captain?" Mollago said as he approached her desk.

"No problem. An opportunity. I want you to take us back towards the area where we saw the Denubbewa fleet. We're going to search for them again."

"But Captain, we searched out to a distance twice as far as we estimated they could have traveled. We never caught sight of a single ship."

"But we were assuming they could travel as fast as us once the unsheathed ships were inside the Dakinium-sheathed motherships."

"Yes, Captain."

"That's where we erred, Paul. I just learned that the Denubbewa don't know they can create a double envelope. Without that capability, they're limited to Light-480. We never even looked for them that close to the original location because we assumed they were twenty times farther away."

"Uh, okay. And how did we learn that the Denubbewa don't know about double-envelope travel?"

"That wasn't made clear. All I was told was that it was extremely reliable information and that we must never talk about it. We can tell the bridge crew, but no one else aboard ship is to know."

"It's going to be hard to keep a secret like that."

"That's why we can only tell the bridge crew. They must know. But if anyone else is told, or learns about it, a full investigation must be held and the guilty party or parties will be sent to the prison colony on Saquer Major to serve sixty years in solitary confinement for passing on Most Secret information. That applies to anyone who learns of a breach in security and fails to report it."

Mollago's jaw dropped and then moved as he repeated the penalty silently. "I guess Space Command is serious about this."

"Deadly, and we'd better take it seriously also. Space Command doesn't want the Denubbewa to learn they can travel almost twenty times faster than they're currently traveling when they go to maximum speed."

"That makes sense. Did Space Command learn this from examining the ship we found?"

"I'd say there's a high probability that's the case. If they checked the helm settings they might have realized the ship was not capable of creating a double envelope."

"Then it was worth everything we went through to get that ship back to Lorense-Three."

"And then some. Okay, this is the last time you and I will discuss this. Right?"

"Aye, Captain."

"Good, because I don't want to spend sixty years in a penal colony. Have the navigator establish a course for us and get us on our way. When the course and destination are set, communicate that information to the other captains. It's not necessary to discuss it with them. By now they already know about the order. It's not necessary to inform the bridge crew tonight, but sometime over the next few days you should relate what I've told you to each and every bridge crewmember on all three watches. You can do it in a group meeting, one watch at a time, or individually. But make them understand that when the meeting is over, they *never* mention it again or *question* it."

"Aye, Captain."

"Good. That's all, XO."

"May I say something, Captain?"

"Of course."

"It's been months since we left Quesann after taking the Denubbewa ship there. We have no idea how far that Denubbewa fleet might have traveled."

"Calculate how far they could have traveled at Light-480 from the date we first arrived near them and add ten percent. That's the maximum distance they can be, and that's the farthest out we'll search. If you were the Denubbewa, had successfully escaped from an enemy fleet, and wanted to continue sheathing your ships with Dakinium, how long would you continue to travel?"

"I suppose I'd want to put some distance from the Space Command ships. I guess I'd travel for at least a month."

"Okay, so by that estimation, the Denubbewa are definitely within the area we're going to search, and the area we did search is well outside that area. Since we know that most of the ships we saw couldn't be sheathed by now, we're going to tear through space until we get a sizable blip on our long-range sensors."

"And if the Denubbewa learned their lesson and are keeping all of the unsheathed ships inside the sheathed motherships?"

"Then it's going to take a lot longer to find them. Let's keep our fingers crossed that they're creatures of habit."

"Aye, Captain."

◆ ◆ ◆

Over the next few days, the bridge crews were all told about the speed advantage. A number of them chuckled when first told they would spend the next sixty years in solitary confinement if they talked about the double-envelope issue with anyone, then blanched when told Space Command was deadly serious on this issue and that it included even discussing it with people who knew about it already, such as other bridge crewmembers. Jenetta had been adamant that the ship's scuttlebutt not include a single word about the issue, and she made the penalty so fearsome that no one would dare breach security. Of course, she was the only one who knew she would never actually imprison someone who violated the rule, but she might dishonorably discharge them from Space Command if letting the secret out could be traced back to them. Maximum secrecy was the only way to maintain the speed advantage as long as possible.

◆ ◆ ◆

For eleven days, the *Koshi* squadron searched for the Denubbewa fleet. And then, on the twelfth day, they got a small sensor hit. There was no guarantee it was the Denubbewa fleet, but they couldn't ignore the chance that it might be. Christa sent one of the CPS-16s in to snap some images at Marc-One.

When the *Mojo* returned to where the squadron had stopped, about eight billion kilometers away, it joined the laser link-up with the squadron. Captain Isladdo said, "It's a Denubbewa fleet, Commander. There aren't nearly as many as we saw at the other site, but there are enough to keep us busy for a few minutes."

"Put your images up, Captain."

Initially, only warships were visible in the small images that filled the large monitor at the front of the *Koshi* bridge. But when the images taken with the Neutrino Measurement Sensor were displayed, they could see all Denubbewa ships present at the location.

"Let's go with image seven," Christa said.

All but image seven disappeared from the screen and that image was enlarged to fill the monitor.

"I only see two motherships," Christa said.

"Yes, but there have to be over three hundred warships waiting for sheathing, and who knows how many are inside the motherships."

"I was really hoping we'd find the entire fleet."

"Fifteen percent or so is better than nothing, Captain," Mollago said.

"When will the other squadrons arrive, Commander?" Isladdo asked.

"We're not going to wait for them. We can't risk losing this group."

"There are an awful lot of ships out there."

"Everyone stand down for fifteen minutes. I'm going to prepare a battle plan and then we'll go in. Now that our hull-hugger is gone, they shouldn't know we're here."

Eighteen minutes later, Christa returned to the bridge and gave the tac officer a file number. A couple of seconds later an image appeared on the front monitor. What looked like a football playbook sketch was immediately broadcast to the CPS-16s.

"Each ship's path through the Denubbewa fleet is marked on the sheet, and it shows which Denubbewa ships each 16 will target and on what pass each warship will be destroyed. At the completion of each run, the ships will exchange roles, just as you've practiced. Since the motherships are so large, a single attack ship can handle each of them. The *Koshi* will target and destroy the two motherships, dropping ten bombs in each. Any questions?"

When no one said anything, Christa said loudly, "Is everyone ready to kick some Denubbewa butt?"

The chorus of shouts from the senior officers throughout the squadron that could be heard over the speakers on the bridge of the *Koshi* seemed to shake the monitor.

"Then let's get in position and prepare to rock the sector."

◆

Some fifteen minutes later, the CPS-16s were spread out in preparation for the attack. Four paths through the Denubbewa shipyard had been established. The area assigned to each bombing path was wide enough so that the 16s had access to every assigned target and they wouldn't have to cross paths with other 16s. With six ships on each flight path, the 16s would always have a target until all warships had been destroyed. Each aligned pair would function as a spotter and a bomber, with the second ship in each pair actually dropping the bomb. The first ship in each pair was controlling the flight of both ships and would release the bomb from the second ship. It was necessary to do it this way because the ships were moving so fast during a bombing run that this was the only way to ensure an accurate drop. Hundreds of bomb drops had taken place in practice areas near Quesann before a pair of ships was qualified to participate in a live bomb run.

While the largest Denubbewa warships were significantly larger than Space Command's battleships, the motherships made them all appear like a swarm of insects at a picnic. Each mothership was capable of housing thousands of warships, so if a mothership were to land on Earth's moon, the ship with its shadow could possibly be visible to the naked eye from Earth.

After releasing the habitat container with the pool and exercise areas so there would be nothing to interfere with the release of its bombs, the *Koshi* led the initial bomb run. Pairs of CPS-16s would deploy from the assembly area in each path less than five seconds apart. The tactical computer system aboard the *Koshi* would actually eject Space Command's most powerful bombs inside each of the motherships. The system would use the new Neutrino Measurement Sensor to calculate precisely when the *Koshi* would enter a mothership, which would determine when the bombs should be ejected beneath the ship. While cocooned inside a double envelope, a Space Command vessel could simply pass through any solid object, including Dakinium-sheathed ships, because it was out of phase with normal space/time. The bombs would be ejected mere nanoseconds apart, but with the ship traveling at Light-9790, the bombs would be properly spaced for maximum effectiveness. As the bombs were ejected from any out-of-phase ship and emerged from the double envelope, they were immediately at a dead stop back in the reality of the vessel being bombed. All Space Command vessels would be long gone before the bombs they had dropped detonated, but the explosions couldn't have damaged them anyway.

The *Koshi* completed its run and stopped to watch the attack site. Suddenly, a tongue of flame shot out of the opening where ships entered or left the first mothership, then another and another in rapid succession until all ten WOLaR bombs had detonated. Flames then shot out of the second mothership just as the first of the warships began to explode. The motherships would have been completely destroyed were it not for the Dakinium hull. As the bombs detonated, the force expelled through the entrance created an effect like a rocket exhaust and the motherships actually began to move. They impacted with warships on their periphery, crushing hulls and causing great damage to some of the ships they hit.

When the 16s completed their first bombing run and turned to attack again, they switched places so the lead ship on the first pass became the bomber on the second pass.

After the third pass, the Denubbewa ships that hadn't yet been bombed or crushed by the motherships finally began to move. That made it slightly more difficult for the attacking 16s, but no Denubbewa ships managed to escape the battle site until the fourth pass of the CPS-16s had been completed. By then, more than two hundred warships had been the victim of a bomb explosion somewhere in its interior. And the bombs weren't pint-sized weapons. They were all WOLaR bombs. It only took one to blow out every deck and bulkhead inside the warship. If the bomb landed in the center of the ship, there was little left inside afterwards. If it landed near the larboard or starboard sides of the ship, it would open the entire side to space. Whether it landed in the center of the warship or towards one side didn't matter. The warship would no longer be good for anything except recycling. The cyborgs inside the destroyed ships had probably been crushed or blown apart, but the Denubbewa working outside the ships were floating in space. Some were flailing as they tried to latch onto any floating piece of debris.

The destruction of the two motherships left the Denubbewa fleet temporarily without any real leadership, so things were obviously pretty confused at first. Despite the valiant effort of the 16s, fifty-one ships managed to get away, but that still left two hundred fifty-two warships and two motherships that remained behind and were now only useful for recycling.

"Well done, everyone," Christa said on a squadron-wide broadcast after the last bombing run. "It's too bad we didn't have a bit more help, but there was no guarantee we would locate any ships so I didn't want to pull the other squadrons away from their assigned territories. I guess we can assume that the rest of the Denubbewa ships we saw at that first site are also still relatively close, so I'm going to send the other squadrons an invitation to come join the party. Before we start to celebrate, we have some cleaning up to do. We have to pull everything together to keep it from spreading out too far, and a couple of 16s will have to babysit this pile of waste until a Ship Transporter like the *Edison* can arrive. Actually, I guess we're going to need every Ship Transporter and Quartermaster ship they can send. There's a tremendous amount of Dakinium here and we can't just leave it untended or the scavengers and smugglers will be sheathing *their* ships with it. All Dakinium-sheathed warships should be pushed into the motherships, if possible, to help ensure we don't lose track of any Dakinium.

"As soon as we clean up a bit, most of the 16s can go after the ships that managed to escape us here. Since none of them are fully sheathed, you should have no trouble locating them from a considerable distance. Again, well done. You did Space Command and the G.A. proud today. Carry on."

Over the next few hours the Dakinium-sheathed shuttles from the 16s gently nudged the floating debris either into a mothership or to the expanding mass of floating scrap. It was harder than it sounded because once set in motion, a moving body in space continues in motion.

◆　◆　◆

Once the mass of scrap was contained, more or less, Christa gave permission to most of the 16s to go after the warships that had escaped the carnage. Of the twenty-four 16s, twenty were permitted to go hunting Denubbewa while four would remain at the battle site until reclamation vessels arrived and took responsibility for the scrap. The 16s guarding the junk pile received orders to immediately destroy anything in the scrap that moved under its own power.

Christa prepared a quick map of the territory where each pair was permitted to hunt and loosed them upon the Denubbewa. She had them check the exterior of every ship to ensure there were no new hull-huggers hitching a ride before it departed.

With the excitement winding down, Christa sent invitations to the other squadrons to come help the *Koshi* track down more of the motherships and warships. She included before and after images of the battle scene because she knew that would convince them better than anything she could say that the Denubbewa were still in the area.

CHAPTER NINETEEN
~ September 10th, 2291 ~

Within two weeks all three of the other squadron leaders had replied, first congratulating Christa on her attack and then announcing that they were underway to join the *Koshi*. The 16s that had pursued the escaping warships had managed to track down and destroy forty-nine of the fifty-one that had fled the battle site. And during the search, two more Denubbewa battle groups had been discovered. The 16s that spotted them completed a flyover, taking images of the ships before continuing to look for the warships that had escaped the carnage of the first attack.

◆ ◆ ◆

"This is just so incredible, Christa," Commander Ashraf said as the four squadron commanders sat in Christa's office aboard the *Koshi* drinking coffee while they discussed the next step in their program to eradicate the Denubbewa. "You came back here and found the Denubbewa fleets and then destroyed a sizable chunk with just your squadron."

"I would have preferred to wait until you could all join me, but I feared a repeat of last time when we hesitated and lost the opportunity."

"In your place I would have taken the same action, Christa," Commander Kalborne said. "We've seen what happens when we delay the attack— we lose our quarry."

"So when do we attack the two battle groups your 16s found?" Commander Fareman asked.

"Is tomorrow too soon?"

"Actually, I'm ready to go right now— before they have a chance to bug out. They might already be gone if they caught sight of your 16s."

"Unlikely," Christa said.

"Why unlikely? They've got Dakinium so they might also have developed ways to sense it, just as we have."

"That's true," Lori said. "I wouldn't put anything past these walking computers."

"They still have a biological brain, so they're not really computers," Christa said.

"Yes, technically they're cyborgs, but they also have all kinds of built-in equipment in those tin bodies to make them supermen and superwomen, or super-whats-its."

"I don't think they have super powers," Kalborne said. "They just get electronic aids for storage and stuff. But hey, we all have viewpads and sensory equipment. It's just not part of our bodies."

"Don't forget our CTs," Fareman said. "They're built into our bodies. And SCI has a plethora of electronic gadgets they put into the bodies of their undercover agents."

"But the insertion is voluntary and can be removed."

"I'd be completely lost without my CT," Kalborne said. "I use it constantly throughout the day."

"There's one thing the Denubbewa get that I certainly don't want," Christa said.

"What's that?" Lori asked.

"A new set of phony memories after the old ones are involuntarily stripped away."

"I agree," Commander Fareman said. "So are we going to put a few thousand of them out of their misery today?"

"Let's do it," Christa said.

◆

Six hours later, after traveling at Marc-One, the four squadrons halted their travel less than ten minutes away from their destination. They had divided into two attack groups, each group proceeding to one of the two locations where the Denubbewa had been seen. A single CPS-16 from each attack group was sent to overfly the area and record images that could be used for planning the attack.

Christa was on the bridge of the *Koshi* when the scout from her group reported in.

"Uh, you're not going to believe this, Commander. They're gone. All of them."

"You're sure you're at the right location?"

"Yes, ma'am. The stars say this is the place. I see nothing and the DeTect sensors confirm there's nothing here. I flew through it six times from different directions with the Neutrino Measurement Sensor running. It didn't pick up a thing."

"Return to the squadron."

A minute later the other scout reported that there were no ships at the second location. Christa turned the bridge over to her XO and walked to her office where she set up a conference call with the three other captains.

"It's déjà vu. The Denubbewa are gone— lock, stock, and motherships."

"This can't be happening again," Commander Ashraf said.

"But it is," Commander Fareman said. "The question is why."

"It has to be in response to the attack at the other location," Commander Kalborne said. "The other Denubbewa must have sent out an alert when the first attack began and the two battle groups moved farther away in case we knew their location."

"We have ninety-six CPS-16s and four SDs, less the four CPS-16s I left to protect the Dakinium scrap from scavengers at the last battle location," Christa said. "We know the motherships are sheathed in Dakinium and that the unsheathed warships are most likely inside the motherships while they're traveling so it's not going to be easy to spot them while they're on the move. But we do have the neutrino measurement devices and we might get lucky. We know we have a significant speed advantage over the Denubbewa so they can't have gotten too far away in the two weeks since they were spotted. Anybody want to start scanning space here rather than heading back to your assigned territory?"

"I'm game," Commander Ashraf said. "I think the chances of finding some Denubbewa are a hell of a lot better here than at the territory I was assigned."

"I agree," Commander Fareman said. "I'd prefer to spend my time here, searching for an enemy we know for a fact is not far away."

"I'm in," Commander Kalborne said. "We *know* the Denubbewa are around here— somewhere. And there's a good chance there may not be any near the territory we were originally assigned if they've really assembled here to have all their ships sheathed with Dakinium. Let's split up and start searching this sector. And when we find them, let's not hesitate. Better that just fifty or so warships escape than we allow the entire battle group to get away."

"Okay," Christa said, "let's assume the Denubbewa wouldn't move closer to the last battle site if they were notified of the attack, and the probability that one or more of the warships that escaped has briefed them is high. Let's divide the remaining part of the sector into four sections and begin a search to find where the Denubbewa that were here— went."

◆　◆　◆

"I've just received a vidMail from Christa," Admiral Holt said to Jenetta when the secure call from his office on the base went through to her office in the A.B. building.

"How is she?" Jenetta asked.

"She seemed in good spirits when she sent this message. After learning that the Denubbewa are limited to Light-480, she took her squadron back to the sector where they'd seen them. When they searched previously, they'd assumed the Denubbewa had traveled much farther than they could have if they'd been limited to Light-480. The squadrons actually by-passed the area where we now believe the Denubbewa could be. So when the squadron returned, they calculated the maximum distance the Denubbewa could have traveled since they were last seen and worked back towards the original site."

"And?"

"And they found a battle group consisting of two motherships and three hundred three warships. Rather than summoning the other squadrons and waiting weeks for them to arrive, the *Koshi* squadron moved in alone. The final kill count is two motherships and three hundred one warships."

"Wonderful, Jenetta said. "That should put a bit of a crimp in the Denubbewa plans for the conquest of Region Three."

"Christa says she's summoned the other three squadrons to return and help mount a thorough search of the sector."

"They should already be there, given the distance the communication had to travel."

"Yes, they should be there already and searching for Denubbewa. Perhaps they've already engaged another battle group. I *really* wish we could get more timely information. These delays are maddening."

"The original sighting was twelve motherships and an estimated four thousand warships. That means ten motherships and thirty-seven hundred warships remain. That's an enormous battle fleet."

"Then we'll just have to keep whittling it down."

Jenetta chuckled before saying, "That works for me."

◆ ◆ ◆

"Fluessa, did you hear?" Senator Witherea asked. "The G.A. Justice Court has ordered that an arrest warrant be issued for Sloasku. They're searching for him."

"An arrest warrant? On what charge?"

"A hundred sixty counts of slavery."

"Slavery? Who did he enslave?"

"A hundred sixty Jumakas."

"But Jumakas can't be enslaved. They're non-sentient animals."

"Not on Taurentlus-Thur. They've been declared sentient there."

"But if he has the Jumakas, they're on Kethewit."

"But the hundred sixty Jumakas were captured and illegally removed from Taurentlus-Thur against their will *after* the export ban went into effect, so he never had a right to remove them. That means they are legally and technically still inhabitants of Taurentlus-Thur, and the government there says those Jumakas are now legal, sentient citizens of their planet. The Justice Court has agreed to hear the case."

"That'll never stand up in court since the Jumakas were removed before the species was declared sentient there. The export ban is immaterial."

"That's up to the courts to decide, but in matters of slavery they almost always go against the slavers. He should have freed his Jumakas as soon as Taurentlus-Thur declared them sentient. I doubt we'll be seeing Sloasku in Council meetings for quite a while."

"Perhaps not ever. Even if he's not found guilty of slavery, no one will want to associate with him and he'll lose the supporters that got him a Council seat."

"No big loss. Who do you think will get his seat?

"Carver!"

"What?"

"Carver. Admiral Carver."

"Nooo. She can't be elected to the Council unless she first gets a seat in the Senate."

"No, I'm not talking about that. I'm talking about Sloasku getting arrested."

"You've lost me."

"This is her work. She's behind this."

"Behind Sloasku's arrest? Do you really think so?"

"Without a doubt. She indicated that she knew who was responsible for blocking the resolution from going to the full Senate for a vote, didn't she?"

"Uh, yeah. I guess so."

"She couldn't force a vote, so she's removed the impediment. And I'd be willing to bet my seat that she's planned things to go this way all along. She purposely presented the

Jumakas at her first A.B. session so the entire G.A. audience would have a chance to assess their sentience long before she filed that request for an official determination and pronouncement. She knew that once citizens of the G.A. saw that little demonstration she put on, they'd be clamoring for us to declare the Jumakas sentient. Oh, I underestimated her. I knew she was a brilliant *military* tactician, but I didn't realize she was this skilled in political matters. We're going to have to watch her much more closely."

"She's an Azula on Obotymot *and* a Lady of the Royal House of Nordakia. She's reportedly handled a number of very important and delicate political issues for the Royal Family. She understands politics."

"Yes, I'd forgotten that. I was viewing her as just another pompous military drone. I won't make that mistake again."

◆ ◆ ◆

"We've completed a basic analysis of every square centimeter of the Denubbewa ship," Admiral Plimley said. "The good news is that their technology is generally inferior to ours. The bad news is that their technology is generally inferior to ours."

"Wait a minute," Admiral Woo said. "The same news is both the good news *and* the bad news?"

"Exactly. Being inferior to ours means that we have nothing to be overly worried about, but— we were hoping to find a number of technological advances in the Denubbewa ship that we could incorporate into our own ships."

"You said *generally* inferior, Loretta," Jen said. "Does that mean you found something we can use to improve our own capabilities?"

"We found one thing we believe is far superior to our technology. We've suspected for a very long time that the original Denubbewa empire is a very great distance from G.A. space. We have no idea where they first came to power, who it was that decided cyborgs would be a good idea, or even why they felt that way. The cyborg prisoners we're holding either don't know or are withholding that information.

However, we found an electronic device aboard the recovered Denubbewa ship that we couldn't identify so we decided to remove it with the intention of examining it closely in a lab. But while trying to remove it from the console on their bridge, we learned that it was connected to a vast assortment of equipment in an engineering space below decks. Nothing else was connected to that equipment so we've assumed that the device on the bridge is a controlling interface."

"What's the function of the equipment down in the engineering area?" Admiral Bradlee asked.

"We don't know— yet. The cyborg prisoners claim total ignorance. We don't believe them, but we haven't been able to ascertain with any certainty what the device actually does or is supposed to do."

"Do you have any *speculations* about the device's purpose?" Jenetta asked.

"We— think— the device might be a long-range telecommunications device. The equipment below decks contains a huge power generator, and based on our study of the interface we're pretty sure it's not a weapon. If the Denubbewa take orders from a controlling government tens of thousands of light-years away or even in another galaxy, they'd have to have a way to communicate that information in a timely fashion."

"Now I'm excited," Jenetta said. "Not too long ago I was talking with Brian about developing a faster method of communication. It can presently take two months for a message to travel from our farthermost border to the opposite side of our territory. With our travel time catching up with our telecommunications time, we'll soon be able to deliver important messages faster than sending them."

"Don't get too excited, Jen," Admiral Plimley said. "First, we're only speculating that it's a communication device. Second, we don't yet understand the technology being employed or the science involved. So third, we haven't been able to make it work. And fourth, we don't even know if the Denubbewa had gotten it to work. They might have installed it, discovered it didn't work as intended or wasn't reliable, and simply left it in a bridge console without ever using it."

"You seem to have settled on the idea that it's a telecommunication device so you must have *some* clue about its operation."

"A famous writer named Arthur Conan Doyle once had a story character say, 'When you eliminate the impossible, whatever remains, no matter how improbable, must be the truth.' We have eliminated most of the impossible, and what remains is that it appears to be a telecommunications device."

"What else haven't you eliminated?" Admiral Woo asked.

"Uh, well, we haven't eliminated the idea that they might have been trying to make a teleportation device."

"The principal cyborg prisoner did admit that the Denubbewa believed we were able to teleport bombs to places inside their ships and detonate them," Jenetta said. "It's possible they were trying to accomplish the same."

"Foolishness," Admiral Burke said. "Sending electronic signals, or even solid matter through space, might someday be possible, but sending a complex piece of electronic equipment like a bomb and rematerializing it is the stuff of sci-fi books and movies."

"A lot of things have been labeled foolishness," Admiral Woo said, "until someone comes along and does it. Look at powered flight attempts on Earth in the nineteenth and early twentieth centuries. People laughed at the people who tried it. Of course, some of the contraptions *were* pretty ridiculous, but every leap forward seems to start with ridiculous ideas. Look at the attempts to break the sound barrier, then a flight to Earth's moon, and then interplanetary travel to Mars. And let's not forget the naysayers, even eminent scientists, who said faster-than-light travel was completely impossible because one man, Albert Einstein, theorized that was the case. And then someone pointed to the fact that he didn't *really* exclude FTL as a possibility in his theories."

"I meant that teleportation without both a transmitter and a receiver to focus the signal is impossible," Admiral Burke said.

"Oh. I admit that makes it much less likely to be possible," Admiral Woo said.

"What other possibilities do we have?" Jenetta asked.

"Well, uh— someone suggested they might have been trying to open an entrance to an Einstein-Rosen bridge."

"A wormhole?" Admiral Yuthkotl asked.

"Yes."

"More sci-fi nonsense," Yuthkotl said.

"As Lon said, all scientific investigation seems like sci-fi until someone proves it beyond a shadow of doubt," Jenetta said. "I prefer to keep an open mind about such endeavors because in my lifetime I've seen scientific investigation that was branded sci-fi nonsense at one time become scientific fact. Teleportation and wormholes would be wonderful, but I'll be delighted beyond belief if we can simply send messages across our space in one day."

"All three of the technologies we're working to prove or disprove," Admiral Plimley said, "involve transmission of a signal and thus require great amounts of power, plus some sort of external antenna so the transmission won't be affected by the Dakinium. Part of the device equipment on the Denubbewa ship included connection to a sort of antenna network that could be either raised or pulled back into the ship as needed. That's why we've focused on these technologies as our possibilities."

"Thank you, Loretta," Jenetta said. "We look forward to your next progress report."

◆ ◆ ◆

"Admiral," the chief secretary to the Senate Council said as the com call began, "I've been told to call and report that the Jumaka Sentiency resolution has been placed on the docket for presentation to the full Senate for a vote."

"Wonderful. Thank you. When do you believe that will happen?"

"Well, there's a great number of discussion topics ahead of it, so it'll depend on how quickly the Senate concludes all previously scheduled business. I'm unable to predict when it'll come up."

"Okay, I understand. Thank you for calling."

Jenetta leaned back in her chair after concluding the call. If the resolution wasn't brought up for discussion during the present session, it would die and have to be reintroduced when the senators returned from their winter break. The recesses always lasted six months because of the distances to their home planets. Space Command vessels would take them to their homes and then pick them up for the return to Quesann because the trips could otherwise take several years if the senators had to rely on regular passenger ship travel. It wasn't lost on her that bills were sometimes intentionally sent to the full Senate for a vote too late to be acted upon in that session and the process would have to start over again in the Council with the next session. In this way, the Council made it appear that they weren't delaying a vote when in fact they were trying to kill a bill surreptitiously.

Jenetta fantasized about how great it would be if there really were a teleportation device like the ones in books and movies where one stepped onto a small raised platform at one place and was instantly able to step down from a platform at the destination. The Senators would then have no excuse for not taking care of business more expeditiously. But then she realized that if the Denubbewa had access to such a transporter device, they could send an entire invading army through it overnight. And it wouldn't be possible to watch every single teleportation connection. Space Command would have to take responsibility for security at every location, with the ability to shut down the platform in an instant if there was a problem. "Perhaps it wouldn't be such a good thing after all," she said.

CHAPTER TWENTY
~ September 18th, 2291 ~

"Captain," Christa heard Mollago's voice state via her CT as she worked in her office, "we just intercepted an encrypted message sent to the *Seeker* from one of his CPS-16s. They've located a battle group and performed a flyover to capture images. Before transmitting the message, they moved a light-year away. We have the coordinates where they're waiting. Do we join them?"

"We most certainly do," Christa said after touching her Space Command ring to establish an outgoing carrier signal. "Send a confirmation to Commander Ashraf that we're on our way to join the attack group, XO."

"Aye, Captain. Navigation has already entered the course into the system and Helm is ready to push the throttle to the stops if you approved. Estimated time of arrival at the assembly area is three hours, eighteen minutes. Now engaging drive."

"XO, how many ships have been reported at that location?"

"The message says three motherships and about a thousand warships."

"Excellent. There will be enough to go around."

"Aye, Captain."

"Carver out."

"Mollago out."

Destroying three more motherships would bring the total to five of the twelve that were originally spotted months ago. But that still left a considerable number of Denubbewa ships in G.A. space. And who knew how many others there were or how many more were on their way. Regions Two and Three were so vast that there could literally be hundreds of

Denubbewa motherships and tens of thousands of unseen warships out there. It was a depressing thought. Fighting an enemy who had no home base, at least not one in G.A. space, was like shadowboxing. You could swing your arms at an opponent forever and yet never score a knockout. Christa had tried to get information from Sywasock regarding the origins of the Denubbewa, but he'd always told her he didn't know. Perhaps he hadn't known, but that seemed just a little unreasonable given that Christa now knew he'd been lying to her about other issues all along.

◆ ◆ ◆

The other three squadrons were already at the rendezvous point when the *Koshi* arrived.

"Welcome, Commander," Commander Ashraf said when a laser communication link had been established.

"We're happy to be here, Lori. What's the situation look like?"

"Three motherships and about a thousand warships, verified four hours ago. I didn't want to alert them to our presence if they're not already aware of us, so I haven't sent another reconnaissance flight yet. I've developed an attack plan along the lines of the one you created for your successful attack. If the situation is still the same as it was when they were discovered and you approve of the plan, we can leave whenever you're ready. I have a pair of 16s positioned twenty minutes out from where the Denubbewa were spotted. I suggest we send them in now, ahead of the main body, to verify the Denubbewa presence and ship locations. The 16s can then wait until we make the first bombing run and join up with us for the second attack run."

"Sounds like a good plan."

"I'm sending you a copy. If you approve, I'll send a copy to the *Khatanga* and the *Ottawa* so they can become familiar with the layout. If you want to make any changes, you can then forward a revised copy to them for distribution to the 16s."

"Great. I'll take a look and get right back to you."

◆

An hour later, all ships had a copy of Commander Ashraf's plan, which had been approved by Christa without modifications after the placement of the Denubbewa ships had been confirmed by the latest reconnaissance flight. As with Christa's plan for the first attack, every ship on the image was in one of four attack lanes, and each had been assigned a target number. The squadrons would not stop once they began their attack until every ship had been destroyed or had escaped. Upon completing a run, the ships would change roles and immediately go at the Denubbewa again. When the attack was over, the 16s would be authorized to pursue and destroy any Denubbewa warships that had managed to escape the carnage and get away from the battle site.

◆

The *Seeker* led the attack, depositing ten WOLaR bombs in one of the motherships. The *Khatanga* and *Ottawa* followed close behind, depositing ten bombs in each of the other two motherships. As the motherships were having their guts literally ripped apart, while any ships still inside were being crushed, the 16s were destroying the warships with one WOLaR bomb in each.

As with the bombing attack performed by the *Koshi* squadron, no Denubbewa warships managed to break out until the squadrons had completed their third run, and by then space was filled with floating hulks and ship sections, making an easy escape impossible. If a warship hadn't been damaged by a bomb, it was almost certainly damaged by collisions with other ships and ship pieces in any location where it hadn't been sheathed with Dakinium.

Also like the previous attack, there were cyborg bodies floating everywhere. Most had been working outside the ships when the attack began. Some were flailing about, trying to snag a floating piece of debris, but most were just incomplete pieces of what used to be working cyborgs.

As the final run began, Christa issued permission for up to twenty 16s from each of the other squadrons to pursue the escaping ships after the run was complete, and each of the 16s had left one of their shuttles to help corral the destroyed ships at the battle site. The squadron's commander would decide who went and who stayed to help with the cleanup. Four of the 16s from the *Koshi* squadron had been left behind at the last battle site, so all of the *Koshi's* 16s were permitted to leave. Within minutes, eighty 16s were leaving the attack area in pursuit of escaping warships.

◆

The four Scout-Destroyers gathered in an area near the Denubbewa destruction while shuttles tried to corral the floating debris. Two of the *Koshi* engineers sent out maintenance sleds with video cameras and guided them remotely into the destroyed motherships. The ten WOLaR bombs had left little that was recognizable compared to the way it had looked before, except for the Dakinium-sheathed warships that had been inside the mothership when the attack began. They hadn't been destroyed but were so entangled in the debris that they wouldn't get out without weeks of effort. And the task force had no intention of allowing them to ever get out.

"Okay, suggestions," Christa said as the four commanders and four XO's of each SD conferred via the monitor in each captain's office.

"How did you handle this problem at the last battle?" Commander Fareman asked.

"We didn't have this problem there," Christa said. "There were no DS warships inside the motherships when we attacked so we assumed that any warships in there had been crushed and were simply part of the scrap materials we saw inside."

"It seems logical then that there are still cyborgs entombed in the crushed ships," Fareman said.

"Yes," Christa admitted. "They will be dealt with when the scrap is separated for recycling at the Lorense location."

"What about the cyborgs that were floating around among the destroyed ships in space?" Commander Kalborne asked.

"What would the Denubbewa have done if the situation were reversed?" Christa asked.

"Probably dissect the Space Command personnel and extract their brains."

"Exactly. So I sent out the shuttles to bisect any cyborgs they located and get in a little target practice at the same time. We left their brains with their metal bodies. When my shuttles returned, there were only dissected pieces of cyborgs floating around."

"I had a couple of friends on the *Salado*," Commander Ashraf said.

"My sister Jenetta once said that when you're fighting an enemy that's totally ruthless, you must be just as ruthless as them if you ever hope to defeat them. I knew someone on the *Yenisei*. They never had a chance. The ship went to greet the strange-looking ship from another nation and was destroyed without ever receiving a reply to their hail."

"I didn't know anyone on either ship," Commander Kalborne said, "but there were friends of friends."

"I vote for more target practice," Commander Fareman said.

"I second the motion," Commander Kalborne said.

"We have a motion that's been seconded," Christa said. "All in favor?"

A chorus of ayes was heard.

"All opposed?"

There was only silence.

"The motion carries. The shuttle crews get target practice."

"Now, what about the Dakinium-sheathed Denubbewa ships that weren't destroyed?"

"When the 16s have completed their task of destroying the escapees, we'll let them have a little target practice of their own. We'll have one of the ships fly through the motherships until all the intact DS warships are located, then we let the 16s finish our work here."

◆　◆

When the 16s returned from their mission to destroy all escaping warships, the battle site had been cleaned up and the scrap was ready to be loaded into a Ship Transporter and whatever else would be sent to take the junk to Lorense-Three for recycling. The Dakinium sheathing that had been prepared for the warships couldn't be used for Space Command vessels since a double envelope couldn't be established, but there were innumerous other useful purposes for such nearly inde- structible materials.

Four CPS-16s would remain at the site to fend off possible scavengers until reclamation vessels arrived to haul the scrap away. The rest of the task force would resume their search for the Denubbewa vessels that were still somewhere in Region Three. It was assumed that the Denubbewa battle group just destroyed had gotten messages out informing other battle groups that they were under attack. The 16s left behind had orders to destroy anything that moved under its own power. Should it appear that any of the ships stuck inside the motherships hadn't been destroyed in the follow-up bombing, the 16s had orders to again pass through the mothership and drop a bomb inside any warship that seemed to still contain life.

Of the twelve Denubbewa motherships that were known to be in the sector, five had now been destroyed. Following a conference call by the four commanders, the squadrons de- parted to renew their hunt for enemy ships.

◆　◆　◆

"So this is the equipment you were telling us about in the executive session?" Jenetta said to Admiral Plimley as she toured the bridge of the Denubbewa vessel in the enclosed dock at the Lorense-Three shipyard.

"This is it, Jen."

"And you still haven't established its true purpose?"

"Not yet. A couple of my people want to turn it on and see what it does, but I won't let them do that until we have a pret- ty good idea of what it's intended to do, and what to expect."

"How do *you* propose to determine its purpose."

"That's the problem. I don't know. But turning it on with- out knowing what it does doesn't seem very prudent. We could destroy the entire shipyard. Perhaps that's what the Denubbewa were hoping would happen."

"Perhaps. Where do we go from here?"

"I honestly don't know."

"Have you spoken with the Denubbewa cyborg?"

"The one Christa brought back?"

"Yes."

"Yes, I did. At least I tried. But the SCI people were there ahead of me. By the time I was allowed in, he wouldn't talk with anyone. I guess the SCI people were a bit threatening or something. All he did was lie on the table and stare at me. He wouldn't even exchange greetings. Roger told me he had stopped responding to questions from SCI after about the fourth session."

"Too bad."

"Perhaps Christa can get him to talk. I listened to all the recordings she made. They seemed to have established a— rapport."

"I don't know. Christa told me she believed he was lying to her at times. I guess she played along and actually fed him erroneous information."

"Yes, I figured that might be the reason for some of the wild things she said about our weapons and travel ability."

"She apparently didn't want to give him any useful information in case he escaped or was released."

"I understand. But maybe it's not too late for her to reestablish their— I guess I don't know what you'd call it."

"Just call it what you already did— a rapport. Do you really think it's worth a try?"

"Why not? Or perhaps you could do it."

"Me?"

"Sure. You look and sound alike. You said you've done it before. You exchanged uniforms with Christa and visited Madu, the leader of the Dakistians."

"That wasn't official. It occurred while I was on leave."

"You can do this, Jen."

"That was before I became the Admiral of the Fleet. I have an image to maintain now."

"It's for the good of Space Command."

"Uh, I'll think about it."

"It's for the good of the G.A."

"I'll think about it, Loretta."

◆ ◆ ◆

"Good morning, Sywasock," Jenetta said as she entered the holding cell where the cyborg was still chained to a table.

"Captain, greetings. It's been a long time since we last talked. Have you been promoted? Your insignia of rank is different."

"I'm not Commander Christa Carver. I'm Admiral Jenetta Carver."

"Ah, yes. The sister. Or perhaps I should say the original."

"Yes, Christa's a clone that was made from me. It's not a secret."

"Yes, she told me how you were drugged many years ago and someone made two clones while you were asleep."

"That's correct. I have two sisters."

"And what can I do for the famous Admiral Carver?"

"I felt it was time we had a talk. Christa tells me you lied to her repeatedly and that you can't be trusted. Is that correct?"

"She said I— lied to her?"

"Yes. She said you claimed not to have information that we know you have."

"What information?"

"You know what information."

"I'm afraid I don't."

"You're lying again."

"I think I'm done talking."

"Very well. I guess the only thing left for me to do is schedule your termination."

"My termination?"

"Yes."

"Captain Carver told me I would be freed if I cooperated, and then allowed to leave G.A. space."

"Yes, I know. And that would have been the case if you *had* cooperated. Responding to some questions accurately and lying to other questions, or refusing to talk, doesn't fall under the heading of cooperation. Christa reported that you've lied, and I see you're still lying."

"I've told the truth."

"What you said about your home planet was truthful. We've verified that with the other cyborgs. But where the rest is concerned, we get a lot of conflicting stories. You really should have spent more time coaching your associates. I'm amazed they made you their leader."

"I'm not their leader. I'm just the first one to be awakened by your Marines."

"Then who is your leader?"

"I haven't seen my supervisor since I was put to sleep on the tables and locked in the hold. He wasn't there when I was awakened."

"Not there?"

"No."

"Is he with the others?"

"I don't know. I haven't seen or spoken with any of the others since before the supervisor put us to sleep."

"This supervisor— is there any way to distinguish him from the rest?

"He has a blue light on his forehead, instead of a red light, as do all supervisors. The higher the supervisor's rank, the more lights he has. I've seen cyborg supervisors with up to five blue lights."

"Why did you lie to Christa?"

"Captain Carver never asked me about our supervisor."

"I'm talking about the special equipment on the bridge."

"I don't know what you're talking about."

"You told Christa you're a maintenance worker. So you must know about the special console on the bridge that's connected to all that equipment below decks."

Sywasock paused for a second before saying, "I have no knowledge of that."

"Is that your final word?"

"Yes."

"Then— I'm sorry. I can't save you. We only spare enemies who are completely honest with us and who renounce their former masters."

"The Denubbewa are not my masters. I'm free. We escaped to be free."

"But you brought along a supervisor who locked you up?"

"We didn't bring him. He was somewhere below deck when he was supposed to have gone back to the main ship."

"Hiding?"

"Probably to avoid work."

"Why would a machine hide from his assigned duties?"

"I was a scientist on my planet. They took my body, but my mind is sharper than it ever was. Still, we get fatigued and we have to rest our brains. When we rest, our minds sleep while the electronic components recharge. We may have metal bodies filled with electronics, but we're not machines. The supervisor is also not a machine. He's just dedicated to serving the Denubbewa cause. I and my people do not share that mindless commitment."

"Yet you lie to protect their secrets."

Sywasock was quiet for about ten seconds, and then said, "I've tried to protect you and your worlds from unspeakable horror."

"Christa reported that you said, 'the safety of the G.A. depends on you releasing us' when you first spoke. But then you backed off and said you were only trying to get her attention. Now you're talking about protecting us and our worlds from unspeakable horror. Are you merely trying to get *my* attention?"

"I…"

"Yes?"

"We really do want to protect your worlds."

"We've gotten pretty good at protecting our worlds on our own. For example, Captain Carver and her task force have located one of the Denubbewa battle groups and destroyed two motherships and hundreds of warships. They know there are ten more motherships and thousands more warships, so they continue to search for them and will destroy every one of them when they're found."

"A drop in the bucket, as your people say."

"Explain."

"The Denubbewa have many, many *thousands* of motherships. So many they are like stars in the sky. And they have many, many *hundreds* of thousands of warships. What word describes a billion trillion?"

"We call that number a sextillion."

"Then the Denubbewa have sextillion cyborgs to do their bidding."

"All of them are soldiers?"

"No, many are production workers who only build military ships and weapons, or construct new cyborg bodies that will contain the brains of people from conquered civilizations. You have to realize that the Denubbewa have been working their way across this galaxy for many thousands of your years, absorbing all civilizations as they go. The tiny invasion force you discovered in your Region Three is only the very tip of the spear. Dozens more such forces are currently being assembled in preparation for coming here. I know because it was my job, and that of my countrymen, to bring them here. I didn't want the destruction of your worlds on my conscience. I've already done so much I'm ashamed of. Our attempt to escape from the Denubbewa was an effort to stop the insanity we'd been forced to perform."

"And how were you supposed to bring these invasion forces here?"

"Eons ago, the Denubbewa conquered a people called the Locculo, who'd developed the ability to travel through what your people call wormholes. The Locculo called it Droux Parchur. Roughly translated that means Cosmic Jump. Captain Carver told me you have the ability to locate naturally occurring Cosmic Jump Gates, so you know what I'm talking about. She calls them Einstein-Rosen bridges."

"You told my sister that the Denubbewa had determined that wormholes are a myth, and that there is no such thing."

"I— wanted to shield you from the truth. I did— lie— about that."

"Even after my sister told you we already had such travel capability using naturally occurring wormholes?"

"It's complicated, Admiral. Wormholes are the most dangerous form of travel ever discovered. The Denubbewa believe it will allow them to establish complete domination of this galaxy in a matter of years. But although the Denubbewa gained access to the technology when subjugating the Locculo, they were never able to make it work the way they wanted it to work. By the time they understood what a momentous discovery they'd stumbled upon, they'd already wiped the minds of the scientists who had developed it, along with everyone who had ever worked on the project. That's why *our* brains were never wiped. They needed scientists who were able to think and reason, unlike the majority of cyborgs, which are mindless drones that perform endlessly repetitive tasks.

"The Cosmic Jump technology the Denubbewa acquired was fully functional from the first day, but it only permitted a few individuals to travel through the gate that was established by the equipment. To send more, you had to open a new gate, which is time consuming. The Denubbewa wanted the capability to send their largest ships through. So they forced my people to learn the secrets of the Cosmic Jump technology and build the equipment that would allow them to send motherships through. With an expanded Cosmic Jump Gate system, they'll be able to send battle groups anywhere in the universe in the blink of an eye. I'm sure you understand the danger that presents."

"You said the process has to be reinitiated for each jump. How much time are we talking about?"

"Not a great deal. I'd say about ten of your seconds. But the Denubbewa wanted to create a gate that would remain open for as long as they wanted. So we were forced to slave for dozens of years to learn and understand the technology that opens Cosmic Jump Gates between any two points the operators choose, and then make modifications so the gates could accommodate enormous ships. Now, once the expanded Cosmic Jump Gate is open, ships can pour through for as long as the power remains stable."

"How do you open your Cosmic Jump Gates?"

"We need to have a ship or satellite station at each end. Once the initiating signal is sent, the Cosmic Jump Gate begins to form and grow. It expands relative to the amount of power devoted to the gate. The size of the Jump Gate we can create is more than enough for a Denubbewa mothership filled with warships. After we arrived here via the original Cosmic Jump Gates of the Locculo, the ships that had come ahead told us about the metal you call Dakinium. They had acquired a small sample and had been working for many annuals to produce it in significant quantities."

"How did the first ships get here if you need a ship or satellite at each end?"

"Centuries ago, the Denubbewa sent ships out in every direction and at least one in each group had the original Locculo equipment that allows a few people at a time to go through. Key supervisors are required to travel back periodically to report their progress. Once the new technology was perfected, my countrymen and I were sent here to build the equipment that would allow the fleets to come here via the new Cosmic Jump Gate. For the first test, they sent three motherships fully loaded with warships."

"They sent ships out *centuries* ago?"

"Yes. Normal space travel is the only way to get anywhere if you don't have a Cosmic Jump Gate network already established or you don't know how to locate naturally occurring Cosmic Jump Gates, as you've done."

"And G.A. space was selected as the first target. Why?"

"The Denubbewa see you as the greatest threat to their plans they've ever encountered. Your Dakinium alone made it imperative they come here first because they want to stop you before you grow too powerful for them to overcome. The Denubbewa plan is to eventually rule the universe. After the first invasion force arrived here, we were supposed to return and then travel to a new location and build another Cosmic Jump Gate emitter somewhere else. But we stole the ship that contained the unit we'd built here so no more motherships could be sent until they built a new emitter."

"How long did it take you to build the emitter once you had arrived here?"

"We worked on it for about an annual because we didn't always have the right materials. When we needed something we couldn't get here, it would be sent though the Cosmic Jump Gate conduit from the Denubbewa home world, provided it was small enough."

"So the Denubbewa will need a year to replace the one we now have?"

"Yes. But possibly quite a bit more because they no longer have us to build it for them. They'll have to find new scientists somewhere and teach them the science and technology. But where we were building something that didn't previously exist, they now have complete plans and documentation for the construction."

"How difficult will it be for them to find new scientists?"

"I really have no idea. The Denubbewa leaders like to quickly subjugate the most intelligent members of any society they conquer because they know the more intelligent members are more likely to lead a rebellion. But they control so many thousands of worlds, they might have some they've held in reserve for just such a situation as this."

"If you only brought three motherships here, where did the other nine come from?"

"The Denubbewa who came here by normal space travel had orders to immediately begin building new motherships and warships whenever they entered a new part of space where materials were available. Then, after the Denubbewa leader here learned about your Dakinium, he summoned all ships in G.A. space to come to a rendezvous location and have a new skin layer applied. That's why you were able to find so many Denubbewa ships gathered in one place.

"Admiral, the Denubbewa want your territory, and more importantly, your technology. Your G.A. is next on their conquest schedule. And once they arrive here in force, you won't be able to stop them. All sentient life here will be crushed or turned into cyborg drones. And if you defeat the first wave, they will send another, and then another, each larger than the last— until there are only cyborgs left in this part of space."

CHAPTER TWENTY-ONE
~ September 20th, 2291 ~

"I had a most interesting conversation with the cyborg named Sywasock this morning," Jenetta said in the afternoon's private executive session of the A.B. held in her office.

"Did you go as Christa?" Admiral Plimley asked.

"No, I went as myself."

"You probably would have gotten more information if you'd gone as Christa."

"Any more information and I would've needed medics to carry me out."

"Medics?" Admiral Plimley echoed.

"Because I would've been suffering from shock. Listen to this," Jenetta said as she placed a data ring on the small spindle of the keyboard on her desk. There was no image, but the sound played through the wall monitor's speakers.

When the other admirals had heard the replay of the full conversation, there was complete silence in the room.

Finally, Admiral Bradlee said, "Oh my God. Many, many *thousands* of motherships, and many, many *hundreds of thousands* of warships, plus a sextillion cyborgs to do their bidding."

"Exactly," Jenetta said. "But we know we can still kick their butts in a fair fight. At least until they learn about the double-envelope capability that allows us to be out of sync with space/time."

"Sywasock said at the end of the conversation that he will work with us and cooperate completely. Do you trust him to keep his word, Jen?"

"We'll see. You heard me tell him that if he wants us to honor the promises made to him by my sister, he'll have to be one hundred percent open and honest from this point forward.

No more lies and no more silence games. He must think of us as his brothers and sisters just as he did of the people on his home world before it was invaded and everyone was turned into cyborgs.

"The first thing we should require of him is to explain to our best experts the use of the Cosmic Jump Gate emitter device he claims to have constructed here with the other cyborgs. Next, we have him or the other cyborgs—or all of them together—explain in minute detail the science and technology behind the Cosmic Jump Gate. If he has any drawings or schematics in his brain or the electronic storage devices in his body, he must make copies for us. When they're done explaining it, our people must understand it as well as he does, if not better. The Denubbewa allegedly got the original device from an alien race called the Locculo , and this group of Elobians were able to piece together enough of the science to create stable Cosmic Jump Gates that allow ships as large as Denubbewa motherships to cross any distance in the universe. We need to have that knowledge now if we're to have a chance of defeating the Denubbewa because one thing seems fairly certain. The Denubbewa will never stop trying to turn us into their slaves. Does anyone disagree with that?"

The other admirals in the room were silent, but as she looked around the room and made eye contact, all shook their heads in response.

"Do we have to call them Cosmic Jump Gates?" Admiral Plimley asked. "I've only called them wormholes all my life."

"I've always hated the term wormhole. An American theoretical physicist named John Wheeler is credited with the term, but I find it a bit repulsive. I'm going to call them Cosmic Jump Gates in all of my official reports to honor the forgotten race of Locculo who defined the science and developed the technology, but you can continue to use wormhole if you prefer."

◆ ◆ ◆

Twenty-five days later, Christa received a long Priority-One message from Jenetta. It contained a briefing of the situation at Quesann and Jenetta's discussion with Sywasock.

When the message was over, Christa stood up and paced around her office, thinking. She'd known the situation was bad, but she hadn't realized just how bad. But at the same time, there was hope. Forewarned is forearmed, and they now knew the basic history of the Denubbewa and the breadth of their plans. She'd had very little compunction about killing the Denubbewa drones before, and now she had none. For the most part, they were, as previously believed, mindless drones with no will of their own. They were no better than robots, doing what they were programmed to do. Some might actually consider it a mercy to destroy them. One thing was certain— the Denubbewa would never hesitate to kill any member of a sentient species and use their brain to create another mindless cyborg for slavery or free labor.

The *Koshi* was still operating in an area roughly twenty-five days away from Quesann for communications and roughly forty-eight days' travel time at Marc-One speed, so Christa realized the message from Jenetta had been sent before she learned of the second battle in this sector. If they'd been substantially closer, Christa would have ordered the ship to Quesann immediately. They hadn't had any more luck finding Denubbewa battle groups since the last encounter so the tally still stood at five motherships and well over a thousand warships destroyed. Any day now she expected to hear that the first of the reclamation vessels had arrived at the first battle site. When that happened, the reclamation ships would become responsible for guarding the scrap from scavengers and her four CPS-16s would return to the hunt. Once Quesann had learned of the second battle, they would have hopefully begun preparations to send reclamation vessels to that second location.

◆ ◆ ◆

"Message from the *Seeker*, Captain," Christa heard via her CT from the watch officer on the bridge. They've located another Denubbewa battle group."

"How large?"

"Four motherships. No warships in sight."

"Have navigation plot a course and engage at Marc-One as soon as it's ready. Send a confirmation message to the *Seeker* and inform me when an arrival time estimate is available."

"Aye, Captain. Edmunds out."

"Carver out."

No warships visible was a new twist, Christa thought as she rose from her bed and walked around her quarters. Two possibilities came immediately to mind. Either the Denubbewa were performing all sheathing operations inside the motherships, which had to be pretty inefficient because of the lack of work space, or they were simply keeping all warships hidden elsewhere while the ships were sheathed in order to provide a smaller footprint for the ships searching for them. A third possibility then occurred to Christa. Perhaps the warships that had already been sheathed had also been sent somewhere else as a way of distributing their resources. If so, it was going to make their effort to locate the Denubbewa three times more difficult.

"Time to the RP is estimated as seven hours, twenty-six minutes, Captain. Edmunds out," she heard via her CT. She hadn't activated a carrier to respond so she didn't have to sign off. Edmunds would know she received the message. She glanced up at the chronometer on the wall and decided to return to bed. It was 0429 so she would already be on duty when they reached the RP.

◆ ◆

"I understand the Cosmic Jump instruction is going very well, Loretta," Jenetta said when she arrived at Lorense-Three and stopped by Admiral Plimley's office.

"Yes, but who told you? Sywasock?"

"You mentioned it to Roger. He mentioned it to me."

"Ah, yes. Yes, it's going quite well. Sywasock is glad to finally be unchained from the table, and he's an excellent instructor. He started with the basics of Cosmic Jump theory and progressed quickly on to the finer points when he got a feel for the level of scientific knowledge his *students* possessed on the subject."

"You've explained to everyone that they're not to discuss envelope travel?"

"Yes. Repeatedly. And I've told them that if they slip up, they shouldn't try to cover their mistake. I've told them to just shut up and not try to talk their way out of it. They should just change the subject if possible. I've also told them that Sywasock believes we already use Cosmic Jump travel in naturally occurring Cosmic Jump Gates, but they may not discuss it with him at all. I told them he may try to compare his method with ours, but they were to say they weren't permitted to discuss our system."

"Very good. Did you also tell them that if they did, I would hang them up by their thumbs and let them stay like that for a full day?"

Admiral Plimley grinned before saying, "Roger told you about that also?"

"Of course. He found it quite amusing."

"I just wanted to impress upon them how important it was not to say anything."

"I understand. I've threatened worse over the decades. But I've developed a sort of paper-lion reputation because I've actually never done anything like that."

"Yes, that's the danger. I guess you just don't have enough Captain Bligh in you."

"No, I guess not. More's the pity," Jenetta said, the remark being punctuated with a wide smile. "So what's your evaluation of everything so far? Are we going to be able to use this technology?"

"I don't see why not. The only real problem is setting up emitters at both ends."

"Is it possible to use the emitters the Denubbewa have set up?"

"Sywasock says yes, but— there's only one pair right now that's capable of creating a Cosmic Jump Gate large enough for a ship."

"Okay. Later on, when there are more, how do you know which destination you'll reach?"

"Each emitter has an identification number. You key in the ID for the location you want and you go."

"So if the Denubbewa change the identification, you won't be able to perform a Cosmic Jump to their gate."

"Exactly. And vice-versa."

"Okay. That's very useful information. Make sure your students know how to do that. We'll want to change our ID numbers periodically so the Denubbewa can't use our gates."

"Of course. Uh, our *gates*?"

"I'm thinking ahead. I know you're just getting started and that there's bound to be a significant learning curve, but do you have any idea how long it will take for our people to learn everything Sywasock can teach them?"

"About the technology of the Cosmic Jump Gate emitters and the science? I'd guess, based on what Sywasock says, not more than another six months for just that part."

"What else is there?"

"While his scientific and practical knowledge of Cosmic Jump physics is extensive, there's a great deal more he can teach us. He has extensive knowledge of every piece of equipment aboard the Denubbewa warships and knowledge of other areas the Denubbewa were investigating. And— there are a number of his associates with practical knowledge we could use. But they're still locked up— by your order."

"Yes, I had to make sure Sywasock was being truthful before I let others loose. Do you believe they can be trusted to roam around this part of the shipyard?"

"I don't know, Jen. It's impossible to read them. And I admit that their ability to communicate with each other while never verbalizing a thing makes them highly suspicious."

"It's not only that fact that bothers me. It's that every other cyborg within range hears their thoughts."

"Sywasock says that's what makes them work so efficiently. They're able to perform work as a single entity with hundreds of eyes and arms controlled by one brain because they don't have to stop and discuss everything."

"He sounds like a recruiting agent," Jenetta said with a grin.

"Well— he also said that the peace and solitude he's had over the past months has been the first time he's been alone with his own thoughts for many years, and once he finally got used to it again, he enjoyed it. He speculated that if he has to remain as a cyborg, he'd like to install an off switch to his communication system so he can be alone at times."

"I can appreciate that. I certainly wouldn't want dozens or hundreds of others hearing my every thought. I guess it would be like on Earth centuries ago where cell phones and social sites combined to evolve into groupthink systems. And then colleges started to use the technology in classrooms to teach students because they said it was a more efficient way of learning, but some schools severely abused the system in the early twenty-first century. Instead of turning out young people who were better prepared to take on the challenges of leading in a world in crisis, groupthink actually turned many students into people who lost the ability to think on their own and who became forever dependent on others to tell them what to do and when to do it. Eventually, people outside the educational system realized what was going on and decided that enough was enough. Those methods were made illegal, but not before a few schools were actually burned to the ground by the student body they'd been trying to control like— mindless drones. At some point people really need a little privacy and don't want every thought in their head coming from someone else's brain or having their own thoughts being broadcast to the world."

"I'm glad I didn't live in those days," Admiral Plimley said, "especially that period when the advertisers got into it and began broadcasting cleverly disguised sales messages, like the way advertisers embraced subliminal messages back in the early nineteen fifties. Some people said it was the same thing but vocal instead of visual, while others said that it was more like hypnosis because you couldn't consciously hear the messages being input into your brain. I hope that's the closest we ever come to anything like that again. What's wrong with individuality?"

"Some people are just so weak-willed or weak-minded that they need someone to tell them what to do, and they usually turn to people in authority for direction. The people who can profit from exploiting that behavior are always ready to take charge— and then take everything else they can get."

"So what are we going to do about that vast knowledge base you have locked up?"

"Let Sywasock meet with them individually and tell them what we need. If they agree to cooperate, we'll allow them to begin training our people in scientific areas where they might be more advanced. But let's do it in rooms where electronic messages can't be sent or received. And let's keep them all separated for now. Only allow them to have contact with Sywasock. And make sure we're monitoring him electronically when he meets with others."

"Okay, Jen, I'll begin working on that right away."

◆ ◆ ◆

When the *Koshi* arrived at the RP, Christa was working in her office and she immediately established a conference call with the other three SD captains via laser com.

"Congratulations, Lori. I understand you found us a major battle group."

"Aye, Christa. We've located four of our missing motherships. But there are no warships in evidence."

"Have you sent a 16 in to get images of the interior of the motherships?"

"Not yet. I didn't want to spook them in case they can sense the penetration. Now that you're here, I'll do that."

"Okay. Let's get prepared. Once we have the images, we attack. There are four of them and four of us, so you each take one, and I'll take one."

"Here's the flyby shot," Lori said as it appeared on the monitor. "I've labeled the ships with the numbers one through four. Christa, since you arrived last, why don't you take number four. The *Seeker* was here first, so we'll take number one. Burl, you arrived second so take number two, and Walter can take number three. If anybody would prefer a different ship, speak up. I'll trade position one with anybody who wants it."

"I'm fine with two," Commander Kalborne said.

"Number three is fine with me," Commander Fareman said.

"And the *Koshi* is fine with number four," Christa said. "Now all we need are those interior shots so we can estimate the number of warships we'll be destroying at this battle before we turn them to scrap."

◆

Forty minutes later, the CPS-16 sent to take the interior shots returned to the RP.

"The ships are empty," the lieutenant in command reported.

"Empty?" the four commanders seemed to echo at once.

"Aye, nothing shows up on the interior shots."

"Are you sure you had the neutrino measurement device active?" Christa asked.

"Yes, ma'am, Captain Carver. We verified that twice after seeing the images. Then we made a second pass through all of the motherships just to be sure. They're totally empty, ma'am."

Christa sat back in her chair and thought for a second before saying, "Did you see *any* sign of life?"

"No ma'am. Nothing was stirring at all."

"Is the entranceway open or closed?"

"Wide open, ma'am."

"Thank you, Lieutenant," Lori said. "Stand by while we discuss this."

"Yes, ma'am. We'll be standing by."

After the lieutenant(jg) had signed off, Commander Ashraf said, "Well, this is one for the books. Thousands of warships have left the protection of their mothership."

"Maybe they decided the mothership wasn't offering very much protection," Commander Kalborne said. "It sure didn't help the other warships when we caught up with them."

"Some of the ones we destroyed must have gotten messages off first so the ones here decided to take their chances on their own," Fareman said.

"Possibly," Christa said. "I wonder how many of them have Dakinium sheathing."

"No more than half, if their progress was similar to that of the other motherships," Lori said.

"Where would they go?" Commander Fareman asked.

"Anywhere but here," Commander Kalborne said.

"Before we go running off to search for warships, we have to conduct a search of the motherships," Christa said.

"Are you kidding, Commander?" Kalborne said. "Searching each of those ships would be like searching a major, occupied city on any planet. It could take months to search all four."

"We don't have to search every broom closet. We'll just let some shuttles cruise around the center where the warships would have been and take some energy readings to see if anything appears to be out of the norm."

"Okay," Commander Ashraf said. "I'll send a dozen shuttles into number one."

"I'll send a dozen into number three," Command Fareman.

"I'll send a dozen into number two," Kalborne said.

"And I'll send a dozen into number four. Let's get this over with so we can go look for those missing two thousand or so warships."

◆

The searches turned up nothing. There was no indication of an energy signature or any sign that anyone had been inside any of the motherships recently.

"Commander," Commander Fareman said to Christa during a conference call following the search effort, "shouldn't we drop ordnance inside these behemoths to prevent them from ever being used again?"

"Yes," Commander Kalborne said, "We should make sure the Denubbewa don't return with expectation of moving in again."

"No, I want to leave them intact."

"Why?" Commander Ashraf asked. "Do you have a plan for them?"

"More like an expanding idea than a plan. I'm not ready to elucidate further just yet. Let's just make sure nothing happens to them yet."

Before leaving to search for the warships, each of the SD commanders assigned one of their 16s to remain behind and watch the motherships in case someone returned or some scavenger decided he'd like to trade up to a slightly bigger ship.

CHAPTER TWENTY-TWO
~ October 2nd, 2291 ~

"It's finally arrived, Adam," Aliana Shanara said excitedly to the Jumaka she'd purchased to be her personal bodyguard and companion as she entered her apartment. The seller had never named him, so she'd decided to call him Adam.

"You wouldn't believe what I've had to go through to get this. It's a proprietary design made for a special and powerful customer, and it includes a translation chip that you can't buy for love nor money. Fortunately, fear and intimidation always win out over love and money."

Adam sat on the carpeted floor, looking on passively as Aliana opened the package. "My contact at the company had to steal this from the R&D lab with the help of an associate in that section so it cost a small fortune, but it should be worth it to both you and me."

With the package finally unwrapped, Aliana opened the box and looked at the collar. "It's attractive," she said. "I might get something similar made for myself so we look like a matched set."

Bending down, she motioned to Adam to come a little closer so she could put it on him. She fastened it loosely about his neck, positioning it so the microphone was over his larynx, then tightened it just enough that it wouldn't slide around. When she was done, she stepped back a couple of feet.

"There. Give it a try. Say something."

Adam made a soft growling sound but nothing came from the collar.

"I didn't hear a thing except your normal growl. I guess there must be a special way to activate it. Perhaps you have to give it a command or something. Let's watch a replay of that video where two Jumakas are talking at the Admiralty Board session. But first I want to change into something a bit more comfortable and then we can relax and see what they do to activate the collar."

◆　◆　◆

"We've found the final three motherships that were part of the original fleet," Commander Lori Ashraf said when the conference call among all four CPS-16 squadron commanders had been established. "Rather than immediately summoning the combined might of this group, I approved some flyovers. When we saw no evidence of Denubbewa presence, I authorized a closer investigation with fly-throughs. When we saw no evidence of warship presence, I sent some shuttles in to investigate. They report there are no warships inside and no indication of life or even any energy sigatures. It appears that the Denubbewa just turned the lights off and ran away, just as they apparently did at the last site. What are your orders, Commander? Do we remain here or leave a small presence here and go searching for the warships?"

Due to the distances involved, there was a slight delay when the conversation shifted to a different participant.

"We should leave three CPS-16s at that location and continue searching. The warships may have scattered to the four corners of this sector, but we know they're out there somewhere. That means that eventually we have to confront them, and it might as well be now. I'm going to notify Quesann, but it will be almost two months or more before a reply arrives here. We could all use a break so if you want to stand down for a week or two, establish a distant DeTect system using CPS-16s and relax a little. I've been notified that the Ship Transporters and Quartermaster ships have finally arrived at the first battle site to begin taking on the scrap so it will be many months before the cleanup there and at the second battle site is complete. I've received orders to return to Quesann so we'll be leaving now that we know about the final three motherships. I'm going to reassign my CPS-16s to temporary duty with you three commanders."

"Aren't we all being recalled, Commander?" Commander Kalborne asked.

"I've only received orders for the *Koshi* to return at this time. You'll receive notification from Quesann when they make a decision regarding your return. In the meantime, if you see any Denubbewa warships, take them down and show them no mercy because those cyborgs sure wouldn't extend any to us."

◆ ◆ ◆

"I've heard there are a lot of people who want to know where they can purchase Jumaka collars," Annette Carver said to her daughter at dinner. Cayla, Tayna, Ruby, and Jake were instantly alert and listening.

"Yes, I'm aware of the interest," Jenetta said. "Some people seem to believe that if they put one of the collars on their pet dog or cat, the pets will be able to talk with them. We've denied it repeatedly and tried to make them understand that if the animal isn't a Jumaka, the collar won't do what they want. But it does no good so I've finally given up and contacted Chamberlain Yaghutol. With the help of our legal people, he's already been working to set up a company to market the collars through stores on Taurentlus-Thur. Now we're also going to be establishing marketing avenues for sales to stores on other planets. The packaging will state in very clear wording that the collars are *only* for Jumakas and that no returns will be honored if the collar is being purchased for any other species. We've received estimates that there might be as many as ten thousand Jumakas off-world so we want to be able to supply collars for them. I've given instructions to the Chamberlain to send most of the collars we received with the initial shipment to the government of Taurentlus-Thur at no charge to thank them for the courtesies they've extended, such as waiving the export prohibition that allowed Dr. Wilkerson to bring Nicky to us."

"Is there any news regarding your request to have the G.A. Senate declare Jumakas sentient beings?"

"No official news. The bill was sent to the full Senate, but so far it hasn't been presented for a vote."

"What takes so long? All they have to do is say yes or no."

"They're politicians. Some have to find out how their constituents want them to vote, while others have to find out how the big companies want them to vote."

"What do the big companies have to do with it?"

"They frequently have interests in political decisions because changes in the law may affect their corporate profitability. If it does, they get their lobbyists to warn the politicians that if the measure passes, they'll cut off all election support and various other funds they give to those politicians so the politicians vote only the way the big companies want them to vote."

"What? That should be illegal. The only thing that should matter is how the people want them to vote."

"It is illegal, but because the people who get the money are also the ones who make the laws, they build in loopholes so they can accept money in devious ways. That's why they work so hard to reelected, while ignoring everything else. Most politicians are quite wealthy when they retire. That's just the way it is, Momma, and the way it's been for centuries in every society, big and small, that have genuinely free elections."

"It's shameful."

"Yes. The only governments where such abuse isn't so rampant is where politicians have term limits. They're voted in, they do their jobs, and they're gone— with no chance of running for office again. The dishonest ones still manage to fill their pockets as much as possible while they can, but they don't have the years and years necessary to develop the schemes and cronyism that allows them make million credit deals for their own personal benefit."

"Oh, have you heard from Christa?"

"Indirectly. She reports to Brian."

"How come she doesn't vidMail us anymore?"

"She's on a special assignment. All private communications are restricted because they might give away the location of her ship. No one on her ship has been allowed to send messages home for many months. I know she's okay, and she should be back here in about a month and half."

"Oh, good. I was beginning to get concerned."

"She's fine, Momma. And she's doing an excellent job for Space Command and the G.A."

◆ ◆ ◆

"I received a message overnight from Commander Carver," Admiral Holt said to the Admiralty Board meeting in closed session in the A.B. Hall. The aides and clerks were there, but the gallery was, naturally, empty.

"She reports that they have now accounted for all twelve Denubbewa motherships that we believe represented the first wave of a massive invasion fleet. As has previously been reported to this Board, five of the Denubbewa motherships were pretty much destroyed in early fighting. Since their outer hull is Dakinium sheathed, they appear to be intact from the outside, but the inside is definitely a different story. Each of those first five motherships was the recipient of ten of our most powerful weapons. After detonation of a WOLaR bomb, there's usually not much left that's recognizable so I leave it to your imagination to visualize what ten would do in an enclosed area. But we have a slightly different situation where Denubbewa warships with a Dakinium outer hull were inside the motherships. Undoubtedly, everything not protected by Dakinium is just a memory, but there's a good chance cyborg drones inside the warships survived the original attack. Commander Carver ordered bombing runs on the warships inside the motherships, so we're hoping all cyborgs have been killed.

"By now, Commander Carver has received orders to return to Quesann. I sent that order before the latest discovery, but I'm sure she was happy to account for all twelve before being summoned to return. However, we still haven't accounted for an estimated two thousand seven hundred warships that were actually spotted at the first Denubbewa assembly area where they were sheathing all ships with Dakinium. We have no idea where those thousands of ships have gone. They may be on their way out of G.A. space, they may be trying to hide, or they may be headed this way.

"That's all I can offer at this time."

"Thank you, Brian," Jenetta said. "How are we doing with the recovery of damaged Denubbewa vessels?"

"Everything that can be packed into a Ship Transporter, a Quartermaster transport, or a reclamation vessel will be returned to Lorense-Three for recycling. Additionally, we've been pre-filling the motherships with as much as we can cram into them. Once we seal the entrance, we'll try to tow the motherships back within an envelope since they're sheathed with Dakinium. We have shuttles standing by to watch for enemy combatants suddenly coming to life. When found, they're terminated on the spot. Although they were once biological beings, they're just killing machines now. We don't have adequate resources for rehabilitating Denubbewa drones. And we were certainly not prepared for the enormity of this task. We haven't even thought about the second battle site yet. I understand that one's going to be twice as bad."

"Thank you for your reports, Brian," Jenetta said.

Addressing the full Board, she said, "We have two priorities: one is to find those missing Denubbewa warships, estimated to be about twenty-seven hundred; and two, we must begin making preparations for a massive invasion by the Denubbewa. We fortunately might have some time before the invasion if everything we've been told by the cyborgs we have in custody is correct. They allege that the Denubbewa warship we have in the enclosed dock at Lorense-Three is the only one capable of establishing a Cosmic Jump Gate opening in G.A. space that's large enough to allow the Denubbewa invasion fleet through. They say the Denubbewa will have to send another scientific team to build a replacement emitter here and that will probably take significant time, if they even have another team capable of building an emitter. The cyborgs we're holding say they don't, but we also know the cyborgs have no control over the dissemination of their knowledge or information so there may be thousands of others that have absorbed the information, even if they're unable to use it at present because of their programming. The actual issue may come down to the fact that few cyborgs are allowed to retain their ability to think and reason. That may be how the cyborgs we have were able to make their escape. It might have been inconceivable to their supervisors that any cyborg would ever try to leave."

"It seems clear that we should concentrate on finding those missing warships," Admiral Bradlee said. "I move that we bring every ship in G.A. space that's capable of Marc-One to Region Three and have them start searching."

"There's that other wrinkle, Roger," Jenetta said. "All ships involved in the search will have to be equipped with a Neutrino Measurement Sensor in case the ships are Dakinium sheathed."

"Then equip them with that device."

"We would if we had a ready supply," Admiral Plimley said. "It will take months to manufacture enough devices and many more months to install them. I'm not saying it's not possible. It's just going to take time."

"The hundred ships we currently have out there have the device installed already, right, Loretta?"

"Yes, Roger."

"Then we should get them started with the search and just keep sending the rest to join the effort as you get them outfitted. Isn't there an old saying that a journey of a thousand miles begins with a single step?"

"Has anyone asked the cyborgs we're holding if they know where the others would go if they needed a place to hide?" Admiral Ressler asked.

"I doubt the cyborgs we have in custody would be entrusted with that information, Shana," Admiral Bradlee said.

"Didn't Jenetta say the cyborgs have no control over the dissemination of information? So if one knows, they might all know."

"You're right, Shana," Jenetta said. "Good idea. We'll ask them. It can't hurt."

"Okay, we have two ideas on how to proceed. Any others?"

When no one spoke up, Jenetta said, "Loretta, how long before you can start turning out those Neutrino Measurement Sensors in quantity?"

"We needed a hundred for the CPS-16s so my people really got rolling after a few days. If we know how many we need, I can come up with a schedule."

"We'll need one for every single ship in Space Command, even if they aren't sent out to look for Denubbewa. If every ship has one, ships that are dark to conceal their presence won't have to turn on their running lights in order to be seen by other Space Command vessels."

"Okay, one Neutrino Measurement Sensor for every ship in Space Command. I'd guess we can fill that order in about eight months, unless I give it top priority over everything else. Do I stop the construction of new ships to make the sensors?"

"Of course not," Jenetta said. "Eight months will be fine as long as we can begin installing the first ones within a month."

"Can do."

"Great, let's do it."

"Who's going to approach Sywasock and the others about possible concealment locations the warships might use?"

"I established something of a rapport with Sywasock during our first talk," Jenetta said. "I'll speak to them."

◆　◆　◆

"Hello, Sywasock," Jenetta said as she entered the room where the cyborg was waiting. Two armed security people accompanied her since the cyborg wasn't secured.

"Hello, Admiral Carver."

"How are you getting on?"

"Quite well, I think. All things considered."

"Good. Do you have any needs I can help you with?"

"I'd like to have a meeting with my countrymen."

"That will be possible very soon. Right now, we need you to continue with the work you've been doing. Once that's finished, you'll be reunited with your countrymen."

"Why can't I be reunited with them now?"

"It's an issue we call cross-contamination."

"You believe I'll influence them in some way and they'll influence me."

"Exactly."

"You're afraid we'll compare notes and decide what to teach you about our work."

"If you're being completely honest, as you've promised, there's no danger of that."

"And if I am not being completely honest and the others don't know enough to remain silent about it, they might say or do something that will provide proof I'm not being honest and forthright?"

"Yes."

"I've promised that I'll be completely forthright."

"Then there shouldn't be a problem."

"Except that I'm denied companionship."

"Only until you've completed the work you've started— for the reason I've already stated."

"So I should get back to work then."

"Yes, but first I've come here to put a question to you. It's the same question being put to all of the others."

"I'll answer it if I know the answer."

"Do you have any knowledge related to possible alternate rendezvous areas where Denubbewa ships would amass if the invasion effort began to fail?"

"Has the invasion effort begun to fail?"

"Wasn't that your goal?"

"Uh, yes."

"Then let's assume you were successful. Where would the Denubbewa ships go to reorganize?"

"I don't know."

"You've told me that the cyborg collective has no secrets. I believe you said it's like a single entity with hundreds of eyes and arms, all controlled by one brain. That means you never have to stop and discuss things because everyone has the same information."

"That's true."

"But now you claim you have no knowledge of alternate plans should things not go as planned."

"That information, if it exists, was obviously kept secret."

"How is that possible?"

"Most information is automatically stored in my body's memory banks so that the data is available to anyone who wants to access it. But some I'm able to retain in my biological brain. The Denubbewa supervisors are only able to keep lesser cyborgs in line because all their information is stored in their memory banks. Any surreptitious plans they try to make would be seen by all. Most cyborgs don't know that I and my countrymen weren't programmed as they were. While their ability to store information in their brains is extremely restricted, the overseers couldn't do that to us or it would have caused problems with our ability to perform the special tasks they require of us. Other cyborgs would constantly be accessing information they shouldn't be aware of."

"I see. Then your answer to my question is that you have absolutely no knowledge of alternate rendezvous areas in G.A. territory."

"No, not exactly. I have no knowledge of rendezvous areas in G.A. space specifically identified for use in case the invasion began to fail."

"But you know of other rendezvous areas for Denubbewa ships."

"Yes."

"How many?"

"Eighteen."

"How many are within five hundred light-years of the invasion point where you arrived?"

"Eighteen."

CHAPTER TWENTY-THREE

~ October 7th, 2291 ~

"You confirmed that information with the other cyborgs, Jen?" Admiral Bradlee asked during the discussion in the closed session of the A.B.

"Yes, Roger, I did."

"And there's no way they could have colluded to provide that information?"

"The cyborgs are all housed separately in areas where electronic signals are absorbed by Dakinium plating covering all of the walls and doors. We can't even use our CTs while in that area. The signal never reaches us. So the cyborgs cannot be sharing information. And what good would it do them to lie? We'd know the truth as soon as we checked out the locations. Statistically, at least one of the locations must be active as an RP."

"And you recorded all the information?"

"Of course. Every word was recorded."

"So do we mount a major offensive immediately?" Admiral Holt asked.

"I think we should hold off until we have enough ships with the new Neutrino Measurement Sensors installed."

"But that could take months," Admiral Woo said.

"Yes, Lon, but if the information *is* accurate, and if all the ships seen by our squadrons happen to be headed to the same location, we're talking about thousands of warships. If we barge in there with limited vessel support, some will escape. I want them all."

"But what if they decide to begin their takeover before we get there?"

"The information we now have suggests that the Denubbewa plans for the immediate future have been thrown into complete disarray. Since the Denubbewa still have the ability to travel via the personal Cosmic Jump Gates, we can probably assume that the remaining fleet here is still receiving orders from their high command, wherever that is. Given the damage our ships have been able to inflict thus far, they've probably received orders to maintain a low profile until they're reinforced by the full invasion fleet."

"I thought we had their only Cosmic Jump Gate emitter," Admiral Burke said.

"We have the emitter that was built here by the Elobian cyborgs," Jenetta said. "Our cyborg prisoners say it's the only one in this part of space capable of opening a Jump Gate large enough for ships to jump. But the Denubbewa still have the original emitters that allow personal transportation. In fact, they may have personal emitters in every single ship. Their senior people may be traveling back and forth daily."

"Oh, right. I'd forgotten about the emitter that only opens a small Cosmic Jump Gate. I wouldn't mind having one of those myself."

"Planning a little visit to the Denubbewa home world, Raymond?" Admiral Yuthkotl asked.

Scowling, Admiral Burke said, "Of course not! I meant it would be nice to have a network of them here so we could travel to Earth or other planets in seconds."

Admiral Yuthkotl chuckled and said, "Calm down, Raymond. I was just trying to inject a little levity into this rather somber conversation."

"Setting up personal travel Jump Gate emitters on various planets is not a wildly imaginative dream anymore," Admiral Plimley said. "Nor is establishing jump points for military or commercial vessel traffic. It will take time to build the equipment and test the reliability of the system, but we've already learned so much from the cyborgs Commander Carver found and brought to us that it's difficult to quantify. However, I would speculate that their information has advanced our science on the subject of Cosmic Jump Gates by many decades or possibly even a century."

"I'm as excited about the possibilities of Jump Gate travel as everyone else," Jenetta said, "but let's stick to the business at hand. We recently discussed the action we would need to take regarding the destruction of those thousands of warships. I would like to amend my recommendations at this time. I still believe we still need a Neutrino Measurement Sensor in every single ship in the fleet. But I wouldn't send every ship in the fleet to search for the Denubbewa warships. What I'd like to do is step up the production of the habitat containers we're attaching to the CPS-16s. I'm referring to the ones that carry and release the WOLaR bombs. The CPS-14s and CPS-15s are already equipped to transport them so all we'd have to do is install the special targeting systems in the CPS ships and train the crews in the bombing procedure. When we send them out, they can join the other searchers and actually participate in the bombing runs when we finally track the warships down. The larger ships, such as destroyers, might only get in the way.

"We should also recall all Scout-Destroyers, equip them with the Neutrino Measurement Sensor and send them to join the other hunters. And I think I'm going to start calling it the NMS instead of the Neutrino Measurement Sensor. We have eighteen likely locations so we should forget about searching all of Region Three until we've checked out those eighteen locations."

"I agree, Jen," Admiral Bradlee said, "on all points."

"Does anyone disagree?" Jenetta asked.

As she looked around the table, everyone shook their heads.

Admiral Woo said, "It sounds like a sensible plan. If we get lucky, we'll find those invading warships at one of the eighteen locations and wipe them out before they know what hit them."

"Would it be wiser to wait until we've checked all eighteen locations before launching the first attack and then attack all locations at the same time?" Admiral Ressler said.

"I think Shana has a point," Admiral Hillarie said. "If the Denubbewa think we've located all their RPs, they might move to an unknown area before we can get to them."

"We'll order the commanders to only send in ships from locations at least a light-year away when performing flyovers, and the ship must return without filing a report before it's back," Jenetta said. "Once all eighteen locations have been checked, the ships can move in and perform their bombing runs in a coordinated attack on the RPs where the Denubbewa are located. Good. Any other suggestions?"

When no one spoke up, Jenetta said, "Okay, we'll have quite a bit of time to think about it. I'm going to appear before the Senate Council because they need to be briefed."

"I wish you didn't have to do that," Admiral Bradlee said. "I don't like passing Most Secret information to them because they have more leaks than a colander."

"I understand, but they're the boss, even if they can't be trusted to keep their mouths zippered."

◆ ◆ ◆

"Good morning, Admiral Carver," the Senate president said. "Did you request this closed session meeting to discuss the Marine ground forces?"

"No, Mr. President. That issue has been dwarfed by other problems facing the G.A."

"Then tell us what you have on your mind."

"Before I do, I'd like to request that all aides and clerical employees leave this chamber and that all recording devices be turned off."

"Why?"

"The information I'm about to share with the Council is too sensitive for anyone other than a senior military officer or an elected official to hear."

"This is most unusual, Mr. President," the elected representative from the planet Sebastian said. "I protest."

"What is this information, Admiral?"

"I'll tell you when the room is cleared. If you decide my request is unwarranted, you certainly have the authority to invite the clerks back in."

The president made eye contact with Jenetta and then with all other members of the Council for a full minute before ordering everyone except the elected officials out of the room. Before his aide left, he gave him orders to turn off all recording devices and ensure that no one in the communications center was listening in or recording anything. When the room was clear, Senate Council President Fluessa said, "This had better be damned good, Admiral."

"It's not good, Mr. President. That's why I requested you clear the room and prevent anyone else from hearing what I'm about to report. I've already informed you of the threat we face from the Denubbewa. After many months of searching for the enemy, our ships located a battle group. We engaged the enemy and successfully destroyed two motherships and several hundred warships. Our forces continued to search and discovered another battle group. Throwing all our combined might at that second location, we destroyed three motherships and roughly one thousand warships. Those battles were a significant accomplishment because we lost no ships or personnel. Our fleet continued searching and finally located the remaining seven motherships. Unfortunately, all the warships were already gone. We estimate the missing warship count at roughly two thousand, seven hundred. Our weapons technology has so far proven to be superior, but we can't possibly protect shipping, or even planets, in Region Three with so many warships on the loose. But we have an even greater concern, and this is why I requested that the room be cleared. It's no secret that someone— or perhaps several someones— is leaking information on matters discussed in this chamber. Whether the information is being traded for favors or monetary gain or it's merely being overheard by waiters and attendants as Council members discuss Council business in the Senate dining hall within the earshot of civilian employees, this issue is far too sensitive to be leaked."

When Jenetta paused for effect, the president grew impatient.

"Continue Admiral." Glaring at the other senators, he said, "I promise you that *no one* will leak *this* information."

"Very well, Mr. President. Here it is— the Denubbewa have developed Cosmic Jump Gate technology that allows them to send an entire invasion force directly from their home space to any point in G.A. space in the blink of an eye. The motherships and thousands of warships we've seen so far represent just a *test* of the new system. We've been convinced by a cyborg who wishes to be free of the Denubbewa that the Denubbewa have many, many thousands of those enormous motherships and many hundreds of thousands of warships, and trillions of soldier cyborgs. They are capable of overrunning Space Command in a matter of days if that new technology is used for an invasion."

"And your source for this information is this defector?"

"Yes. He tells us that cyborgs are not volunteers. They were once biological beings. Their brains were extracted from their biological bodies and placed into mechanical bodies. Most have been brainwashed and reduced to the level of mindless drones. He reports that the Denubbewa have been on a mission for thousands of years to control this entire galaxy and eventually the universe. When they find a society with advanced technology, they absorb it and use the technology to further their goals."

"And you believe this defector?"

"I do."

"You believe he's being totally honest?"

"I believe much of what he's told us. He's been teaching our scientists about the Cosmic Jump Gate technology the Denubbewa acquired from one of the civilizations they conquered and destroyed."

"But you've said the Denubbewa reduce these cyborgs to mindless drones."

"That was always our belief, based on the available intelligence. Normally, they do turn the conquered into mindless drones, but now we know that's not always the case. They still need a small number of intelligent individuals to further their goals when science, medicine, and complex technology are involved. The cyborg who wants to defect, along with his fellow scientists who were also turned into cyborgs, were sent here to construct special equipment that would aid in the invasion. He's defected with the equipment they built so now the Denubbewa will have to send replacements to build the equipment they require. That buys us a little time to prepare— perhaps as much as two years."

"What do you require from us?"

"We must substantially boost our fleet strength. We need more ships and people. This threat is a thousand times greater than the one we faced from the Raiders, the Milori, the Tsgardi, and the Uthlaro put together."

"I figured that's where you were heading."

"Funding is, after all, the one thing only you can provide. With adequate resources, we can protect the G.A. from almost anything. Without the resources, all we can hope for is to slow the eventual takeover by the Denubbewa."

"And if you get the funding, what will you do with it?"

"My goal is to strike a blow to the enemy that will reverberate throughout their entire nation and show them that further attacks on us will lead to their doom."

"And how do you propose to do that?"

"I want to use their own Cosmic Jump Gate technology against them. I want to open a Cosmic Jump Gate to *their* home planet and send as large a force of our ships as we can muster to show them that coming here was the dumbest thing they've ever done."

◆　◆　◆

"Loretta, what would you do if you learned your budget was suddenly doubled?" Jenetta asked the next day in an executive meeting of the A.B. held in her office.

"Doubled? Well, after I picked myself up off the floor, I'd start making calls and spending money. First, I'd arrange to double the size of the Lorense-Three shipyard. I'd arrange for new enclosed docks, with at least two being twice the size of the largest dock we have at present in case we have to house any more Denubbewa warships. It also appears we may need a few Ship Transports which are even larger than the *Edison*. Then I'd start contacting firms we have contracts with and telling them to immediately double all outstanding orders for CPS-16 materials and equipment."

"Okay," Jenetta said. "Do it."

"What? Are you serious?"

"Perfectly. The Senate Council has authorized doubling our appropriation for the next five years."

"I can't believe it. How did you manage that?"

"All I did was tell them the Denubbewa plan to invade this part of space with thousands of motherships and hundreds of thousands of warships, turning everyone they capture into cyborgs."

"And they bought that?" Admiral Burke said.

"We have proof of the invasion beginning, and I reinforced that by playing a partial recording of what Sywasock told me. It took a little time, but they finally believed we're facing the greatest threat they could imagine. And I guess they can imagine pretty good. The CPS-16s have worked out really well for us. I proposed we expand that program significantly."

"I agree," Admiral Holt said. "We already have enough Scout-Destroyers to function as command vessels for fifty more squadrons. So we need twelve hundred more CPS-16s and the required habitant containers for ordnance to complete that function."

"So in doubling the shipyard size, most of the new docks will be devoted to CPS-16s and habitat container construction," Jenetta said. "Do we have a consensus on it? Or does anyone have a different point of view?"

One by one the admirals all acknowledged that construction of CPS-16s should be the primary focus of the expansion.

"Loretta," Jenetta said, "where do we stand on the Cosmic Jump Gate education? Are your people picking it up? I mean, are we going to have a cadre of people capable of guiding the new discipline through the development stages?"

"The people I assigned to the program are the best we have. I would have to answer yes to that question. When Sywasock is finished, they should all understand it as well as he does, and he was the lead for the Denubbewa Cosmic Jump Gate expansion effort."

"Good. And how much longer do you expect that to take?"

"It's difficult to say. The science is so new and so foreign when compared to everything we've accepted for so long. But I would say that within ninety days our people will be able to begin putting together a new Cosmic Jump Gate emitter. They might even have ideas for improving the one we have now."

"I think we should have a backup and a backup to the backup before we start improvising," Admiral Hillaire said.

"I agree," Admiral Yuthkotl said. "We should learn to crawl effectively before we attempt to walk and run."

"I've been hoping we could do both," Admiral Plimley said. "That's why I assigned everyone I could spare to this effort. We're not only going to do this, we're going to do it better."

"How are we going to explain the sudden increase in our annual budget to the media?" Admiral Ressler asked.

"With an honest and forthright reply that's a bit light on specifics," Jenetta said. "I don't think we should initiate a conversation about the budget increase, but someone is sure to notice the increased appropriation at some point and ask. So we tell them that the first priority of the G.A. Senate, Space Command, and the Space Marines is the safety and security of all G.A. citizens and the planets on which they reside. The increased appropriation will enable the military to greatly improve the security situation in Region Three, which has been only marginally protected since the Uthlaro ceded the region to us following the war they declared against the G.A."

"I like it," Admiral Burke said. "It's the truth, and yet we don't mention the predicted invasion. If people hear a massive invasion by the Denubbewa is imminent and we're all going to be turned into drones, there'll be riots in the streets of every planet and people will be boarding ships headed out of G.A. space."

"If we can develop a Cosmic Jump Gate emitter and we can use it to send a fleet of our CPS-16s to Denubbewa space, we should never have to worry about invasion again," Admiral Woo said. "We simply swoop in and trash their infrastructure so badly that they'll have to spend the next ten thousand years rebuilding."

"But will that stop them for good?" Admiral Ahmed asked.

"It didn't stop the Milori," Jenetta said. "As soon as they got over the shock of their first defeat, they came at us again."

"But after you laid waste to their home world, they called it a day," Admiral Burke said.

"They only stopped because the people rose up and killed Maxxiloth," Jenetta said. "If he had lived, he would have come at us again and again and again. But the Denubbewa might not have a group that can take down their supreme leader or leaders. Our biggest problem is a lack of intelligence. We don't *really* know who the Denubbewa are or where they come from. We don't know who's in charge or even the form of their command structure. We don't even know if the Cosmic Jump Gate used to support the first invasion experiment is in this galaxy. We're flying totally blind here, and it's damned uncomfortable."

"Somebody has to know," Admiral Hillaire said.

"Yes, but who? You've all heard the recordings Christa made and the ones I made. We both tried to get that information, but the cyborgs who will talk to us say they don't know."

"There was one conversation you had where the cyborg talked of a supervisor having a blue dot on his forehead instead of a red one."

"Yes, that was with Sywasock. He said the first level supervisor cyborgs have one blue dot on their foreheads, a ship's captain might have three, and the highest level supervisor cyborgs he knew of have five blue dots. So the more dots, the more responsibility and the more knowledge the supervisor has. We'd love to get our hands on one with five blue dots, but how do we find him— or it? We usually can't even get close to cyborgs. They open fire as soon as they see us and we're forced to return fire and destroy them."

"We need an inside drone," Admiral Bradlee said. "An agent drone."

"How do we find one who'll cooperate?" Admiral Woo asked.

"We don't," Admiral Bradlee said. "We make one. If the Denubbewa can program a drone, why can't we? We have a number of drones in those packing containers. Sywasock said some were there so they'd have spare parts. We just take one of the drones to be used for spare parts and reprogram it to work for us."

"And just how do we reprogram a drone?" Admiral Burke asked.

"And how do we insert it into a Denubbewa ship without them being aware of our presence?" Admiral Woo asked.

"Well, I don't know—yet." Admiral Bradlee said. "Hey, I never said it was going to be easy. Does anyone else have a better idea how we can locate and then retrieve one of those top-level supervisors with five blue dots on its head?"

CHAPTER TWENTY-FOUR
~ November 21th, 2291 ~

"Christa's here," Jake said excitedly as Christa and Annette entered the nursery. "Hi, Christa."

Celona stood up and smiled as Ruby rolled over and said, "Hi, Christa."

"Hi, Jake. Hi, Ruby. Wow, you guys have gotten so big since the last time I was here. You're as big as your parents now."

"Kyle and Kaycee are getting bigger too— but not as fast," Jake said. "Momma keeps reminding us we must be very careful around them, as if we didn't know."

"They're still babies, Jake."

"We know. And we're always careful. We know it will be several more years before we can really play, but we'll wait. They're able to walk a little now, so we're patient."

"I don't mind a bit that they're still babies," Ruby said. "I just like being with them all day. And I'm teaching Kaycee to talk."

Christa smiled at her surprise. She never expected the children would learn to talk from the two Jumakas, but it made perfect sense since they were together most of the day.

"The babies are doing wonderfully," Annette said. "They can stand without falling over and even walk a little, even though they're a bit unsteady on their feet. That'll improve quickly as their leg muscles strengthen with use."

Christa walked over and picked up Kaycee. "Hi, Kaycee. Do you have a smile for your Auntie Christa?"

As if she understood every word, Kaycee's face lit up with a big smile. Christa smiled back and then hugged the baby.

"Oops, someone's a little wet," Christa said as she held the baby in her arms.

Celona was by her side almost immediately. She took Kaycee and carried her to the changing table.

Meanwhile, Christa moved over to where Kyle was playing and picked him up.

"Hi, Kyle," Christa said as she held him out in front of her. "Do *you* have a smile for your Auntie Christa?"

Kyle's smile was as wide as Kaycee's. Christa wondered if the babies understood that she wasn't their mommy or if they thought she was Jenetta.

As Celona finished changing Kaycee, she brought her back to where Annette and Christa were standing.

Annette took the child and said, "Why don't you take a break, Celona. Christa and I will be in here for a while with the children."

"Okay, Missus. I'd like to freshen up a bit."

As Celona left the room, Christa and Annette sat down in two of the overstuffed chairs. Ruby and Jake came over and sat at their feet.

"Christa, have you heard?" Ruby said. "The resolution to declare us sentient has been sent to the Senate for a vote."

"No, I hadn't heard, Ruby. I just got in today. I've been far away in Region Three."

"Yes, we know. Jenetta has shown us maps of where you've been. It doesn't look so far away on the maps, but then she explained how long it takes for light to travel from there to here. It's a very long way from here."

"Yes, it's very far away. Uh, Ruby, have you ever considered going to a school?"

"Yes. Jake and I would love to go, but Jenetta says that has to wait until we're recognized as sentient. Jenetta says if that doesn't happen soon, she's going to hire a tutor for us. The tutor can also work with Kyle and Kaycee when they get a little older."

"Yes, they're still a little too young to understand. Terran babies don't usually start school until they're about five."

"That's a long time."

"Yes, but every species is different."

"We know. But it's difficult to wait."

"That's what most children say. They can't wait to grow up. Jenetta, Eliza, and I were the same."

"Did I just hear my name?" Jenetta said from the doorway.

"Hi, sis. I was just telling Jake that all children are anxious to grow up and be treated as adults."

"Yes, and once you're an adult you have days when you'd love to be a child again without a care in the universe."

"Yes, Jake honey," Cayla said. "Don't be too anxious to grow up. Enjoy your carefree days while you have them."

"Hi, Momma," Jenetta said to Annette.

"Hello, dear. You're home early."

"I heard Christa was in port."

"Uh oh," Christa said.

"What?"

"Whenever you hurry home to talk with me, I know I'm going to be saddled with a mission that will make me wonder if I should have taken my time getting here."

"Well, now that you mention it…"

"I knew it."

"Let's go have dinner and we can talk later."

◆ ◆ ◆

"How long will it take us to travel to all of those eighteen possible locations?" Christa asked after learning of the RPs where the Denubbewa might have gone.

She and Jenetta were sitting in Jenetta's study.

"We, meaning you and the other squadron commanders, must visit all of them, but you all don't have to visit every one of them. Knowing, as we do now, that the Denubbewa summoned all ships to come have their outer skin replaced with Dakinium, this is our best opportunity to clean house, so to speak. It's imperative that we destroy every single Denubbewa warship. Plus— we need to take one of the senior

Denubbewa supervisors prisoner. One with all five, or more, blue dots would be best."

"What? And how are we supposed to find a Denubbewa with five blue dots on its head among the millions of cyborgs that are either trying to escape from us or kill us?"

"We're still working on that one."

"I can't wait to see what you come up with."

"Roger Bradlee took one of the cyborgs designated as re-placements parts by Sywasock and his countrymen and turned it over to his electronics experts. They've downloaded its in-struction set and are now trying to replace it with a new set of operating instructions."

"And?"

"No success yet, but they continue to work on it."

"What does Sywasock think?"

"He says he doesn't know if it's possible but that it might be."

"But even if it is, how are you going to embed your cyborg into the infrastructure of the Denubbewa in such a way that they'll never realize it's a spy?"

"As I said, we're still working on that one."

"Why not just drop it into one of the warships like we do with the WOLaR bombs? We stuff it into a bomb tube and then hit the eject button while we're inside the ship. As it leaves the double envelope, it's immediately back in normal space/time and at a complete rest."

"Christa, that's brilliant. I'm surprised I didn't think of that."

"Okay, can the sarcasm."

"I'm serious. It's brilliant."

"*Enough* already."

"I'm really serious, sis. We've been discussing ways of putting it onto a maintenance sled just outside their scanning range and letting it fly into the Denubbewa fleet area where it would then climb into a ship when maintenance crews returned from outside. But it would take forever to reach the fleet on a sled if it started outside their scan distance. They might see it and question what it was doing so far away, or it might be noticed that there were too many cyborgs returning in the work party. Then we talked about moving one of the wrecked warships into an area where an emergency signal could be picked up by the Denubbewa ships at the RP and having our cyborg as the only one aboard. But we sort of dismissed that because having a wrecked warship even within a light-year of the RP might cause the RP ships to immediately vacate. But your suggestion is brilliant. The cyborg would already be aboard the ship so no one would question its presence there."

"Sis, I was joking," Christa said. "We can't drop a cyborg into a Denubbewa ship. Traveling at the speeds our ships attain while in a double envelope means we can't place the cyborg properly. It might come out of the double envelope and be inside a bulkhead. Or it might rematerialize in the overhead of a large storage hold. Or when the envelope dissolves, it could fall a hundred meters and be smashed. Should I go on?"

"Let me respond to those two. The first one will require some thought, but the second one isn't a problem. We put the cyborg into a Dakinium container like an eggshell to protect it. When the shell stops moving, the cyborg opens it and steps out."

"Okay but emerging inside a bulkhead is a very real possibility."

"Yes, it is, but then— maybe not."

"What do you mean?"

"Our goal has always been to travel as fast as we could."

"Of course. Go on," Christa said.

"Why do we need to travel as fast as we can?"

"We don't. We can travel at normal light speeds within a single envelope."

"But in a double envelope, it's always been a choice between Light-9793.48 or Marc-One at Light-14,685.7. However, we can build our double envelope and simply sit there without engaging the drive."

"Are you saying we should stop while we're inside the Denubbewa warship and then expel the cyborg?"

"Why not?"

Christa started laughing uncontrollably, and Jenetta joined her.

When they started to get their laughing under control, Christa said, "I think we just redefined the entire procedure. We've been traveling at full speed because that's the normal reaction to a WOLaR bomb that's about to detonate. But they can't harm us while we're in the double envelope, unless..."

"Unless what?" Jenetta asked.

"Unless the explosion had some effect on the double envelope, such as causing it to fail. I mean, we're talking about one of the most deadly forces in warfare."

"Yes, there would have to be some serious testing before we tried that. But that isn't an issue here. With your idea that we stop and release the cyborg inside the warship, there's no explosion to consider."

"You know, this raises a new question," Christa said.

"I'm listening," Jenetta said.

"Why do we need two ships for each bomb dropped? If we stop, drop a bomb where we know it would do the most damage, and then go on to the next ship, it would effectively double our capability. We'd only need one CPS-16 for each target."

"Hmm. All of our Dakinium-sheathed ships have the ability to create either a single envelope or a double envelope. We originally required that travel in a double envelope could only be engaged at maximum speed because we had learned that trying to create a second envelope over a first envelope caused a massive short-circuit. That's what happened when I commanded the *Colorado* during the initial space trials. And normally we want full power when establishing a double envelope. But now I see a need to change that. I think I'll have a lot to discuss with Admiral Plimley tomorrow. Want to come?"

"Heck no," Christa said. "I'm on leave. I want to stay here and visit with Mom while I play with the kiddies. But I'll come if you want me to."

"It's not necessary. I just thought you might want to come and hear what she has to say. It was your idea, after all."

"I'll let you tell me all about it tomorrow night after dinner. Now, if we're done here, let's go visit with mom and the gang."

◆ ◆ ◆

"What do you think, Loretta?"

"You came up with all this by yourself?"

"Christa came up with the idea of stopping inside a Denubbewa warship and ejecting the cyborg from a bomb port. Then we got talking about bombing in general and the fact that perhaps we no longer needed two ships for each bomb dropped into a warship if we can simply stop while inside the Denubbewa ship."

"Talking with Christa is like talking with yourself."

"Not really. And people are suspicious of other people who have conversations with themselves. Christa is an entirely separate individual with a separate life and separate friends. We simply share the same family, as do all brothers and sisters. I always think of her and Eliza as sisters who shared the womb with me after the fertilized egg split once and then again. We began to have different lives and experiences after we left Dakistee. We're completely different people now, even though we tend to have similar thought processes."

"I'll have to think about this. Off the top of my head, I can't see any difficulty with stopping inside a Denubbewa warship while maintaining the double envelope to drop off the cyborg Roger's people are trying to program. We stop now without dissolving the envelope to ensure there's no danger of collision when we emerge in normal space/time. But I'd be concerned about one of our ships being too close to a

WOLaR explosion, even while inside a double envelope. We'll have to determine a minimum safe distance from the force released in such an explosion. But— we should be able to slow the ship considerably as long as we create an effective lockout between single envelope and double envelope and then resume full power as soon as the bomb is dropped rather than maintaining a consistent high speed as we do now."

"I'll gladly accept that restriction of a lockout to improve our flexibility. Anything else?"

"Not right now. Let me think about this and share it with a few of my top people so I can get their ideas. But so far, I think the idea has great potential, Jen. The idea that we can immediately double our bombing capability is inspired. It's as big an advance forward as when you developed the idea of bombing enemy ships to begin with rather than assaulting them with missiles and laser arrays."

◆　◆　◆

"Loretta liked your idea," Jenetta said as she and Christa sat in her study after dinner.

"Which one?"

"Dropping the cyborg into the ship while we're stopped within the Denubbewa vessel. She liked the other ideas as well, but she wants to check with her people to see if anyone believes there's a danger from being in the proximity of the bomb when it detonates even when inside a double envelope. However, she was in favor of the variation where we slow down, or even stop, then apply full power to get clear before the bomb explodes."

"That works for me."

"Me too."

"How soon will I be heading back to my squadron?"

"In a hurry?"

"Yes and no. I'm enjoying this little break, but I also want to wrap up this business with the Denubbewa."

"We're on the verge of wrapping up business with this initial invasion fleet, but I suspect this war is just beginning. The

Denubbewa want our technology just as much as, or more than, we want the Cosmic Jump Gate technology they stole from the Locculo civilization. I haven't admitted it to anyone but myself, but even if we manage to locate their home world and flatten it, I don't believe they'll stop while even one Denubbewa still lives."

"I sort of feel that way myself, and it's the impression I got while talking to Sywasock. But I'm still anxious to wipe out every single one of the Denubbewa warships that are currently in our space."

"You'll be headed back soon enough. The shipyard is busy converting every CPS-14 and 15 they can get their hands on so those ships can function as bombers, and all ships are having the Neutrino Measurement Sensors installed. The four squadrons gave us one hundred ships to find and destroy the Denubbewa. When the next attacks begin, we expect to have over four hundred attack vessels. I'd like to have a thousand, and in time we will, but we can't wait around forever. As soon as we learned of the eighteen RPs, Admiral Holt sent orders to the CPS-16 squadron leaders to dispatch two CPS-16s to each possible RP location and perform flyovers to determine if there were any Denubbewa ships there. All ships were to be thoroughly checked to ensure there were no hull-huggers or beacon emitters on their hulls before they left. So we should be able to assemble a picture of what we'll be fighting without having alerted them to our presence."

"Do I at least get an estimated date?"

"Just be patient." With a smile, she added, "I'll give you at least an hour's notice before your ship has to be underway."

◆　◆　◆

"Good morning, Jen," Admiral Holt said as he greeted her in his office on the base. "Coffee?"

"Always. I'll get it. How about you?"

"I have a fresh cup on my desk."

As Jen walked to the beverage dispenser, Brian walked to the informal area of his office with his coffee and sat down in an overstuffed oh-gee chair. When Jen joined him, she took a chair facing his.

"Good coffee, Brian," Jen said as she took a sip.

"The beverage synthesizer was just replaced with a new model. It's now easier than ever to adjust the flavor to one you like."

"I've spent so much time tweaking mine since I arrived, I won't let them near it unless it breaks. I've got it just the way I like it."

"I like the coffee in your office. Now, what brings you here so early? Hiding from the Senate Council?"

"No, not today. I have a very important matter to discuss with you. It's one we've talked about before—Operation Springboard."

"Springboard?"

"Yes."

"I thought we decided never to talk about that again."

"As I recall, we said we'd never talk about it unless it was imperative that we do."

"And it's imperative?"

"Sort of."

"Okay, you have my undivided attention."

"In order to get the assistance of the cyborgs Christa found, she made certain promises."

"What kind of promises?"

"The cyborgs that are teaching us about the Cosmic Jump Gates the Denubbewa use are the last unbridled members of their society. The only other remaining Elobians have been turned into mindless drones. So Christa promised them that in exchange for their help we would reconstruct their original biological bodies from their DNA and put their brains into the bodies we create."

Brian didn't say anything at first. He just sipped at his coffee and stared at Jenetta. Finally he said, "I thought we were never going to create a clone unless the original body was dead."

"Their original bodies are dead."

"But not their brains."

"No. But we'll be putting the brain into the new body we create."

"I don't think it works that way. Our greatest medical minds say we can't perform brain transplants. I don't even know if we can create their original bodies without having the original to copy."

"We have their brains so we have their DNA. Does the equipment need more than that?"

"We don't know if it will work for their species."

"No, but it worked for Terrans, Nordakians, and Dakistians."

"According to the doctor in charge, those species are not that radically different."

"Brian, I'd like to have the people who duplicated Christa give it a try with the Elobians. You know what that Cosmic Jump Gate technology would mean to us, and we wouldn't do this until they've got the Cosmic Jump Gate technology working for us. If they did get it working, it would be worth every second we spend replacing their cyborg bodies with biological bodies. Will you do it?"

"How could I reject such an impassioned plea?" he said with a smile. "I'll contact the lead people from Project Springboard and bring them here to investigate the possibilities. But I can't promise we'll be able to create their bodies, much less install their brains in the biological bodies."

"All I ask is that you try. And please try hard. This is very important to the G.A."

CHAPTER TWENTY-FIVE
~ November 26th, 2291 ~

"Hello, Sywasock," Christa said as she entered the quarters where the cyborg was living. "How are you doing?"

"Captain, it's nice to see you again. I'm doing well. You?"

"I'm doing well also. I've heard you're making good progress with the Cosmic Jump Gate education. I understand your class will be building a personal transporter station as a sort of final examination test."

"Yes. They're brilliant scientists and they've picked up everything very quickly. It took us years to understand it, but of course we had no one to teach us. We had to work from lab notes and through examination and testing of the personal transport device."

"It does make it easier when you can ask questions of someone who knows."

"Yes. Have you finished destroying the invasion force?"

"We've eliminated all of the motherships, but we're still tracking down the warships."

"You've destroyed a dozen motherships? That's impressive. I don't believe any of the innumerous species conquered by the Denubbewa has ever destroyed more than one or two. And the defenders lost all of their fighting forces just accomplishing that."

"The Denubbewa are formidable, but we're far more formidable when someone enters our space with an intent to conquer us and turn us into cyborgs."

"I wish my people had been better prepared. When can we begin the process of recreating our former bodies?"

"Work has already begun on that. That's the reason I'm here today. In order to prepare for the process, the scientists will need a sample of your DNA, or at least the DNA from one of the other Elobians."

"DNA?"

"Deoxyribonucleic acid. It's a polymer found in the nucleus of a cell. It provides the genetic information they need to begin creating an Elobian body. The scientists will take a miniscule piece of your brain to examine and reproduce enough to begin testing."

"I see. I know what you're talking about. We have a different name for it."

"That was to be expected."

"How large a piece of my brain?"

"They only need a few cells, unless your cyborg body contains any other flesh from your original body."

"It doesn't."

"Then it will have to come from your brain. For initial testing, it can actually be from the brain of any Elobian. But when it comes time to produce bodies identical to the one you had on your home planet, they'll need a tiny sample from everyone. It's the only way they can produce bodies that are identical to the ones you had originally."

"And Admiral Carver agreed to this when she was cloned?"

"I told you she was drugged by an assailant beforehand, so no. I understand the process was slightly different with Jenetta and the other cloned people. The chamber where the process was started got samples of DNA skin flecks sucked up by air filters. But your metal body doesn't have any cells that flake off so they'll have to open the chamber where your brain is located and gently scrape a *miniscule* amount of cells off your brain. I'm assured it won't hurt and won't harm you in any way."

"I see."

"Anyway, that's a couple of months down the road. The scientists who'll be doing this have to plan every step before they start, and conduct a lot of tests on the DNA samples. Oh, and since none of us have ever seen an Elobian, they'd like to know what to expect so they know if the process is proceeding properly. Can you draw a picture of what your biological body looked like? And include basic measurements. It doesn't have to be a work of art. They just need an idea. For example, were you air breathers? Did you have arms and legs? How many of each, etc. That sort of thing."

"Yes, we were air breathers, but we didn't require the rich oxygen/nitrogen mixture you require. Instead, we ingested a significant amount of water each day and some of that was used to fuel our bodies. We originally had four legs. It took us quite a while to get used to balancing on just the two that are part of this body. We also had two arms culminating with hands that contained eight fingers. There were six fingers on one side of the hand and two opposing fingers."

"Any other appendages, such as tentacles?"

"No, just the four legs and two arms."

"How tall were you?"

"About your height."

"So that would make you a little under two meters."

"Yes."

"And how big around at the largest part of your torso?"

"A little over one meter."

"I see. Okay, I'll pass that on. And if you can draw a basic shape so the scientists know what to expect and plan for, it will help."

"I can do that."

"Wonderful. Before I go, is there anything you need?"

"Nothing you can provide, I'm sorry to say. I would love to have contact with my countrymen."

"I assure you they're well."

"I know. I've been able to view them in vids on a fairly regular basis, and some people here have recorded vids of me so they can see I'm well. We don't doubt your sincerity and we realize why you don't fully trust us yet. I have only to look into a mirror to realize that. I wouldn't trust me either, knowing what I do of the Denubbewa."

"We have a saying— 'Trust must be earned.' But from what we've seen so far, you're making a great deal of progress in that direction."

"I hope one day to fully earn your trust."

"I look forward to that day as well. Ya know, after I discovered that you'd lied to me, I suggested to my sister that you be terminated."

"Lied to you?"

"About your knowledge of Denubbewa plans and technology."

"Yes, I regret that. I didn't know you or your people well enough and I didn't think I should share the Cosmic Jump Gate knowledge with another government that seemed warlike."

"I realize we do seem warlike, but it's not the appearance that counts, it's the actions. There was once a leader on the planet of my birth who had a favorite slogan. 'Walk softly but carry a big stick.'"

"A stick is a branch from something called a tree. Is it not?"

"Uh, yes. A tree is a tall, perennial, woody plant. It has a main trunk and branches. The slogan means that you shouldn't act aggressively but always be prepared for aggressions from others."

"I see. A wise person, your leader."

"He was. Unfortunately, among politicians there are as many fools as there are wise people. The true leaders lead with dedication, intelligence, and sincerity, while the fools obfuscate, obstruct, and make outlandish and impossible promises, such as increasing free services dramatically while always promising to cut taxes. The fools only seek personal wealth or power, but the voters who believe those promises are the real fools because it's not possible to give more while taking less. There's another old saying from the same time period as the one I just mentioned. 'There's no such thing as a free lunch.'"

"I understand that one," Sywasock said. "Someone always has to pay for what others receive for free. And I know that power is like a narcotic to some. They are the ones to be wary of."

"It sounds like your society had its share of fools in powerful political positions."

"It did. The crime is not being a fool. The crime is being a fool who believes you're wise enough to lead when you are obviously only interested in enriching yourself."

◆ ◆ ◆

Admiral Holt stood up as Captain Lawrence Frederick Gavin, commanding officer aboard the battleship *Ares*, entered his office. The men were old friends. Captain Gavin could have been promoted to admiral a very long time ago but he refused to give up his command and swap his bridge chair for a dirt-side desk.

"Larry," Holt said, "welcome back."

"Good morning, Brian. Hey, what's going on? I haven't seen so many ships around Quesann since the Uthlaro armada attacked."

"It's all because of another invasion attempt. This time it's the Denubbewa."

"The Denubbewa? I thought we kicked their metal buns out of G.A. space."

"Some alien cultures just never learn. They're back."

"When are they expected to arrive?"

"They're not. We're going after them. And I want you to lead the charge."

"I'm ready. When do I leave?"

"Soon. Grab a coffee and have a seat."

Holt took his coffee from his desk and moved over to the informal area of his office, sitting in his favorite chair there. When Gavin had prepared his coffee and sat down, Holt began.

"The Denubbewa have a new weapon. They can send a massive armada through a Cosmic Jump Gate large enough for motherships."

"A Cosmic Jump Gate?"

"What we used to call a wormhole."

"Ah, I see. So someone finally made the theory into a practical reality."

"Yes. The Denubbewa tested it by sending several motherships filled with warships into Region Three. Luckily for us, the scientists who created the Cosmic Jump Gate device defected. They were supposed to return to the Denubbewa home world and build another one somewhere else, but they decided they'd had enough of working for the Denubbewa and stole the ship that contained the emitter they'd been sent to construct. Allegedly, the one they've built is the only one capable of generating and sustaining the enormous gate needed to send a fleet through. They decided it would be better if the Denubbewa never got to use it again."

"Interesting. And they defected to the G.A.?"

"Not exactly. They were hoping to get clear of G.A. space and eventually make it to another galaxy. Unluckily for them, they stopped to rest and recuperate just as Christa Carver happened to stop near them to check out a derelict they'd seen on their sensors."

Holt continued retelling the story until he reached the present.

"So that's the situation, Larry. We have about twenty-seven hundred Denubbewa warships sitting in Region Three. We believe they're waiting for the rest of the invasion force to arrive, but that might be delayed because we now have the Cosmic Jump Gate emitter they need."

"And Christa Carver knocked out twelve Denubbewa mother ships with just four squadrons of these new CPS-16s you told me about?"

"Yes. And with three other SDs as well."

"Then why not just let her finish them off?"

"Because of the size of the Denubbewa force. She's a commander, and we're sending every SD and CPS-14, 15, and 16 we can assemble. In total, we should have a little over four hundred vessels. I can't put that kind of responsibility in the hands of a commander, even though I know she's capable of handling it. I was stretching things a bit when I made her mission commander of the four squadrons, and that was only a hundred ships."

Gavin chuckled. "I understand, but it seems a bit— odd. As you say, she's capable of taking on that responsibility. But I also understand that you don't want the Senate Council to be second guessing your decision. And I know Christa understands. It won't be that many more years before she has that fourth bar on each shoulder."

"And when she does, there won't be any task I'll hesitate to assign to her."

"So when do I leave?"

"I expect to have the ships ready to travel in two weeks. By then the *Ares* will have one of the new Neutrino Measurement Sensors installed so you'll get a visual representation of all Dakinium-sheathed ships in your vicinity. Orders were issued to the squadron commanders already on location to send ships out to check every one of the eighteen RP locations I mentioned to you earlier. By the time you arrive at your assigned location, which will put the *Ares* in a centralized area relative to all the RPs, we'll know which RPs to attack and you'll be able to direct the actions of the four hundred ships assigned to your command. We've divided them into squadrons of as many as twenty-five vessels. An SD will lead each squadron and may also participate in the bombing if necessary."

"Have all of the crews practiced bombing with this new technique you say Jenetta has devised?"

"Yes, they have. The crews that had been trained in the old procedure say it's substantially easier and far more accurate. They simply fly into the target using the double envelope, come to nearly a complete stop for a moment, eject the bomb, and then engage the drive again. A second later they're far enough away that they couldn't be damaged even if they did-n't have the double envelope protecting them."

"How long after they release the bomb does it detonate?"

"About three seconds, which doesn't leave enough time for someone aboard the targeted ship to even think about disarming it, if that's what you're thinking."

"It was."

"There's no danger in that regard. If a Denubbewa did see a bomb fall into their area, there'd be nothing they could do. They couldn't disarm it and they couldn't escape the explosion. They wouldn't even have time to report it or say a prayer to their god, if they have a god to pray to."

"Poor bastards. If I was in their situation and still had some ability to reason, I think I'd say, 'Thank God.'"

◆ ◆ ◆

Since the *Ares* was in port, Eliza managed to get a couple of days' leave from her duties as Executive Officer. After playing with the children and having dinner, she joined Jenetta and Christa in Jenetta's study.

"Ah, this is the life," Eliza said. "Go to work in the morning, then go home at night to family and home cooking."

"I can arrange for you to be permanently stationed on Quesann, Eliza," Jenetta said.

"Uh, no thanks. I was just joking."

"I kind of figured that was the case."

"You know me as well as you know yourself."

"And I would love to be back aboard ship again, but I also love my children and love seeing them every night when I come home."

"Kaycee called me 'Mommy' earlier," Christa said.

"I imagine they're pretty confused about now," Jenetta said. They'd gotten to the point where they recognized me as Mommy, and now they suddenly have two other mommies. I guess it'll be a few more months before they can understand why they have three mommies."

"Maybe sooner," Christa said. "Both of them are really sharp."

"Yeah, before you know it they'll be entering the Academy," Eliza said.

Jenetta laughed before saying, "We just celebrated their second birthday two and half months ago, and you have them entering the service already."

"The years will go quicker and quicker. Have you decided what you're going to do after they leave home?" Christa asked.

"Leave home?"

"To enter the Academy. Are you going to continue as Admiral of the Fleet?"

"I don't know. I still have sixteen years before I start thinking about that. But I know what I'd like to do if I had to decide today."

"What?"

"I'd take a fleet of ships to the Denubbewa home planet and do what I did to the Milori home planet. Except with the Denubbewa, I wouldn't go easy on them and I wouldn't stop while any of them lived."

"Wow, sis," Eliza said.

"Wouldn't you? After what they've done to our people aboard the *Yenisei* and the *Salado*? And to all the innumerous civilizations they've crushed and turned into mindless slaves? And for all the civilizations they'll destroy in the future if someone doesn't stop them? These monsters have one goal. Everyone must think and act like them or they're destroyed. There have been Terran animals like that on Earth. You either accept their way of life or you die."

"They're gone now," Christa said. "Most of them died when that terrorist group got a nuclear bomb and used it against another terrorist group seeking to control the world, starting a nuclear war that stretched from the Mediterranean to the Pacific."

"I'd like to destroy the Denubbewa before they can come here and establish that same kind of twisted population control."

"We don't even know where the Denubbewa come from," Eliza said.

"We may soon," Jenetta said.

"What? How?"

"Thanks to Christa, we have cyborg scientists teaching us the secrets the Denubbewa have claimed from civilizations they've conquered."

"Cyborg scientists? I've never heard of such a thing. It sounds like an oxymoron. I thought cyborgs were all mindless drones."

"So did we until Christa brought us several dozen cyborg scientists. Even the Denubbewa have a need for creatures that can think, develop products, and translate things."

"Christa brought them to you? And neither of you ever thought to tell me?"

"It's not the kind of thing we can explain in a vidMail."

"You could have sent me a Priority-One message."

"No, I couldn't," Jenetta said. "You're not the captain of the *Ares*, and I can't send Priority-One messages to the XO unless Larry first authorizes it. And I couldn't bring Larry into it yet. That's for Brian to do. Protocol, Eliza. We must all follow it."

"Oh, okay. You're right. So tell me now. Tell me everything. Where did Christa find dozens of cyborg scientists and how did we convince them to work with us?"

Over the next hour, Christa and Jenetta told Eliza everything that had happened while she was away.

"Wow," Eliza said when Jenetta finished the story. "While the *Ares* has been cruising around on routine patrol in Region Two, you guys have been up to your eyeballs in cyborgs and Denubbewa warships."

"You're about to be in it up to your own eyeballs soon."

"What do you mean?"

"The *Ares* is going to oversee the destruction of those twenty-seven hundred Denubbewa warships."

"What?"

"Captain Gavin has been chosen to lead the task force of some four hundred ships. You won't actually be in the action, but the *Ares* will be coordinating the attacks and then responsible for cleaning up the mess afterward."

"Am I losing my squadron?" Christa asked.

"No, of course not. You'll probably have responsibility for directing the action at one of the RPs. And of course you'll have the responsibility of inserting a cyborg into one of the ships there."

"You mean like we discussed?"

"Yes. In the months since you first arrived here with the Denubbewa ship, SCI has downloaded all of the information from the data storage devices in every cyborg."

"Including Sywasock?"

"Including Sywasock. We have, literally, trillions of terabytes of data. Of course much of it is a boilerplate copy of data loaded into all cyborgs."

"What's a Sywasock?" Eliza asked.

"He's the lead scientist among the cyborgs. He's been instructing our people in the creation and use of Cosmic Jump Gates."

"Cosmic Jump Gates?"

"Wormholes," Christa said.

"I thought that was just a subject for discussion in theoretical physics since no one's ever been able to establish a— Cosmic Jump Gate— and certainly has never traveled through one."

"It *was* theoretical. It isn't theoretical any more. According to Sywasock, the Denubbewa fleet we're planning to destroy traveled here via a Cosmic Jump Gate he and his associates created."

"Seriously?" Eliza asked.

"Seriously."

"Has that been proven?"

"We're working on it. Our scientists involved in the effort have stated the science rings true and they now believe it will soon be a reality here. Imagine, we can use it to zip across G.A. space from one end to the other between any points where we have paired Cosmic Jump Gate emitters in the blink of an eye."

"Wow!"

"Exactly."

"Does the Senate Council know about this?"

"Most of it," Jenetta said. "They know about the Cosmic Jump Gate technology. But I didn't want to cloud the main issue by announcing possible plans to build Cosmic Jump Gate emitters throughout G.A. space. I'm sure they'll leap to that vision on their own."

"You're serious about building emitters throughout G.A. space?" Christa asked. "Isn't that inviting disaster? Criminals and enemies of the G.A. will be able to commandeer the facilities and use them for illegal or deadly purposes."

"I thought that at first. But I've given it a lot of thought and decided that the benefits far outweigh the costs of making the emitters completely secure. Both ends of all Cosmic Jump Gates will have to be strictly controlled by Space Command. Security will have to be tight, and only authorized users can open a Cosmic Jump Gate. And there will have to be the most formidable of penalties facing anyone who tries to use or appropriate the technology. But there'll be plenty of time later to think about that. Right now, we have a lot on our plate.

"Christa, you'll be leaving in two days. It'll be your task to plant our undercover cyborg in a Denubbewa warship for the purposes of kidnapping a senior commander."

"In the way we discussed? We deliver our cyborg like a bomb into a warship?"

"Yes. SCI has worked with the shipyard to develop a container to hold the cyborg like a baby chick in an egg. You drop it off, and the cyborg hatches from the container that protected him. It will be made from Dakinium to make sure he isn't damaged."

"Is that wise? Should we be sending our Dakinium to the Denubbewa. They might find it and discover that our formula is different than their own."

"The Dakinium being used is recycled scrap from the Denubbewa warships. It's what they have now so they're not getting anything new. And besides, the ship where the egg is laid will soon be scrap itself."

"Okay. What happens after I drop off your little surprise?"

"You pull back and wait until you're signaled by our undercover cyborg. It will attempt to kidnap the highest ranking cyborg on the ship and escape in a shuttle. If it's successful, it will signal you and you send a shuttle to pick them up."

"With thousands of Denubbewa warships all around us?"

"Our shuttles are sheathed in Dakinium. They'll never see it."

"Unless they have something like our Neutrino Measurement Sensors."

"Are you saying you don't want the mission?"

"No, I'm just thinking out loud about all the possible obstacles. How much time will we have before the main force moves in to destroy the warships?"

"Three weeks after your drop, the task force can move in and destroy the rest of the Denubbewa ships that came here as part of the invasion force. If our cyborg hasn't gotten out by then, it probably won't be getting out. Captain Gavin can give the command to attack anytime after that date."

"Three weeks. That should be enough. I hope our cyborg can find the most senior officer aboard the ship we select. Any tips on how to identify which ship contains the most senior cyborg?"

"None. According to our cyborg scientists, there are no markings to indicate the senior leader is on board. Perhaps the captain of the ship you select is the best we can do."

"Hopefully, the cyborg can deliver," Christa said.

"Yes."

"I've been saving a present for you, but since I'm not going to be here for the holidays, I might as well give it to you now."

"A present?"

"Well, sort of. You know we found no warships at the third and fourth Denubbewa battle group sites we located."

"Of course."

"Well, in my report I didn't mention that I ordered my squadrons to stand down and not destroy the motherships."

"All seven?"

"Yes."

"No damage at all?"

"No, I thought we might have a use for them later on so I ordered my ships not to destroy them. I left a CPS-16 with each of the motherships. I also forbid all target practice at or near the ships. I told them I wanted to find them in perfect condition when I returned."

"In your report, you said you had located the motherships and moved in to destroy the Denubbewa there."

"Yes, we did and we did. But there were no Denubbewa there."

"An act of omission can be construed as a lie in some cases."

"I realize politicians and lawyers use that tactic all the time to avoid telling the truth, but I only did it as a surprise. I figured you'd forgive me when I told you why I ordered my group not to damage those vessels."

"You have my full attention. What was your reason?"

"One of the major problems we have in Region Three is that we lack a real presence there. Mainly, that's because we have no bases in the region. Well, now we do. We have seven of the most enormous bases possible, and they are bases that can be moved to any location under their own power. They can't do better than Light-480, but they're sheathed in Denubbewa Dakinium and therefore completely resistant to attack by anyone who doesn't have double envelope capability. And they're each as large as the two asteroid bases you liberated from the Raiders and then turned into Space Command bases."

"And there are no cyborgs inside? Remember what happened when we commandeered those motherships discovered in Region Two?"

"Well— we haven't searched every room and corridor. Actually, we haven't searched any rooms or corridors. Do you have any idea how *enormous* those things are?"

"Yes, I have an idea. They'd dwarf Stewart if you removed the asteroid shell."

"Well, then don't I deserve a thank you for saving the G.A. the trillions of credits it would cost to build seven bases like that?"

"I'm still working on how I'm going to explain to the A.B. why my sister intentionally misled the high command."

When Christa frowned, Jenetta smiled and said, "On behalf of Space Command and the G.A., thank you, Christa."

CHAPTER TWENTY-SIX
~ December 8th, 2291 ~

"Have you ever seen so much wreckage in your life?" the senior reclamation officer said to his aide as they stood near a viewing port in the Reclamation Control Station that orbited Lorense-Four. All wreckage from the battles in Region Three was being brought to this location for separation and recycling. The station was in a higher orbit so they could see the inhospitable planet behind all the scrap as the third Ship Transporter began pushing its cargo out of the hull.

"I read in the orders that each ship could be making dozens of trips."

"That agrees with what I was told. According to reports there are, or will be, thousands of ships brought in."

"I wonder how many ships we lost in this battle."

"I heard we didn't lose a single vessel."

"Really? How many people did we lose?"

"None. At least that's what I heard."

"That seems impossible. I mean— look at this mess."

"Well, if we did lose people, that will come out eventually. You can hide damage to ships, but when people die, they're gone— and eventually someone will miss them and start talking about them."

"I suppose we'll hear something if a lot of people suddenly show up with serious wounds at the base hospital on Quesann. Do you think we could fight a battle like this and not suffer casualties?"

"With Carver as Admiral of the Fleet, anything is possible. That woman is amazing. Ya know, I was a cadet at NHSA when she was there."

"Really? Did you know her?"

"Unfortunately— no. I was two years ahead of her so I didn't associate with anyone in her class year. I heard a lot of mixed things about her though."

"Really? What kind of mixed things. What did you hear?"

"Some cadets were always putting her down, saying that she was a joke and should have been expelled at the end of her first year."

"Really?"

"Yeah. But others had a different take. They claimed she was the most brilliant cadet ever to attend NHSA and that the detractors were just jealous."

"Wow. Why the discrepancy?"

"I'm not sure, but I heard she played some kind of practical joke on old Hubera that made him so angry he flipped out and began screaming at her in class. People say that anyone other than her would have been kicked out the same day but that the officers in charge recognized her brilliance and let the joke slide. And Hubera wasn't very well liked by the academy superintendent or anyone else. They might have even been applauding her action, secretly. Anyway, her supporters must have been right because she graduated from the academy with the highest math and science grades ever earned. She still holds that distinction."

"I've heard she has a genius for tactics."

"That's the story I've heard as well. But the practical joke she played on Hubera did cost her in a major way. Instead of sending her to the Warship Command Institute when she graduated from the Academy, they made her a science officer and immediately shipped her out on a quartermaster's ship. Quartermaster ships need a science officer like I need a heavier beard."

"Yeah, I know the story after that. The ship blew up because of a fault in the antimatter system and Carver was believed lost for more than ten years. And now she's the top officer in all of Space Command and still looks like a recent graduate of the Academy because the Raiders did something to her to enhance her value as a whore in one of their sex colonies before she escaped and blew up their entire hidden base."

"Yeah. Pretty amazing story, eh? Well, the transport is closing its hull so I guess it's empty. Let's get the crews in the yard tractors out there so they can start separating the good from the bad. And remind them to keep a *sharp* eye out for those chambers Admiral Plimley wants."

"Okay. What are they, by the way?"

"Damned if I know. I saw old black & white pictures once from the mid-twentieth century that showed something they called phone booths back then. Supposedly you stepped into the booth to call someone. I have no idea why anyone would need a tiny booth to make a call instead of just calling from wherever they were sitting, standing, or walking. Anyway, these chambers look sort of like those, except they're about five times larger and don't have a door. I was just ordered to find them if they exist, and we'll do as ordered. They're all supposed to be the same size— two meters square by four meters high— so they'll be difficult to spot in all this mess. But the admiral wants them even if the chamber has been crushed flat or destroyed in the battle. And all cyborg bodies are to be saved in a separate area without being ripped apart."

"The yard guys only started doing that because some of them started to move their arms and legs after the first ship unloaded."

"If any move, have our guys notify security. Some of their people are standing by in donkey tractors in case they're needed."

◆　◆　◆

"Welcome back, Christa," Commander Ashraf said when the *Koshi* rendezvoused with the *Seeker, Khatanga, and Ottawa*.

"Thanks," Christa said with a smile. "I wish I could say I was happy to be back. I missed the holidays with the family again, just as all of you have missed the holidays with your families."

"It's just part of the job," Commander Kalborne said. "The worst part is that we're unable to contact family members because of the com blackout rules for an engagement area."

"Space Command sent holiday messages for everyone here and informed the families that although you were unable to send personal messages, everyone here is healthy and safe."

"Yeah," Commander Fareman said, "this is the third year in a row that holiday message has been sent to my family. I hope next year I can send my own."

"We're going to ensure that the Denubbewa aren't responsible for ruining our holidays next year," Christa said. "Have we determined where they're hiding?"

"It's kind of funny to suggest they're hiding," Commander Ashraf said. "There are so many ships congregated at one location that it looks like a Denubbewa convention."

"How many occupied RPs are we talking about?"

"One."

"One? Just one? We expected them to be spread out over the eighteen RP locations we learned about from the cyborgs we took back to Quesann."

"I guess they feel safer in numbers," Kalborne said. "It's like the first images we saw when we arrived. The rows of warships just keep going on forever, except there are no motherships."

"So when do we attack, Commander?" Fareman asked.

"The *Ares* is underway for this location by now. Captain Gavin will take command of the mission."

"Why?" Kalborne said. "Have they lost faith in us because we allowed the warships to get away from us while we were busy destroying the others?"

"Not at all. Admiral Holt is extremely pleased with our performance. Gavin is bringing another three hundred ships to the mission."

"Three hundred?" Commander Ashraf said.

"Yes. Every CPS-14, 15, and 16 that could be spared has been altered to perform as a bomber using the new technique. Every available SD is also coming. Admiral Holt wants to ensure that not a *single* warship escapes this time. In addition to the ships that attack directly, there will be ships waiting on the periphery to chase any that manage to get away from the RP. The intelligence info they've gotten from the cyborgs aboard that ship we captured indicates that every single Denubbewa vessel in G.A. space was summoned here to have its hull sheathed with Dakinium. If we destroy every ship here, G.A. space should be completely clear of Denubbewa vessels— at least until more arrive."

"So we're going in with enough ships that the ratio is less than seven to one," Fareman said. "I like that, but it's going to be pretty crazy in there for a while."

"Yes," Christa said. "We weren't expecting the Denubbewa to be congregated at just one location."

"Is that going to be a problem?" Commander Ashraf asked.

"It's going to confuse things a little. I have orders to drop off a package inside one of the ships as soon as possible."

"Can we ask what kind of package?" Kalborne asked.

"It's a cyborg."

"Carrying coal to Newcastle?"

"What?"

"Oh, just an old expression from my hometown on Earth. Newcastle was our first coal exporting port in the UK. The expression refers to someone performing an unnecessary task."

"In this case, it's not an unnecessary task. The cyborg we're carrying is an SCI creation. They took one of the spare cyborgs from the ship we found and gave him a new identity and memories. It's sort of like what the Denubbewa did to him originally. He's now an undercover operative for the SCI, with all his loyalty going to the G.A. His job is to infiltrate one of the Denubbewa warships and kidnap the highest-ranking officer he can. The captain will be the main target unless there happens to be a Denubbewa fleet commander aboard. Someone like an admiral would be ideal."

"Does SCI think they can force a Denubbewa admiral to talk?" Commander Fareman asked.

"I don't know. I'm not even sure if the rules of war allow us to do what we're doing. We're treating the cyborgs as machines rather than biological beings."

"How do they expect this cyborg to enter one of the Denubbewa ships?" Kalborne asked. "He can't exactly just drift over and knock on the hatch."

"No, he can't. That's where we come in. The *Koshi* is going to bomb him in."

"What does that mean?" Commander Ashraf asked.

"SCI and the shipyard people created a casing, like a bomb casing, made from recycled Denubbewa Dakinium. It will protect him as we drop the bomb casing inside one of the warships. Hopefully, no one will question his presence and he'll be able to select his target and escape in a shuttle or something."

"That's got to be the craziest plan I ever heard," Fareman said.

"Crazy?" Christa said. "Maybe. I think of it as audacious. Who knows? It might work. If it doesn't, we're no worse off than we are now. And if it does, we might have access to information that could help us tremendously in the fight ahead."

"It'll help us with destroying the two thousand, seven hundred warships?" Commander Ashraf said. "How?"

"I don't mean in this battle. I mean the overall fight for the survival of the G.A. This attack by the Denubbewa was only a test of their new wormhole equipment. If it was successful, a massive armada of Denubbewa vessels was assembling to attack. We've interrupted their plans, but they're not going to stop until one of us is out of the game. We're fighting for our very existence as free-thinking biological beings, and we're not going to stop until the Denubbewa are dead, or we are."

"Where did you hear all this?" Kalborne asked.

"From the cyborgs we brought back to Quesann. They unburdened themselves and told us everything. The Denubbewa mean to crush us and turn us into cyborgs. Even if we destroy every Denubbewa warship at the upcoming engagement, the war won't end. This is a fight to the death— their death or ours. And this is privileged information you're not to pass on to anyone. It could create panic if it ever got out."

◆　◆　◆

Christa held a conference with the entire first watch bridge crew to ensure that everyone knew was what going to happen when the *Koshi* entered the area where the thousands of warships were sitting.

"We're going to plant a special bomb inside a Denubbewa warship. It's special because it doesn't contain any explosives. Instead it contains a cyborg prepared for this mission by SCI. We will fly into the Denubbewa area encased in a double envelope and come to a halt inside a warship that is not Dakinium-sheathed. That's critical. I'll make the selection when we enter the RP. Ideally, we'll be able to stop in an area of the ship where no other cyborgs are present and the drop to the deck won't exceed four meters after the special bomb casing passes through the double envelope. If the casing opens properly and the cyborg is okay, he'll send a signal to indicate he's beginning his mission. We can't receive a signal if the Denubbewa ship's hull is Dakinium sheathed. By then we should already be on our way out of the area. Any questions?"

"Just so we're perfectly clear, Captain," the tac officer said, "we will not be dropping any ordnance?"

"Affirmative. No ordnance this trip. This is just to deliver an undercover operative and return."

"And we're going in without cover?" XO Mollago asked.

"Yes. We're in no danger. We'll be protected by the double envelope. This is just a quick in-and-out mission. With luck, no Denubbewa will ever know we were there."

"May we know what the undercover cyborg is going to do?" Mollago asked.

"He's going to attempt to kidnap a senior Denubbewa cyborg. We need the intelligence data it might have stored in its electronic memory component."

"How does our cyborg get back to us with the other cyborg? Do we pick them up?"

"He's on his own. He'll have to find a way back to us, such as with a shuttle. When he's away from the ship, he'll signal us and we'll go pick him up. Hopefully, he'll have a second passenger for us to bring to SCI."

◆ ◆ ◆

As the *Koshi* entered the area where thousands of warships sat, it was difficult for the bridge crew not to feel a little nervous. But the mission went off without a hitch. The phony bomb casing protected the cyborg and opened as it should. Once the cyborg was out, it picked up the pieces of the casing and dropped them into a waste disposal tube. Then it sent the signal to the *Koshi* and began its mission.

◆

"Okay," Christa said to the bridge crew, "the excitement's over. Helm, take us back to *our* RP."

As she leaned back into the command chair, she thought about the SCI cyborg. It had no memory of its past life. She knew that when SCI activated it, it had resisted even though it was simply a drone programmed with a specific task it was to perform repetitiously until ordered to stop. It was living, but it had no life. Christa kept reminding herself it was just a drone so she shouldn't be saddened if it was lost. But she just couldn't help herself because it was no longer the enemy. In reprogramming all of its memories and mission parameters, the SCI undercover operative was now, effectively, a comrade in arms.

◆ ◆ ◆

When the *Ares* arrived a few weeks later, Captain Gavin immediately summoned all squadron commanders to a conference aboard the battleship. The sixteen Scout-Destroyer captains enjoyed the opportunity to renew old friendships and talk about their previous postings until Gavin entered the room with Commander Eliza Carver and an aide. The captains quickly came to attention and remained that way until Gavin told them to find seats. After sitting they gave Captain Gavin their full attention.

"I've seen images of the Denubbewa fleet of warships," Gavin said. "It appears they're simply waiting for orders to begin their attacks in G.A. space. We're not going to let that happen. We're here to destroy every ship at that RP. Some will make a run for it when we arrive and begin our attack, but several squadrons have been tasked with showing those Denubbewa there will be no escape. No matter which way they turn, our ships will be waiting for them and they will meet the same fate as the ones who are destroyed where they're currently sitting."

Gavin nodded to an aide and a prepared drawing of the RP appeared on the large monitor at the front of the room.

"All commanders will receive a copy of this diagram when you return to your Scout-Destroyers, along with specific instructions for your attack. As those in the know can see, we're adopting the attack strategy of Commander Carver and the three squadron commanders who've been out here for some time showing the Denubbewa they've picked the wrong nation to attack."

Gavin paused as a laugh rippled through the assembly.

"All ships will approach the Denubbewa RP on the same heading and remain within their assigned lane. In the past, the bombing was performed by two ships—one targeting and the other dropping the bomb. Single envelope travel for SC vessels is now history, except in special situations. The modifications made by your engineering teams actually locks out single envelope capability and allows us to travel at any speed

from a full stop to Marc-One while encased in a double envelope. In the future, ships involved in interdiction efforts can
drop their double envelope and an engineer can switch the
lockout in seconds so that only single envelope travel is then
possible. That's only necessary so the ship being stopped can
see our vessel. With the ability to vary our speed in double
envelop travel, our new bombing strategy only requires one
ship for both targeting and bomb deployment. You've all
practiced the procedure until your accuracy reached a level
that permitted you to become part of this task force. It's time
to put that knowledge to use. The Denubbewa have the advantage in numbers, but we have a distinct advantage in technical superiority. If each ship in your squadrons destroy just
seven warships, not a single Denubbewa ship will escape
their RP. That's not so many when you consider that the average number of kills for the four squadrons that have been
working this area for the past half year is currently thirteen
per ship. Now let's go out and finish mopping up this part of
G.A. space. Any questions, ladies and gentlemen?"

After a few seconds of silence, Captain Gavin said,
"None? Then let's get out there and get this job done. Dismissed."

The ship captains all jumped to their feet as Captain
Gavin left the conference room, followed by his aide. Eliza
remained behind for a few minutes to talk with friends.

"Eliza," Commander Dillon Wilder of the SD *Tigris* said,
"I bet you wish you were commanding an SD like Christa."

"I'm happy right where I am, Dillon. I'm going to kick
back and watch the action from the Auxiliary Command and
Control center. Any bets on how many ships you'll destroy?"

"I guess I'll have to do thirteen to keep up with Christa."

"Ambitious. I like that. Don't forget that Christa is also
going to be out there working to improve her score."

"That's right. I guess I'll have to do a lot better than thirteen."

"Do I hear my name being slandered?" someone said from behind Eliza. Eliza turned and said, "Hi, sis. Dillon is calculating what he has to do to beat your score."

"Can't happen. Dillon, you might have a great ship and crew, but I'm going to be out there today also."

"I realize that. I just told Eliza I'll have to do better than thirteen."

"A lot better. I estimate my ship took down over a hundred in one attack."

"A hundred? When?"

"During the first engagement, my ship dropped ten WOLaR bombs inside each of two Denubbewa motherships. It was impossible to tell how many warships were inside when the detonation occurred, but there were at least a hundred hulks in there afterward."

"That doesn't count," Dillon said with a grin. "You can't claim collateral damage."

"I must have missed that in the rule book," Christa said, also adding a grin. "Can you tell me what page that's on?"

"I'll have to look it up and get back to you. Right now I have to get back to my ship before my XO leaves without me."

"Okay, Dillon. Good luck."

"You also, Christa. Hey Eliza, enjoy the show," Dillon said as he backed away towards the door.

"Thanks. That reminds me. I have to make some popcorn."

When Dillon left the room, only Christa and Eliza remained.

"Good luck, sis," Eliza said.

"Thanks. Unless something totally unexpected happens, it's a turkey shoot."

"But you never know. Have you been able to recover your SCI undercover cyborg?"

"No. We haven't received his signal. I guess he'll die along with all the other cyborgs today, unless he's already dead."

"It was a long-shot to begin with."

"I know, but I feel sad for him."

"Don't be. He was murdered a long time ago on some forgotten planet when the Denubbewa extracted his brain and tossed the rest of his body away."

"But we resurrected him and gave him a new purpose in life, even if he was only substituting one master for another."

"Think of it this way. For a couple of weeks he was his own person again, able to think and act according to his own wishes even if he had no choice in the overall mission."

"I guess," she said with a sigh. "Hey, I'd better get going or my squadron will be leaving without me."

"Good luck out there."

"Thanks. Enjoy the popcorn."

"I would never say this to Dillon, but I envy you right now."

"We've both seen our share of action."

"Yes, we have." Eliza said. "And I'm grateful I've never been shot."

"Ouch. Don't remind me." The sisters hugged and then Christa hurried out while Eliza looked around the room and thought about the upcoming engagement and the poor cyborg who'd gotten his humanity back, although limited and only for a short time. After a couple of minutes, she shrugged and headed towards AC&C.

CHAPTER TWENTY-SEVEN

~ February 16th, 2292 ~

Christa sat in the command chair on the bridge, staring at the huge monitor at the front while the crew prepared for the attack. The ships about to participate in the organized chaos that would follow were currently positioning themselves for departure from the assembly area. More than a light-year away, the fleet of Denubbewa warships sat quietly, hopefully unaware of the destruction about to befall them. The arrival at the battle site and the first detonations from the attack would occur within seconds of the scheduled time for all Space Command vessels.

As far as anyone in Space Command knew, the Denubbewa didn't have Neutrino Measurement Sensors, so the Dakinium sheathing of the SC fleet would keep their presence from being observed by the enemy fleet while sitting at the RP. Every ship in the attack group did have the sensors, so the position of every other SC vessel within ten kilometers was visible on their monitors.

The course to the Denubbewa fleet had been entered into the navigation computer of every ship, and their double envelopes would be built three minutes before deployment. The chronometer on the helmsmen's consoles, synchronized with the chronometers of all ships participating in the battle, would actually engage the drive at the correct nanosecond. One full second before the first bomb was to be dropped, the Alpha-Twelve rotating-frequency ship-protection code would begin being broadcast by every Space Command ship in the sector. This wasn't to prevent a Space Command vessel from being damaged by friendly-fire but simply to track the positions of all Space Command vessels because the signal could identify all fleet ships out to a distance of eight billion kilometers using the DeTect system. The Denubbewa might become aware that an unidentified signal was being broadcast, but they wouldn't know what it meant until their ships began exploding in their midst. At that time, many command officers might begin to suspect it was indicative of the method Space Command used to teleport bombs directly into their ships.

As the chronometer neared the departure time, all talk ceased on the bridge and all eyes were on the time displayed on the front monitor. With exactly three minutes left, the double envelope finished engulfing the ship. When the chronometer reached zero, the ship attained Marc-One without anyone feeling the slightest movement. The chronometer immediately reset to thirty-six minutes, the time it would take to reach the Denubbewa RP.

Activity on the bridge returned to normal after that. When the time ticked down to single digits again, it would almost be time to begin the destruction of the Denubbewa armada. Once the attack began, the helmsman on each ship would head directly for one of the ships in their 'lane.' As the ship slowed and entered a Denubbewa ship, the tactical officer would release a bomb, whereupon the helmsman would apply power and proceed to another ship after bypassing about a hundred. The ship behind the SD would target the first ship after the one that was currently blowing apart. And so on and so on for all the ships behind the SD. It wouldn't matter if a ship or two or twenty was missed. Other squadrons were waiting for any ships that made it out of the RP area. None would escape because the Space Command vessels could travel more than thirty times the speed of the fastest Denubbewa ship.

"Captain," the Com Chief said as the *Koshi* ejected its fourth WOLaR bomb, "we just received that signal."

"What signal, Chief?"

"Like the one we received right after we dropped off that special package a few weeks ago."

"Where did it come from?"

"It seemed to come from the third warship we bombed."

The most recently ejected WOLaR, the fourth, detonated as the chief petty officer spoke.

Christa sighed and said, "Thanks, Chief."

Where previously the SC ships had completed the initial bombing run and then turned to make pass after pass until there were no more targets, most of the Denubbewa armada fell victim to the attackers on just the first pass. Naturally, some warships managed to escape, but the SC ships lying in wait were in hot pursuit as the Denubbewa ships only briefly managed to escape death from the attack at their RP.

"Well done," Captain Gavin said in an announcement to all ships after the fleet paused to regroup. "Not one ship has survived our attack. I guess we can call this a clean sweep. We still have a lot of work to do. We must clean up this mess before we rest. So send out your shuttles to push the destroyed ships back into the central area. And again, well done."

"You heard the boss," Christa said to her squadron commanders. "We've done this before. We have to get this mess cleaned up and ready for the ships from Quesann to collect it for recycling."

"What do we do with the cyborg, uh, bodies we find?" Commander Fareman asked. "Do I have my people bisect them?"

"No, SCI now wants us to preserve all of them that are still alive."

"Are we starting our own cyborg battalion, Commander?" Commander Kalborne asked jokingly.

"I certainly hope not. I believe SCI is hoping to gather intelligence. They've learned how to download the information the cyborgs possess in their electronic memories. That data may help us in future engagements. This war isn't over. In fact, some think it's just beginning. As evidenced by the fact that they were sheathing their ships with Dakinium, the Denubbewa continually evolve, and so must we. We have to stay well ahead of them."

◆ ◆ ◆

Even with the shuttles from four hundred ships working to clear the site, it took a couple of weeks to round up all the pieces of the Denubbewa ships and drag them to a collection point. Engineers from one of the SDs strung cable between a few of the larger sections initially to keep them together and then others started cabling additional large sections as they were pushed to the quickly expanding pile. As the pile increased in magnitude, the cabled sections added a degree of stability to the collection of scrap. Denubbewa bodies collected during the effort were put into a separate area. If the Denubbewa appeared to still be alive, they were brought to the *Ares*. Christa warned Captain Gavin that the Denubbewa had the ability to pick up all electronic signals within the ship, including CT transmissions, so Gavin had the engineers completely enclose one hold with a wire grid that would interfere with electromagnetic signals. The grid didn't totally block the signals, as Dakinium plating would, but it distorted the signals so much that the messages were unintelligible. Then the engineers began working on sheathing a hold with Dakinium plates from the Denubbewa ship scrap.

With the entire Denubbewa advance armada destroyed, along with all of the Denubbewa warships that had already been in G.A. space, there was no further reason to block unnecessary communications so all restrictions were lifted and military personnel were permitted to send vidMails to family and friends. The normal time limit was extended to ten minutes per day for the first week.

◆　◆　◆

There was no way of knowing when the Denubbewa would attempt another invasion or even where they would try, so once the RP was somewhat orderly, Captain Gavin began releasing most of the CPS-14s and 15s so they could return to their regular duty assignments. Gavin retained all of the SDs because each had, at a minimum, a full Marine platoon on board. The *Ares* itself had come close to cleaning out Harrat Island Marine Base and brought a full brigade of four thousand Marines for this mission. The base had temporarily acquired the look of an abandoned base, with the remainder of the needed Marines acquired by temporarily reducing by half, the Marine complement on all warships at Quesann.

Battleships normally had one or two companies of Marines on board because of the inability to predict a situation that would require ground troops, but a brigade was unheard of. The reason there were so many Marines on the *Ares* on this occasion was simple. Jenetta wanted the motherships Christa had saved from destruction thoroughly searched. Her orders had specified that no corridor, no hold, no room, no locker, and no access tunnel was to be marked as clear until it had been checked. Gavin told them that as each area was checked, it had to be signed off by the senior officer or enlisted person in charge. And further, if an area was later found *not* to be clear, the officer in command and everyone else in that unit would forever regret the day they stepped foot on the *Ares*.

◆ ◆ ◆

Searching seven motherships, each the size of a small city, was going to take time— lots of time. But Gavin had made it clear that if anyone ever wanted to get back to Quesann or Harrat Island Marine base, they would have to complete this job. So the Marines threw themselves into the task. They had equipment that could detect the heartbeat of a mouse at a hundred meters, but they had nothing for detecting cyborgs that hadn't yet been activated so the entire mothership from sail to keel and larboard to starboard had to be visually checked.

To save time, the Marines decided to first occupy each mothership to be searched. There seemed to be an infinite number of holds from which to choose for their bivouac, and they found one with fresh water for their mess hall with another enormous hold next to it for their sleeping accommodations. The Denubbewa didn't need oxygen, but there was oxygen/nitrogen capability throughout the ship and it was activated in all areas other than the port in the center of the mothership where ships docked. One officer speculated that they must have needed the systems to keep slaves alive until they could turn them into cyborg drones. Or perhaps the original Denubbewa population were air breathers. Whatever the reason, a breathable atmosphere throughout made the job substantially easier. The Marines were all wearing their personal armor throughout the day, but they relied on the air in the ship for breathing unless their armor warned them of a problem. If that was to occur, the suit would automatically close the vents to outside air and fall back on the rebreather units and small oxygen replenishment supply.

◆ ◆ ◆

When the first of the motherships was declared totally clean of any Denubbewa cyborgs, Gavin assigned a squadron of CPS-16s to drag it to one of the locations established by the A.B. Knowing that the double envelope created by a single CPS-16 could be extended to completely eclipse the mothership, one was tethered to the Denubbewa vessel and departed, with much fanfare. Once at their new location, the squadron would remain there until relieved. As soon as Quesann received notification that the mothership was on its way, several destroyers at Quesann would leave to meet them and the CPS-16's new homeport would become the newest space station in G.A. space.

◆ ◆ ◆

"Commander Christa Carver, reporting as ordered, sir," Christa said to Captain Gavin as she entered his office and braced to attention in front of his desk. Christa managed to hold her stolid stance until Gavin said "At ease, Commander," despite the fact that the ship's executive officer, Commander Eliza Carver, was grinning at her from an oh-gee side chair next to the desk. She stood up when Gavin rose from his chair.

"Christa," Captain Gavin said, "you and your four squadrons have done an incredible job out here. The people of the G.A. owe you a debt of gratitude. None of us believe this is the end of the Denubbewa effort to absorb this part of space, but we're better positioned to fight off their invasion attempts now than at any time in the past, and we'll continue to get stronger with each passing day. We will continue to drive them back or destroy them whenever they come at us again. Unfortunately, the cyborgs are about as close to being machines as anything could be, and machines have just one objective. They will continue to perform whatever jobs they've been created or programmed to perform to the exclusion of all other considerations. With the Denubbewa cyborgs, this means they'll continue to prosecute this war until one or the other of us are no more. By securing those seven motherships for our use, you've helped us tremendously. Once they're checked and moved to a strategic location, we'll begin using them to give us a better presence in this part of space. And having a better presence, as happened with Stewart, can make all the difference when it comes to extending the rule of law and order, not to mention being better prepared should an outside force attack."

Christa had been trying to figure out where Gavin was going with the little speech, but he hadn't yet made the point he seemed to be working towards. Was he going to tell her that her squadron was going to be stationed out here? Or, even worse, that she was going to be placed in command of one of the new space stations as had happened to Jenetta when she managed to capture the Raider base that eventually became Stewart Space Command Base?

"Christa, when you stepped slightly outside the orders instructing you to destroy every Denubbewa ship you encountered, you showed the courage that real commanders always exhibit. We don't want machines in command of our forces. We want intelligent commanders who know that sometimes they must briefly obey the true spirit of our objectives. Before we left Quesann, Jenetta told me that all members of the Admiralty Board were delighted you hadn't destroyed the seven motherships. The G.A. Senate has approved substantial increases to the Space Command budget to allow us to prepare for the war with the Denubbewa, and having these seven bases almost ready to occupy will mean that more funds can be devoted to ships and manpower. The A.B. was already making preparations to occupy the seven new bases before the *Ares* left Quesann. I want to thank you on behalf of the G.A. for your loyalty and dedication to the G.A. and Space Command, and your superb performance out here. I wish I could bestow a more tangible sign of our appreciation, but promotions and medals are the province of the A.B. However, I have written a letter of commendation that will be placed in your file."

"Thank you, sir. I appreciate that."

"You're most welcome. Now, my XO has something to tell you. XO?"

"Christa, I've been told that a cyborg has been asking to meet with you— alone."

"A cyborg? With me? Alone?"

"Isn't that what I just said?"

"Yes, I guess I was taken a little aback. Why me?"

"I'm sure I don't know. Would you like me to accompany you?"

"Uh, no, that's not necessary. Where is it?"

"Down on the security deck in one of the shielded rooms."

"Okay, I'll stop down there and see what it's about."

"It might be one that learned you led the forces before the *Ares* arrived and wants to promise they'll leave the G.A. for good if we release the surviving cyborgs."

"If that's what it wants, it's going to be disappointed. I'm the one who ordered that all cyborgs be destroyed— until Quesann overruled my standing orders." Looking at Gavin, she said, "I'll go down there now if that's all, sir."

"You're dismissed, Commander."

"Yes, sir." Christa said as she braced to attention and then turned and left the room.

There were both advantages and disadvantages to having a face and appearance identical to the Admiral of the Fleet, who was also the most famous person in G.A. space. One advantage was that no one ever questioned your authority once you passed a retinal scan, if your rank permitted you to issue such orders.

"I'm here to see the cyborg that's been requesting to see me, Staff Sergeant," Christa said as she completed the retinal scan necessary to enter the security area.

"Aye, Commander. This way."

The Marine noncom led Christa to a secure holding cell, then said, "The cyborg is secure, Commander, but do you wish to have a guard accompany you?"

"As long as it's unarmed, I should be fine."

"Oh, it's definitely unarmed, ma'am," the Staff Sergeant said with a mostly suppressed snigger.

"Then open the door and leave."

The noncom ordered the guard to unlock the door and saluted Christa, then turned and left.

Christa pulled the heavy door open and entered the room. There was only one cyborg in there, and as soon as Christa saw it, she understood the guard's comment about it being unarmed. It had no arms, only partial stumps where its legs had been, and its chest-protection plate was bent and scarred.

"Commander Carver," the cyborg said. "At last."

"Uh, you requested to see me?"

"I've been requesting to see you for weeks."

"Why?"

"I'm M934CVY9274NT209W."

"Is that supposed to mean something to me?"

"Sorry. I'm D01 of SCI."

"D01? The cyborg I brought out here?"

"The very same."

"Prove it. Where did you come from originally?"

"I don't know. My memory was wiped clean, erasing all knowledge of my homeland. The SCI took me from the Denubbewa warship you found that was being used by the Elobian scientists in their getaway."

"Okay. You pass the test. Uh, are you in pain?"

"Not any more. Cyborgs do feel pain when they're first injured. It's necessary so we know when we've been injured, but we have the ability to turn off the pain receptors once we acknowledge the injury. I feel quite comfortable, except I can't get up and move about."

"What happened to you after we dropped you off?"

"I hid the pieces of the bomb casing and was then able to move about freely on the Denubbewa warship without question. Since I wasn't listed as being part of the crew, no one tried to assign me to any work details. I located a likely target— a security officer with two blue dots— and waited for my chance to kidnap him. When your fleet attacked, I was just about to render the security officer unconscious. I never got the chance. Suddenly the whole ship was destroyed around me. I wasn't injured in the explosion but I was damaged when the overhead collapsed onto the deck where I was. The security officer was critically injured because the casing that contained his brain was damaged. As he died, he grabbed me and entered an encrypted message into my memory in case I survived."

"What does it say?"

"I don't know. It's encrypted. Perhaps the decryption officers at Quesann will be able to decipher it."

"I'm sorry we injured you."

"As you Terrans say, I was just in the wrong place at the wrong time."

"I believe it was a bomb from my ship that destroyed the ship you were on. As the bomb exploded, my Com Chief got the signal you sent."

"I never sent any signal. The transmitter was in the concealed opening in my left leg where SCI hid it. I suppose the explosion was responsible somehow, or perhaps when the overhead crushed my legs and they were broken off."

"Apparently. I'll be right back."

Stepping out of the cell, Christa said to the Marine guard, "Corporal, have this prisoner taken to Shuttle Bay 2."

"Uh, I'll have to check with the officer on duty in the security office first, ma'am, and get authorization for a prisoner transfer."

"Corporal, do you know who I am?"

"Yes, ma'am."

"Then you should know that I'm operating under the orders of the Admiral of the Fleet. Now, once you issue instructions to begin moving this prisoner, you go check with whomever you want. But I order you to begin moving this prisoner. NOW!"

"Yes, ma'am," the corporal said, saluting. "Right away, ma'am."

The corporal signaled to two guards, who came over quickly. They had probably heard the exchange.

"Prisoner transport," the corporal said to them. "Take it to Shuttle Bay 2."

While the gurney was being pushed out of the security area, the corporal was on the com speaking with someone, but Christa ignored him.

As the gurney reached the shuttle bay, Eliza approached Christa.

"You've got all my security people on edge."

Christa grinned. "I don't usually have to throw my weight around."

"It's okay. They need a little discipline like that from time to time. They shouldn't have questioned the orders of a senior officer moving a prisoner who represents no possible physical threat to anyone. There was plenty of time to verify permission for the transfer once it had been initiated. Where are you taking it?"

"To the *Koshi*. This is the cyborg that SCI reprogrammed and sent in."

"Really? I thought you said it had been killed during the battle."

"I thought it had. As you can see, it's not in too good a condition."

"Yeah. It's needs a bit more than a new coat of paint."

"Technically, it's one of ours, Eliza, so I'm going to do whatever I can for it."

"Okay, sis. Good luck."

"Talk to you later."

CHAPTER TWENTY-EIGHT

~ March 6th, 2292 ~

"Where are you taking that— thing," the young doctor asked as two enlisted rolled the gurney into the sickbay aboard the *Koshi*. Christa was a few paces behind them and heard the challenge.

"I need you to patch it up, Lieutenant," Christa said.

"What? Oh, sorry, Captain. I didn't see you back there."

"I want you to do everything you can to help this cyborg."

"Why?"

"Because I've ordered you to do it."

"But Captain, I'm a doctor, not a mechanic."

"It needs help, and I can't very well take it down to engineering. But I'll get a couple of engineers to come up here and work on it. And you will assist. Perhaps you'll learn something they didn't teach you at the medical college."

"But Captain..."

"Are you resigning your commission and requesting to be released from Space Command?"

"What? No! Ma'am."

"Then you have your orders, Lieutenant. Carry on."

The doctor looked up into her eyes for a second before saying, "Aye, Captain."

The doctor directed where the two enlisted were to take the gurney. When they reached an examination table, the cyborg was lifted off and gently laid onto it. Then the two enlisted left the sickbay. The doctor turned and walked into his office.

"D01?" Christa said.

"Yes, Captain."

"Are all cyborg bodies built to the same specifications?"

"Not all, Captain. There are tiny cyborgs that work in the engineering access tubes and very tall cyborgs that work in the holds. But most cyborgs, according to my electronic memory files, have been built to the same physical specifications for decades. Materials for the body may vary slightly, depending on what's available at the time of construction."

"So if I gather a few of the expired cyborg bodies that have good working parts and we replace your damaged parts, your body will operate properly and won't reject them?"

"The parts from most Denubbewa cyborgs are fully interchangeable."

"Excellent. That's what we'll do then. Uh, D01, do you understand gender in biological life forms?"

"You're referring to the difference between males and females and how the females have eggs to produce the young when the eggs are fertilized by sperm from the males?"

"Yes."

"Yes, I understand. You are a female, Captain."

Christa smiled. "I'm not talking about me. I wanted to know if your original body was male or female."

"I don't know, Captain. My memory has been erased. I don't know what sex I was, what species, or even how old I was."

"That's terrible. I'm so sorry."

"You had nothing to do with it, Captain. Nor did your species. That much I do know."

"I was expressing empathy, not apologizing for what happened to you."

"Oh. I understand."

"The main reason I wanted to know was to give you a proper name."

"Is D01 not a proper name?"

"Uh, it's a bit too generic. How about the name Lucky?"

"Lucky?"

"Yes, because you were lucky to be selected for this mission and lucky to have survived the bombing of the ship you were on."

"Lucky. Lucky. Yes, I like it. My name is now Lucky instead of D01."

"Let's keep D01 as your official identifier."

"Okay. Should I be D01 Lucky, or Lucky D01."

"I think I like Lucky D01."

"So do I."

"Okay, Lucky. I'm going to make arrangements to get you some arms and legs, and perhaps a new chest plate."

"Thank you, Commander."

◆　◆　◆

"There you go, Commander," Lt. Hudden said. "Your cyborg has arms and legs again, and we replaced the chest plate."

"Excellent work, Lieutenant. Lucky, how does it feel? Move your arms."

The cyborg stretched its arms out and wiggled its fingers, then rotated its arms to the stops.

"Are your receptors working?" Christa asked.

The cyborg stopped moving for a second and then touched its fingertips together.

"All receptors in my hands and arms are active and normal, Captain."

"Good. Now move your legs."

The cyborg stretched out its legs and wiggled its toes.

"Everything feels normal, Captain. The receptors in my feet and legs are working properly."

"Good. Stand up."

The cyborg grabbed hold of the edge of the examination table and twisted its body so its legs were over the edge, then bent at the knees and moved to place its weight on its legs and stand. As it stood and rose to its full height, Lucky said, "It feels normal, Captain. And it's a pleasure to stand up

CHANGING OF THE GUARD

again. I had begun to think I was going to have to be on my back for the rest of my life."

"You know, Commander," Lt. Hudden said, "I bet we can put together some casings for its arms, legs, and torso to make it appear more Terran and less intimidating to crew-members."

"What do you think, Lucky?" Christa said.

"As long as they don't interfere with my mobility, I have no objection."

"We'll make them from a flexible material so they bend when you move," Lt. Hudden said to the cyborg.

"Like Terran skin?"

"Somewhat. Naturally, you won't have the sense of touch that Terrans have."

"It would be nice to blend in a little more. At Quesann, Terrans always leaped out of the way when I approached. They seemed to expect me to attack them."

"That's understandable, Lucky. Most only know the Denubbewa cyborgs to be merciless killers."

"Yes, I understood, but it didn't make the situation any more comfortable. Lt. Hudden," the cyborg asked, "can you change my eye color to something a little less intimidating such as blue or light green?"

"That might be possible. I'll check the eyes on the expired cyborgs who donated your body parts to see how the eyes are constructed. Perhaps we can even produce a full head mask as well."

"With synthetic hair?"

"Of course."

"Wonderful."

"Okay, Lucky, Lt. Hudden will begin work on making your appearance less intimidating to Terrans. And this Marine will show you to your new quarters and stay by you to see you aren't disturbed. A Marine will plug you into your power supply each night and unplug you the next day."

"Am I to be treated as a prisoner?"

"It will seem like that for a while— until the crew gets used to having a cyborg in our midst. I know you're not like the cyborgs we've just spent many months chasing down and fighting, but not everyone sees things the same way because they know most cyborgs have been programmed to destroy this nation and its sentient population. Just be patient and continue to be cooperative. You'll see attitudes eventually change."

"I understand, Captain."

"After you arrive at your room, a com chief will come to download the message the Denubbewa security officer uploaded into your electronic memory. It's going to be transmitted to SCI so they can have a crack at decrypting it."

"I understand, Captain."

"Good. That's all for now, Lucky."

"Captain, thank you for everything. I know I'll never be considered a member of the crew, but since SCI resurrected me, I've felt like I have a life. When I was aboard that Denubbewa ship and saw all those cyborgs mindlessly doing what they were programmed to do, I realized how lucky I was to be rescued."

"Uh— yes, Lucky. You go along with the Marine now and he'll get you settled in."

"Okay, Captain."

◆

As Christa sat in her office a short time later, she thought about the situation with Lucky. She feared that with its mission completed, SCI might decide to return it to the spare parts inventory. She had tried to avoid any personal attachments, but she'd felt some responsibility since it was first deposited in the Denubbewa ship. She decided that if SCI tried to send Lucky to the scrapheap, she would talk with Jenetta about a better disposition for the cyborg.

◆ ◆ ◆

"Come in, Christa," Captain Gavin said when she appeared at his office aboard the *Ares*. As the doors closed behind her, he added, "Let's skip the formalities. Have a seat."

Eliza was there, seated in a side chair. She looked up from her viewpad without expression.

"I sense bad news," she said.

"No," Gavin said. "Not bad. Not exactly. We've completed the searches of all the motherships. Not a single cyborg was found anywhere. We did find enough spare parts to build an enormous army of cyborgs, but no brains. I guess they figured they'd pick up the brains here."

"That's a gruesome thought," Christa said.

"No doubt about that," Eliza said. "We know what they intended for us."

"Have all of the motherships now been sent to their designated locations?" Christa asked.

"All but the last one," Gavin said, then lapsed into silence.

"Here's where I get the bad news, isn't it."

"I'm afraid so, sis," Eliza said. "You drew the short straw."

"And I don't even remember getting to draw a straw."

"I represented you."

"Then *you* should have to get stuck aboard that new space station."

"You're not getting stuck aboard the station," Gavin said.

"I'm not? I don't understand."

"Your ship, the *Koshi*, and your squadron, are being assigned to the station, not you. At least not on a permanent basis. You'll be in command of the station, but only until a new administrator arrives."

"Isn't that what happened to Jenetta on both Dixon and Stewart?"

"Uh, yes, but it won't happen here."

"Can I get that in writing, sir?"

Gavin smiled. "Jenetta knew you'd feel this way so she ordered me to assign you to the last of the space stations so the permanent administrator would already be on their way here."

"Who is it?"

"I don't know. The individual hadn't been named before we left Quesann, and I haven't received any updates that included that information. But Jenetta said the person would be underway by the time you had to take command of the station. Since travel time from Quesann is forty-eight days, that should be the most you'll have to wait."

"I suppose that's not too bad, as long as the new administrator is underway and doesn't get sidetracked."

"Your sister is not in the habit of lying."

"No, but my sister can't control everything. I have no doubt that the administrator is on his or her way here, unless the Senate intervened or some other such problem arose."

"We'll learn soon enough if that's the situation. In the meantime, you'll move the new space station to its designated area and wait for the contractors, supply ships, and new administrator to arrive. Once you turn over control of the station, you'll return to patrol duty in this sector until you receive new orders. Six CPS-16s will remain in the station at all times as a protection force, and be rotated as you see fit."

"Yes, sir."

"It's about lunchtime. Why don't you ladies join me in my quarters for lunch? My steward is preparing one of my favorite meals. It's grilled chicken breast fillets coated with breadcrumbs. The sides are broccoli and baked potatoes."

"I'm in, sir," Eliza said. "I love the way Bertram prepares chicken."

"I'm in also, sir. Today is pizza day on the *Koshi*, and I do enjoy it, but we have that every week. It'll be nice to have something different on Pizza Friday."

◆ ◆ ◆

"We're here, ladies and gentlemen," Christa said in a ship-wide announcement that also went out to all twenty-four CPS-16s in her squadron. The *Koshi, Seeker, Khatanga, Ottawa*, and three other Scout-Destroyer squadrons had been assigned to each of the seven motherships, with orders to move them to new locations in Region Three in preparation for becoming Space Command's newest bases. And until further notice, those space stations would be their home port.

After the *Koshi* and all but one of the CPS-16s had entered the newest space station in the G.A., the giant doors had been closed. The one CPS-16 was enough to tow the former mothership to its destination. Once they arrived, the doors would be opened wide enough for the CPS-16s to enter or leave and eighteen would begin patrolling space around the new station to a distance of four hundred light-years. That meant that no ship would ever be more than ten days' travel time from the station. The *Koshi* would have to remain at the station until the new administrator and three destroyers arrived. The destroyers would serve as the protection force until the space station became a regular port with multiple Space Command vessels assigned there.

◆ ◆ ◆

The following day, many of the squadron officers and enlisted were wandering around the enormous space station. It was already underway to its newly assigned location. The Space Command and Marine personnel had been instructed on how to open and close doors and how to use the lifts but had strict orders not to touch anything else as they wandered around.

Christa was touring the station with her XO, Lieutenant Paul Mollago, Lucky, and one of the Marine security guards who normally spent their days standing outside the cyborg's door. Lucky, excited about the opportunity to do something other than sit in his quarters all day, had practically jumped for joy when Christa invited him along. It would be the first time he'd have an opportunity to walk around in the new synthetic skin that now covered most of his body. And with baby blue eyes, he appeared a lot less intimidating now. He'd also been given a Space Command uniform similar to those worn by the enlisted men and women.

The group had been walking for well over an hour when they came to a door with a large sign on it. Usually, the doors just had numbers and letters.

"Can you read that sign, Lucky?" Christa asked the cyborg.

"It says 'Interactive Dispatch Hub.'"

"What does that mean?"

"I don't know, Commander. My electronic database allows me to translate the Denubbewa language, but I don't always know what the words refer to."

"XO. Any ideas?"

"None, Captain."

"Let's take a look," she said as she tapped the control that caused the two doors to slide into their pockets.

The interior of the area looked quite ordinary. There were several worktables around the periphery where Denubbewa were to stand while doing whatever they were supposed to do, and a large cabinet— two meters square and four meters tall— in the center of the room. It had a single entrance but no door and no other openings. The two officers studied the control panel mounted on the outside for several minutes.

"I can't make any sense of this," Christa finally said.

"Nor can I, Captain."

"Lucky, does anything look familiar?"

"It's very confusing, Commander. I can translate some of the words, but I don't understand their meanings, except for these two," the cyborg said, pointing to the two words next to a button.

"And what do they mean?"

"On and off."

"But what do they turn on and off?"

"I don't know."

"One way to find out, Captain," Mollago said.

"Okay, but no one walk into that opening."

Everyone backed away from the cabinet except Christa. She took a breath and then depressed the button that Lucky reported as being the 'on' button. A soft white light came on inside the cabinet that illuminated the interior and a panel on the outside surface glowed with a series of Denubbewa symbols. The same symbols were visible on a side wall inside the cabinet. Nothing else happened for about fifteen seconds.

Suddenly the interior of the cabinet glowed with an intense white light that made the Terrans wince. Then it returned to normal, but as the light dimmed, everyone was astounded to see an individual wearing a Space Command EVA suit standing inside the cabinet. The EVA suit sun visor was down so they couldn't see who or what was inside.

The EVA-suited individual looked at the four individuals outside the cabinet without moving. Christa, Mollago, Lucky, and the Marine stood equally transfixed.

At least thirty seconds passed before anyone moved. The person in the EVA suit was first, and the Marine was second as he pulled his handgun from the holster and pointed it at the chest of the EVA suit. The person in the EVA suit froze, then very slowly raised his hands. He was carrying some sort of a large viewpad, but no weapons were in evidence.

Christa gestured towards the helmet, trying to indicate that the individual should raise the sun visor. The individual responded by removing the helmet completely. It was a Terran so the four outside the cabinet breathed a little easier. The individual stepped out of the cabinet.

"Who are you?" Christa asked.

"Uh, Admiral? Is that you?"

"I'm a Commander. The insignia of rank is quite a bit different."

"Yes, ma'am. That's why I'm confused. You look just like Admiral Carver."

"Admiral of the Fleet Carver is my sister. I'm Commander Christa Carver."

"Commander Christa Carver? You can't be. You're not supposed to be here."

"What do you mean? Who are you?"

"Sorry, Commander. I'm Chief Petty Officer Dorithy. Franklin Dorithy."

"I don't recognize you. Which ship are you posted to?"

"Uh, no ship, ma'am. I'm assigned to the maintenance section of the shipyard."

"Shipyard? What shipyard?"

"This shipyard— at Lorense-Three. Actually we're at Lorense-Four right now because that's where all the scrap is being brought."

"Lorense-Three and Four are in Region Two."

"Yes, ma'am. Right here in Region Two."

"Tell me, Chief, what's the last thing you remember before seeing us?"

"Well— I was examining this cabinet here at the scrap yard. We have orders to collect all the cabinets like this one we could find in the scrap and prepare a condition report on each."

"At the scrap yard?"

"Aye, Commander. I apologize for my confusion a minute ago. I wasn't aware the *Koshi* had returned from Region Three. Welcome back, ma'am. Everyone is talking about your great victory over the Denubbewa. Anyway, as I always do, I turned on the light inside the cabinet to better see the condition of the interior and had started to make notes when the cabinet suddenly shifted slightly. That happens a lot during salvage operations. I put out my hand to steady myself. Then the interior glowed so bright I had to lower the sun visor in my helmet. When the light returned to normal, I saw all of you standing there. Uh— this room looks completely different now. It looked like a disaster scene before, and now it looks brand new."

"What did you touch when you put out your hand to steady yourself?"

"I guess I touched the display panel inside the cabinet."

"Why are you wearing an EVA suit?"

"We have to. Because this cabinet is inside a part of a damaged ship that's open to space. But— uh— uh— where are your EVA suits? And just how are we able to breathe in here now?"

Christa chuckled and said, "It's because you're not in Kansas anymore, Dorothy."

"It's Dorithy, ma'am."

"Not today," Christa said with a grin. "Today it's Dorothy and you've just soared over the rainbow." Gesturing to XO Mollago and then the Marine, she said, "This is our Lion, and our— Scarecrow. Next to him is our Tin Man. So I guess that makes me the Wizard. Welcome to the Land of Oz. Or if you prefer, Region Three."

~ finis ~

The exciting adventures of the three Carver sisters will continue...

I hope you've enjoyed this installment of the AGU series. Watch for new books on the websites of online booksellers, in local book stores around the world, or check my website. Sign up for my free newsletter to receive email announcements about future book releases.

APPENDIX

This chart is offered to assist readers who may be unfamiliar with military rank and the reporting structure. Newly commissioned officers begin at either ensign or second lieutenant rank.

Space Command Officer Hierarchy:

Admiral of the Fleet (5 Star)
Admiral (4 Star)
Vice-Admiral (3 Star)
Rear Admiral – Upper (2 Star)
Rear Admiral – Lower (1 Star)

Captain
Commander
Lt. Commander
Lieutenant
Lieutenant(jg) "Junior Grade"
Ensign

Space Marine Officer Hierarchy:

General (4 Star)
Lt. General (3 Star)
Major General (2 Star)
Brigadier General (1 Star)

Colonel
Lt. Colonel
Major
Captain
First Lieutenant
Second Lieutenant

The commanding officer on a ship is always referred to as Captain, regardless of his or her official military rank. Even an Ensign could be a Captain of the Ship, although that would only occur as the result of an unusual situation or emergency where no senior officers survive.

On Space Command ships and bases, time is measured according to a twenty-four clock, normally referred to as military time. For example, 8:42 PM would be referred to as 2042 hours. Chronometers are set to always agree with the date and time at Space Command Supreme Headquarters on Earth. This is known as GST, or Galactic System Time.

Admiralty Board:

Carver, Jenetta Alicia - Admiral of the Fleet

Bradlee, Roger T. - Admiral - Director of Intelligence (SCI)

Ressler, Shana E. - Admiral - Director of Budget & Accounting

Hillaire, Arnold H. - Admiral - Director of Academies

Burke, Raymond A. - Vice-Admiral - Director of GSC Base Management

Ahmed, Raihana L. - Vice-Admiral - Dir. of Quartermaster Supply

Woo, Lon C. - Vice-Admiral - Dir. of Scientific & Expeditionary Forces

Holt, Brian D. - Vice-Admiral - Commander of the Second Fleet

Plimley, Loretta J. - Rear-Admiral, (U) - Dir. of Weapons R&D, and SC Shipyard Management

Yuthkotl, Lesbolh - Rear-Admiral (U) - Dir. of Nordakian Forces Integration

Hyper-Space Factors:

IDS Communications Band - .0513 light years each minute
   (8.09 billion kps)

DeTect Range - 4 billion kilometers

Ship Speed Terminology:

Plus-1	1 kps
Sub-Light-1	1,000 kps
Light-1	299,792.458 kps, or,
	(*c*) (speed of light in a vacuum)
Light-150	150 times the speed of light
Light-450	134,906,606.1 kps
Double Envelope	Light-9793.48 = 2,936,011,441.57384 kps
	26.81308692711052 light years per day
Marc-1	Light-14,685.7 = 380,390,005,478,931.8 kps
	40.2072553045859 light years per day

Sample Distances:

Earth to Mars (Mean) - 78 million kilometers

Nearest star to our Sun - 4 light-years (Proxima Centauri)

Milky Way Galaxy diameter - 100,000 light-years

Thickness of M'Way at Sun - 2,000 light-years

Stars in Milky Way - 200 billion (est.)

Nearest galaxy (Andromeda) - 2 million light-years from
   M'Way

A light-year - 9,460,730,472,580.8 kilometers (in vacuum)

A light-second - 299,792.458 km (in vacuum)

Grid Unit - 1,000 Light Yrs^2 (1,000,000 Sq. LY)

Deca-Sector - 100 Light Years^2 (10,000 Sq. LY)

Sector - 10 Light Years^2 (100 Sq. LY)

Section - 94,607,304,725 km^2

Sub-section - 946,073,047 km^2

The map on the following page shows Galactic Alliance space when maps were redrawn following the end of hostilities with the Milori, and the war with the Uthlaro, Tsgardi, Gondusan, and Hudeerac. Unclaimed territories between the three regions were claimed in order to have one contiguous area. Regions Two and Three are so vast that exercising control and maintaining law and order has been largely impossible to this date.

The only purpose of this two-dimensional representation is to provide the reader with a basic feel for the spatial distances involved, and the reader must remember that G.A. territory extends through the entire depth of the Milky Way galaxy.

.jpg and .pdf versions of the maps created for this series are available for downloading at:

http://www.deprima.com/ancillary/agu.html

should the names be unreadable in your printed or electronic media, or if you simply wish to gain a better overall perspective.

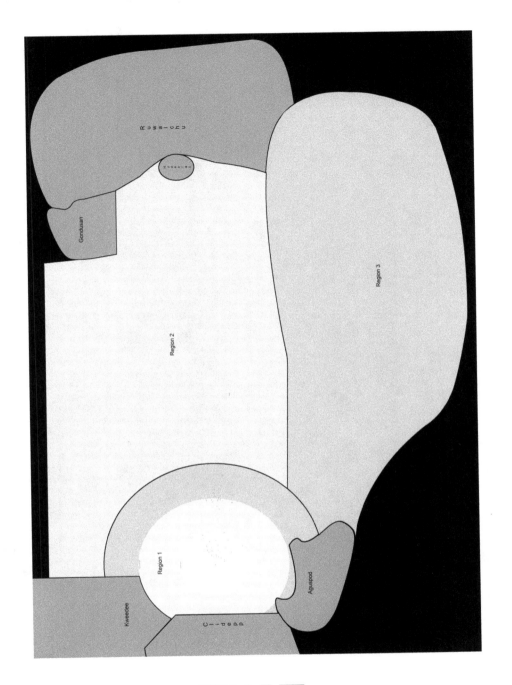

Region 1

Region 2

Region 3

Gondusan

Kweedee

Aguspod

Printed in the USA
CPSIA information can be obtained
at www.ICGtesting.com
LVHW021654280124
770181LV00044B/610